Praise for
the Dark Tides Novels

Siren's Desire

"[With] a root-able heroine, a divinely sexy hero, and a really cool bad guy (bad gal?), Devyn Quinn's *Siren's Desire* has pretty much everything you need to curl up and get lost for hours."
—MaryJanice Davidson, *New York Times* bestselling author of the Undead series

"This triumphant conclusion to the story of the three Lonike sisters and the men that fall hard for them is sure to engage both romance and fantasy readers!"
—A. C. Crispin, *New York Times* bestselling author of *Pirates of the Caribbean*

Siren's Surrender

"A genuinely unique tale of magical mermaids. The characters are people you can cheer for, and the story line really keeps the pages turning. Thought-provoking historical insights give a sense of realism to a fantastic, romantic story that will have readers hoping for a happy ending for all."
—*Romantic Times* (4 stars)

"[A] fast-paced and exciting book." —Fresh Fiction

"A passionate, action-filled thriller." —Night Owl Reviews

"A wonderful second book to the Dark Tides series . . . full of adventure and romance." —Sizzling Hot Book Reviews (5 stars)

Siren's Call

"A thoroughly mesmerizing ride—Quinn throws open the doors to an unbelievable world where nothing is as expected. At once terrifying and fascinating, and unbelievably entertaining, this is a book you won't forget."
—Kate Douglas, bestselling author of *Wolf Tales 12* and the Demonslayers series

continued . . .

"Devyn Quinn writes her stories exactly the way I like to read them: rich, detailed, and a touch poetic. You can practically smell the wind, feel the passion, and taste the tears."
—Morgan Hawke, author of *Insatiable*

"More than a paranormal romance where the star-crossed lovers must battle huge obstacles, *Siren's Call* quickly serves up a main course of interesting characters with a side dish of archaeological and historical intrigue. The novel does not delay the inevitable, nor does it retread the oft-trod, predictable lines of many paranormal romances. Instead, as the story develops, so do intriguing questions about privacy, relationships, and what the world may have a right to know."
—Fresh Fiction

"The questions, feelings, and issues discussed made this unlikely story more real and believable. . . . I felt that the author fully pulled me into her world that she created . . . I am definitely interested in reading the next book in this series."
—Night Owl Reviews

"I love this book . . . overall a very enthralling novel that made me definitely want to keep reading!"
—*Publishers Weekly* Beyond Her Book Blog

Praise for
the Vampire Armageddon Series

Darkness Descending

"[A] unique world to enjoy being lost in. The alternate reality is made realistic by the detailed setting and rawness of the characters."
—*Romantic Times* (4 stars)

"Filled with captivating excitement and chilling thrills, this book will keep you on the edge of your seat. . . . This is an extremely fast-paced story that will keep you alert and waiting for the next word."
—Fresh Fiction

"An exhilarating action-packed thriller from the opening graveyard battle until the climactic finish. . . . This is a terrific opening act."
—Genre Go Round Reviews

ALSO BY DEVYN QUINN

The Dark Tides Series
Siren's Surrender
Siren's Call

The Vampire Armageddon Series
Darkness Descending

Siren's Desire

A Dark Tides Novel

DEVYN QUINN

A SIGNET ECLIPSE BOOK

SIGNET ECLIPSE
Published by New American Library, a division of
Penguin Group (USA) Inc., 375 Hudson Street,
New York, New York 10014, USA
Penguin Group (Canada), 90 Eglinton Avenue East, Suite 700, Toronto,
Ontario M4P 2Y3, Canada (a division of Pearson Penguin Canada Inc.)
Penguin Books Ltd., 80 Strand, London WC2R 0RL, England
Penguin Ireland, 25 St. Stephen's Green, Dublin 2,
Ireland (a division of Penguin Books Ltd.)
Penguin Group (Australia), 250 Camberwell Road, Camberwell, Victoria 3124,
Australia (a division of Pearson Australia Group Pty. Ltd.)
Penguin Books India Pvt. Ltd., 11 Community Centre, Panchsheel Park,
New Delhi - 110 017, India
Penguin Group (NZ), 67 Apollo Drive, Rosedale, Auckland 0632,
New Zealand (a division of Pearson New Zealand Ltd.)
Penguin Books (South Africa) (Pty.) Ltd., 24 Sturdee Avenue,
Rosebank, Johannesburg 2196, South Africa

Penguin Books Ltd., Registered Offices:
80 Strand, London WC2R 0RL, England

First published by Signet Eclipse, an imprint of New American Library,
a division of Penguin Group (USA) Inc.

First Printing, February 2012
10 9 8 7 6 5 4 3 2 1

*To the readers who stuck with my mermaid sisters
through thick and thin, to the end.*

This one is for you.

ACKNOWLEDGMENTS

I've always told anyone who asked that it takes more than a single individual to produce a book. Now that we've reached the close of the Dark Tides trilogy, I believe that more than ever. This book—and any other I have ever written—simply would not exist without the collective persons that are always necessary to bring any book together.

Therefore I would like to thank my "team," which includes my fabulous agent, Roberta Brown. Without her on the job there would have been no Dark Tides trilogy to begin with. Mermaids were not even on my mind when Roberta put them on my radar and began the process that would lead to an eventual submission—and acceptance—of the material.

But that's only the beginning of the process.

Although I may produce the manuscript, it is always in the rawest of formats. That's when my terrific editor, Jhanteigh Kupihea, steps in, rolls up her sleeves, and begins the real work. Her red pen separates the wheat from the chaff, and offers me a clearer picture of what the characters are doing and where they should be going. She's quick to point out what's good, what's bad, and what just has to go. Her efforts pull the book together and make it make sense from beginning to end. I have appreciated her hard work since day one.

Never to be left out is copyeditor Jane Steele. Her sharp eyes fix the clunky sentences and bad grammar, and she always makes sure every detail is correct—even if it means additional research on her part. It's at this point that we'd better get the book right, and I truly hope we have.

I'd also like to thank my beta readers, those ladies who are brave enough to read early drafts of my books and offer me their feedback. Sometimes I don't like what they tell me, but they're always honest. And I value their opinions enough to try to fix what they think I've messed up. So Lea Franczak, Tracey Anderson, Kelly Muller, and Marissa Dobson deserve a big pat on the back for their hard work.

And then there are the ladies I call my "rah-rah" cheerleaders, who give me a kick in the rear when I start whining. Sara Reinke, Sarah Parr, Anya Howard, Vanessa Hawthorne and Kate Douglas, I thank you all for being there for me when I need you. You are all the best. Ever. And Del Garret, you knew me way back when, so I'm tossing you in just because I can. So there.

And lastly, I need to write something for my readers. Thanks for coming along for the ride. It's been fun. Let's do it again sometime soon.

Chapter 1

Port Rock, Maine
Present Day

*T*his doesn't look promising, Addison Lonike thought as the twenty-seven-foot Boston Whaler headed toward the orange life raft bobbing on the choppy waters. Now that summer was coming to a close, people were attempting to squeeze a few more precious days of sailing out of the season.

Her heart sank as she performed a quick head count. When the distress signal had come in to harbor patrol, the pilot of the crippled yacht had radioed that four people were aboard. "I see only two survivors," she called as Sidney Rawlings guided their rescue boat around the raft, attempting to use the larger vessel as a break wall to give the smaller dinghy a little relief from the gusty wind and pummeling water. As far as pilots went, Sidney was one of the best. If anyone could handle navigation in a dangerous situation, he was the man. A few seconds later the raft scraped the side.

"We got 'em!" Addison called as she threw out a line to secure the smaller craft. Joined by a second crewman, she worked to bring the survivors aboard.

Two sopping wet people, a man and a teenage girl, collapsed on deck. Both were shivering and blue from the cold. Addison quickly snuggled them both in thermal heat wraps.

"My w-wife," the man stuttered frantically, "and m-my s-son are still in the boat."

Paramedic Jim Witkowsky quickly scanned the water. "I don't see anything," he called over the lashing gale. "What happened?"

The man shook his head in confusion. "I don't know. We were cruising along just fine, heading toward the mainland. Then there was some—"

"Some sort of explosion," the teen filled in, eyes welling. "From the engine room, I think. There was a lot of smoke and fire."

The kid's father broke back in. "I sent a distress signal that we were going under. I—I managed to get the life raft out and inflated, but the cruiser started sinking." Face contorting with pain, he shrugged helplessly. "It just went over on one side."

The boat wasn't what concerned Addison. The fact that two people were still in the water did. Unless they had life vests, there was little to no chance of survival. "You said your wife and son were still aboard," she broke in.

Still half in shock and suffering the effects of hypothermia, the man nodded. "Brenda and Sheldon. They were belowdecks, in the galley fixing lunch. Barbara w-was with me. I'd been giving her lessons on piloting the boat."

The girl's face scrunched up as the realization set in. "They never had a chance," she said, sagging to the deck. A tear slid down her pale cheek, and then another. "There was a big hole in the hull and it just went under."

Addison winced. *Damn it.* The rescue effort had just turned into a recovery mission. If there was one thing she hated, it was fishing dead bodies out of the water. The Mayday call had come in roughly half an hour ago. Though they'd headed out within minutes, the exact location of the wreck was unknown, preventing them from reaching the area sooner. The chances of locating more survivors had just gone from slim to none.

"It must have gone down fast, and straight to the bottom," Witkowsky continued. "There's no way—"

Jaw tightening, Addison elbowed her crewmate. The last thing to say in front of the family was that there was no hope. But Witkowsky was a newbie, and he still had to learn the finer points of empathy when in an emergency situation.

"There's always a chance. Last year a woman survived underwater, in an air pocket of a sunken boat, for more than twenty-four hours." She cut a glance toward the shivering man. "How much time has passed since the boat went under?"

Still a bit dazed, the man shook his head. "I—I'm not sure. Fifteen, maybe twenty minutes. It didn't go under fast but kind of rolled on one side and floated. Then it went under."

Addison did a quick mental calculation. The average person had six to ten minutes for survival if completely immersed. Given the frigid temperature of the bay, hypothermia and shock would immediately set in, lowering the body's temperature. It also meant that cellular metabolic processes would begin to shut down, slowing heart rate, pulse, and respiration. At this stage, the body would actually take longer to undergo brain death. That factor alone might have bought the victims below a few precious minutes.

But those minutes were quickly ticking away.

The girl looked up at her, desperation written across her young face. "Is there any way to get down to them?" she asked hopefully. Even as she spoke, her gaze found and fixed on the diving equipment the rescue vessel carried.

Witkowsky shook his head. "We should probably wait for backup from the coast guard before we proceed with any diving."

Addison wasn't listening. Her mind had already been made up. The girl couldn't be older than thirteen, fourteen at the most. Having lost her own parents at an early age, Addison knew how it felt to suddenly have family members ripped away far too prematurely. There was no way she'd let the chance pass without attempting to do all she could to change the course of an already tragic day.

Stripping out of her EMT uniform, she began to put on her diving gear. Every minute that ticked away was another one lost. Though she usually didn't bother with a wet suit, today she'd awoken with a nagging feeling she should be prepared to go into the water. She was already wearing hers when the distress signal came in. *Call it Mer-tuition,* she thought, putting on the heavy oxygen tank and mask.

"Tell Sidney to hold it steady," she called.

The pilot was already one step ahead. "I've got it here," Sidney yelled back, throttling the engines down into idle.

Addison gave him the diver's signal for "all systems go." "I shouldn't be long, Sid."

Sidney nodded. "Will do. I've radioed the coast guard that we've made contact and are commencing with recovery efforts. We've got the go-ahead if we think we can handle it."

Witkowsky speared them both with a look of pure disbelief. "Sending a single diver down into an unknown situation definitely isn't a good idea. At least two need to be in the water in case something goes wrong."

Addison tossed him a nod. She already knew what Witkowsky didn't—that the sea was a mermaid's natural environment. She was actually safer in the water than out of it. Nevertheless, it always took an event like this to break in a new member of the team. A freshly minted paramedic, Jim had fewer than two weeks with harbor patrol under his belt.

"It's your first time out with the team, so I'll cut you some slack for your disbelief in my diving capabilities."

"Lonike is our most experienced diver," Sidney cut in. "And since she's the captain of this vessel, she outranks both of us. Going into the water is her call." He paused a moment, then added, "If she can't handle it, no one can."

Witkowsky shook his head. "Fine. But I want my protest logged."

"Your concern is duly noted." Addison hated to pull rank, but when lives were on the line, she'd do whatever it took to do her job. The chief had wanted to gauge how well Witkowsky performed under her authority before letting him in on her true identity. The guys she worked with had to be trusted to watch her back when she went into the water. "When we return to the mainland, we'll sit down with Harbormaster Ashford and have a little talk."

Witkowsky pulled a sour face. "You bet we will."

Addison ignored him. She didn't have the time or the inclination to quibble. Recent events concerning her kind had made it necessary to keep a very low profile. Now that the Mer had begun to emerge from Ishaldi, the powers that be weren't exactly welcoming to the newly revealed species. Mer were still viewed as aliens and were treated as such. One of the conditions for release from the government's A51-ASD complex was that she and her two sisters had to keep a low profile among the civilian population. They would be allowed to resume their lives in Port Rock—as long as they lived and acted like regular people.

But that was proving to be difficult. As much as she tried to mimic landlubbers, she just wasn't human.

Heading down the side boarding ladder, she eased into the water. Although she'd learned years ago to dive the human way, she found all the heavy equipment annoying. Disappearing beneath the waves, she stopped when she was about fifty feet below the surface, deep enough under the water where no one could see her.

Without hesitating, she ripped off the mask and mouthpiece. Giving the unnecessary items a wink, she quickly worked a little Mercraft. A small flare surrounded the items, and then they were gone. The heavy tank across her back soon followed.

Freed of several things to carry, Addison stretched

out and made a slow roll through the water. The change
from her human form to that of a Mer occurred in the
blink of an eye. One moment she had two legs. The next
moment a spark of bright colors raced like wildfire across
her skin. Her wet suit melted away, leaving her completely
naked. The lower half of her body had also changed, becoming a beautiful multicolored tail. It took less than
thirty seconds for the metamorphosis to complete itself.
She was, again, a creature who belonged and thrived in
the cerulean blue waters of the deep sea.

Addison nodded with satisfaction. All those hours
she'd spent practicing her magic had finally paid off.
With just a thought and a little push of energy from the
crystal she always wore around her neck, she could make
small objects appear and disappear at will. Tessa, her
older sister, had taught her that trick. Although it had
taken much trial and embarrassing error, she'd finally
gotten the hang of the spell. She had no clue where it all
went, but when she wanted it again, she simply had to
think about it and everything would return.

Free to swim unencumbered, Addison dived toward
the bottom. The waters were cold and murky, strangely
devoid of fish and other sea life. It was as if the creatures
sensed something had gone terribly wrong and had
abandoned the area.

Minutes later, the wreckage of the yacht loomed into
view. The craft had turned almost completely upside
down as it sank.

Putting her tail in motion, Addison swam toward the
crippled vessel. As the girl had stated, there was indeed
a gaping hole in the hull. A thin stream of gasoline and
oil eddied up from the exposed engines. The sight sad-

dened her. A family outing had turned tragic in the blink of an eye. No doubt the coast guard would salvage the yacht to determine the cause of the accident.

Why the vessel sank wasn't her concern. She needed to locate the remaining passengers. Even though it had been foolhardy, she'd practically promised the girl a miracle. She intended to deliver one, if at all possible.

And with a Mer in the water, anything's possible, she reminded herself.

Reaching the interior of the cabin wasn't going to be easy. A diver wearing full gear would find it almost impossible to wriggle beneath the yacht and into the interior of the cabin. It was a tight fit even for a mermaid, but Addison somehow managed to squeeze through.

Amazingly the galley's emergency lights were still functioning, lending an eerie illumination to the swamped interior. The body of a woman floated nearby.

Addison swam through the narrow space, checking the woman's pulse. Nothing—she was cold, motionless. One look at her empty expression and gaping mouth told her the spark of life had been snuffed out.

But the child . . .

Addison looked around. It took a few moments for her sharp gaze to pick out the little boy floating among the debris of cushions from a nearby bunk. With soft blond curls fanned out around his head, he looked like a doll abandoned after a day's play.

Her heart squeezed painfully. *Oh no.* He couldn't be more than five or six. She reached out, laying the tips of her fingers at the pulse point of the boy's throat. *Please, oh, please,* she thought, stilling her own breath and striking out with her sixth sense. The final sparks of life were rapidly fading. She wasn't sure how long he'd been deprived of oxygen, but deep inside she felt his desperate struggle and sensed his lungs burning with the need to drag in a precious breath of air.

Giving thanks to the goddess that the child still had a chance to survive, Addison pressed her mouth over lips that were cold and unmoving. As an empath, she had the ability to generate energy within her own body and then remanifest it in physical kinetic form. The soul-stone around her neck began to glow softly as she filtered living electricity from her body into the boy's motionless figure.

Seconds later the child's eyes fluttered. He coughed, then gasped for air. The lungs in his chest expanded, filtering out seawater and taking in pure oxygen. He was awake, but only on a peripheral level.

Relief whirred along her nerve endings. *You'll be all right,* she mentally telegraphed. Under the enchantment of a mermaid's kiss, the boy was capable of comprehending her silent words. The spell was only temporary and would last until his lungs again drew oxygen above the level of the water. He would have no memory of her in Mer form.

Smiling with relief, Addison gathered the little boy into her arms, though it took a bit of creative maneuvering to get back through the narrow passage and away from the sunken wreck. Guiding the child toward the surface, she quite forgot that she'd doffed her diving gear.

Seconds later their heads popped above the water. Bobbing with the waves, Addison swam toward the rescue boat. She saw Jim Witkowsky lean over the edge, pointing her way. "There she is," he called, "and she's not alone."

Catching hold of the ladder, Addison hefted half her body out of the water before lifting the limp child toward Witkowsky's waiting hands.

The man and his daughter stumbled toward the semiconscious boy even as Witkowsky began resuscitation efforts. "Sheldon!" the man cried from behind the paramedic. "Come on, son. Breathe."

A moment later the child heaved out a stream of bile mixed with water. A splutter, followed by a healthy wail, rolled past his blue-tinged lips. And then he was breathing, above water and on his own.

Witkowsky gave a quick thumbs-up. "I think he's going to make it."

The man gathered the boy into his arms. "Thank God," he murmured against the wet matting of hair pasted to the child's forehead. "He's alive."

But not everyone's eyes were on the rescue efforts taking place. Even as she clung to the ladder while watching events aboard unfold, Addison had the uneasy feeling she was being watched. She looked up to see the girl's gaze fixed upon her. A look half of horror mingled with fascination colored the teen's expressive features.

Addison winced, giving herself a quick mental slap. She'd just made the worst blunder a Mer could make: She had let humans see her in her true form.

The teen raised a hand and pointed her way. "D-Daddy, something's not right," the girl exclaimed in a shaky voice. "That lady has a tail!"

Everyone looked—and gaped.

"Holy Mother of God," Witkowsky exclaimed, eyeing her exposed breasts and slender hips. "She's naked as a jaybird."

For a few beats, Addison couldn't think to react. The tension throbbed between them for a minute or so. It didn't take a mind reader to know what everyone aboard was thinking.

Sidney Rawlings gave his errant crewman a slap upside the head. "Stop staring. You're being rude."

Regaining self-control, Addison belatedly pressed an arm over her bare breasts as she slid back into the water. "Shit," she grated under her breath. Talk about having one's stupid hanging out. Even though her elaborate scale pattern afforded a bit of modest cover, above the waist she was still completely exposed.

During those gut-wrenching minutes when she'd been underwater, her only concern had been to save the boy's life. Eager to get him to the surface, she hadn't given a second thought to making sure she came up in the same equipment she'd gone down in.

It really was a megascrewup.

Washington, DC

"Are you kidding me?" The words popped out of Captain Mason McKenzie's mouth before he had a chance to even consider the repercussions.

Secretary of the Navy, Adam Webber, raised a single disapproving brow in response. "Do you see a smile on my face, Captain?"

Mason quickly shook his head. That was not the right way to respond when speaking to a superior officer. "No, sir." He didn't dare say another word. Instead, he silently chastised himself. *Pull yourself together,* he thought. *This isn't a joke.* It wasn't his job to question the judgment of a superior.

Even if he didn't agree with his instructions, he'd follow them to the letter.

Webber nodded. "Then I take it we're on the same page as to your orders?"

Suppressing a flinch, Mason didn't hesitate. "Yes, sir. I am perfectly clear on the matter. You want me to recruit a mermaid to the USET team."

This time Webber allowed the briefest hint of a smile to cross his weathered, craggy face. "It sounds as if I've gone mad, I know, but this comes down from the highest level. And we both know who that is." Giving his balding head a scratch, he tapped the paperwork spread out on his desk. "I have to admit I was more than a bit skeptical when I got word the A51 sciences division of the bureau had gotten hold of a living, breathing alien life-form. But given what has recently transpired over these last few months, we can no longer turn a blind eye to the facts. The Mer, as they call themselves, are here, and they're here to stay. How we deal with them through the coming months is going to be crucial."

Mason nodded. "I understand, sir." To keep his mind focused, he did a quick mental review of all the classified information he'd managed to ingest since agreeing to lead the Undersea Search and Exploration Task Force, the US government's first step toward first quelling and then controlling the threat of the Mer who had created a stronghold for themselves in the Mediterranean.

Barely four months had passed since the initial discovery of the species, which seemed to center around the lost civilization of Ishaldi. Concealed under the sea for almost two millennia, and guarded by a mysterious sea-gate, the indigenous species was not friendly toward humans. The team Mason led had been implemented to operate outside naval operations already in place in the Mediterranean. To date, the USET team's attempts to engage the Mer in diplomatic talks had been unsuccessful.

Webber kept on going. "We already know that the leader of the rebel Mer, Queen Magaera, doesn't wish to negotiate with our representatives at this time."

Mason inwardly winced.

Every time they'd sent a diver into the waters surrounding the sea-gate, one of Magaera's soldiers had responded with an immediate intercept. A couple of his men had come close to drowning when their equipment was sabotaged. The rogue Mer were fast, sneaky, and ruthless.

Secretary Webber shuffled through his paperwork. "According to the boys at the A51, they have technology and abilities we can't even begin to touch. Short of lobbing a nuke toward the island, we have to be very careful how we proceed in the future." A snort escaped the crusty old sea dog. "That damn fool acting as adviser to the queen—what's his name?"

"Massey," Mason filled in. "Jake Massey. He's the archaeologist who put together the initial team looking for that place." According to intelligence, Massey was acting as some sort of ambassador to Magaera.

Webber shook his head. "Right. Anyway, given their actions, we're regarding the Mer as a potential enemy. We can't forgive the recent attacks on our soil, along with the loss of human lives. The biggest disadvantage is that we don't really understand what we're up against."

"It's true our first contact wasn't successful, though we did get to see the, ah, creatures in action in their natural environment. They are quite impressive."

"Formidable would be a better word," Webber groused. "We can't touch them in the water."

Mason forced his features to betray not a hint of incredulity. "And so you're asking me to recruit a mermaid?"

Webber looked at him, unperturbed. "Exactly."

Nonplussed, Mason leaned back in his chair. He needed a few minutes to digest the request.

A lot of things had winged through his mind when he'd been summoned for the meeting. The emergence of the Mer was still very hush-hush, known only to those in the upper echelons of government. And despite recent failures to breach the island, they weren't giving up. The covert operation, presently known only under the code name "Sea Horse," would go forward.

There was a new island on the map in the Mediterranean, one that had seemingly appeared overnight. Somehow, using technology beyond human comprehension, the Mer had lifted from the bottom of the sea the remnants of an island that had once served as the gateway between the human realm above the water and the Mer ecosphere beneath the waves. A landmass measuring an estimated nine miles in length and girth, the island was shielded by an electromagnetic signal powerful enough to shut down even the most sophisticated electrical equipment. The A51 sciences division had recently identified the energy as radiating from a wormhole at the bottom of the ocean that connected the two diverse worlds. Through a feat of inexplicable engineering, this wormhole led to a Mer domain that literally existed in the center of the planet, albeit on a slightly different dimensional plane.

As it turned out, the area wasn't exactly unknown. Pinpointed in the late 1950s, it was referred to as the M441966 site. Scientists had already noted the area's intense concentration of electromagnetic energy. At the time, theories to explain the presence of this energy ranged from the area's being a geothermal field due to volcanic activity, to the energy's coming from some sort of alien homing signal or beacon. A recent earthquake in the area had apparently shifted the stability of the sea-gate guarding the entrance to the wormhole, which made the area even more volatile.

Mason struggled to keep his thoughts straight. As incredible as the story might sound, it was the absolute truth. And truth, as the old adage went, was often stranger than fiction.

Nobody was expecting these facts that had emerged months ago, thanks to three courageous young women determined to find out the truth behind their origins.

As far as the rest of the world was concerned, the anomaly in the Mediterranean was scientific. The navy's Sixth Fleet, which kept an American naval presence in the Mediterranean, was presently on patrol to keep busy shipping lanes moving without too much disruption. It was proving to be a difficult balancing act, as no fewer than three continents with thirteen nations had direct access to those waters. Soon enough the truth about the Mer would become known to the entire world. The diplomatic and political ramifications would probably take decades to untangle.

If early encounters held true, then the Mer absolutely intended to reclaim their place in this world as a major seagoing power. Queen Magaera appeared more than ready and able to fight for her people. With Massey's help, she'd recently reclaimed a piece of Mer technology that reportedly gave her control over land and sea. The appearance of the island was proof positive that whatever she'd managed to lay her hands on worked.

Realizing his silence had dragged on too long, Mason cleared his throat. Webber was waiting for a response. "Permission to speak freely, sir?"

Webber flagged a hand. "Of course. As you're the commander of USET, I do want to hear your thoughts on the matter."

The response emboldened Mason. "With all due respect, since we honestly don't know what we're dealing with, would we want to involve a mermaid in a tactical operation against her own kind?"

Webber didn't hesitate. He'd obviously made his decision. "It's as you said, Captain. We don't know what we're dealing with. Logic would dictate that we recruit someone who does. The A51 scientists have an idea, but they're in no position to call themselves experts despite all the tests and experiments they've run on these creatures."

"Then I take it the two hostiles they have in custody are still refusing to cooperate?"

The older man nodded. "Correct. Those women remain firmly dedicated to their queen, and they would rather die than help us out. That leaves the Lonike sisters. As Mer born and raised in our society, they have done their utmost to cooperate with us since their kind, uh, emerged."

Mason had a thought or two about that fact. "In my opinion the government should have kept the sisters confined and controlled instead of releasing them back into society. Yes, I am aware they are basically peaceful and have lived their entire lives in Port Rock. They are even productive citizens, who hold jobs and pay taxes. But that doesn't change my mind about the species. To the core of their DNA, they are still part of an alien life-form that has proven to be particularly deadly. At this point, I consider *all* mermaids to be suspects."

Webber's expression betrayed a hint of annoyance. "Your concerns are noted, Captain—and overruled. These orders have come down from the top, and that's the way it's going to be." His brown eyes narrowed. "If you have a problem with that, you will be reassigned—immediately."

The idea tempted him, but Mason quickly pushed it out of his mind. Being cherry-picked for the command of the covert USET team was more than an honor. If he brought the operation in as a success, the rating of rear admiral, lower half, bestowed by Naval Special Operations, would surely be his next step up the ladder. Intending to go all the way up the chain of command, he had his eye on the chair Webber presently occupied. In his mind it was time for the old-guard politicians to hand over the power to the young pups who actually had experience with the jobs they oversaw.

Alas, those dreams of future glories would have to wait. He needed to focus on the present, and on the unusual circumstances he'd been thrust into.

Mason offered a sharp nod. "I have no problem, sir."

"Off the record, I'm half inclined to agree with you," Webber grumbled beneath his breath. "But whatever prejudices you've got against the Mer, keep them to yourself. We've got a job to do, and we're going to do it right."

Mason squared his shoulders. After twelve years in the service, he was an expert at performing above and beyond expectations. He might not agree with his superiors, but he'd carry out his duty to the bitter end. *Even if it means going down with the ship,* he reminded himself.

He acknowledged his superior's admonishment with a nod. "Absolutely, sir."

Webber picked through some plain manila folders. "Of the three Mer sisters, we believe this one," he said, passing the selected folder across his desk, "Addison, is the best choice."

Mason took the file, which contained all the pertinent information the government had on Addison Lonike. Although he'd already studied up on the sisters after joining USET, it probably wouldn't hurt to refresh his memory.

Webber still hadn't convinced him that asking one of the girls to join the team was the correct way to go. Sleeper agents were known to be benign for decades before being activated by those they served. The Lonike sisters' integration into the human world could have been something the Mer planned a long time before their sudden emergence back into the mainstream. Hundreds, perhaps thousands, of their kind could already be spread throughout the world, just waiting for the call to arms.

He had no doubt that his superiors had considered all the options as well. Still, they'd chosen to proceed.

"She's a good candidate for this mission," Webber

filled in. "She is the youngest, approximately twenty-six years of age."

Mason thumbed through her profile. "This is pretty basic," he commented. "On paper nothing looks out of the ordinary."

Webber shuffled through his own massive pile of notes on the Mer sisters. "On the surface they seem as normal as any human." He began reeling off the stats. "Her father, David Lonike, was human. Half Scots-Irish, half Native American from the Abenaki tribe. He had a small fishing business—one he inherited from his father. His wife, Jolesa, was full-fledged Mer."

Mason inwardly blanched. The idea of a mermaid tail and human legs didn't mesh in his mind. How did they manage that, anyway? He didn't dare contemplate the answer. "It says here that Mer offspring are always female."

Tilting his head, Webber peered over the black rims of his glasses and scanned a few more pages. His folders were considerably thicker than the one Mason held, and he'd obviously gone through the intelligence forward and backward, then forward again. Considering the delicacy of the situation, his couldn't have been an easy decision to make. He had superiors to answer to, as well. "It seems to be a genetic quirk with their species, a way of ensuring the Mer DNA doesn't die off and become extinct," he noted. "From what we can glean, this particular bloodline has been in Port Rock for centuries."

More than a little uneasy, Mason closed his own folder. He didn't like the way Addison Lonike's flashing green eyes seemed to home right in on him through her photo. Nor did he like the fact that interspecies breeding didn't exactly sit well with him. "It's amazing they've managed to hide in plain sight for so long," he commented as a way to remain neutral on the matter.

"The Lonike sisters have done their best to be cooperative," Webber said, making sure every word was precise and clear. "And without their assistance, we wouldn't have any idea what we're up against. But for all we do know, there are still too many gaps to fill in. That's why I want a Mer on our team. ASAP. We haven't got the time to guess what's waiting for us out there in the Mediterranean."

Mason handed Addison's folder back. He had to admit the more he learned about mermaids, the less he liked them. "When do I leave?"

Webber's expression turned grave. "Immediately. A seaman is waiting outside my office to take you to the airfield. I expect you to be back in Washington within twenty-four hours. With Miss Lonike in tow." He dug through his pile of paperwork and extracted a second folder. "Here are the details of the position we're prepared to offer her as MTA."

Mason's brows rose. That was one he hadn't heard before. "MTA?"

"Mer Tactical Adviser," Webbed filled in. "It's noncommissioned, and she won't have any rating in the team, but she will be compensated. As an EMT and experienced search and rescue diver, she'd be a good fit even if she weren't a mermaid."

Without betraying his unease for a second time in front of his superior, Mason pushed to his feet and tucked the folder under his arm. "Understood, sir." Drawing in a deep breath, he snapped out a neat salute.

Adam Webber halfheartedly returned the gesture. "You are dismissed, Captain."

Mason nodded once before turning toward the door. There was nothing more for him to say. It wouldn't have done any good anyway. The decision was made. He had his orders. His opinion had no place beyond this point.

Personal prejudices aside, Mason felt confident he could handle the assignment. If he did his job right, everything would be fine.

Chapter 2

Queen Magaera was restless.

Although she had achieved her desired goal of securing the scepter that would allow her to raise Ishaldi from the seafloor and into the human world, she wasn't happy.

Jake Massey glanced toward the agitated monarch. Draped in silk so fine it might have been spun from cobwebs, she presently wandered the halls of her temple, a wraith who could find no succor in her recent success.

Cloaked in mists that shrouded it from the eyes of the curious world, the island paradise she'd worked so hard to restore in Earth's waters had also become her prison. The kingdom she'd single-handedly resurrected from the depths of the sea was an empty one, devoid of subjects. Most of them were still trapped in a hidden realm within the ocean, where they'd been ever since the Lonike sisters' grandmother, who had once been Queen Nyala of the Mer, sealed the sea-gate to prevent her kind from overtaking humanity. This world was accessi-

ble only via a sea-gate, a sort of wormhole that could
be accessed only if one had the correct key. That key
had once been a diamond choker and crystal orb, both
of which had been destroyed when Tessa opened the
sea-gate for the first time. Now that the pieces were destroyed, Tessa had somehow reset the sea-gate to recognize only her psychic imprint. If she went through first,
others could follow. If not, the sea-gate rejected those
attempting to breach it, spitting back bones. Magaera
and eight of her soldiers had managed to follow Tessa
as she escaped the realm, but the rest of the Mer were
left behind. Magaera could not open the sea-gate to return home and retrieve her people—not without Tessa
Lonike.

Though Jake struggled to keep his brow smooth and
untroubled, his thoughts were racing a mile a minute.
He knew that to assume control of the sea-gate, Magaera
would have to fool it into thinking she was Tessa. Normally, such an energy output was unique to each individual, as personal as a fingerprint. However, all Mer
carried a psi-kinetic gene that allowed them to communicate on a cerebral level. Normally this gift was used
when submerged. But it could also be manipulated for
more nefarious purposes.

Although the practice was forbidden, a Mer could
make the electrical forces of her brain resonate on the
same wavelength as another's, thus mimicking the exact
frequency until the two were impossible to tell apart.

Jake inwardly frowned. *Magaera needs Tessa's soul-
stone,* he thought. *Without it, she has no way to bring her
people through the sea-gate.*

And a queen needed her subjects—to worship her

and for her to command. A queen without subjects was like the Sahara in high summer—empty, arid, and dry.

He frowned. *Paradise without peons is boring.* Twiddling his thumbs on an island was not what he signed on for when he'd agreed to become Queen Magaera's guide in the human world. As the archaeologist who'd returned the long-lost mermaids to the earth's surface, he'd imagined not only reclaiming his standing in the archaeological world, but also receiving an ambassadorship. He'd be an important man—feted; toasted for his brilliance; significant.

As things presently stood, he was a gigolo; the reluctant lover of a seven-hundred-year-old cranky Mer queen with four—count them, four—Mer subjects to serve her every whim and command.

Although the island provided for every physical need a mermaid might have, its options were limited when it came to conjuring up some entertainment and eats for a human being. How he longed for a wide-screen television with satellite, and a computer with Internet access. A decent bottle of whiskey and a steak would be welcome, too. In his mind, an ambassador such as he deserved much better lodgings and luxuries. He'd cut off a limb to be aboard a yacht; sitting on deck and sipping a margarita while watching the sun slip in a leisurely fashion behind the faraway horizon.

Since that wasn't possible right now, he had to think of something else.

I need some action.

It was time to put his foot on Magaera's ass and give the bitch a push in the right direction.

Sauntering over to the object of his ambition, he

came to a stop a few feet behind her. Lately, the most casual of conversations was guaranteed to send her into a rage. "You have something on your mind?"

Magaera did not glance his way, nor did she cease her pacing. "These days of leisure have begun to grate upon my very nerves." Her hands suddenly balled into angry fists. "The whole world is out there, and I cannot yet touch it."

"We agreed it was best to let the humans think we are in retreat," he reminded her. "By acting too quickly last time, too many mistakes were made. Good soldiers were lost and our number was effectively halved."

Magaera froze, regarding him through an icy blue gaze. "Which I did upon your advice," she shot through clenched teeth.

Jake hurried to explain his grievous tactical error. "There was no way they should have been able to beat your soldiers. How they managed it, I don't know."

The queen turned her head, gazing through the murky fog enveloping the edges of their island fortress. Through the last few days she was moody and volatile, driven by the twisted thoughts writhing in her mind. The revenge she was planning against the human race would probably make men shudder. "Humans today are not as weak as they once were. They have command of these waters now, and technology we do not yet understand. They watch us now, curious as to our next move."

Jake tracked her gaze, though it did little good. To his eyes the glittering mist surrounding the island was impenetrable. "The Mer, too, are an enigma they don't yet understand," he reminded her.

For several weeks, several navy ships had patrolled

the perimeter of the island, sending out reconnaissance teams in order to investigate the anomaly that had suddenly appeared in Mediterranean waters. There was no doubt in his mind that the United States government now knew about the Mer. The feds had taken Tessa Lonike and her family into protective custody after Queen Magaera's ham-fisted attempt to take her hostage. Of the four soldiers she'd sent to reclaim Tessa, none had returned. They, too, had been taken into custody.

He imagined the feds were trying to digest the existence of the Mer and to decide what to do now that they had come out of the water.

At this point, Jake knew the island was being watched, and closely. The US Navy had even sent in an exploratory ship, and divers had attempted to enter the waters around the island. They hadn't gotten very far. Magaera's remaining four soldiers made sure the waters around the island were well patrolled. It also helped that the electromagnetic field generated by the wormhole beneath the water kept their ships at a respectable distance. Anything electronic went haywire. He'd gotten an inkling into the energies emanating from the sea-gate when his BlackBerry blew up. It was fried—toast.

Their stamina, however, was beginning to wear thin. Five weeks had passed since their queen had reclaimed Atargatis's scepter, the very thing that had allowed her to raise Ishaldi from its watery grave. It was time to decide on their next move.

Jake cleared his throat. "It's only a matter of time before the navy figures out a way to penetrate the island's perimeter."

His observation seemed to amuse her. "You think I

do not know that?" she snapped through a scowl. "It is true we are well shielded. But it is not enough. I must have my missing piece."

Jake felt the fine hairs on the back of his neck prickle. "It always comes back to her," he murmured.

Tessa . . .

Thinking about her caused his heart to skip a beat and his chest to tighten. He briefly closed his eyes, allowing cloying memories to seep back into his mind. If there was anything on his conscience that bothered him, Tessa was it. She was the best thing that had ever happened to him. Letting her go was the biggest mistake he'd ever made.

At one time they'd been lovers, and she'd trusted him enough to invite him into her secret world. It was an honor and a privilege, and there really was a time he thought they'd be together forever. There was only one problem, and it wasn't that Tessa was a mermaid.

He was totally screwed up inside.

Deep down, he harbored a mistrust of the female sex. Women were unstable, emotional, even hysterical. And with such a notion embedded in his psyche, there was no way any relationship he entered into could ever succeed.

Jake had always longed for a mother who'd rescue him from his own bat-shit crazy father. His mother hadn't done jack, though. Three years after giving birth to her son, Beth Massey had taken the proverbial walk for cigarettes and never come home.

Left on his own with a young son to raise, Jake's dad had drifted from woman to woman. Some he married; others he merely took up with to have a convenient babysitter. Most of the females he picked up were trash—loose women who weren't interested in another woman's child. When he wasn't getting the better side of a leather belt from one of his many stepmothers, Jake was completely ignored, thrust aside whenever his dad had the misfortune to knock up another broad. He had so many half bothers and half sisters that he couldn't even keep count.

A swirl of nausea caused his stomach to tighten. Watching his father cycle through wives the way an elephant devoured peanuts, he'd never learned what a true relationship looked like. In his mind, women were disposable. He had no respect for their sex whatsoever.

And then one woman had stopped him dead in his tracks.

When he'd met Tessa, he'd actually believed he'd have a real honest-to-God chance of making a relationship work. Tessa wasn't human; she was Mer. And, in the beginning, everything seemed perfect.

But then he discovered a female was a female, no matter her species. Once a woman got those nesting instincts, everything changed. The strings tightened. Once they cut into the skin, they began to strangle. Instead of remaining his magical and ageless princess of the sea, Tessa wanted to get married—and make some spawn.

Jake supposed his resistance to the idea of children was the catalyst that caused Tessa to question her choice of a husband. Once a Mer took her *breema*, her breedmate, it was for life. When she'd suggested they postpone their forthcoming nuptials, he'd persuaded her to go through with their plans.

His pulse rate bumped up a notch. Myriad emotions

caused his chest to tighten in a most uncharacteristic way. Instead of honoring his commitment to Tessa, he'd walked out on her the night before the wedding. And despite what people might presently think of him, he regretted the decision to this day. He'd even tried to make it up to Tessa by locating the ruins of Ishaldi, perhaps giving her and her sisters proof of their place in the human world.

The idea backfired—terribly. Once they learned that he intended to bring his search for the Mer into the academic realm of archaeology, Tessa and her sisters had accused him of taking advantage, and of seeking to exploit them and their kind.

I wasn't always a backstabbing fuckup, he thought. Even though he hadn't intended to, he'd somehow become a carbon copy of the father he'd never respected—insensitive, reckless, heartless.

But it was too late for regret now. He'd made his choices—and his enemies—and all he could do now was follow the path to its end. After breaking up with Tessa, he'd prided himself on being cold, emotionless, and detached. Archaeology became his god, filling the void he'd let himself be sucked into. It also kept him from having to think about the pieces missing in his life, those tiny details that gave a man a sense of purpose and fulfillment.

Any chance he had to redeem himself in her eyes was long gone. To save his own sorry ass, he'd aligned himself with Queen Magaera.

The queen's voice shattered his internal contemplations. "Your mind drifts, my consort. I have yet to hear your thoughts on the matter at hand."

Jake quickly snapped back to attention. Judging by

the displeasure laced around her words, he knew the queen was not pleased. Instead of focusing on the matter at hand, he'd let his memories amble on.

He looked at her, feeling an odd quiver in his gut. In so many ways she reminded him of his father. She was determined to satisfy her own whims no matter the consequences.

For one crazy moment he wished her dead. Intuition warned him that she held no allegiance to him and would discard him when the opportunity arose. It was to be expected. He was used to walking the fine line between insanity and delusion. When he fell . . . Well, he always landed on his feet.

That, and the scars on his own damaged psyche were too deep to ever heal.

"Forgive me, my liege," he answered in a smooth drawl. "Like you, I know we can't remain immobile much longer." He forced himself to banish the old memories. The past was dead and gone. He needed to look forward, to the future. The Mer weren't going to crawl back into the obscurity enveloping their kind for almost two thousand years. They had a place in the modern world. And it was his job to help Queen Magaera define and rebuild her civilization.

Shifting in her place, Magaera cocked her head, studying him. "I am glad you agree. It is time the girl learned her lesson."

Aware that his pulse was beating double time through his veins, Jake stared back at her. Once again, she was sizing him up and scoping him out. "I know it is vexing that she continues to elude you. My thoughts are on how we can remedy that in the shortest time possible."

The queen smiled, but cruelty glinted in the depths of her eyes. "Her defiance will cost her everything by the time I am done." Her strident tone was charged with menace.

Ignoring his early feelings of empathy toward Tessa, Jake hardened his heart. At this point in his life, it wasn't difficult to manage. He'd had a lot of practice holding a grudge through the years. "The next time we go after her, it must be with a show of real force."

Her gaze taking on steel, Magaera nodded in agreement. "This time I will not send my soldiers." Her full lips stretched into a self-satisfied smirk. "I will go myself." Her mood abruptly shifted, and she laughed. "And humans will tremble in my wake."

Chapter 3

Now that the drama of the day had come to a close, Addison sat in Harbormaster Ashford's office. Jim Witkowsky had a seat beside her. Now and again his gaze would surreptitiously sidle her way, though he hadn't looked directly at her since they'd returned to port with the survivors aboard.

Uncomfortable that Witkowsky kept giving her the stink eye, Addison finally had enough. Looking directly at him, she smiled broadly. "Just because you've seen my bare breasts once doesn't mean I'm going to show them to you again, Jim."

Shocked by her outburst, Witkowsky turned beet red. His head dropped. "I wasn't lookin' at your tits," he muttered under his breath. "You might have given me a heads-up you were a mermaid."

"Can it, you two," Linda Ashford admonished from behind her desk. "Now that it's out, we have to deal with the fallout."

Addison pursed her lips, keenly aware that Witkowsky presently considered her to be some subhuman thing that had just crawled out of the primordial ooze. "He was going to have to know," she said in her own defense. "Most of the people who work with me do." On an unconscious level, she supposed the slip wasn't just part of her fervor to prove the new guy wrong. Truth be told, she was tired of hiding behind a human façade, suppressing her extraordinary abilities in order to appear average. There was so much more she could be doing with her Mercraft. The power was there, boiling furiously inside her core.

Lacing her hands together, Ashford leaned forward. "Yes, I know. And I thought we'd agreed I would be the one to break him in gently."

Addison stuck out her lower lip. "There wasn't any time. I was the most qualified diver to go into the water, and I did. There's no way a human could have handled that rescue."

"While I am aware that your, uh, unique abilities in the water give you an advantage over the rest of us peons, Addison, I was also under the impression that we had an agreement that you would stay out of the water as much as possible. And that during those times when you had to be submerged, you wouldn't pull out the tail. You were supposed to have the same limitations as any diver."

Fighting the impulse not to bang her hands against her head, Addison struggled to rein in her temper. It was true that her and her sisters' release from the A51 government compound had come with several stipulations attached. The girls would be allowed to resume their lives among the human population of Port Rock—but only if they refrained from Mer-related activities. This included not only keeping a check on their Mercraft but also rolling up their tails and keeping them tucked away.

Given her line of work, this was something Addison considered supremely unfair. Sure, it wasn't a problem for Tessa. Now married to Kenneth Randall, she'd recently discovered herself to be pregnant—with twins, no less. Gwen, too, didn't have much of a reason to go into the water. Her hotel on the mainland was thriving. Business was so good that she and Blake Whittaker, her new main squeeze, were scouting sites for a second hotel.

Although Blake and Gwen hadn't yet tied the knot, they had set a date in the fall. Gwen was also busy trying out the mommy ropes on Blake's son, Trevor. Debra, Blake's ex-girlfriend, had recently agreed to let Trevor spend more time in Maine now that his father was in a blossoming relationship.

Addison sighed. *And that leaves me.* It was true she had a career of her own to look after, but her love life remained barren.

"I put on my gear before going under," she explained in her defense. "I just forgot to put it back on before surfacing. I did have the child's welfare on my mind at the time."

"But she forgot to put it back on," Witkowsky broke in. "And boy, did we get an eyeful." His voice was so laced with innuendo, there was no doubt about the gander he'd taken, either.

Addison felt her cheeks heat. In the water, it was natural for a Mer to be as naked as the day she was born. When in her mermaid form, she'd never given her nudity a second thought. Neither did the rest of the men who worked with her and knew what she was. In their eyes, it was perfectly ordinary for her to surface in a tail.

Harbormaster Ashford shot the crewman a sour look. "Get your mind out of the gutter, Witkowsky. You've been a part of the team for only a brief time. There was no way I was going to fill you in until after you'd satisfied your probationary period."

Witkowsky shook his head with a combination of hostility and suspicion. "I have a right to know *what* I'm working with."

Addison's embarrassment quickly drained away, replaced with a surge of white-hot anger. "Who!" she snapped. "I am a *who*, not a *what*." Hands flying into motion, she pointed at herself. "I might not be human, but I have a brain and I have feelings, you jerk. So you can take your narrow little prejudices and stick 'em in your socks for all I care."

Ashford pounded her desk to restore order. "Enough, you two. The cat's out of the bag, and there's no putting it back."

"You can't keep hiding something like this," Witkowsky said. "I wasn't the only one who saw her. The people we rescued got a good look at her, too."

Belatedly recalling the one little fact, Addison felt her nerves prickle. A dozen different scenarios rushed through her mind, most of which concerned federal agents appearing to whisk her back to the A51 compound. There, she would be euthanized and picked, preserved for scientists to dissect.

That's what they'd like to do to us, came the unsettling thought. The notion wasn't as far-fetched as it might seem, either. A couple of the Mer soldiers taken into captivity after they'd attacked Little Mer Island had come uncomfortably close to being butchered in the name of science.

Thank the goddess above that Blake Whittaker had the nerve to blow the whistle. His testimony before a closed congressional committee had really pulled their alien asses out of the fire. His bravery had cost him his government career, which didn't seem to bother Blake at all. Though a human, he'd done the right thing.

And although the upper echelons of the United States government were now very aware of the existence of Mer in the water, it was nothing the powers that be were hurrying to release to the general public. Gwen was absolutely right when she'd stated her belief that the majority of people were afraid of things they didn't understand. Being different and existing outside the mainstream still carried a stigma.

Never missing a beat, Ashford filled them in. "An agent from the bureau's sciences division is on-site at the hospital now. Under his supervision, doctors have administered a mild sedative that will blur their recollections of the incident. In this instance, the sighting will be explained away as shock from the trauma induced by the accident."

Witkowsky snorted. "In other words, their memories are being erased."

Addison sighed. "It was my fault they saw me. If I had put on a bit of the Mercraft before I surfaced, they wouldn't have caught sight of my tail at all."

Another sound of disgust followed. "It's not right to hide the truth from people." Witkowsky paused and thought a moment. "And what the hell is Mercraft, anyway?"

Addison didn't feel like explaining the whole complicated process. "It's just something I can do." She doubted her coworker could handle the truth.

Ashford broke in. "That isn't our decision to make," she reminded him. "For the time being, the Mer are to remain a closely guarded secret." She narrowed her eyes. "If you can't get with the program, you will be assigned elsewhere. I can't promise that it will be anything you'd like, either."

The disgruntled man glowered. "I'm not liking any of this at all," he muttered. "The government already has too much control over our lives as it is."

"Doesn't matter if you like it, Witkowsky," his boss answered. "That's the way it's going to be. All that matters is that you do your job."

As Witkowsky folded his arms across his chest, his gaze sidled back to Addison. "I don't want to work with her."

Having been pissed on enough for one day, Addison pulled a face. Crossing her eyes, she stuck out her tongue. "I don't want to work with you, either, asshole."

Her boss wasn't amused. "Can it, Lonike. The best thing we can do right now is take the mermaid out of the water. I'm pulling you off harbor patrol and reassigning you to the fire department. The only water you'll be touching will be spurting out of the end of a hose."

Addison's jaw dropped. "You can't do that."

Ashford smiled, then pointed to the second patch sewn on her crisp white oxford shirt. "I believe this thing here means I am in charge of you."

Resisting the urge to roll her eyes, Addison mumbled, "Yeah, I guess so."

"Fire Chief Williams is short a few EMTs," Ashford informed her. "He could use an extra hand, and, until the province of Port Rock can find the funding for a few new hires, we're swapping city personnel between departments. You'll go where you're needed."

It wasn't right. It wasn't fair. Her temper got the better of her. "Why not send Witkowsky? He's the newbie. I've got seniority, damn it."

Ashford didn't blink an eye. "Because you knew better, and he didn't. As much as you don't like it, Addison, you are the one in control of your own actions. You might be a Mer, but that doesn't make you more special than the rest of us. *You* have to take responsibility for yourself. If you can't play by the team rules, then you're the one who'll have to be removed."

Meeting Ashford's gaze, Addison recognized the truth behind her words. The older woman was right, of course. When she'd first joined harbor patrol as an eager young recruit with certification in hand, she'd been hesitant to reveal her true nature in the water. Once she'd become confident enough to share her secret with the people she worked with, she was adamant that she be considered no different than any other member of the team.

Her anger at the injustice of it all drizzled away. "You're right," she allowed. "I knew better and I screwed up."

Ashford nodded but didn't have a chance to answer. A knock on her office door interrupted further conversation.

A secretary poked her head in. "I'm sorry to interrupt your meeting," she said by way of an apology, "but there's a Captain Mason McKenzie here to see you. He says he's been sent by the navy, and he wants to talk to Addison as soon as possible."

The statement sparked through her ears like a hot wire, sending a surge of adrenaline straight into Addison's veins. "Oh, shit . . . ," she muttered under her breath. This couldn't be good. She had a feeling she was in trouble—trouble so deep, not even a mermaid could swim her way out of it.

What the hell does the navy want with me?

Mason's heart pounded hard and fast as he shut the door to Ashford's office. Without giving away the details behind his mission, he'd requested a private place to speak with Addison alone. Ashford clearly wasn't happy, but she'd withdrawn without argument.

Addison Lonike was waiting in the room for him. Arms folded across her chest, she crossed her legs, swinging one foot back and forth in a manner of clear agitation. "If you've been sent to not so subtly remind me I was supposed to keep my tail tucked between my legs, you're too late. I've already had my ass chewed up one side and down the other."

Mason had not a clue about the incident she spoke of. He really didn't care. His first fleeting thought was that he'd just set eyes on the most beautiful woman in the world.

He stared at her, barely aware of his pulse beating in his temples. He knew he should answer her, but his senses were so overwhelmed, he could barcly speak. All he could think of was that Addison wasn't merely pretty. She was gorgeous, possessing the angled cheekbones and strong jawline of a top cover model. A mop of short red curls sticking out in every direction framed her face. Her eyes were her most outstanding feature. They weren't just green. Their color was like that of polished emeralds; bright, vivid, almost electric in their intensity.

A strange sense of discomfort blossomed in Mason's chest when he looked into those eyes. If a simple look made him squirm like a worm on hot cement, he didn't even want to imagine what actually talking to her would do to him.

Every word he'd rehearsed on the flight from Washington tangled in his throat. The effort to spit them out now was like chewing shards of glass—painful and almost impossible to accomplish.

"No, ma'am," he finally managed to answer after an infinite moment. "I have no interest in your tail."

The words came out all wrong.

Keeping a steady rhythm with her restless foot, Addison tilted her head back and directed an audible sigh toward the ceiling. "I can always tell the first time a human realizes he's staring at an honest to goodness mermaid," she commented drily. "Well, if you're waiting for me to break out in scales, it's not going to happen." Righting her head, she stuck out one arm. "Though if you want to see my scale pattern, here it is." She turned her arm one way and then another. "Pretty, isn't it?"

In other circumstances, Mason might have been inclined to agree. The arm she offered was decorated in swirls of black. Had he not known that mermaids had skin decorated in quite interesting ways, he would naturally have mistaken the design for an elaborate bit of needlework. It was certainly nothing out of the ordinary. Having served in the navy most of his adult life, he was accustomed to seeing sailors with tattoos much more striking than hers. He even had a few, though nothing quite so revealing.

Mason hurried to gather his thoughts. She was right. So far, the only thing he was managing to do was make a gaping fool of himself. He hadn't meant to stare. And he certainly wasn't staring because she was an alien entity. He stared because she was an eyeful and he liked nothing more than admiring an attractive woman. She looked bubbly, the kind of woman who laughed easily and liked to have fun.

He cleared his throat. If he'd believed in love at first sight, Mason would have considered himself smitten. "Uh, it's very attractive." Before she could respond, he hurried to add, "But I'm not here for the reasons you believe, even though I have a pretty good idea what those might, uh, entail."

Addison let her arm drop, and, without warning, she broke into a wide grin, revealing the split between her perfectly white teeth. "Forget the tail part of me, okay? I've got a much nicer ass."

Mason's heart skidded to a stop. Once again she'd cut him off at the pass with a well-placed quip. His mouth went bone dry. Damn it, she looked absolutely adorable. And he had no doubt about her figure. The white EMT T-shirt she wore clung to her full breasts, and her snugly fitting khaki pants emphasized her flat abdomen and gently flared hips. Every curve looked perfect.

This one is trouble with a capital T, some inner voice of preservation warned. Keeping her at arm's length was going to be hard, but he'd just have to bite the bullet and keep everything that occurred between them on a professional level.

Mason immediately forced himself to crush the attraction he felt toward Addison Lonike. She definitely had charisma, that special something that most would define as flesh impact. In the back of his mind he briefly wondered what it would be like to hook up with a mermaid ...

He cut the thought short with practiced precision. Why the hell was he even thinking that way? He hadn't come here to propose to the woman, for God's sake. He'd come to talk her into joining a vital mission that might well determine the way Mer and humans regarded each other in the future.

Mason coughed discreetly into his hand. "With all due respect, ma'am, I have to let you know I'm not interested in your, ah, finer attributes."

The playful spark immediately left her eyes. Uncrossing her legs, she sat up straight. The air around her chilled more than a little. "Okay, cut the bullshit, shall we? What does the government want with us now? Except for that little slipup today, I haven't done anything wrong. And thanks to the wonders of medical science, the victims who saw me today won't even remember it once the docs get finished playing mad scientist."

In lieu of an immediate answer, Mason indicated the chair across from her. "May I?"

She nodded. "Knock yourself out."

Mason sat, placing the briefcase he carried within easy reach. "In order not to waste any more of your time, ma'am, I will let you know that acting on orders from the Secretary of the Navy, I have been sent to inquire about your availability to serve your country."

Addison Lonike's eyes widened. "Are you asking me to join the navy?"

Mason nodded. He opened his suitcase, pulling out the folder he'd been given. "The secretary is offering you a civilian's position as an MTA, which would be Mer Tactical Adviser." He handed over the folder. "The details are inside, along with the financial compensation and what your first assignment would entail."

Addison eagerly accepted the folder. Flipping it open, she quickly scanned the few pages she'd been given. Her face darkened as she read. "Gee, you guys don't pay very much," she commented. "I make more as an EMT."

Mason shrugged. "Budget cuts. And we are already fighting wars in two other countries. The Middle East is keeping us busy."

Addison read a little more. "It says here I'm to be assigned to USET. Which is?"

"Undersea Search and Exploration Task Force," Mason filled in. "Our present assignment is to scout out a location in the Mediterranean where we believe some of the rogue Mer have established their stronghold."

A deep frown pressed her full lips together. "Is that what you consider the Mer to be?" she asked sarcastically. "Rogues? Or maybe you think of us more like terrorists." She thrust the folder back at him. "My answer is no. The pay stinks. No matter what you humans might think of the Mer, we still have to put a roof over our heads when we aren't in the water."

Mason checked his sigh of exasperation. He decided to try another tactic. "Our mission will be more ambassadorial than military. If at all possible, we would like to make contact with Queen Magaera and her adviser." It wasn't precisely the truth, but at present Addison Lonike was only going to get the basic facts. If she didn't need to know it, she wouldn't be told—period.

Anger sparked in the depths of her eyes. "That would be Jake 'the Jerk' Massey," she spat without hesitation. "The asshole who dumped my sister at the altar and took advantage of our heritage to further his own stupid archaeological career."

Mason made a mental note of her emotional outburst. In a way, he didn't want her to accept the position. Unless she could learn to conduct herself accordingly, she would make a piss-poor tactician. If she showed any sign of weakness, no one serving on the team would take her seriously at all. She'd be disrespected, an oddity who'd been consulted solely because of her alien status.

Still, he had his orders. "Which is why we would like you on our side," he said. "You know how Massey thinks. And you know how the Mer think."

She didn't receive his words well. Her brow furrowed. "Despite what you may think, my sisters and I have very little in common with the Mer who have emerged from Ishaldi," she said. "They were raised in a whole other society, one that doesn't view human beings worthy to survive as more than slaves and vessels for breeding. They are a fierce warmongering race, and, unless their current queen is deposed, the Mer will fight to the death." She snorted. "I am afraid you're going to discover Queen Magaera isn't of the mind to be diplomatic in any way."

Her words didn't seem to faze him. "I understand that you and your sisters are actually of royal lineage yourselves."

Addison shrugged. "So I've been told."

Mason searched his memory for details of the intelligence report gathered by researchers in the A51 division. "I understand that an ancestor of yours, a Queen Nyala, was actually one who made the decision to seal the sea-gate in order to prevent a war between humans and Mer."

She nodded. "That's what Magaera told Tessa. Of course, I'm sure Nyala didn't intend for the Mer to become extinct in Earth's waters. She didn't leave Ishaldi alone. I'm sure the Mer who accompanied her simply integrated into the human population as the centuries passed."

"We're under the impression there are more out there," he allowed. "It only makes sense that some of the Mer escaped before the wormhole closed."

Addison let her head dip back toward the ceiling before releasing a long sigh. "It has felt that way sometimes." Her head bobbed back into place. Humor sparked in the depths of her eyes. "Hey, I bet if you put out an advertisement, a few will answer." Her grin was one of pure mischief. "Then you can recruit them."

Mason was disinclined to be baited. He wasn't here to indulge in shits and giggles. "I imagine they're like your sister Gwen," he chided her gently. "Afraid to come out for fear of being ridiculed."

Her grin vanished. "It's not an easy thing to do." Her knowing gaze connected with his. "You have to trust the person you're letting into your life before you roll out the tail. We're pretty lucky, because the people who do know have always been supportive."

"Not to mention it helps bring in the tourists. Port Rock is famous for its stories of mermaids living in the bay." He leaned forward in his chair. "Seriously, if you were to estimate the numbers, how many Mer would you guess might be living among humans now?"

Addison nibbled her lip in thought. A few minutes ticked by in silence. "I couldn't tell you," she finally admitted. "It's kind of complicated, but Mer aren't born with the realization that they're mermaids." She tugged the uncut, unpolished stone hanging from a gold chain around her neck. "A Mer must be given a soul-stone in order to manifest her powers. My sisters and I all received ours at birth. It allows us to tap into our shifting abilities, as well as our psi-kinetic abilities. Without it, we're just normal people. There may be hundreds of women out there who have no idea what they really are because they never received their stones. Their heritage has been lost to them over the centuries."

A sliver of sympathy knifed Mason's heart. He couldn't even begin to imagine what it might be like to go through life not knowing who or what you really were. The closest he could guess was that it would be like losing a limb. The loss of an arm or a leg was usually devastating to people; yet somehow the human spirit found a way to compensate and to survive. It must be the same with Mer who weren't aware of their abilities. They would probably always feel pieces of themselves were missing.

For the first time he began to think the Mer might have more in common with human beings than he'd first allowed.

But it was time to steer things back around to his reason for coming to Port Rock. "One thing we're pretty sure of is that the Mer aren't going to go away."

Addison allowed a small smile. "No shit, Sherlock."

Mason ignored her attempt to prod him and continued. "We know it's to our advantage to try and establish diplomatic relations with Queen Magaera. Our position isn't to try and deny the Mer a place in Earth's waters, but to help their, uh, nation through its growing pains as they hopefully come to embrace democracy. We feel our attempts to reach out will be met with more seriousness with a mermaid on our side."

Addison settled back in her chair. "Somehow I feel there's more to the story than you're letting on. Magaera's got Atargatis's scepter, which gives her a lot of power, from what I understand. I'm guessing she's got you guys by the balls, and you don't know how to handle her."

Mason decided to cut through the bullshit. "If I said that was true, would it change your mind about joining USET?"

The buzzing of a cell phone interrupted Addison's answer. Reaching into her back pocket to retrieve the phone, she read the text. "Shit," she muttered. "It's Tessa. I was supposed to meet her and Ken for lunch at the mall." She glanced at the time. "I'm almost a half hour late." She quickly flipped open the cover of her Sidekick and typed back a brief reply.

"So you're blowing me off?" Mason asked as she tucked the phone away.

Addison shook her head. "Honestly, this is a decision I couldn't make without talking to Tessa and Gwen, anyway. We've always stuck together, and if it affects one of us, it affects all of us." She pushed to her feet. "Come to lunch. We'll talk it over and see what shakes out."

Mason tucked the folder back into his briefcase.

"That's fair," he agreed. Despite Webber's insistence, it wasn't right to ask her to make such a life-changing decision on the spur of the moment.

And, truth be told, he was actually looking forward to spending a little more time with her. Although his mind wasn't made up just yet, his opinion of the Mer was beginning to change.

There might be more to the species than met the eye.

Chapter 4

"What do you think of these two, honey?"

Pushing SEND on her cell phone, Tessa Randall raised her eyes from the screen. For the last ten minutes, she'd been tied up in a texting conversation with Addison. So astute in the business of saving lives, her little sister was one of those people who just couldn't show up on time to save her own. "That girl will be late to her own funeral," she muttered, tucking her phone back into her purse.

"Honey, look . . ."

Tessa sighed. She should have known better than to bring her husband to shop for baby clothes. Kenneth had practically taken to glowing since she'd shared the news that had surprised even her. She hadn't expected to become pregnant immediately after going through the Mer ritual that would synchronize her body's biological clock with that of her human mate. *Apparently I'm a very fertile Myrtle.* The ink on their marriage certificate wasn't even dry; yet here she was, knocked up with twins.

Amazing.

She glanced at the cute pink pinafores Ken had clutched in his hands. "They're very pretty, babe," she said, "but they're for toddlers. We're shopping for infants."

Her words didn't deter Kenneth a bit. "They'll grow," he countered, flashing a cheery smile as he added them to the growing pile in their cart.

Tessa had to smile. Every time she looked at her rough-hewn husband, she wanted to pinch herself. She couldn't believe how lucky she'd been to find Kenneth Randall. The love he'd offered her came with no strings attached. He adored her for who she was, not what she was. Discovering she was a Mer hadn't deterred him one bit. In his eyes she was perfect, and he treated her like a princess.

She had to smile at his sensible nature. "Yes," she agreed, "they will."

Kenneth leaned over, offering her a quick peck on the cheek. "And how are all my girls today? You're not too tired, are you?"

Tessa quickly shook her head. "I'm fine." It was true she'd had a bit of an energy lag lately, but she attributed it to the morning sickness she'd recently begun to suffer. "I could use something to eat, though."

She glanced down at her still-flat stomach and grimaced. She hadn't yet begun to show, but that would soon change with two babies taking up space in their new rental. "Will you still love me when I'm bigger than a house and all moody from hormones?"

"Absolutely," he insisted with all the enthusiasm of a man who'd never been through the process. Once the twins were born, he might change his mind about the miracle of birth.

Despite his reassurance, Tessa had her doubts. When she got agitated, she tended to be a little on the mean side. And, oh goddess! Soon there would be more than one baby to deal with. While she had no doubt that Kenneth would be a hands-on dad, the idea of actually giving birth to these babies was scaring the ever-loving daylights out of her. A true Mer didn't have her babies in a sterile hospital room with a nice doctor in attendance and an epidural to kill the pain. Young mermaids were birthed in the water, where they'd be immediately acclimatized to their natural environment.

She'd already picked out the girl's stones, as she and Kenneth had both decided they wanted their children to be aware of their natural heritage. Although she and her sisters—and so many other Mer—had hidden their true origins, Tessa had a feeling that was about to change. Slowly but surely, the Mer were beginning to emerge from the shadows of obscurity. The sea-gate was open again, and more Mer were eager to return to Earth's waters.

Kenneth checked his watch. "It's almost one, and I'm definitely ready to eat. Let's get this paid for and head on down to the food court. Addison can find us there."

Tessa nodded in agreement. Breakfast was long past, and it had been hours since she'd indulged her craving for caffeine and sugar. She was sure a root beer float with an extra scoop of vanilla ice cream was lurking somewhere in her immediate future.

They'd just begun to push their cart toward the checkout stand when a strange high-pitched whistle

pierced the air. The whine got louder and louder until
the air around them began to tremble from the intensity.
The entire building began to shake. Screams and shouts
mingled with the sound of stone tearing asunder.

Wincing in pain, Tessa slammed the palms of her
hands against her eyes. So did everyone else shopping in
the boutique.

"What the hell is that?" Kenneth shouted.

They were about to find out. The pitch grew louder,
deafening. Seconds later, a massive explosion filled the
air. And then, without any warning whatsoever, the rear
of the building crumbled.

Tessa stood rooted in her place, stunned by the eerie
sight of seeing an entire brick wall vanish right before
her eyes. The screams of the shocked and wounded reverberated through the frightening scene. She stared in
disbelief. One minute everything had been perfectly
normal. And then the world exploded. It was like being
picked up and thrown into the middle of a battlefield.

Tendrils of smoke rose from the remnants like ghostly
fingers. Two figures swirled into sight amid the damage.
They began to advance, their movements propelled by
purpose. The first figure seemed to be a blond woman
carrying a glowing stick. A taller man followed in her
wake. They glided amid the debris and the wounded
people as though taking a stroll through the park on a
warm summer day.

The fine hairs at the nape of Tessa's neck rose to attention. A gasp of recognition tore past her lips. Oh, shit!
Speak of the devil, and here she comes, came the wild,
disconnected thought.

Queen Magaera had returned, this time in person.

And she had to rub it in by bringing Jake Massey along for the ride. The fucker—he would have to come along, just to rub it in.

Whether or not they wanted it to, round two was about to commence.

Adrenaline mixed with anticipation surged straight through Tessa's veins. Her first instinct was to protect the two precious babies in her womb. But there was no way she could make a run for it—not when innocent people were still trapped amid the rubble. The wounded needed help. The plaintive whimpering of a child hurt in the detonation grated against her ears. Sirens wailed in the distance. Help was on the way, but it couldn't arrive fast enough.

Suddenly Kenneth was there, placing himself between his wife and the advancing enemy. His hands were raised in a defensive stance. Except this time he wasn't unarmed.

Tessa winced. Kenneth had recently applied for, and received, a permit to carry a concealed weapon. He'd also undergone extensive training and was a dead-on shot.

Given that they'd been attacked and almost killed before, it seemed a wise decision. In the back of her mind, she wished the A51 division had returned her Ri'kah, which agents had confiscated when they'd taken her family into protective custody. With such a piece of Mer weaponry in her hands, she could do some serious damage. As it stood, she'd just have to do the best she could with her own Mercraft. And a little was all she had. Pregnancy had almost sapped her completely dry.

Kenneth thumbed back the safety on his pistol. "Stop right there," he warned.

Jake Massey stepped forward. Tessa slowly came apart inside at the sight of him. *That fucking bastard!* Fury sizzled within her. He deserved to have his heart ripped out and fed back to him, piece by poisonous piece.

"Don't even think about it, Randall," Jake called across the smoldering ruins. "You haven't got a chance."

Kenneth kept his weapon level. "That's what you think."

"You know why we're here. Just give us Tessa and we'll go." A wide grin crossed his face. "Otherwise my liege here might be inclined to do a little more redecorating. And humans, as you know, have little value to her."

"Not going to happen, Massey," Kenneth grated. "I'll die before you'll take my wife."

Queen Magaera smirked. "That can be arranged, I am sure." She raised the scepter she carried. The jewels embedded in its golden staff glittered with the intensity of a star gone nova. It was a breathtaking thing, frightening yet awesome at the same time.

It was also powerful enough to send Tessa's hope of escape plunging to the pit of her stomach. Nothing they had on hand could match it. It was like trying to fight a wildfire with water balloons—ineffective and a little bit laughable.

Tessa reached out to put a hand on Kenneth's arm. Resist and more people would be hurt. She couldn't risk that. Too many people had already been injured or killed by the rogue Mer. "I'll go."

But Kenneth wasn't listening. The last time they'd been attacked, he'd failed to protect her and her sisters. It hadn't been his fault. He was outgunned and outarmed.

Not this time. He was prepared to defend his family. "No way."

"Don't," she started to say, but it was it too late. Kenneth squeezed the trigger, sending a shot straight toward Jake Massey.

Jake screamed as the missile tore into his shoulder. One hand flying to cover the wound, he dropped to his knees. "You shot me, you fuck!"

"They can't take you to prison if you're dead, Jake. Behind bars is where I want to see you next." Kenneth aimed the gun toward Magaera. He wasn't afraid and he wasn't messing around. By the look on his face, he would shoot with the intent to kill. Seconds later another shot rang out.

At that exact moment, everything seemed to decelerate, turning every action and reaction into a slow-motion ballet.

Queen Magaera laughed as she raised her free hand. The bullet slowed, so much so that Tessa was able to clearly follow its trajectory.

Without so much as blinking, Magaera simply reached out and plucked the bullet out of the air. Holding the small projectile between thumb and forefinger, she examined it from every angle. "Is that all you humans have?" She laughed, flicking it away.

"Hurry up," Jake howled in pain and rage. "I'm going to fucking bleed to death here."

"Let me go," Tessa said, realizing that she was pleading and that her voice was shaking uncontrollably. "If I don't, she'll kill everyone here."

Kenneth shook his head. "No way." He fired again—and again. The gun in his hand recoiled. Violent flashes and the smell of gunpowder seared the air.

The Mer queen merely swatted them away. And then, with the most casual of moves, she turned up her palm. A small orb of light burst into life above her hand. It blazed with the intensity of a live coal.

Tessa gasped. Magaera was powering herself up from the crystals embedded in the scepter. Fighting panic, she knew there was no way anyone would survive once the blast hit its mark.

Magaera smiled. The soul-stone around her neck blazed with a luminescence that lent her pale skin an unearthly glow. She seemed to tower above them all, a goddess stepped down from the realm of heaven to wreak havoc on the lesser mortals.

"For your defiance, I'm going to burn your man down into a little cinder." The orb in her hand took flight, winging its way straight toward Kenneth. With each passing second it got bigger and menacingly brighter. There was no way to dodge it.

Without thinking, Tessa threw herself in front of her husband. Vaguely she was aware of the high-pitched whine cutting through her ears. The atmosphere around her crackled with an eerie glow.

Aware that her heart was pounding hard against her ribs, she lifted her hands. It was a panicked reaction, done without rational thought. A moment of consideration would have reminded her she wasn't strong enough to ward off the threat. Drawing on every ounce of energy she had, even that of her unborn children, she threw up a shield around Kenneth. A shower of blue sparks twinkled in the air around her.

But it wasn't enough.

An instant later the world exploded.

"Tessa!" She heard panic in Kenneth's voice but couldn't respond. The terror ripping through her overrode her sense of self-preservation. She would die to protect her husband.

The concussion whacked Tessa like a giant's fist. Heat seared through her, burning the clothes off her body. Vaguely aware that her feet were no longer touching the ground, she flew through the air.

The violence of the impact crushed the air out of her lungs. Struggling to breathe, she couldn't catch her breath before wave after wave of pain flashed brutally throughout her entire body. The only sound she heard was a low moan, and it was her own.

Tessa blinked, disbelief and horror rising inside her. All she could do was stare in shock at the flames, smoke, and debris surrounding her. *Where's Kenneth?* she first thought, dazed but coherent.

Concern for his safety overrode agony, giving her the strength to sit up. She got one arm under her, but when she tried to move, a white-hot spike burned its way through her shoulder and up her neck. She would have cried out, but there was suddenly no oxygen to breathe.

Clamping her jaw, Tessa rode the wave, struggling to remain conscious. But the pain was too much for her abused body to endure. Unable to stop the assault, she spiraled into pitch-black darkness . . .

Chapter 5

Heart pounding a mile a minute, Addison hurried toward the wreckage of the Itty Bitty Baby Boutique. The last text she'd received from Tessa had said she and Kenneth were shopping there.

The next message she'd received hadn't been from Tessa, though. A 911 call had come through on her work pager, instructing all available emergency personnel to report to the mall. Details were sketchy, but word of a terrorist attack was going around.

She didn't remember getting out of the car; nor did she exactly recall the fire chief's warning that rescuers should proceed with all due caution. Putting her feet into motion, she'd dodged around the barriers police were in the process of setting up. And even though she hadn't invited him along, Mason McKenzie was managing to keep up with her.

People stumbled past her, unaware where they should go or what they should do. Some were sobbing piteously. Others were blank faced with shock.

Addison's fear ran so thick, it made her light-headed. "My sister and her husband were in there," she yelled at Mason.

As an EMT and search and rescue worker, Addison had witnessed her share of tragedy. But she'd never beheld such utter devastation firsthand. What had formerly been a beautiful little shop snuggled amid many others in the midsized mall was presently a wreck, little more than ruins. Everywhere she looked, chaos prevailed. People were still hysterical and confused.

"By the goddess," she gasped, "it looks like a war zone."

Aid workers were already on the scene, performing triage on those who had been injured in what looked like an intense blast. The entire rear wall of the store was gone. An empty space gaped out into the parking lot behind the mall. The moans and groans of the wounded people surrounding her threatened to rip through her sanity.

Addison swore under her breath. A dozen scenarios ran through her mind. She didn't care what had happened or how. All she cared about was finding Tessa and Kenneth. She'd already tried both their cells a dozen times but had received no response. *If they were safe, Tessa would answer,* she thought.

Aware that her heart was bashing against her ribs, Addison began to search through the victims. Since she was still in uniform, nobody questioned her presence. She couldn't begin to think where to look for them in the rubble. "My sister," she asked any and every aid worker. "Have you seen a Tessa? Or a Kenneth?"

Mason McKenzie gently took her arm. "The paramedics are working on a man named Randall," he said quietly. "That's your sister's last name, isn't it?"

His words were as sharp and painful as a hot blade shoved between her ribs.

Addison whirled. A couple of paramedics from the hospital were bent over a man stretched out on the floor. A battered mess, he was evidently the victim of a horrible scorching. Most of his clothing looked as if it had been burned away. What little remained had been torn away so rescue workers could administer CPR. An oxygen mask covered his face.

Instant recognition slammed into her brain. She stared in dazed horror. The shock of seeing her big strong brother-in-law little more than a helpless victim was so sudden and so deep that she couldn't take a breath.

More terrified than she'd ever been in her life, Addison stared at him for in interminable minute. Somehow, she managed to shake off the numb feeling and hurried over to the paramedics. "That's my sister's husband," she said briskly, fighting to keep the emotion out of her voice. "How is he?"

One of the medics glanced up. "It's not good . . . He's got burns over sixty percent of his body. He's already flatlined once. We've got him stable and are waiting for transport." Even as they spoke, two rescue workers bearing a stretcher were heading their way.

Addison's gaze zeroed in on Kenneth's torn, seared skin. A tear slid down her cheek. She swiped it away with an angry hand. *Not now*. Her personal feelings had no place in the middle of an emergency. "His wife, Tessa, was with him. Have you seen her?"

The medic shook his head. "Could be she's still in there. We haven't gotten everybody out yet."

Addison glanced toward the ruins of the store. Racks of merchandise still smoldered amid the deep piles of rubble. The parts of the roof that were still intact looked unstable, ready to crumble at any given second.

"If Tessa's in there, I've got to find her." She refused to consider the possibility that Tessa might be dead among the rubble. It was something she would *know*.

"Tessa . . ." She'd intended to shout her sister's name, but it came out as little more than a sob between numb lips. She'd never lost it in the middle of an emergency. But then again, members of her family had never been involved. Her thoughts were so jumbled that she couldn't think straight.

She headed toward the debris.

Mason McKenzie grabbed her arm. "This isn't the time to play hero." He nodded toward the medic lifting Kenneth onto the stretcher. "You need to go to the hospital with him."

Addison immediately broke away, shaking her head. "My sister's in there." Her voice cracked briefly before she was able to continue. "If anyone can find her, I can."

Captain McKenzie's features might have been carved of stone for all the emotion he revealed. His intelligent blue gaze assessed the chaos around them in a calm and efficient manner. "She might already be on her way to the hospital," he noted. "She'll need you there."

Forcing herself to focus, she drew a steadying breath. The acrid odor of smoldering merchandise scorched the air around them. "Other people still need help," came her stubborn reply. "My job is to help them."

Although she couldn't be sure, Addison thought she saw a glint of admiration in Captain McKenzie's eyes. Clad in his full dress blues, he towered over her like a mountain. With his blond crew cut, high cheekbones, and square jaw, he looked like the epitome of the all-American male. His tan emphasized that this was a man who spent a lot of time out of doors. Broad shouldered, narrow hipped, and with legs that stretched for a mile, he definitely looked like the peak of physical perfection—like a Roman god stepped down from the heavens.

A shudder whisked down her spine. The sheer presence of the man was overwhelming.

Her chest tightened in a most uncomfortable way. *Pull yourself together,* she warned herself.

Captain McKenzie nodded gravely. "I'll help," he answered without hesitation.

Addison blinked and tried to refocus. Having a teammate helped. McKenzie even had the good sense to grab a trauma bag, something that had completely escaped her. Hers was still in the car.

As they approached the destruction, Fire Chief Williams motioned for their attention. "Good to see you, Lonike," he said, lowering the walkie-talkie pressed against his ear. "I'm sorry this is your first call on the department's team. We'd hoped to break you in easy."

Addison didn't waste any time. "I'm ready, sir. But I need to let you know that my sister and her husband were shopping here when the blast occurred."

"Aw, shit," Williams muttered. "That's not good news."

"They're taking Kenneth to the hospital now, but I can't find out anything about Tessa." She risked another glance at the devastation. By the look of things, anyone who'd survived was damn lucky. "Does anyone know what happened?"

"Just that there was some crazy-ass woman with a glowing stick," the fire chief answered. "If that makes any sense. Witnesses have reported that one of the invaders was shot. Past that, nobody seems to remember anything. There was some kind of second explosion, like a fireball tearing through the place." The chief shook his head as if he could hardly believe what he was saying.

Captain McKenzie shook his head. "Looks as if they lobbed a handful of grenades around in here."

Williams eyed the uniform. "You here for a reason, Captain?"

"Just to help render assistance to the wounded," McKenzie answered. "I have training in first aid."

"He's with me," Addison filled in.

Her answer seemed to satisfy Williams. His attention shifted back to the matter at hand. "The feds are on their way now. This has been declared a terrorist attack, and all personnel are on red alert. All security precautions are being implemented now." He cocked his head, giving her a knowing look. Of course, he knew she was a Mer. He'd been aching to snatch her from harbor patrol for years. "You know what this means."

Addison stared at him with dawning comprehension. The implications of what he'd said began to hit her.

For ten, maybe twenty, seconds she couldn't react. How could she not have known? Her heart had to be pushing more than a hundred beats per minute. The blood roaring through her veins all but deafened her. It took only seconds for her to put two and two together.

Queen Magaera had come back. And Jake Massey was apparently still acting as her faithful lackey.

Her shoulders sagged in relief. "Tessa's not in there," she murmured to no one in particular. But any sense of relief she might have felt was short-lived. There was no doubt in her mind that the vengeful monarch had achieved her objective of taking Tessa hostage.

They had all known this day would come. They should have been ready; better prepared. The first rogue Mer attack on their family should have warned them Magaera would stop at nothing to gain what she wanted.

Now Tessa was in more danger than ever before.

The ER was in chaos. The small county hospital didn't have enough resources to deal with such a major public emergency, and victims of the attack lined the hallways. Most weren't hurt badly, suffering mostly from shock and the trauma of having a perfectly normal day go haywire right before their eyes.

Mason hurried behind Addison as she frantically tried to find out about Kenneth. The facility was already crammed with sick adults and crying babies brought in for other reasons, making navigation difficult.

"My brother-in-law just came in," she said to anyone who would listen. "Kenneth Randall."

A nurse clad in scrubs paused to answer her. "The burn victim?"

Addison nodded eagerly. "Yes, that's him."

"He's in trauma room three," the nurse answered.

"Thanks." The words had barely left Addison's mouth when a redheaded woman carrying a little boy hurried their way. A tall, dark man followed at her heels. They were, Mason assumed, Addison's sister, Gwen, and her fiancé, Blake Whittaker. Two more men trailed behind him. Their dark suits and impenetrable sunglasses immediately pegged them as federal agents.

Protection, he thought. *That was fast.* Since the first attack on the Lonike girls, and their subsequent release back into the human population, A51 undercover agents had been assigned to keep an eye on the girls and their family. Both fellows did a double take at the sight of his dress blues, but they said nothing. They were, for all intents and purposes, on the same team.

Both his cell phone and pager were buzzing wildly, but he ignored them both. Adam Webber had probably received word of the attack. But he wasn't in the position to talk or answer any questions. Right now he was sticking close to Addison.

"We got here as fast as we could," Gwen said, shifting the child on her hip to a more comfortable position. The little boy's arms were clutched around her neck in a death grip. By the look on his face, the child was obviously frightened. "The agents . . . They're saying we've been attacked again by the Mer."

Addison grimaced. "Kenneth and Tessa were in the middle of the blast. Kenneth's in trauma room three. But Tessa—" She choked, unable to make herself say more.

Everyone went pale. "By the goddess . . . ," Gwen murmured. "We knew they'd try again, but not so soon. Where's Tessa?"

Addison ducked her head to hide the tears welling in her eyes. "They got her," she mumbled under her breath. "Magaera and Jake. They did this."

"Jesus Christ." Blake Whittaker cast a glance over his shoulder. "No wonder we've got company. The boys in black have been hot on our tails since we left the hotel."

Gwen's jaw tightened. "I was afraid this would happen. As long as Magaera's out there, she's going to be a danger to all of us."

Addison nodded in agreement. "I don't think they will hurt her. She's the key to the sea-gate. They need to keep her alive."

Gwen pressed her lips together. "We can deal with only one thing at a time. Kenneth's the one who needs our help now."

Although he felt a little bit guilty about eavesdropping on the family in their time of tragedy, Mason was aware that every little piece of knowledge he gleaned might help when the USET team went after Magaera again.

This time we're not going to lose, he told himself. The devastation these creatures could cause was enormous. What's more, they did so with little regard for human lives. After witnessing the aftermath in the mall, he was more convinced than ever that eliminating the Mer entirely would be the wise thing to do.

Mason glanced toward Addison and her sister. He didn't fail to notice that Gwen Lonike took a lot of care to make sure her scale pattern was concealed. Addison, on the other hand, didn't seem to care if other people gaped at the design covering her arms.

But still another question begged for an answer in his mind. What should be done with the Mer already integrated among the human race? Should they be dealt with differently from the rogue Mer, or should the entire species be lumped together?

But there was no time to ponder the question. They arrived to find doctors and nurses streaming out of the ICU.

Addison muscled her way to the front of the group. She caught a woman dressed in scrubs. "Dr. Jiminez, can you tell us what's going on with Kenneth Randall? He's married to my sister."

"He's stable. Though there for a while it was touch and go because his heart couldn't keep its rhythm." Jiminez shook her head. "He must have sustained a massive shock, something that entirely short-circuited his system. He's a strong man, though, in good health."

Eyes shadowed with worry, Gwen broke in. "But he's going to be okay?"

Dr. Jiminez nodded. "I think so, but we can't know for sure. He also suffered burns across sixty percent of his body. His clothes offered some protection, but there's still a lot of damage. We're preparing to move him to the burn unit now."

"Take Trevor," she told Blake, handing the boy over to his father. "Kenneth needs my help."

The child immediately began to cry. "Don't go, Gwennie," he bawled piteously.

Gwen ran a hand through the child's tousled hair. "I'll be back as soon as I can, honey."

"Hush, kiddo. You aren't being abandoned." Blake cradled his frightened son. He looked to Gwen. "What are you going to do?" She straightened her shoulders. "He'll need help healing. I can give him that, using Mercraft."

Jiminez looked at her in confusion. "Mercraft?"

Gwen pursed her lips. "It's a form of crystal healing," she explained, without giving away too much.

The doctor's face took on a skeptical look. "If you don't mind, I'd rather stick to medicine I understand."

Gwen insisted. "You'll just have to trust me when I say I know what I'm doing." She cocked her head toward the agents still shadowing their movements. "I'm sure they will be more than glad to explain."

Jiminez pursed her lips. "You are his family," she allowed, "so I can't stop you from visiting him. But I will put a stop to anything I believe is harming my patient."

"You are welcome to watch," Gwen invited her. "I'm not hiding it anymore."

Addison grabbed her sister's arm. "Are you sure you want to do that?"

Gwen nodded. "It's time for the Mer to come out of the shadows. After today's attack, there's no way they can keep us hidden much longer. Going after us on Little Mer Island is one thing, but Magaera deliberately widened the arena today. It's just a matter of time before we're exposed."

"You don't seem upset," Blake commented.

Gwen smiled gravely. "I'm not. I've been thinking about this for a long time, and I'm ready." She reached for her fiancé's hand. "As long as I have you, I can take anything they throw at us."

Addison blew out a breath through pursed lips. "Looks like we're going to have to."

Blake nodded. "We'll be in the waiting room."

There was nothing they could do now but wait. The group parted.

Although he wasn't sure if it was appropriate at this point, Mason followed them into a lounge area where family members could wait for word on their sick or injured loved ones. A convenience area offering coffee, tea, soda, and other nonperishable snacks reminded him that the morning's breakfast was long gone. Although he wasn't a regular coffee drinker, he surely could use a boost of caffeine to revitalize his mental faculties.

"Anybody want coffee?" he asked.

Blake flagged a hand. "I could use a cup."

"Me, too," Addison chimed in.

Mason pointed to an empty table near the coffee bar. "That's okay?"

"I'll go for that." Settling Trevor in a chair, Blake busied himself finding something for the child to eat, finally settling on a banana, an oatmeal cookie, and a pint of milk out of the vending machine. The cup of coffee he claimed for himself was black and unsweetened.

Addison went for the coffee and a packet of pretzels. She frowned. "I had my mind set on tacos for lunch."

Mason settled on coffee, heavily lashed with cream and several packets of sweetener. When he sat down beside Addison, Blake made a face. "You drink sissy coffee."

Mason recognized the challenge behind the ex-agent's comment. Along with the dossiers on the Lonike sisters, he'd also been given the history of the men in their lives. Whittaker's story was an interesting one.

He sipped his brew. "I take my coffee with cream and sugar," he drawled, "because I don't need any more hair on my chest."

Blake guffawed as he unwrapped the cookie for Trevor and handed it over. "Yeah, this stuff is strong enough to peel the paint off a car," he agreed. "I think it's been sitting for at least a day, maybe two."

Oblivious to the drama around him, Trevor immediately stuffed one big bite into his little mouth. "Mmm, good, Daddy."

Blake barely turned his head. Parents seemed to know what was going on whether they looked or not. "Don't be rude, Son."

Addison tore into her own packet of food. "He's from the navy." Imitating Trevor, she stuffed a couple pretzels into her own mouth. "Tasty, huh?"

Trevor giggled wildly, snorting his milk.

Mason tried to hold his annoyance in check. Kids just weren't his thing. He didn't like them and couldn't imagine wanting any in the future. He liked being unattached, going wherever his next assignment might take him.

Blake rolled his eyes. "I can see that. Is there a reason he's with you?"

Mason decided to answer for himself. "I've been sent by the Secretary of the Navy to recruit Addison to join our team in the Mediterranean."

Blake immediately shifted into agent mode. "Then you know where Magaera's base of operations is?"

"We have a good idea," he allowed carefully. "But we can't get close due to the magnetic interference generated by the wormhole, or the sea-gate, as you call it. It's shutting down our equipment."

"I'm aware of the effects," the former agent returned drily. "I'm also going to guess that things in the water are more than a little bit treacherous for your divers."

Mason decided to answer honestly. There was no point in trying to hide anything from her family. "The Mer have proven to be a threat to my men," he confirmed.

"So you're trying to even up the odds a little?"

He sneaked a little glance toward Addison, who continued to tease the kid with her antics. Her messy red hair looked like a halo of flames around her pert face. No doubt about it; she was a real cutie. Every time he looked at her, he felt something deep inside his stomach squirm.

Nerves, he told himself refusing to think it might be anything else. Certainly he wasn't attracted to her . . .

Mason reined in his recalcitrant thoughts. This wasn't a time to get distracted from the task at hand. "That's exactly what we want to do," he confirmed. "Although the A51 has provided us with all their intelligence, we're still up against something we don't understand. And though their technology seems primitive, we have discovered it to be very effective."

Blake sipped more of his coffee. "That makes sense." He didn't have a chance to add more. Spotting them across the waiting area, Gwen hurried into the snack area. Pulling up a chair from another table, she plopped down beside Blake. Her face was unusually pale, and she suddenly looked exhausted.

"How's Kenneth?" he asked.

Gwen managed a wan smile. "Good. He's weak, but he responded well to my touch. I think I was able to ease some of his pain."

Although he didn't understand exactly how Mercraft worked, Mason knew the Mer's psi-kinetic manipulations of crystal energy to be both effective and dangerous.

Whittaker reached for his fiancée's hand. "I knew you could help, honey."

"After our experiences in the compound, I swore I'd never use my Mercraft to hurt people," she explained. "I'm a healer."

Addison's face darkened. "Well, you may be into doing good things, but I'm not," she suddenly declared.

All eyes turned her way.

Gwen frowned. "What are you saying?"

Addison jerked her thumb toward Mason. "I've been recruited by the navy to serve as a tactical adviser in all Mer matters. I'll be joining his team in going after Magaera and Jake."

Gwen stared, speechless. "Surely you're not signing on?" she asked after an infinite moment had passed. By the expression on her face, she didn't agree with the idea at all.

"Are you sure that's what you want to do?" Blake chimed in.

"I am," Addison stated without hesitation. "Tessa's been taken, and Kenneth was almost killed. I can't just stand by and let other people fight our battles, even if they've already signed up to do so. This mess all began because we meddled in things we didn't understand. We opened the sea-gate, and now it's up to us to close it."

Gwen visibly struggled to gather her emotions. "Is that true?" she finally asked, directing her question toward Mason.

Mason nodded. "The navy would like to take advantage of Addison's expertise as an EMT and diver. Her insight as a mermaid would assist the USET team."

"And that would include the goal of taking Magaera and her consort into custody?" Blake asked without mincing words.

Mason reminded himself that, even though he was dealing with a former agent of the A51 division, the civilians were operating on a need-to-know basis. "That has yet to be established."

Blake recognized the government doublespeak. He nodded, saying only, "I see."

Mason turned to Addison. "I don't believe I have to stress the importance of our mission. You, more than anyone, are aware of the danger Magaera presents now that she has successfully managed to capture your sister."

Addison didn't hesitate. "I'm in, Captain."

Chapter 6

"Are you sure working with the navy is what you want to do?"

Addison met her sister's gaze across the narrow expanse of Kenneth's bed. He lay unconscious, blissfully unaware of the fate of his wife. Three hours had passed since the attack on the Port Rock shopping center, and the chaos was nowhere near to settling down.

News agencies across the nation were already abuzz with speculation about the incident, and newscasters and pundits had already weighed in with opinions and speculation as to which extremist organization would claim responsibility. Addison was aware the extra security was necessary because later in the evening the government was going to lift the veil of secrecy about aliens living among humans. Although she and her family would not be directly identified, plans were in motion to bring the Mer into the public eye. They had no choice. Six more people had been killed and several more injured by Queen Magaera's attack.

Though Kenneth wasn't out of the woods yet, he had stabilized. For a few critical hours his physicians were worried that his heart, which had stopped twice, would be permanently damaged from the blast.

"How could I not?" she replied. "Tessa's in danger. If I can help find and rescue her, then I should. As much as we might not like the thought, we've got to help humans even the odds against—"

"Us," Gwen finished quietly.

Addison shot a surreptitious glance toward the dark-suited agents guarding Kenneth's room. Although the feds had insisted the guards were in place for their own safety, she couldn't help but wonder when or if they'd be ushered back into custody and returned to the A51 compound.

Watching her older sister wrestle with her emotions meant Addison didn't have to think about her own. Her feelings were in flux, but right now wasn't the time to lose her grip. In a way she was glad she'd be able to dodge the firestorm about to hit. Her role as a member of the USET team would continue to be confidential and top secret. After a quick phone conference with his commander, Mason had informed her that Magaera's act of terrorism would be met with equal retaliation. The mission now was to neutralize the Mer queen—at any cost. Further violence from the species would not be tolerated.

Gathering her frazzled nerves, she forced herself to remain positive and upbeat. "You have to remember that not all Mer are like Magaera," she reminded, trying to lighten Gwen's mood. "And if they're going to be emerging through the sea-gate soon, it needs to be under a monarch who will lead them in a peaceful manner. We're supposed to be part of Grandmother Nyala's Tesch dynasty, so it's our responsibility to help restore our kind to Earth's waters in a way that will be beneficial to humans and mermaids. I'm willing to do my part to make that happen."

Gwen sighed. "You're braver than I am, kiddo. I couldn't imagine signing on to a military mission."

"If they hadn't asked me, you can bet I'd be volunteering about now." Addison nodded toward the stones Gwen had placed on a table at Kenneth's bedside. "I see that you're a little more comfortable with working out in the open," she pointed out. "Didn't you say more and more people were seeking you out for crystal-healing therapies?"

Gwen rubbed the small greenish blue stones she presently worked with. Small and round, about the size of a robin's egg, the quantum-quattro silica was a stone used in the healing of trauma. Though the work was slow and painstaking, she was drawing the charge from inside it and then redirecting its energy over Kenneth's blistered skin. Although it would take time—as the long healing sessions took a lot out of Gwen's own inner reserves—Kenneth wouldn't even have a scar when she was done. She was that good.

Gwen allowed a shy smile. "I'm building a small but dedicated clientele," she admitted. "Thank the goddess that Blake's here to handle the hotel for me. More people are calling every day."

"I think what you're doing is a good thing," Addison said. Unlike her older sisters, she still hadn't found a way to focus her Mercraft in a way that would be beneficial.

She wanted to do more with her power, too. Joining the USET team, she felt, would finally give her the outlet she'd been searching for. The crew she'd be working with would all be perfectly aware she was a mermaid. At this point she had all the advantages.

She just hoped they wouldn't hold it against her.

A little embarrassed, Gwen dropped her eyes. "I hope I'm doing the right thing. Though I can't really explain it, I feel it's been my calling all along. I was just never willing to listen to my inner Mer." Although Dr. Jiminez had been wary about letting someone with no medical degree touch her patient, she'd soon come around as a believer once Gwen had offered a demonstration of her crystal-healing techniques.

"At least you're not trying to hide it anymore. And you do look happier, if I do say so myself. Of course, I'm sure getting a little love on the side has helped," Addison teased. It was nice to leave the trouble at hand alone for a moment. Discussing something sane, something normal, gave them both a chance to relax for a few precious minutes.

Her older sister's cheeks reddened. "I never thought I'd find a man who loved everything about me."

"Sounds as though it's working out."

Gwen's smile lit up. "I think it is. And though it's not firm just yet, we've been thinking about giving Trevor a sister."

Addison's eyes widened. "So soon? You're not even married yet? Are you sure you're ready to take that step?"

Gwen pursed her lips. "Well, we're getting married this October, and I wouldn't want to wait too much longer." A hot blush stained her cheeks. "Definitely within a year."

Addison shook her head. Her mouth felt dry, as if she'd swallowed a few mouthfuls of sand. "I never thought I would see both my sisters married with kids."

Gwen's gaze connected with hers. "That just leaves you," she said softly. "I hope you find the love of your life soon."

She flagged a disinterested hand. "Oh, please. Don't wish him on me too soon. I like being single, playing the field. There are a lot of men out there. I'd like to sample a few more before I make up my mind."

Despite her words, the image of a very tall, very Nordic blond Mason McKenzie wormed its way into her mind. He sure was good-looking—no doubt about that. Although Mer always gave birth to girls, they usually took on the genetic features of their fathers. Her own father had a shock of bright red hair, which he'd passed on to all three of his girls. There was no mistaking that they were sisters. Spaced roughly two years part, the Lonike girls could have passed for triplets.

She allowed a brief thought to creep in. *He would make some pretty blond babies.*

Not that she was ready to make any. She put Mason McKenzie out of her mind for the time being. Not that it was easy to forget those cornflower blue eyes of his.

Kenneth stirred suddenly, pawing helplessly at the IV tubes inserted in his veins. "Tessa," he moaned piteously. "Where's Tessa?"

Gwen looked panic-stricken. *"What should I say?"* she mouthed. They hadn't decided what to tell Kenneth when he awoke and his wife wasn't present.

A vague sense of uneasiness rippled through Addison. "I don't think he's in any shape to take it," she whispered. "Tell him Tessa's okay. When he's stronger . . ."

Gwen nodded and immediately bent over him. She caught one of his bandaged hands in an attempt to soothe him. "Ken, this is Gwen. Tessa's not here right now. She's, uh, she's resting. For the babies."

"She okay?" His voice was thick and slurry from the medication doctors had administered to control his pain.

Even though he really couldn't see her through the bandages covering his scorched face, Gwen nodded emphatically. "She had a little scare, but she's doing well. The doctors want her off her feet for a few days, just to make sure everything's okay with the babies."

Kenneth released an audible sigh. "I did my best . . ." He struggled to speak a little more but couldn't seem to form a connection between his brain and vocal cords.

Gwen laid a calming hand on his shoulder. "Everything's fine," she said to reassure him. "You need to concentrate on getting better. Those girls are going to need their father." She blinked hard as she spoke, squeezing back the tears forming at the edges of her eyes.

Kenneth half nodded before his eyes slipped shut. "Tell my lady I love her," he slurred before unconsciousness claimed him.

Addison's chest constricted as his words echoed through her mind. The emotion she felt was tangible. Kenneth had been a true blessing, not only for Tessa but for the rest of them as well. She couldn't imagine life going on without him.

She blinked hard, refusing to let any tears fall. Damn it. She hated to cry. She was stronger than that.

Kenneth wasn't finished. "Bastard," he mumbled. "I shot him. Jake . . . Shoulda killed him."

The girls exchanged a simultaneous look. By the time rescuers had arrived, there hadn't been a sign of Magaera or Jake—only the wreckage.

Addison reached for her soul-stone, concentrating on opening a psychic channel so that she and Gwen could converse without being heard. Both of them had also tried to communicate with Tessa, but they hadn't had any luck.

If he shot Jake, that could have slowed them down a bit, she signaled.

Gwen frowned deeply. *I hate to wish anyone ill,* came her silent reply, *but if there's anyone who deserves it, Jake definitely qualifies.*

Dead would be too good for him, Addison shot back. *I'd rather see him behind bars.*

Their brief conversation was interrupted by the arrival of Dr. Jiminez. Stethoscope looped around her neck, she reached for Kenneth's chart. "How's he doing?"

"He's drifting in and out of awareness," Gwen filled in.

"He needs all the rest he can get. A patient responds better when calm." She stroked the smooth skin of his hand and lower forearm. "Healing's going well, too. Almost all traces of the blistering are gone."

Jiminez moved to examine Gwen's work. When he'd first been wheeled into the ER, Kenneth's face, neck, and upper torso were terribly scalded, as though he'd been hit dead on by the blast from a furnace. "Amazing," she murmured under her breath. "I still can't believe this is all accomplished with crystal energy."

"The earth offers us everything we need to heal ourselves," Gwen said quietly. "We just need to understand how to tap into those energies and use them."

As she watched her sister consult with the doctor, Addison folded her arms over her chest. A smile tugged at her lips. It was amazing to see how much Gwen had blossomed since she'd accepted her Mercraft.

Jiminez nodded. "I have other patients who would definitely benefit from this therapy," she said thoughtfully. "Would you be willing to consult on a few cases?"

Gwen practically beamed with pride. "I would be happy to try and help."

Yes, her older sister had finally found her calling in life.

"So, what does your sister think about your shipping out so soon?"

T-shirt in hand, Addison paused a moment before stuffing the article of clothing into her travel bag. "She isn't happy about being left on her own, but Gwen understands if I've got a chance to help find Tessa, then I should take it." She crammed more into the bag, taking no time to fold. Everything went in hodgepodge until the case bulged to overfilling. "We've always stuck together, you know. If one of us has problems, we all do."

Mason inwardly winced at her packing technique. As one who'd lived under military discipline for a good portion of his life, he was used to everything being perfectly in its place. And though he certainly wouldn't brag, he could arrange a suitcase with such precision that his clothes wouldn't have a single wrinkle when retrieved.

Addison, on the other hand, didn't seem to know the

meaning of the word neat. Her small apartment on the second floor of an old brownstone was a mess. Empty take-out containers filled the trash, the bed was a rumpled unmade mess, and the carpet looked as if it hadn't been vacuumed in ages. Housekeeping clearly wasn't her forte.

His fingers itched to take over. He didn't mind the discipline behind a job well done. If it was done right the first time, there wouldn't be any problems. Slipshod work annoyed him. "I think that's admirable you and your sisters are so close."

She shrugged. "You've got family, I suppose. Don't you show up when one of your brothers or sisters is in trouble?"

Mason sucked in a deep breath. He had a sister, but they'd never been particularly close. His father, a long-time drill sergeant in the US Marines, had spent the better part of Mason's childhood bossing him around like a soldier. When the old man was around, he'd made everyone miserable by trying to run his family the way he did his platoon. Promptness, precision, and perfection were his father's watchwords. Not being able to make the grade wasn't acceptable. His mother, the poor woman, never had a say about how her children were raised. Like a good soldier she fell into line and did her duty.

It was a foregone conclusion that the son of Mark McKenzie would join the military. Raised right beside Camp Pendleton in California, he'd grown up with the military in his blood. Of course, he'd disappointed his father by not following in the old man's footsteps into the marines, but he'd been eager to take advantage of his love of the sea and diving. With a degree in marine engineering, he'd gone into the navy with an officer's commission at the not-so-tender age of twenty-two.

And once he'd shipped out, he'd never looked back. Save for the cards he sent his mother three times a year—her birthday, Mother's Day, and Christmas—he had no other reason to communicate with his family. He wanted to live his own life and make his own way in the world, under his own terms. Nothing he did suited his father, and he hated the criticisms that never failed to come his way whenever they did meet.

"I'm not close to my family," was all he deigned to say. They weren't here to swap personal stories.

Addison shook her head. "I couldn't imagine not having my sisters around. Even though they give me a hard time because I'm the youngest, it's always nice to know they're there for me when I have a problem."

It was his turn to shrug. Once he'd graduated from high school, he'd more or less taken care of himself. He worked full-time, went to college, and still managed to indulge his passion for diving. He was proud that he hadn't taken one cent from his old man to pay for his education.

The only thing he hadn't managed to find time for was a girlfriend. There never seemed to be enough hours in the day to ask a girl out, and every penny he earned was spent before he got it. Yeah, he'd had his flings. Women couldn't seem to resist a man in uniform. But to actually think about settling down with someone in a steady relationship just wasn't on his list of things to do. He was only thirty-four. He had plenty of time before he'd have to think about making a commitment, if ever. The bachelor life had treated him pretty well so far. As the old saying went, there was a girl in every port. And most were willing to have a little fun, with no strings attached.

Preoccupied with digging something out of her crammed closet, Addison bent over, giving him a prime view of her pert backside. "I know my extra pair of tennis shoes is in here somewhere," she groused.

Mason felt his heart accelerate. Though he'd never admit it aloud, Addison Lonike had everything he liked in a woman. Red hair, snapping eyes, and a spitfire personality. He'd felt an attraction the moment he'd laid eyes on her photograph, but he'd dismissed it as inappropriate. Now that she'd accepted the commission, he certainly had no business entertaining any personal thoughts about her.

The idea of serving in such close quarters with her was more than a little unsettling. If they could just have one night, a little fling, he was pretty sure he'd go for it, no holds barred. That damn tattoo, which she called her scale pattern, intrigued the hell out of him. He wanted to trace it with the tips of his fingers and follow it wherever it might lead. Of course, that meant she'd have to take her clothes off . . .

But, oh no. That kind of indulgence would be a mistake. First, it would be crossing a hazardous professional line. Second, he knew, in the back of his mind, that he didn't want to get sucked into a relationship. And something about Addison made him think she was the committing kind.

Mason cleared his mind of thoughts related to seeing Addison naked, though he supposed it was inevitable in a way. As far as he knew, mermaids swam in the buff, as naked as the day they were born. Although he would never say so aloud, and would never want to embarrass her, he was curious to see her in the water.

All wet, slippery and . . .

No. Don't go there.

Addison came up with one shoe. "Found one," she said, giving a cry of triumph. "Now I just need to find the other."

"Maybe if you cleaned up a little," he suggested.

She crossed her eyes and stuck out her tongue. "Who the hell has time to clean?" she demanded. "It's just my crash pad. Tell the two other pigs that live here they need to clean up."

His brows rose. "Two other people live here?"

"Yeah, I share it with Shane and Shawn, two other EMTs. You ought to see it when we're all crammed into one bed."

Mason's brows rose at the thought of Addison squirming between not one but two hard male bodies. A little bit of jealously rose with it. He tamped it back. "Maybe that's something I shouldn't see," he said, coughing discreetly into one hand.

Addison's grin widened. The little gap between her teeth made her look that much more adorable. All he wanted to do was bend over and kiss those delectable cherry red lips of hers. Despite her tomboy ways, she was definitely all female.

Regardless of his attempts to cool his internal temperature, the attraction insisted on simmering.

"Shane and Shawn are gay," she informed him without blinking. "When we're all in bed together, it's to sleep. Usually our shifts don't overlap, but when they do, there's a lot of fighting for the better side of the bed. That mattress is a lumpy old mess."

Mason felt relieved. "It's a good thing you're used to cramped and small, then. The cabins aboard ship aren't big, and the bunks are pretty narrow."

"I can handle that," she said, then paused a moment. "But how do you think the rest of the crew will handle me?" A frown wrinkled her forehead. "I guess they will all know I'm a Mer."

Mason scrubbed a hand over his jaw. It was well past five p.m. now, and the rasp of stubble made him wince. They really needed to get a move on. He was aware the seamen who waited outside were getting antsy. In truth, he was, too. He didn't want to be anywhere near Port Rock, Maine, when the president made his shocking announcement about the Mer to the American people. It was scheduled to take place in less than an hour during the six o'clock news.

"The crew will be aware," he affirmed. "And if anyone has a problem with it, he can keep it to himself. No prejudice of any sort will be tolerated."

Her expressive features took on a look of inward contemplation. "I guess people are wary about things they don't really understand."

"You tell me. How did your crewmates take being told?"

Addison nibbled her lower lip. "Most of the people I work with are cool about it, once they understand that I'm really only different underwater." A smile tugged at one corner of her mouth. "A few people, such as Witkowsky, kind of freak."

"What about the Mercraft?" he asked. "You can do that anywhere, right?"

She laughed. "Oh, I'm not half as good as Gwen and

Tessa. I can move a few things from here to there, but it's nothing spectacular." She flexed her finger. "But put a Ri'kah in my hands, and I can do some serious blasting."

"We have requested the ones confiscated by the A51 agency to be returned," Mason replied.

Addison's eyes widened with delight. "Really? I'd love to get my hands on one again."

"You will. But only under my supervision. We're not planning to turn you loose in the Mediterranean to blast your way through Magaera's defenses."

Addison ran her fingers through her hair, making it more of a wild mess than it already was. "But that's kind of what you're hoping I can do, isn't it? Blast that bitch back into the arms of the goddess herself."

Mason worked hard to suppress his smile. Yeah, in a way he was hoping that was exactly what she'd do. Even though he'd never admit it aloud, he was aching to get even with the Mer in the waters around Magaera's island fortress.

Her soldiers had embarrassed the hell out of his men, and they'd been forced to retreat. As sailors, they should have been forewarned about mermaids, based on the lore alone. Once a mermaid got a man into the water, she'd do her damnedest to drown him, disabling his equipment and dragging him to the depths of the sea.

He didn't even want to contemplate what might happen if hundreds or even thousands of the Mer flooded the seas. In the water, mermaids were unstoppable, vicious creatures with no regard for human life. Magaera's attack on innocent civilians had proven the Mer queen was committed to following through with her intention to return her people to the waters she felt rightfully belonged to Ishaldi and its people.

"Our intention was to resolve this peacefully," he said quietly, "though I have a feeling that isn't going to be possible."

Addison's eyes took on a strange look—one of anger mingled with abject sadness. "Unfortunately, I think you're right."

Chapter 7

Magaera's Island
Mediterranean Sea

Emerging from a world of churning nightmares, where a dragon queen shot laser beams from the tips of her fingers, Tessa opened her eyes to an even stranger sight. A dense mist, scented with the pungent salt of the nearby sea, wove its way through white marble columns. The ground, too, was an ocean of pale stone, stretching endlessly.

Heaven? The vision had no basis in her reality. *Did I die?*

Unwilling to accept the possibility, Tessa closed her eyes and attempted to distance herself from such an unacceptable oblivion.

A light slap stung her cheek.

I'm dreaming, she thought vaguely, and ignored it.

Another slap followed, harder and more insistent.

This time Tessa opened her eyes, blinking hard to focus her blurred vision. "Stop that!" she snapped, annoyed that Kenneth would be bothering her when all she wanted to do was sink back into the blissful oblivion of sleep. Didn't that man understand she was exhausted?

An unfamiliar female voice, right beside her, said, "Wake up, inferior!"

Tessa's head swiveled. Short blond hair shaved in some sort of odd Mohawk style ruled over blue eyes so light, the color was almost clear. A jumpsuit fashioned from fish leather covered her sleek, well-muscled body.

Tessa gasped as recognition seeped into her beleaguered brain. Although she didn't know the woman's name, there was no mistaking that she was one of Queen Magaera's soldiers.

And it wasn't a nightmare.

Images of Magaera and Jake Massey in the mall flashed across her mind's eye. One minute she and Kenneth were shopping for new clothes for the babies; the next minute she'd been blasted ass over heels as she'd attempted to protect her husband from the Mer queen's wrath.

Struggling to sit up, she recoiled violently. "Don't touch me, bitch!" she shouted. The sudden move brought a wave of dizziness. For a brief scary moment her stomach rolled with nausea. As she fought back the urge to vomit, her hand flew to her mouth. Unfortunately, her morning sickness wasn't confined to the early hours of the day. She was bound to be stricken whenever she got nervous or upset.

Another voice interrupted. "Leave her alone." This was a man's voice.

The Mer soldier nodded in acquiescence as Jake

Massey ambled toward her. Shirtless, he was dressed only in a pair of wrinkled well-worn slacks and boots.

Her instinctive fear of the man washed over her, drenching her with her own nervous perspiration. The look he'd long cultivated, that of the preppy professor and man of adventure, was long gone. In its place stood a man with a ragged haircut grown out just enough to reveal his blond roots. The time he'd spent with Magaera had added muscle to his lanky frame. He was broad shouldered and narrow hipped, with an abdomen hard as rock, and his darkly tanned skin emphasized the white flash of his teeth.

"Jake?"

"Tessa." He nodded. "How are you feeling?"

Tessa performed a quick inventory of her ailments. Her whole brain was numb. Her body ached from head to toe. That, added to her nausea and confusion, made her feel, well, shitty. "I'm okay," she grated. She glanced around, trying to figure out where the hell she was. The place appeared to be some kind of Grecian-style temple surrounded by wide lawns, enclosed gardens, and cool fountains.

"Where am I?" she asked disjointedly.

Jake allowed a small smile. "We're on an island in the Mediterranean, just above the sea-gate. The ruins once scattered across the bottom of the sea have been restored."

Tessa was almost inclined to scoff. "No way," she snapped. She'd made the initial dive and witnessed the ruin and devastation of the sunken landmass for herself. Lost beneath the water for centuries, the entire place was little more than pieces.

Jake's grin widened. "Way," he confirmed.

"Then it's true. You did really find the scepter?" Tessa's jaw tightened.

He stuck his hands in his pockets and rocked back on his heels. "Yep. We did. Amazingly, it was hiding in plain sight. Your cousins had it. Can you believe they'd donated it to a damn museum?" He laughed, as if saying the words amused him. "And it really does give a Mer queen control over land and sea."

Her blood chilled. "Where's my husband?" she demanded, desperate to rally her brain into functioning mode. "Where's Kenneth?"

His brows rose in surprise. "You married that big ape?" He smirked. "He must not be very memorable if you're just now getting around to asking about him."

An abrupt image of Kenneth attempting to defend her emerged from the haze. The sound of a gun firing echoed through her brain. Kenneth, she was sure, had shot Jake. She thought she remembered Jake yelping in pain before going to his knees. Yet he didn't seem to be wounded. *How could he have missed?*

Jake followed the line of her vision. He pressed his fingers beneath his right collarbone. "Yeah, the fucker shot me." He rubbed the area, which showed no trauma whatsoever—not even a scar. "You know Mer can heal, as well as harm."

She nodded slowly. Although she'd never dabbled in that side of her Mercraft, she knew Gwen had begun working with the healing side of their extraordinary gift.

"Where's Kenneth?" she repeated. She attempted to keep the fear out of her voice, but that was almost impossible to do. There was no doubt in her mind that Jake had somehow gotten even with her husband.

Jake's hand dropped as he shrugged. "Most likely he's in the hospital, if not already dead. Magaera blasted him pretty good." He eyed her. "You took a bit of that yourself. If you'd been much closer, it probably would have charred your skin."

A flood of tears immediately rose behind her eyes. She remembered throwing up a shield in front of her husband, but was it enough? The twins she carried had sapped so much of her energy, and she wasn't at her strongest. "He'd better not be dead, you son of a bitch."

Jake shrugged again. "Dunno," he said with a flippant wave of his hand. By the way he spoke, they might have been discussing the weather. He seemed totally unconcerned that he'd just taken part in an attack that might have killed or wounded innocent people. "Don't care. The only thing that matters is that we got what we wanted."

"Me," she finished for him. She didn't need to look down to know that her soul-stone, which hung from a thick gold chain, was nestled firmly between her breasts.

They can't kill me, she thought. They needed her alive in order to use her stone. If she died, the stone was useless. She had no doubt they were still intent on opening the sea-gate.

Jake suddenly closed the distance between them, taking a seat beside her on the low pallet. He leaned close to her, his gaze focusing on her mouth as if he contemplated kissing her. "I know you don't believe me," he murmured, "but I did all of this for you, Tessa."

She could hardly believe her ears. It took her a moment to work her way through what he'd said. "For me?"

He nodded emphatically. "I found the Mer for you. To prove how much I loved you."

Tessa immediately pulled back, far enough to see the sincerity in his gaze. Jake actually believed what he was saying. No fucking way. "No, I don't believe that. You just took advantage."

Hands catching her shoulders, his strong fingers dug deeply into her skin. "I did, too," he insisted. "You were always so unhappy, wondering about your people, what had happened to your kind. I wanted to give you the answers so that you'd want to be with me again. Of course, that was before you tried to kill me. I've had a lot of time to think about how I wanted to get even." His smile turned savage. "I'll enjoy taking Randall's place in your bed."

Cold-blooded rage suddenly surged through her. Without her even thinking, her hand shot out, latching on to his neck. "Lay one hand on me, and I'll drain you dry. There won't be anything left of you but an empty shell by the time I'm through." She didn't like using the D'ema, or death magic. Normally it was forbidden, to be invoked only rarely and with the greatest of caution. But in this case she'd make an exception. Just as Mer could pull energy out of a crystal, they could also suck it out of humans. Right now the only thing she wanted to do was make Jake shrivel up like a paper cup tossed into a bonfire.

Jake froze as her nails dug into his vulnerable jugular. His pulse lurched beneath her palm. "Take it easy!" he gasped, his hands scrabbling helplessly toward his neck. "I was just kidding."

Tessa tightened her grip. She wasn't messing around, either. "I don't think so."

Jake gagged. "S-stop, Tessa. Please . . ."

Queen Magaera glided into the chamber. Two of her soldiers marched at her heel. The queen halted a few yards away. A cruel glint lit her arctic gaze. "Let him go," she said calmly, low in her throat.

Tessa's grip tightened. Given another moment, she'd crush Jake's larynx. The energy she consumed from him surged through her veins, revitalizing her exhausted body. She'd been aching for a rematch, and here it was. *Time to deal with the bitch.* "Make me."

Magaera merely smirked and snapped her fingers. "Gladly."

The two soldiers following behind her sped toward Tessa. They lunged from different sides, each catching an arm in an attempt to pry her off Jake.

Freed, he stumbled back, gasping for breath. Unable to control his shaky limbs, he collapsed in a heap on the floor.

Caught between the two women, Tessa fought and scratched like a wildcat. Teeth snapping, she kicked one woman in the gut. She barely avoided the second soldier's jab at her face.

A fireball out of nowhere struck her dead on. Something that felt like vibrating tentacles wrapped around her, lacing her up from head to foot. Suspended in midair, she hung like a fly wrapped neatly in a spider web.

Magaera sauntered up, casually waving her soldiers away. "Don't even think about trying something like that again."

Tessa writhed inside her invisible bonds. "Fuck you."

The Mer queen released a leisurely yawn. "If you want to live to see your children, you won't fight me," she continued in a tone laced with acid. "Otherwise, I will have you tied down and let my soldiers beat you until you haven't a hope of bringing children into this world—ever."

How did she know? Tessa thought in panic.

Jake finally managed to crawl to his feet. His face was pale and his neck bruised and scratched, but he seemed no worse for wear. "What do you mean?" he spluttered. "Is she pregnant?" The look on his face was one of disgust.

Queen Magaera nodded. "Obviously." She casually closed the distance between them, reaching up to finger the crystal hanging around Tessa's neck. It glowed softly against her skin. "A Mer's soul-stone changes color when she is with child. Yours is no longer clear, but it has a dark pink hue to it. By the tint, I judge at least two children." She paused a moment and closed her eyes. "Or is that a third heartbeat I'm sensing?"

Tessa's brows rose. *Oh, shit. Three?* Surely that couldn't be right . . .

But what if it was? That was definitely something she didn't want to think about.

Magaera cocked her head. "If you want your children to live, I suggest you cooperate. I wish to proceed to the sea-gate, immediately. It is time for my people to come out of the shadows of an unwarranted exile."

Tessa felt the oxygen seep from her lungs. If she'd been on her own, she'd be willing to fight like hell to take Magaera down. But it wasn't her safety that was at stake. The presence of the precious babies she carried effectively crippled her ability to resist. She couldn't keep pushing herself physically, not while her pregnancy was still so uncertain.

Tessa took a deep breath. "I won't fight you," she said quietly. "I'll help you open the gate. Just don't hurt my babies, please."

Magaera's eyes glittered with satisfaction. She'd acquired exactly what she wanted, with minimal fuss. "Good. You are less stupid this time."

To her surprise, Tessa suddenly felt Magaera's psychic presence in her mind. She flinched against the invasion, which hit her smack between the eyes as a blinding mental blow. She struggled to keep her eyes open, but noticed Magaera concentrating intensely on the waves of energy emanating from her soul-stone. The black stone around Magaera's own neck began to lighten.

She was matching soul-stone resonances with Tessa. *By the goddess, she's going to mimic my psychic resonance to open the sea-gate.*

Had she not already been otherwise restrained, she would have dropped to her knees. The Mer queen was mentally devouring her.

"Don't fight me," Magaera warned. "I will burn you down to a crisp."

Tessa let herself go limp. The crystal around Magaera's own neck glowed like a live coal now, bright and powerful. "Just don't hurt my babies," she managed to mumble through ragged gasps. The clarity of her own thoughts began to drizzle away. All her senses were screaming in revolt, and there was nothing she could do . . .

And then it was over, just like that. She had nothing left inside—not a single drop.

Giving a hard jerk, Magaera snapped the gold chain holding the pendant bequeathed to Tessa by her mother on the day of her birth. "That wasn't even hard," she said through a cruel smirk.

The invisible tentacles holding her abruptly vanished. She dropped to the cold stone floor in a heap. All her senses felt muted, as if some connection between her brain and body had been snipped in half. She moaned in pain and confusion. Every nerve in her body was torn to shreds. She felt like a useless, dead thing.

Jake dropped to one knee. Catching her chin in one hand, he wrenched her head back, forcing her to look at his face. He was smug with pleasure and easy success. "You lose," he whispered.

But Tessa was far past listening. Exhausted by defeat, she slipped into a deathlike void of unconsciousness.

Chapter 8

Addison was wasted. She hadn't had a moment's sleep since leaving Port Rock, now going on twenty-four hours and counting. Since agreeing to join the USET team, she hadn't had a moment to herself. She'd been photographed, fingerprinted, and provided with an ID that would give her access to most of the areas aboard the ship she'd be working on, which was currently docked off the coast of Crete.

USET's ship, which carried the moniker of *Sea Horse*, was a blue-water research vessel recently launched into service just a few months before.

At two hundred eighty feet in length, the *Sea Horse* was the largest vessel in the USET fleet. The hull of the ship was hardened against ice to allow for Arctic and Antarctic research. The vessel had a total of sixty bunk spaces and could seat thirty at a time in her mess room.

The ship also included a six-bed hospital facility and had a full medical staff ready to handle any emergency. She also carried a full crew.

The deck equipment featured three winches, two fixed cranes, a portable crane, a hydrographic boom, and an A-frame. This equipment gave the *Sea Horse* a lifting capacity of up to forty-one thousand pounds as well as up to ten thousand meters of cable that could pull up to eight thousand pounds. One of the winches was specifically for use with specialty cables such as optical fiber cables or coaxial EM Cable.

As it was an undersea research vessel, a substantial amount of the ship was dedicated to laboratories. Included in the forty-one hundred square feet of lab space were an electronics lab, a biochemical lab, and a wet lab.

"What do you think?" Mason McKenzie asked.

Addison smiled. Although she'd much rather have been touring the sights and sounds of Crete, the ship itself offered a pretty good substitute. "It is, in a word, awesome."

He smiled. "Glad you like it."

Addison swiped a nervous hand over her new jacket. "I just hope the crew likes me." So far everyone she'd met was polite and respectful. The only thing she'd noticed was that no one would look her in the eyes. Everyone was looking through her, doing his best not to stare directly. They were all curious, and more than a little bit afraid. Word of the Mer had begun to seep out through media sources, and people were clamoring for more information. Nobody really understood the complications. In their eyes she wasn't just a new member of the team. She was a member of a species that hadn't exactly made itself welcome.

To them I'm the enemy, she reminded herself.

Though she was serving only in an advisory capacity, it was decided she would wear a civilian's version of what enlisted personnel wore: khaki trousers paired with a blue cotton T-shirt, a black web belt with a closed buckle, and black smooth leather boots. Aside from a few personal belongings, everything she needed would be supplied while she was aboard ship. She'd asked Gwen to handle her finances while she was away.

It really was a grand adventure—and it scared the hell out of her. Aside from their brief incarceration at the A51 facility in Virginia, she'd never been out of Port Rock. Her whole life was tied up in that small fishing community. It was easy to be a Mer there. Those people were her friends or coworkers, and she trusted them. Those who didn't know certainly wanted to believe that mermaids swam in Penobscot Bay. The lore definitely helped encourage tourism. More than one person swore he spotted a mermaid or two in his day, even though it wasn't true ninety percent of the time.

Mason gave a small nod. "I think they'll like you once they get to know you. If you don't mind, I'd like to be able to give them a demonstration of a mermaid in the water soon."

She tucked away her uncertainty. "I think I can handle that."

A lanky young man approached, pausing to snap a smart salute. "We have clearance to ship out at any time, Captain," he reported.

Mason nodded. "Make it so, Commander."

The officer glanced toward Addison. "Quarters have been prepared for Ms. Lonike," he continued.

"Thank you, Hawkins," Mason said before dismissing his second-in-command. He turned to Addison. "I know you haven't had much time to rest since all this began. Why don't we get you settled in?"

Addison was grateful for his suggestion. It would give her a chance to stow her things and take a much-needed breather to herself. "Thanks. I could use a break."

Mason escorted her belowdecks, leading her down a narrow set of steps that would take them to the living quarters. Due to space limitations, many of the crew were doubled up, two people per cabin. Because she had requested no special treatment, Addison expected that she, too, would have a bunkmate. In a way, she was looking forward to having a buddy. She was surprised when the captain opened the door to a cabin clearly marked for himself.

"This is yours—," she started to protest.

Mason ushered her inside. "I thought you would like a little more space and privacy away from the rest of the crew." He nodded across the narrow hall. "I'll be bunking with Commander Hawkins."

Addison's grip tightened on her travel bag. This was exactly the kind of thing that riled her. "Really, that's not necessary. I can share a room."

Mason's lips thinned. "I'm going to try and be tactful," he said slowly.

It didn't take a psychic to figure out what he was about to say. She cut him off. "Don't tell me. Nobody volunteered to share."

"I'm sorry, but after their recent go-round with Queen Magaera's soldiers, my crew members are more than a little wary about the Mer. Yes, they understand you're not the same as those who recently emerged through the sea-gate, but—"

"But I'm a Mer and they don't trust me," she finished for him.

"Exactly."

Addison shrugged. It wasn't the first time someone hadn't liked her because of what she looked like or what she was. There was no reason to let it bother her. She'd just have to prove to the crew members that she was on their side.

Hefting her travel bag, she headed toward Mason's bunk. The captain's cabin was well-appointed; it was not necessarily more luxurious than the rest, but it certainly offered the advantage of complete privacy.

She was just about to toss her single piece of luggage on his bunk when the sight of something odd stopped her dead in her tracks. She stared in disbelief. "What the hell is that?"

Mason hurried over to take a look. His hand immediately slammed into his forehead. "Oh God, no," he moaned. "I can't believe they did that."

Addison couldn't help but admire the ingenuity of the perpetrator. Some genius had taken the top half of a male Barbie doll and combined it with the bright fish tail of a stuffed animal. A can of sardines lay beside the transformed toy. A neatly typed note was propped beside both.

She picked it up. "*Dinner and a date for our newest crew member,*" she read aloud. "*Welcome aboard.*"

His skin taking on a distinct flush, Mason struggled to keep a straight face. "I'm sorry," he said briskly. "That is totally inappropriate."

She picked up the mutant doll. In a way it was kind of cute. "So, does this mean I'm being hazed?" It was all she could do not to crack a grin. She liked watching Captain McKenzie squirm with embarrassment. Apparently things weren't all business under his command.

He cleared his throat. "We, uh, have a little tradition when a new crew member comes aboard. You know, give him a little razzing to see how he handles the situation. Long tours of sea duty can get a little stressful, and it's a way to find out if a person fits in."

Addison looked at the doll. "Well," she deadpanned, "this just won't work for me. For one, he's not my type." She tossed the doll back on the bunk. "Send me one of those big strong sailors, please. Preferably naked." She waved the can of sardines. "And I hate fish with a passion. I'd prefer a bottle of red wine."

Much to her relief Captain McKenzie allowed a small grin. His eyes glinted as he drawled back, "I can probably arrange the naked sailor, but there's no alcohol aboard this ship."

Addison couldn't resist. She waggled her eyebrows in an obscene manner. "Then send me two naked sailors and we'll call it even."

He shook his head. "As much as I would like to grant that request, I'm afraid it won't be possible. I don't allow any canoodling—"

The captain didn't have a chance to finish his sentence. The ship suddenly lurched, knocking them off their feet. Addison stumbled back onto the bunk, landing in an inelegant sprawl. McKenzie tumbled right on top of her. His arm shot out, catching his weight before he sank completely between her thighs. His mouth wasn't more than a foot away from hers.

A little gasp of surprise rushed past her lips. *Good God!* The feel of his body pressed against hers sent a hot tremor through her. Oh, man, he was big—and strong. For a moment the energy pouring off him threatened to send her internal temperature straight into the red zone.

A thrill of something forbidden and dangerous zipped down her spine. His own breathing accelerated.

Struggling to sit up, she shifted beneath him. His body was rock hard, well muscled, and sleek. He was all man—and damn delicious.

Regaining his balance, McKenzie pushed off her. Regaining his footing, he straightened his uniform. The captain was back to business.

Addison's checks flushed, but she felt an unpleasant emptiness as he took a few steps back.

"Sorry if that was awkward for you," she mumbled under her breath.

McKenzie gave her a quick nod. "I think I need to go and check on the damn fool crewman piloting this ship. That was certainly not the way we leave dock." He spoke in a precise, clipped manner, and his voice sounded more than a little bit strained.

She tried not to smile. Yep. She'd gotten to him. A Mer always knew when a man wanted to mate. The pheromones were practically pouring off him. He was more than a little bothered. "I could use a few minutes to rest."

The muscles in Mason's jaw rippled. "Certainly." He then beat a hasty retreat. The cabin's door closed behind him with a firm click. He didn't look back as he departed.

Settling her legs over the edge of the bunk, Addison sat up and shook her head to clear it. The last thing she should be thinking about was getting involved with a human when her species and his were practically at each other's throats. She hadn't come all this way to partake in a pleasure cruise.

First we find Tessa, she reminded herself sharply.

Her gaze drifted toward the Mer doll. It was silly but cute. But the note reminded her that it had been a long time since she'd had a steady lover. And it sure was hard to ignore the way her heart kicked whenever she looked at Mason. She didn't believe in love at first sight. But lust—yeah, the good captain had everything she liked about a man. Every time she was around him, something inside her clenched with need.

She sighed and let herself fall back on the bunk. Sleeping in his bed wasn't going to make things any easier. Even though the bedding had been freshly made, her acute senses still picked up his unique masculine scent. It tickled her nostrils, unspooling all sorts of naughty images across her mind's eye.

She forced herself not to indulge. At this point, the best she could hope for was a speedy capture for Magaera and Jake.

"Man, I can't get off this boat soon enough."

His senses still abuzz from his brief encounter with Addison Lonike, Mason stomped into the control room. Every man present had a shit-eating grin on his face.

Realizing something was afoot, he shot them all an irritated frown. "Who the hell is piloting this ship?" he demanded. "Knocking everybody ass over heels isn't the way to leave dock."

Commander Hawkins shrugged. "Take it easy, Cap," he replied, grinning and flinging something shiny into the air. "We just wanted to give you a friendly shove in the right direction. It's been a long time since you've had a little shore leave."

Mason caught the flying missile. Opening his hand, he recognized a familiar brand of condom—ribbed and lubricated, extralarge. "Ha, ha. Very funny." Without giving it a second thought, he quickly tucked it into his pocket. Out of sight was out of mind. "It's shit like this that can cost a captain his command. And if I go down, you can sure as hell bet I'll be taking a few of you funny guys with me."

Hawkins spread his hands in apology. "Sorry, sir. We just thought you could use an excuse to get a little more friendly with her." His eyes narrowed slyly. "You haven't taken your eyes off her since she arrived. And you certainly won't let anyone else get very damn close."

Mason blinked in surprise. Had it been that damn obvious? "I was simply trying to be polite," he said, coughing discreetly into his hand.

Jesus. Was he truly acting like a lovesick pup? There really wasn't a reason to, either. He had a little black book full of women willing to show a sailor a good time when on shore leave. He could hook up anytime he wanted.

Maybe that was the trouble. Most of the women he'd slept with all fell into the same category: easy, good-time girls who weren't interested in him for who he was, but for the uniform he wore. And there was a time when he was willing to settle for one-night stands.

But those times had begun to wear thin lately. He rarely picked up the phone anymore, preferring to spend his time alone rather than indulge in another shallow bout of sex with a woman whose last name he didn't even know. He wasn't sure what he was looking for, but he'd recently decided to go without until he figured out the answer.

He had to admit that Addison was definitely a departure from all other women. She was something special, unique. And it wasn't just because she was a mermaid, either. She was funny, blunt, open, completely without guile or deception. What a man saw was what he got.

And Mason liked what he saw—a lot.

One of the seamen smirked. "If you get any more polite, Captain, you're going to smother the girl to death. Back off and give the rest of us guys a chance."

"Yeah," Hawkins added. "The rest of us want to see what these mermaids are all about. Looks as though they're not all vicious bitches."

Mason immediately shook his head. Yes, he was perfectly aware of secret trysts on long assignments at sea, but it was something he refused to indulge in. It was the cost of doing business in a gender-integrated military. And while male and female soldiers were not allowed to be in the same room with the door closed or be "out of uniform" anyplace, people still found a way to sneak off for private time.

It was something he wouldn't mind doing with Addison. The idea of actually getting her alone again caused his stomach to twist into painful knots. Even now all he could think about was the feel of her sleek body pressed beneath his. She was so close, and so willing. He'd wanted to kiss her and was surprised he'd managed to keep himself from doing so.

But it was neither the time nor place to think about his attraction to Addison Lonike. First and foremost he had a job to do. And that included getting his crew members to act like professionals instead of little boys let loose at summer camp.

"Not going to happen, fellas," he said behind a stern frown. "You all know the rules. I can't stop you from eyeing the lady, but it's strictly hands-off. Ms. Lonike is here serving in an advisory capacity, nothing more. The last thing she needs is to be mauled by a bunch of horny sailors."

"It would be a good way to find out more about those mermaids," Commander Hawkins suggested. "There's nothing like a little naked interrogation to find out an enemy's secrets."

The men around him laughed.

Mason didn't think it was very funny at all, and he suddenly found himself feeling protective.

"Every one of you is aware that this isn't the time for funny business," he said, forcing a measure of steel into his tone that made everyone present snap to and pay attention. "Ms. Lonike is here to help us gain the advantage. But if her presence is going to be a distraction, she will be removed."

One of his crew members piped in. "Our apologies for making light of the situation."

Mason narrowed his eyes, staring down the control room. "Do I make myself clear?"

Commander Hawkins and the rest of the men nodded. "Absolutely, sir," his second-in-command answered.

The buzzing of an intercom interrupted.

The commander answered. "Hawkins here."

"Dr. Bessimer here," came a crisp female voice. "I'm down in lab two with Ms. Lonike. We're preparing to give a demonstration of Mer shifting capabilities." An experienced marine biologist, Elizabeth Bessimer was also a commissioned lieutenant and lead scientist on the ship. Any further study of the Mer species would be done under her inquisitive eye.

Mason squelched a desire to wince. The last thing he wanted to do was see Addison so soon after an embarrassing incident.

Apparently he wasn't going to have that luxury. There was no way he'd miss the demonstration. When he'd encountered Magaera's soldiers, they were already in the water, in full Mer form. He wanted to see for himself how the shift from human to mermaid actually happened.

Where were they hiding that damn tail?

"I'm on my way," Mason informed her.

The commander looked askance. "Permission to accompany you, sir?"

Turnabout was fair play. "Permission denied. Divers and science personnel only."

A chorus of groans filled the control center.

Mason nodded toward the man piloting the ship. "Ensign Collins, what's our ETA?"

Consulting his computer, the ensign rattled off the answer. It would take about forty-eight hours to reach their destination.

"Full speed ahead, then," he said, then added with a small smile, "And this time, no hot-rodding the engines."

The ensign blushed. "Aye, aye, Captain."

Leaving the control room behind, Mason wove his way through the ship. The day was clear and the weather perfect for sailing. They should have no problem reaching their destination on time.

This time we'll be ready, he thought. Two men had come close to losing their lives to Magaera's soldiers.

A group was gathered in lab two, which boasted a roughly sixteen-by-sixteen-foot observation tank. All that could be seen of it was the wide, flat viewing pane set into the wall.

Mason deliberately positioned himself at the rear of the room, out of her line of sight. His only intention was to observe.

Addison headed toward the tank, stopped, and eyed its girth. "How do I get into this thing?"

One of the divers volunteered to show her. "This is the observation side," he explained. "The actual entrance is on the other side."

Addison nodded. "Let's go, then."

Expectation buzzed through the divers and scientists. Everyone stepped closer to the glass.

A few minutes later, Addison lowered herself into the tank. She'd changed into a wet suit but wore no other diving gear. She glided beneath the water, doing a few flips and turns.

Pausing only to give onlookers a saucy wink, Addison stretched out and made a slow twirl through the water. The change from human to Mer occurred in the blink of an eye. One moment Mason saw two legs; the next moment he caught a glimpse of bright colors racing like wildfire across her skin. The wet suit melted away, disappearing completely. By the time he managed to focus his vision again, her transformation was complete.

The lower half of her body had completely changed, becoming a beautiful multicolored tail. Now that she was stripped to the buff, everyone could see the elaborate markings that covered most of her body.

The lab around him had fallen deathly silent.

As a diver, Mason had experienced some of the most awesome sights the sea had to offer. But nothing could even come close to the beauty of a mermaid. Her scales shimmered and sparkled like thousands of tiny crystals. All he wanted to do was stand and admire her.

A light shiver moved up his spine. A thrill of purely male appreciation swept through him. *This is it. There's no going back.*

Giving her tail a saucy flick, Addison swam up to the window. Extending her arms over her head like a ballerina, she did a series of graceful rolls so they could observe all angles.

Everyone stepped closer, noses almost pressed against the glass. They were practically gawking. No one could pull his gaze away.

"Amazing," Dr. Bessimer breathed. "Simply stunning."

A diver named Cox pointed. "Look at the fine scaling over her torso and arms."

Bessimer nodded. "The pattern is absolutely breathtaking."

Mason held himself back, watching the people watch Addison. The lab suddenly felt overcrowded, hot, and suffocating. He couldn't miss the way her flesh glowed in the water, and his hands ached to stroke the satiny smoothness.

As it was, he couldn't look at Addison without yet another hot tremor passing through his body. Unbidden and unwelcome, a series of erotic images swirled through his mind. Heat began creeping up his neck.

Mason closed his eyes in sheer frustration, forcing himself to exhale. Just thinking about her supple figure was tying him in knots. The memory of his body pressing against hers filtered through his mind.

Slipping out of the lab, he groaned under his breath. This attraction wasn't good—not good at all. He'd be a damn fool to give in to his lust. He was going to blow this mission if he didn't concentrate and get his mind out of his pants. Because of who and what she was, messing around with Addison Lonike would be career suicide.

You can't have her, he warned himself.

Chapter 9

"Everything okay, Captain?"

Mason opened his eyes. He'd only meant to step outside of the lab for a few minutes, just to take a breather.

He nodded. "I'm fine, Ensign," he said, casting around in his memory to recall the man's name. Ah, Johnson. Lifting his hand, he rubbed his tired eyes. "Just a little tired."

Ensign Johnson nodded. "These are exciting times, sir. Imagine, being on the forefront of the discovery of a new species."

Mason let his hand drop. As a diver and explorer, he had to agree that uncovering the existence of the Mer was one of the most important discoveries of the twenty-first century. Only the discovery of Noah's Ark or perhaps the Holy Grail would rate on the same scale. Certainly it opened up a messy can of worms, as creationists would want to duke it out with scientists over whether or not the Mer were to be considered an alien or indigenous species. Theologians would chime in with their two cents, of course. Did a mermaid have a soul?

It was almost too much to think about.

"Kind," he reminded his subordinate. "The Mer are to be referred to as a kind, not as a species." Already the politically correct language was beginning to fall into place. No one wanted to risk offending what could, in the future, become a major seafaring power.

Ensign Johnson peeked through the small glass pane in the lab's window. "She's awesome, isn't she?" He wasn't a diver, and therefore wasn't in on Addison's demonstration. Not that he could have found a place to stand, anyway. The lab was crammed to the max. If the ship were to sink right now, more than half the crew would probably drown.

But he had to agree with the ensign. It was definitely hard to keep his concentration when Addison was in the next room, water caressing every inch of her tempting curves. Even though her scale pattern afforded her some cover, she was completely nude.

And, God, oh so beautiful.

Mason braced a palm against his forehead. Blood thudded dully in his temples, drowning out sounds of the ship's engines. She was so close and so naked, and just thinking about tracing his hands along her lithe body was enough to send his libido into overdrive.

"That she is," he said, making a show of rubbing a small crease between his eyes.

Unable to stand still another second, he tossed a quick salute of dismissal toward his crewman and headed back above deck. He needed a few minutes to himself, just to clear his head.

Out of habit, he headed toward the diver's platform. Until this latest assignment he'd spent most of his career in the water. It was where he felt most comfortable. Putting on his equipment and sinking below the surface gave him a sense of peace and serenity he just couldn't find anywhere else. The beauty of the ocean, its mysteries, had always piqued his curiosity. He'd always believed there were yet more discoveries to be made in the endless depths. Technological advances were allowing man to plumb those shadowy depths now, to go deeper and farther than ever before.

Mason stared down into the depths. It actually wasn't hard for him to accept the existence of a water-bound species. The lore surrounding mermaids had existed for centuries, with many an ancient sailor reporting the sight of sirens in the water. The fact that the Mer were exclusively female seemed to lend credence to the stories of seduction. Tales of mermen were few and far between.

The ship cut through the waves, its diesel-powered engines humming along at a comfortable eleven knots. It had only a sixty-day endurance, which should be more than plenty of time to breach Magaera's island. Of the crew, twenty-nine members were divers—thirty-one if he counted himself and Addison.

Mason winced. As captain and lead tactician, he was forbidden to go into the water.

His hands clenched. *Bullshit on that!*

There was no way on God's green earth that he would send any man into the water without knowing firsthand what he'd be facing off against. With the Mer, no one knew.

And so on their first ill-fated mission, Mason had gone into the water.

At first there was nothing—just a calm, peaceful sea.

But when he and his men ventured inside the magnetic zone surrounding the island, all hell had broken loose. Their equipment began to fail, forcing everyone to the surface. Not that they'd had a chance of staying there. Like sharks gliding beneath the waves, four long silhouettes appeared out of the impenetrable depths.

Mason closed his eyes. A flash of arms and tails punctuated by laserlike beams burning through the water was all he remembered. His life could have ended at any time when he'd gone under the crystalline depths.

The idea of going back wasn't pleasant. But it was his job, and he intended to do it. At least this time around they were a little more knowledgeable and better prepared.

At least he hoped that was the case.

The sound of footsteps caught his attention.

"Hi."

Mason turned. "Hello." Addison was thankful to be back in her clothes. Her red hair curled in damp strands around her face. Free of all makeup, her skin was absolutely flawless. Only the slightest pink flush colored her fair and translucent angled cheekbones, which were clearly a part of her father's Native American heritage. The figure he'd admired was now hidden by shapeless slacks, a loose T-shirt, and a jacket almost a size too large.

Commander Hawkins stood beside her. If the man had stood any more rigid and correct, he would have snapped in half. "Demonstration's over, sir," he announced.

"I finally got them to let me out of the water," Addison added with a grin.

Mason allowed a nod. "How did it go?"

She thought a moment. "I tried to answer all their questions as fully as I could. I know there are things they still don't understand, but unless you experience it for yourself, there's really no way to explain."

"Such as?"

"For instance, how a Mer can share her breath with a human in a way that allows the human to breathe under the water."

That one definitely piqued his interest. "You can do that?"

She nodded. "Of course."

Her answer set the wheels of his mind in motion. "How long can a human breathe underwater, then?"

Addison shrugged. "I've never really timed it, but I suppose as long as they're under the water. The spell breaks once you breathe air again. Most people don't even remember."

"I'd like to find out what that's like," Hawkins said with a grin. "I'd be the first to volunteer."

"How would you even do that?" Mason asked. "Share your breath with a human?"

She shrugged. "Well, it's like a kiss. But it's not, uh, you know, meant to be an intimate thing." She cleared her throat. "It's a lifesaving device."

Mason had to wonder if it could be intimate, then chased the errant thought away. He hadn't known Addison even three days; yet already she'd invaded his every waking thought. It didn't help that she was starting to seep into his dreams. Waking up with a raging erection wasn't a pleasant way to start the day. Masturbating in the shower was for teenagers, not grown men.

But the picture of her lithe body undulating through the observation tank cut across his mind's eye. Heavy awareness pulsed through his loins. It was getting harder and harder to put her out of his mind. If anything, in the past couple of hours he'd become even more sensitive to her presence.

Mason turned his attention back to the water. He'd never mixed his work with pleasure—especially when the risk might cost him more than his career. The Mer were still very much part of uncharted territory. Nobody knew how to handle them.

He inwardly sighed, but the insistent longing squeezing his heart couldn't be denied. There was nothing holding him back from being with her except . . .

My oath as an officer and a gentleman.

Now that his eyes were off her, Addison took a moment to sneak a peek at the captain. He had a penetrating stare and a presence that made her heart flutter. Even when immersed in water, she'd felt his stare among all the others, burning its way through her with an intensity she'd never encountered.

Something simmered beneath his reserve, and it was all too easy to identify—raw, sexual attraction. The good captain fancied her—no doubt about it.

But for all her bravado, Addison wasn't as secure in her Mer identity as she would have liked others to believe. Being different from other people had taught her not to trust too easily, especially men who oozed sex appeal. Tessa's go-round with Jake Massey had shown them all how vulnerable they really were.

She glanced at Mason McKenzie through wary eyes. *This is something I shouldn't be messing with,* she warned herself. Pushing him out of her mind might have been easier if he were a total dud instead of a tall, strapping hunk of pure male.

Commander Hawkins chose that moment to break into her thoughts. "Does it feel strange not to be in hiding anymore?"

The commander's choice of words brought Addison's brows up.

She shook her head. "We've never been *in hiding*," she pointed out. "We've just kept a low profile. People have known about us for years. They've just had the good sense to keep the information to themselves." She sighed.

"Though I guess it isn't a secret now that Mer are on the nightly news," Hawkins commented.

Her brows rose. "Really?"

Mason shook off his mantle of silence. "Yes, it's true. Word of the Mer has begun to leak out to the general public. Although the identities of you and your sisters are closely guarded, I doubt your anonymity will last."

Her grip tightened around the rail. "You're probably right." Port Rock was a small community, and sooner or later, locals who did know about the Mer would be tempted to blab to the journalists. The chance for fifteen minutes of fame was irresistible to some people. "Guess we'd better get used to being stared at."

"At least you're inaccessible as long as you're aboard ship. And while you're here, you're no different than the rest of us." Mason speared Commander Hawkins with a pointed look. "In fact, I believe some of us are on duty and would be well advised to get back to it."

"Right away, sir." The commander made himself scarce.

Addison watched the officer depart. Since she'd come aboard, everyone had treated her well, even though now and again she'd caught more than one person blatantly staring. *Now I know what a sideshow freak feels like.*

She shook off the disquieting notion. "I'm grateful to be here," she said in reply to Mason's remark. With Tessa's life in danger, she doubted she would have been able to stand up under the deluge of security that had most likely enveloped Gwen, Blake, and Kenneth. At least she had a chance to do something.

Mason's gaze settled on her, intense and focused. He seemed to be following her line of thought. "I understand that mermaids are low-level psychics. Have you been able to sense your sister since we set sail?"

It was eerie how well he read her.

Addison shut her eyes against the tremor of awareness seeping through her body. Mason McKenzie affected her on more than a physical level, and that made the dynamic between them all the more dangerous. "I can, but I can't."

Surprise laced with confusion crossed his expressive face. "Which means?"

"It's as if her vibe has changed," she said, pausing to find the right words. "Her resonance is no longer clear and identifiable, but muddied. She's not herself. Maybe it's because she's pregnant and the twins are interfering." She shook her head. "I really don't know. Our mother never really taught us about our Mercraft, so learning it has been a bit hit-and-miss. More miss, than anything."

He paused a beat. "So you weren't formally trained?"

She shrugged. "Not really. Our mother wanted us to be as much like humans as possible. She always warned us to keep our abilities under wraps and our tails tucked away, if you know what I mean. I think if it hadn't been for our father, we might have never known we were Mer."

"So your father encouraged you to learn?"

Mention of her father always made her smile. "Dad was cool. He used to say he wished he were a merman, so he could swim, too. We'd laugh because it was so funny to think of men with tails. Can you imagine? I mean, where would the penis go?" Realizing what she'd said, heat crept into her cheeks.

He had the audacity to grin. "Seems it would be a pretty funny sight."

She couldn't suppress a giggle. "I think so."

"Your father sounds like a pretty good guy," he commented. "Fisherman, wasn't he?"

"Yeah. Shrimp and lobster, mainly. He loved everything about the sea. After he died, Uncle Jay sold the boats. He had to, I guess."

"That's too bad. Seems as though it would have been a good business for mermaids."

Addison forced a casual shrug. She didn't like thinking about the past. Along with the memories came the suspicion that she'd somehow been responsible for his death. "I guess it wasn't meant to be."

"Is that why you became an EMT?"

She was startled by the question. "What?"

"Because of your parents, I mean."

Her throat tightened. "I don't like to see people in pain. My parents were killed, you know, in a car accident."

Mason nodded tightly. "I was aware of that."

She closed her eyes against the sting of tears that had begun to blur her vision. "I've always felt it was my fault because I was whining about spending my birthday money at the mall. Some kid ran a red light—"

He lifted his brows in surprise. "You were in the accident?"

Addison swiped at her eyes, refusing to cry. "I was in the backseat. I wasn't hurt or anything . . . But my parents were. Both of them were gone in an instant." She paused, drawing in a steadying breath. "I never forgot the guys who pulled us out of the wreckage. I wanted to be like them when I grew up. I wanted to help make things better."

"Must have been tough on you and your sisters to lose your parents when you were so young."

She ran her hands through her damp hair. "Uncle Jay took us on. Not much family on Mom's side. That Mer extinction thing, you know." Her stomach coiled into a tight knot. She hated the raw, wounded tone in her voice. He made her think about things she'd rather forget.

But that was the trouble with Mason McKenzie. He bothered her in so many ways, none of them good.

"I suppose it must have been hard, growing up in the human world."

Addison would have swallowed, but her mouth was suddenly dry. The tension of the last few days began to build behind her eyes, thudding at her temples. Her head throbbed in time to her words. She suddenly couldn't remember the last good hour of sleep she'd gotten since all this trouble had begun. Every time she tried to rest, her keyed-up nerves defied her.

It was too much, too soon.

She didn't want to be having this conversation and wished it would end. How had they even come around to discussing her parents, anyway? She studied him, but had a hard time gauging his neutral expression. There were times when she thought she'd piqued his interest, as in his cabin when they'd fallen into a tangled heap. At other times she thought she sensed distance in his attitude, as though he'd rather be anyplace but around her. The signals he sent were confusing. She wanted to like him—hell, she wanted a lot more than that—but if he couldn't make up his mind about her, then being forced to work together would be pure hell.

She sighed. Once again everything seemed to boil down to the fact that humans were, and would continue to be, afraid of the Mer until they knew exactly what they were dealing with.

She lifted her chin. "No harder than it must be for humans to find out mermaids are real."

A wary look touched his expression. "Truthfully?"

Addison swallowed hard and moistened her lips. "Sure. I can take it."

An ironic smile tugged at his lips. "It is tough finding out there's another species in this world; one that's not only just as intelligent but even more technologically advanced than anyone could have ever imagined. All of a sudden there's a threat in our waters, and we have no idea how to deal with that."

She raised her brows. "I guess it is true that people are afraid of what they don't understand."

He spread his hands. "It's a natural reaction." He couldn't help a rueful chuckle. "Human nature, so to speak."

Addison had to bite her bottom lip to keep from saying something rude. "I just wish Magaera would have some sense. Why can't we all just get along and share?"

Mason's gaze caught and held hers. "Maybe because nothing worth having comes easily."

She was close to launching into her thoughts on that matter when an ensign hurried up to the diver's platform. He tossed off a quick salute. "Sorry to interrupt you, sir, but Lieutenant Russell is requesting that Ms. Lonike join him to explain Mer weaponry and its use in and out of the water."

"Tell Russell we will join him shortly," Mason instructed.

The ensign nodded and hurried off.

The captain quirked a brow. "Guess it's time to get back to work." Pushing away from the rail, he ran his hands through his short blond cut. "No rest for the wicked."

Addison's jaw tightened. She was exhausted and stiff, but she forced herself to ignore the fatigue. Even though she didn't feel like giving any more demonstrations, there was no way she was going to refuse the request.

"Let's go," she said. "You guys have a lot to learn about Mer."

Chapter 10

When Tessa had rekeyed the sea-gate to her psychic resonance, she'd accidentally given Queen Magaera an unexpected advantage. The magnetic energy radiating from the wormhole proved to be an effective deterrent to the outside world. Anything electrical shut down, which meant ships unlucky enough to drift into its radius would be immediately disabled—ditto aircraft. It was an effective wall of defense as yet to be breached.

Jake Massey glanced up at the swirling mass of energy awaiting them at the top of a long staircase. When Ishaldi had a presence on the face of the earth, the sea kingdom had originally existed in two parts—that of an island settlement above the surface of the water, and a second below, accessible only to the Mer themselves. The temple on the ocean floor, which guarded the sea-gate that led to this hidden realm, was one of the few places that had remained untouched through the centuries by seismic activity.

Jake stood before it now, protected by a bubble of oxygen that encircled the temple. "The Temple of Thiraisa," he murmured.

Magaera stood smugly beside him. Tessa's soul-stone was in place around her neck. "It is time to return my people to their rightful place in these waters."

Jake nodded. "I always felt it was possible."

Shackled between two of Magaera's soldiers, Tessa hissed and spat like an angry cat. "You had no right to meddle with something you didn't understand. None of us did. We should have left well enough alone." Since losing her soul-stone, she'd become vicious and hard to handle. For her own safety, she'd had to be restrained. He'd heard that losing a soul-stone was the equivalent of a death sentence for a Mer. Robbed of the ability to manifest energy outside of herself, she was essentially powerless.

Jake didn't blink. He'd gambled his entire reputation and won. He'd no longer be a laughingstock of the archaeological community; instead, he would be a star, forever known as the man who'd revived an extinct species. "I would think you above all others would want to see the Mer survive and thrive."

Tessa's lips curled. "Once they get into the water, it's over."

Magaera lifted an annoyed hand. "Shut your mouth now, or I shall have my soldiers toss you through the gate just for the pleasure of watching it spit out your bones."

Jake grimaced. Ugh. That wouldn't be a pleasant sight at all. The gate had a way of disposing of those it didn't see fit to grant passage to. "Stop fighting it, Tess," he advised. "You're just wearing yourself out."

Tessa bared her teeth. "I hope the fucking thing grinds you up and spits you out, asshole."

He allowed a benign smile. "That's my girl. I think that's why I was drawn to you in the first place. You've got spunk."

Tessa's face twisted with anger. "Bite me!"

"Enough of your natter. It distracts me." Scepter in hand, Queen Magaera began to mount the stairs leading up to the eye of the sea-gate. "Come," she said. "It is time."

Jake felt a little tingle of exaltation as he ascended the stairs behind Magaera. He had defied all the odds, overcome all the derision of his colleagues, to break through the wall of secrecy surrounding the Mer and their disappearance from Earth's waters.

The closer he got to the sea-gate, the more the magnetic tension deepened. His skin prickled, the fine hairs on his arms and neck rising in response to the energy generated around them. The gate itself resembled the single eye of an angry god; lightning flicked within its sphere, flaming out now and again as if trying to keep them at bay. It throbbed, a vibrant force guarding the entrance between two very different worlds.

Queen Magaera stepped closer. As she did, the core of the sea-gate darkened spasmodically. Tendrils of lightning sped from its center, striking the small crystal pendant hanging around her neck. A tremendous crash of thunder snapped the air apart when it made contact with Tessa's soul-stone.

Teeth clenched with anxiety, Jake winced. Would the gate recognize and accept Tessa's psychic imprint and allow them to pass—or would it devour their bodies and spit back bones?

The answer came sooner than expected.

Magaera's body suddenly arched backward, rigid as a pillar, as the tendrils of lightning unexpectedly wound themselves around her body. Jagged flickers of color darkened, then glowed brightly again. A scream tore from her lips.

A wild thought zinged through his mind. *This is what happened when it first took Tessa.*

Without thinking, Jake rushed forward. He'd barely taken two steps before a layer of red-hot fire enveloped him, lifting him off his feet and dragging him toward its flaming center. The electric tension grew, throbbing. The eye of the sea-gate glowed, turning almost transparent enough to reveal a hazy glimpse of the world waiting on the other side.

The force suddenly pulled them forward, propelling them like two rocks in a slingshot. Jake barely heard himself scream as the sweep of an otherworldly power bore them toward their destination.

Tumbling through the air, he landed with a thud on a hard stone surface.

Jake shivered, feeling cold, empty, and void. He was sure every molecule in his body had been torn apart and reassembled, perhaps incorrectly. Moaning in delirious agony, he slowly lifted his face off the cold surface beneath his cheek. The movement caused his stomach to roll. Shaken by fine tremors, he was sure he was about to vomit. The sound of scuffling limbs alerted him that another had arrived in his wake.

A moan filtered through the ringing in his ears. "Oh God, I'd forgotten what dimensional travel feels like." Tessa groaned again. "I can't believe I'm back here."

Jake barely spared her a glance. Since he'd found out she carried Kenneth Randall's brats—three of them, no less!—he'd lost all interest in her.

"Get used to it, babe." Clamping his teeth against the rush of nausea, he forced himself onto his knees. Blinking hard, he glanced around. Although he couldn't be sure, he seemed to be on some kind of platform inside a stone sanctuary. Recognition filtered back into his scrambled brains.

A smile parted his lips. They'd made it through intact. His tongue felt like a dry wad of cotton. "We're back." His eyes searched for and found Queen Magaera, who seemed to be suffering no ill effects from her own passage through the sea-gate. The atmosphere around them was oppressively silent.

The Mer queen gazed down on the great hall. As was to be expected, this sanctuary of worship was crowded with women on their knees before the great dais. Since the queen's departure, her minions had kept watch, waiting for the time when the sea-gate would again reopen.

Gaining sight of their revered leader, the Mer women rose to their feet. Hushed murmurings spread throughout the temple. Nobody present blinked for fear of missing a single detail.

Composed mostly of stone and crystal, Ishaldi looked much as he remembered from his first visit to the lost city. There had been a time when lush forests teeming with wildlife and cold streams of pure water spread throughout the land. But the beauty of the city was an illusion, as transient as a phantom in the mist.

In sealing the wormhole between Ishaldi and Earth,

Queen Nyala had doomed her people to a slow and inexorable death. Because the natural resources could not be replenished, the animals died off, water became poisoned, and plant life shriveled. Though the Mer would learn to adapt by drawing their sustenance out of the stone, the humans left behind fared less well. Famine forced the culling of the weak, the sick, and the inferior. Only the strongest, most desirable males were kept for breeding. The rest of the men, and a few women, were consigned to slavery.

As he looked around, a sense of accomplishment filled him. The perilous times were at an end. *I did it,* he thought smugly. He imagined he would be well rewarded.

Flinging back her head and squaring her shoulders, Magaera slowly crossed to the front of the dais, from where she could be seen and from where she could see—all angles. Her blond hair and shimmering white weblike robes gave her an unearthly appearance. The scepter of Atargatis glimmered, a star plucked from the heavens. Her impassive eyes betrayed nothing of her thoughts.

The queen spread her arms. "My people, as I promised, I have returned," she said, addressing them in the Mer language. She raised the scepter. "I have retrieved that which has been stolen, and with it I shall grant the freedom that has been taken from us. Once again we shall rule Earth's waters as Atargatis intended."

A deep, booming cheer rolled forward. *"We believe! It is proven to our eyes!"*

Jake's brow furrowed as he struggled to keep up with her words. English was not the language of the Mer.

Since becoming acquainted with Magaera, he'd picked up bits and pieces of their strange dialect. He'd found that much of the language was based on dialects of ancient Greece and Egypt, two seafaring nations the Mer would have been in contact with for trade and commerce. As an archaeologist who specialized in the Mediterranean countries, he had enough training to follow along.

Magaera smirked. "Have I earned your faith?"

"Our queen has provided well and truly," the women roared back.

The queen raised her hand for silence. "And what is your will?" she questioned gravely.

Again came the thunder of female voices, en masse: *"We shall serve!"* The temple was no longer a place of meditation and contemplation. Peace was shattered by the rallying cry for war.

Without warning, Magaera gestured for her soldiers to bring Tessa forward. Still reeling and weak from passing through the sea-gate, Tessa stumbled, falling to her knees. Her long red hair was a tangle around her face, as bright and damning as the mark of Cain. Any Mer who did not have blond hair and blue eyes was considered to be of an impure bloodline.

"This is the inferior who betrayed us," the Mer queen said, pointing an accusing finger at Tessa. "She is a descendant of the Tesch dynasty, of the queen who chose mankind over her own people. She now carries the seed of a *husla*, a human male, whom we would not deem worthy for breeding."

A hiss rose through the crowd.

Magaera's strong voice rang out. "What is your will?"

"Condemn her to death!" the collective roared. The judgment reverberated through the voluminous temple with a grim finality.

Feeling his blood turn to icy chips, Jake winced. This wasn't what he'd been expecting at all. "If Tessa dies, her soul-stone dies with her," he reminded Magaera.

Her frigid blue eyes met his. "I need her soul-stone only a little while longer," she said in a low and curiously level voice. "Once we have established ourselves in Earth's waters, there will be no need to return to this realm. Besides, we cannot allow the spawn of an inferior to survive. Our race is a pure one, and we intend to keep it that way."

Jake gazed back at her in consternation. The future he'd envisioned had suddenly turned pitch-black before his eyes. The Mer had no intention of adapting to the modern world. No, by the look in her steely gaze, she was hell-bent on going to war. The power vested in her was a very real thing.

There would be no peace, no mediation.

And no place for him, except as a consort for her pleasure, and perhaps breeding.

A voice from behind snapped through his silence. "Looks as though you've fucked us all, Jake."

He turned his head and looked into Tessa's eyes. Her features were etched with despair and the finality of the death sentence Magaera had leveled on her head.

"I'm sorry," he whispered, though his lips barely moved. He knew then that he would suffer for his stupidity. His own blind pride and foolishness had generated endless, bad karma, for which he and many other innocent people would now pay. As much as he wanted to, he couldn't deny his responsibility for what had happened.

Slumping forward, Tessa ignored his apology. "I hope you got what you wanted, Jake." She covered her face with her hands and shuddered. The pain in her voice penetrated deep. "You've just killed my children."

Chapter 11

"Why are you hiding in a utility closet?" Mason McKenzie asked.

Pulling her legs closer to her chest, Addison wrapped her arms around her knees. "I just wanted to be out of sight," she mumbled toward the tall figure silhouetted in the doorway. "I needed a place to myself."

He checked his watch. "It's almost midnight." Consternation creased his smooth forehead. "I would think my cabin would have provided the same function, albeit a bit more comfortably."

Addison shook her head. If nothing else, being in McKenzie's quarters only made her that much more jumpy. Everything she looked at only made her think of him; from the shower where he would soap his naked body, to the bunk that supported his lanky frame. Since their brief encounter earlier in the day, she couldn't get the feel of his body pressed against hers out of her mind. She had no doubt that Mason was a man capable of fulfilling every fantasy she'd ever had—and maybe even a few she hadn't dreamed up yet. Just the thought of his strong hands skimming her skin made her senses hum with a sexual awareness she couldn't ignore.

And yet she still couldn't figure out how or why this man had wormed himself inside her brain. She didn't even like blonds!

Addison drew a deep breath. "I like it here. Nobody bothers me."

Stepping into the narrow space, Mason closed the door behind him. It took him only a few steps to narrow the distance between them. He knelt, folding his long legs beneath his weight. The dim light from the bare bulb above cast strange shadows across his face, giving him an unearthly look. "Is something wrong?"

She pressed back against the wall, wishing her hiding place were a little bit deeper and darker. "I don't like the way they're looking at me," she said after a moment's pause. "They keep eyeing me as if I'm some kind of a magical wonder. As if I can wave my hands and make it all better."

One side of his mouth curled up. He chuckled, emitting a deep masculine sound. "In their eyes you are magical. Imagine how they feel seeing something so incredible and amazing."

Addison huffed. "Imagine how I feel, being gawked at like a sideshow freak." She shook her head. "Sometimes I think Gwen was right. That it would be better if the Mer were to stay hidden."

"Too late for that," Mason pointed out. "Whether or not you like it, the genie's been let out of the bottle. You're going to have to accept that some people are simply going to stare. It's rude, I know. But it's also human nature. I'll speak to my crew and tell them to lay off."

"Don't do that. It's my problem, not theirs."

His gaze never wavered. Eyes she would willingly drown in, locked and held with hers. "They're pretty good at following orders."

A swirling ribbon of desire unfurled deep within her all over again. She suddenly felt cramped, hot, and definitely uncomfortable. "It's not their fault, I suppose." Shaking her head to clear away thoughts of Mason naked and aroused, she raised her chin a notch. "Why can't they understand that I'm not anything special? I'm just me, Addison. The girl who sometimes wears a tail when she swims." In her secret heart she longed to be approached by a man who'd treat her like a regular woman. She wanted a man who could look beyond the Mer and find the woman.

Mason moved to one knee, leaning closer. His aftershave smelled crisp and fresh, a sensual combination that reminded her of the ocean after sunset. "Don't be so fast to put yourself down," he murmured. "You're a lot more than a girl who wears a tail."

Addison tilted her head back and found herself staring into his eyes. Awareness bubbled up inside her, growing hotter and more intense with every beat of her heart. She couldn't help but wonder how many women this handsome man in uniform had charmed.

He doesn't look like the kind who spends a lot of nights alone, she thought.

She forced herself to swallow, suddenly aware of how parched her mouth was. She hadn't had a thing to eat or drink in hours. "I am?"

Mason's gaze settled on her face, intense and focused. "Absolutely."

"Then why do I get the feeling you'd rather not have me here?"

Surprised, he drew back. "What?"

"Mermaids aren't psychic, but we are empaths. The vibrations emanating off you are strong enough to knock me over."

Her words seemed to strike a chord. The sudden hitch in his breathing seemed to prove her right. "And what do my vibes say, if I may ask?"

Addison attempted to focus her concentration, something she found difficult to do, given their close proximity. "I make you uncomfortable," she said quietly. "You're wary. Maybe because you don't know what to make of a mermaid that isn't trying to blast you to bits. It isn't personal, I think. You just don't trust the species."

"It's true," he countered wryly. "The first time I saw a mermaid, she was trying to drag me to the bottom of the sea."

She winced. "Shit. We'll never live that down, you know. Everyone thinks that all mermaids do is sing prettily and lure sailors to their deaths."

He thought a moment. "Well, there must be some truth to the legend."

Addison speared him with a disgruntled look. "I admit, Mer are known to be a little grouchy," she allowed.

He rocked back on his heels. "A little bit?"

Hot blood rushed into her cheeks. "Oh, hell. A lot. We're bitches, okay? We gotta work to control our instincts. Just like anyone else has to learn to keep his cool." Glancing at his handsome face, she forced a casual shrug. "But things still simmer beneath the surface, fighting to break out. You're the same way. You fight hard to keep control, but even now it's getting the better of you."

He didn't blink. "Is it?"

Her heart rate bumped up a notch, even though his face was one of composure. Desire shimmered in the depths of his gaze, just as it hammered insistently inside her. There was no mistaking it. The unspoken connection was strong and unmistakable.

"I think so." She paused a moment. Did she really want to open *that* door? Once she said the words, they couldn't be taken back. Something inside her warned that she'd be taking a risk, but she decided to ignore it. "You'd like to know more about me," she ventured slowly. "But you think it's inappropriate."

He raised a skeptical brow. "And you can tell all that just by being around me?"

Addison allowed a small smile. "Well, that, and the fact your first officer thinks you're trying to hog me to yourself."

His eyes darkened subtly. An immediate frown followed. "Hawkins told you that?" He cursed under his breath.

Yes, she was right. She'd definitely piqued his interest. There was no mistaking when a man was interested in a Mer. "No. I overheard him talking with a couple of the other crew members. He says you told them hands off. He thinks that's because you want me for yourself." She paused, then added, "Am I right?"

A long pause ensued. The silence between them was maddening.

Just when Addison was beginning to believe she'd taken things too damn far, Mason reached out, brushing her face with the tips of his fingers. "I shouldn't," he admitted in a low voice, "but I do."

She licked dry lips. Her hand rose, fingers curling around his wrist. Just touching him made her feel so intensely alive, vital, desired. "We could . . ." She'd never heard her own voice sound like that, throbbing with need.

Mason regretfully shook his head. "I can't, Addison. The worst sin any officer can commit is to do anything remotely wrong regarding sex."

Her grip tightened. The sudden hitch in his breathing proved to her that he was tempted. A shiver took hold. Overwhelmed and consumed by his physical presence, she closed her eyes. His pulse raged beneath his skin, matching her own heart's frantic beat.

She'd never been the kind of woman to wait around for a man to make the advances. Mer were sexual, sensual creatures. And she had to admit that she'd never before encountered a man who filled her with such carnal longings.

Anticipation burst like a bubble. She let her hand fall away, destroying their physical connection. Breaking contact wasn't easy, but she managed. "I understand." She'd opened herself up, and now she had to take the consequences. His rejection was like a jab to the gut. It hurt, but she would survive.

He climbed to his feet. The distance between them was immediate and striking. "What I want and what my job says I can have are two different things," he whispered. His gaze settled on her face. "As much as I want you, I can't put my career on the line."

She had to respect his honesty. He wasn't turning her down because he didn't desire her, but because he did. "You don't have to explain. I understand the chain of command."

Mason quickly pushed his hands into his pockets. As if he didn't trust himself, he stepped back to put a little more distance between them. "Yes," he admitted, then tried to make light of his answer by adding, "I've always been a traveling man."

She could practically hear the wheels grinding in his head. "It's always going to be duty first with you."

He gave another stiff nod. "I'm afraid so. Forever and always."

An awkward pause ensued.

Addison eyed him from head to foot. *It was only a passing fancy,* she reminded herself. She was a big girl. Rejection was par for the course when navigating through the tricky relations between men and mermaids.

An ironic smile tugged at her lips. "Gotcha."

"I'm sorry."

"Don't be."

He offered a hand. "Let me help you up."

Addison reluctantly accepted. His hand practically swallowed hers. It was the first time she could ever remember being around a man whose own size dwarfed hers. At five foot ten, she wasn't exactly a shrinking violet.

He tugged her to her feet. "You going to be okay?"

Nodding, she reluctantly let her hand fall away from his. She was tired, weary to the bone. A shower and a snooze would go a long way toward clearing her head. And it didn't even matter that she'd struck out with Mason McKenzie. It wasn't as if she'd been looking for more than a fling. And she felt a little selfish for letting herself put aside the reason she'd agreed to join USET in the first place.

Focus, she reminded herself. *Tessa needs your help.* Knocking boots with Mason McKenzie wasn't any way to accomplish that. "I guess this is where we should say good night." Mentally cursing the narrow confines of the closet, she tried to slip past his tall frame. Used for storing cleaning supplies, the space was barely big enough for one person, much less two. "Excuse me, Captain."

Mason's breath caught noticeably when her body pressed against his. "Shit," he swore under his breath.

Her heart jumped into her throat. She suddenly felt as if she were burning up. "What?"

Without warning, he caught her in his arms. His grip was sure and possessive. His hips shifted against her in the tight space. "Damn it, Addison. You aren't making this easy."

Addison didn't know whether to laugh or cry at the comment. The heat from his touch seemed to pour straight into her veins, spreading like wildfire across dry prairie grass. The connection between them was so strong that it felt as though some magnetic force had drawn them together. "Just let me by."

His fingers tightened. "I can't."

Her spine stiffened. "This isn't funny. Don't play games with me." Getting out of there looked to be harder than expected.

"I don't play games." His tone was husky now—strained.

Addison tipped her head back. She looked at him, expecting him to let her go and apologize at any second.

The unabashed desire in his eyes said something else. "Then what are you doing?"

Mason stared down at her. "I shouldn't want you, but I do."

Fighting to maintain her composure, she swallowed hard. "Don't tell me," she murmured. "Show me."

Mason pulled her closer, his mouth capturing hers. One of his hands curled warmly around her neck even as his tongue slid along the seam of her lips, pressing for more intimate contact. Their hips collided as their kiss deepened. A shaft of white-hot heat shot through her, hard and fast. There was no mistaking her body's reaction to his mastery.

She wanted him.

Bad.

Mason wasn't exactly sure when he lost control. One minute he was acting like a perfect officer and gentleman. The next moment he was pulling Addison Lonike into his arms, determined to lay one hell of a kiss on her sensual lips.

The situation was spinning out of control—fast. But he couldn't help it. Desire throbbed as hard and as fast as his rapidly beating heart. The only thing he was aware of was how much he wanted her.

All of her.

When their kiss broke, she let out a low groan. "What are we doing?" Despite her question, her bright green eyes glittered with pleasure.

Mason shook his head. So much for the idea that he'd take a sabbatical from sex and cleanse his mind and body while he concentrated on taking his career to the next level. Meeting Addison had set his libido right back on edge. Her image persisted in buzzing around the back of his brain like a gnat that wouldn't shoo. Why she attracted him couldn't be summed up in words. Still, everything about her was appealing, from her allure to her uncertainty, to the steely determination in her green eyes.

The only thing on his mind was increasing her pleasure as soon as he possibly could. "I don't know." His hands moved, claiming her slender waist. Her T-shirt was tucked into the waistband of her khakis, cutting him off from the feel of bare skin.

Her hands rose to his chest, fingers digging through the material and into his skin. Their eyes locked. The air between them crackled with strange electricity.

She stared at him, her lips parted, moist with anticipation. "We could stop." She laughed, her sparkling eyes dancing with mischief.

A lump formed in his throat, almost cutting off his oxygen. She was so beautiful. The ache inside grew fierce, and his erection strained to break free of his slacks.

Mason bit his tongue, gritting his teeth. A shiver curled around his spine, then crept lower. God, the pressure, the need, the wonderful anticipation.

"I don't want to." Lost in the haze of sheer lust, he pressed her back against the wall. It was as if the whole world outside had ceased to exist.

Mason McKenzie, you are in over your head. But in his crazed, impassioned state he didn't care.

Letting out a long breath, he ignored the self-serving admonition. He was tired of playing it safe.

Mason felt the fine hairs at the back of his neck

prickle. He opened his mouth to say something, then closed it again.

Addison moved her hand and cupped him intimately. Her fingers curled around his shaft. "By the goddess, you feel so good."

Mason's scalp prickled as the heat from her palm seeped through his slacks. Attraction. Need. Desire. All were communicated between their aching bodies. All sense flew out of his mind, and his sole thought was of how badly he wanted her—now. Hers was a warm, living force, a magnet he couldn't resist.

Every inch of his body tingled with anticipation. Without a word, he aligned their bodies so she could feel every inch of him, hard and full.

As he fought back an agonized moan, his hands moved to her breasts. His fingers teased the erect tips of her nipples, made all the more tantalizing because of the material separating his skin from hers. "This is so wrong," he breathed. Illicit sex in a utility closet wasn't even his style, either. He liked to think he had enough class to treat a woman right—a nice dinner, a good bottle of wine, dancing to a live band at a local club in her hometown. If he was lucky, and he usually was, he'd end up at her place, in her bed. If not, he didn't mind a hotel room as long as it wasn't a roach trap.

She tipped her head back, staring up at him through a heavy-lidded gaze. Her breath came in shallow gasps. "But it feels so right." Pressed back against the wall, her legs were bracketed between his strong thighs.

Mason tugged her T-shirt out of her slacks. He pulled it over her head, and her sports bra followed. Her skin was soft and pliant. "I can't get you out of my head," he breathed. He wouldn't be finished until he'd caressed, licked, and sucked every inch of her.

Addison laughed low in the back of her throat. "So I see."

His swollen erection pushed insistently against his slacks. "I can't tell you how tempted I was when we were in my cabin. I damn near lost it."

Her eyes crinkled around the corners. "I know." Her voice trailed off as she fumbled with his belt buckle. "I was thinking you were overdressed."

Her eyes never left his. "Looks like you're taking care of that now," he whispered. The buckle fell away.

Heat pulsed through his veins. His stomach muscles contracted with need as he unbuttoned the top of her khakis. The zipper crunched down. "So are you," she murmured in his ear.

"There's no stopping now," he warned.

"Definitely not . . ." Her mouth came down on his with a slow deliberation. His tongue pressed past her lips to explore her mouth.

Addison moaned a second time, arching her body against his. "Oh, yes . . ."

Mason took full control. He caressed her breasts, teasing the hard little beads. His head dipped. With a merciless drag of his tongue over the tips, he continued his exquisite torment.

The gentle pressure made Addison's entire body shudder. She gasped and tangled her fingers in his thick hair, pressing him closer. "Damn, you're good."

Mason laughed low in his throat and began to suckle harder, taking each nipple in its turn and giving them slow long licks. "I'm about to get better."

Her body trembled with pleasure. Her sigh was like the chorus of a thousand angels' voices in his ears, the most heavenly music in the whole world.

He ran curious fingers over the design etched into her skin. It felt smooth, as soft as silk. Although he'd seen it when she was in the tank, he'd been aching to see the design up closer, and on a much more intimate level. He admired the way the pattern traveled its way up her arms and over her shoulders before beginning a looping descent over her breasts and down her abdomen and hips. The pattern ended at her ankles. "Your scale pattern is amazing."

Kissing his way down her abdomen, Mason nibbled at the soft skin below her navel. He parted her legs, and Addison opened for him willingly. A whimper broke from her throat. "Please," she breathed.

Mason's mouth landed in the soft wetness between her legs and continued his slow assault until her breath came in shallow gasps.

Spasms wracked her. Catching a utility bar above her head, Addison writhed until exhaustion claimed her. A sob of surrender escaped from deep inside her throat.

Mason gazed into her eyes. She opened up to him; she trusted him. He knew then he would do everything in his power to protect her.

Fighting his way out of his own tight T-shirt, he dug in the pocket of his unzipped slacks for the condom Hawkins had tossed his way. He'd almost forgotten about it.

Manna from heaven, he thought gratefully. His men might think with their dicks, but at least they had sense to protect themselves and their partners.

"Prepared for every emergency, Captain?"

He grinned. There was no way he'd ever tell her the truth. "I was a Boy Scout." Ripping the foil packet with his teeth, he eased the rubber over his aching shaft, then lifted her off her feet. "Wrap your legs around me, babe."

Addison obeyed. A moan filtered past her lips as he lowered her onto his waiting erection. She was wet and hot, and his glide into her waiting depths was as easy as it was right.

No more words were needed between them.

What followed next defied anything he'd ever experienced with any other woman. Like a wildcat in heat, Addison drew him in with rocking, twisting motions that had the effect of pulling him in, each time deeper and harder than the last. She writhed in his arms, uninhibited in every way. Shuddering as his hands clenched her ass, she ground her hips against his, begging for more.

Bracing her back against the wall, Mason responded in kind. His penis was a steel shaft, throbbing with heat. With every gliding motion, he thrust deeper inside her, claiming her, branding her as his own.

A shiver went through him when Addison's sharp nails dug into his sweat-slicked back. "Don't stop," she gasped. "Don't ever stop."

A feral growl rumbled deep inside his chest. "Never," he grated between gritted teeth. "You're mine."

He meant what he said—absolutely and completely.

Passing the point of no return, Mason gave himself to the waves building inside him, a relentless tide crashing onto a jagged shore. He rode the peaks, letting the power of his need tumble him end over end. It was all too much; yet it didn't feel like enough.

Countless seconds later, the heat in his loins melded with hers. Physical and emotional sensation melted into a single profound ache even as a sense of the most exquisite rapture branded his heart. All control shattered.

Mason pummeled her harder—faster. Beyond their bodies, beyond sex, he felt himself blending into her. At the same time, Addison's fingers convulsed, her sharp nails tearing into his shoulders as she clung to him. Their shared excitement grew, spreading out in shivering ripples, engulfing every last inch of their physical selves.

A cry of wild abandon ripped from his throat. Addison's name tore past his lips even as his orgasm seared through his veins. Pleasure overflowed, spreading all around him like a wave of fire; a scalding, shivering explosion of white-hot desire.

As Mason let himself drown in the magnificent abyss of pure passion, it vaguely occurred to him that he'd been snared.

Hook, line, and sinker.

Chapter 12

The aftermath of sex was the hardest part for Addison. Now that the intensity of the moment had passed, the inevitable would occur. She felt empty, deflated.

Mason lowered her to her feet, holding her steady. "God, that was terrific."

Unable to look him in the eyes, Addison reached for her discarded clothing. The narrow space didn't give her much room to maneuver.

Damn it! This wasn't any time to be fooling around. She needed to focus on finding her sister instead of dallying around with the delectable Captain McKenzie. *Tessa needs me.*

Mistaking her silence for assent, Mason pulled her against him before delivering a nip to the nape of her neck. "Give me a minute to catch my breath and we'll do it all over again."

Addison stiffened, wriggling out of his hold. Nerves strung as tight as a piano wire, she felt miserable because she was miserable. Everything was piling up on her at once, and she was powerless to stop the destruction. Like an earthquake victim, she saw no way to dig herself out of the rubble.

Unbidden tears blurred her vision—so much for remaining detached. "That's okay," she said, turning away so he couldn't see her face. "I've had enough."

Mason's touch immediately fell away. "Something wrong?"

Mustering her inner strength, she put on a cool and aloof manner. It was just sex—nothing more. Just because they'd shared a few moments of intimacy didn't mean they had any obligation to share their feelings. She'd had an itch and Mason had scratched it. Besides, he probably just wanted to see what sex with a mermaid would be like. "Nothing's wrong." Slipping on her slacks, she snagged her sports bra. "We've had our moment."

As he reached for his own clothing, bemusement colored his features. "Wow. You don't waste any time brushing a guy off. We had sex. Now we're done. End of story."

Pulling her T-shirt over her head, she poked a finger into his chest. "You were the one who said duty comes first." She shook her head. "I'm not a clingy woman. You don't have to give me a cuddle afterward."

A frown spread across his rugged face. "So that's it?" he asked. "Now that I've serviced you, you're dismissing me?"

Addison ran her hands across her numb face. Talk about putting her foot in her mouth. She was trying to offer him a graceful exit, but he didn't seem willing to take the hint.

"I didn't mean it to come out that way. What I meant was, we've relieved the tension and now it's time to get back to formalities."

His brow furrowed as he pulled his slacks up his slender hips and zipped them up. "That's usually something the man would say," he noted wryly.

"What I'm trying to tell you is that we don't have to get personal here. We gave in, and now that we've satisfied our curiosity about each other, we can get back to work."

He paused a moment. "Is that all men are for Mer?" he asked slowly. "Curiosities?"

Everything she said was coming out sounding negative. It wasn't supposed to be that way. She wanted to tell him she'd just had the most mind-blowing sex of her life, with the sexiest man she'd ever met.

Yet something inside kept holding her back, tripping up her tongue, and sending out the wrong signals. She didn't want Mason to feel obligated, as if he'd somehow taken advantage.

"I could ask you the same question," she countered. "Weren't you wondering what it would be like to be with a mermaid?" A little laugh escaped her. "I know you guys are always wondering what we can do with the tail . . ."

He gave her an odd look. "I actually wasn't thinking about your tail. But I get what you're saying. It was a one-time thing." His words came out a lot cooler than hers.

Addison winced. That wasn't what she'd wanted to say at all. But since he was going to take it that way, maybe she should take the easy way out. "Yeah." Good. That made things easier—less complicated.

Mason's gaze searched her face. "Are you wishing we'd never done it?"

Addison looked at him, his body half in shadow and half in light from the gentle illumination flickering from the naked bulb overhead. She'd never been good at being a distant bitch who used men and then tossed them aside. That was the trouble with being the kind of woman who wore her heart on her sleeve. She wasn't good at hiding her emotions.

"I don't regret what we did," she admitted after a moment's silence had passed. "I just wish the circumstances had been different."

Mason's big frame relaxed. Stepping closer, he turned her around and put his hands on her shoulders. His touch was familiar and soothing, a knowing and intimate one. His thick fingers went to work on the knots of stress and strain. "We both know there's something going on here," he speculated as his fingers probed a particularly sore knot. "I felt it the second I set eyes on you."

As she melted under his talented manipulations, a swirling ribbon of desire unfurled in Addison's belly, igniting her desire all over again. She relished everything about him—his scent, his touch, his closeness. She swallowed the lump rising in her throat, feeling a thousand-watt jolt go surging all the way through her body. She was like putty in his hands, willing to be molded into anything he desired.

The pressure felt so good, she groaned in relief. The pain receded a bit, and she focused on the rhythmic motion of his hands. A comforting rush of heat traveled between his fingers and her skin. "I have to admit, the feeling was pretty strong," she said softly.

Mason continued the soothing massage, pressing the tips of his fingers into the slender curves where neck and shoulders came together, the soft pads of his thumbs rubbing at the hollow at the base of her hairline. "And I have to admit that now isn't the best time for us to discover we have a mutual attraction. I'm breaking every damn rule in the book, being here with you now."

Her throat tightened again. "Technically I'm not a crew member under your, uh, command, Captain."

His low deep laugh brushed across her ear. "Technically, you're right. But you can't deny that being involved with you is something much more explosive."

Addison's heart stalled. She broke away from his delicious hands, turning around to face him. He was right, of course. "That little problem with Queen Magaera . . ." The rapid flutter of a pulse beating in her throat betrayed her nervous tension. "Which must mean you're fraternizing with the enemy."

"In so many words, yes. It's true you've been recruited to help breach the queen's island, but—"

"I'm still one of *them*." She waited a beat, but he didn't speak.

Mason simply nodded.

Addison felt her throat tighten. The warmth and tenderness in his touch caused a tidal wave of emotion surging through her, the need to have him all over again almost overwhelming.

She reluctantly pulled away. "Oh, damn . . . We just made a huge mistake."

"It didn't feel like a mistake to me," he said. "But the timing isn't right. It's just too much, too soon."

She grimaced. In other words, they should have been

adults who were able to hang on to their hormones. "Tell me about it."

Although she'd had her flings, tumbling into the nearest utility closet for a hot sex session wasn't usually the way she took on a new lover. She had to admit it was a bit easier this time. There were no awkward explanations about her scale pattern and no unveiling of the tail. Mason knew exactly what he was getting.

Yeah, he was definitely getting her. *And so much more,* her mind silently filled in. So far Mer females had proven to be a handful for their partners. The men who chose to be with them usually ended up sacrificing everything. Kenneth Randall had practically rebuilt his whole life around Tessa. And Blake Whittaker had not only ended up chucking his entire career for Gwen; he'd taken on the federal government to do so.

As for Mason McKenzie . . . Although she didn't know him well—ha! hardly at all—she had a feeling he wasn't going to be the kind of man who'd willingly put aside his ambition for a woman.

"So, what do we do?" she ventured.

His gaze narrowing, Mason looked at her long and hard. "We have to stop thinking about ourselves." As he reached for her hands, his fingers curled over hers. "We've both got jobs we need to focus on, and we can't let our emotions get in the way. Too many lives depend on cool heads and steady hands."

Cool and steady was the last thing she felt. A better description of her emotional state would be dazed and confused.

Knowing he was right, Addison felt cruel hands twist her heart into knots. It was all she could do to keep

breathing. "And that means keeping business and pleasure separate."

He cocked his head to one side. "I think that's the
best thing we can do."

The constricting grip throughout her chest tightened.
Her gaze darted away from his. Hysterical laughter
threatened to bubble to the surface. She rarely lost control and had always managed to keep her head and her
emotions separated.

*Maybe it would be easier to walk away now. I don't
have to look back . . .*

As if reading her thoughts, Mason cupped her cheek
in his hand. "We're not going to pretend this never happened." His deep voice wrapped around her.

A wonderful pulsing sensation settled between her
thighs. His musky scent filled her nostrils, the smell of
him sexy and definitely alluring. Desire threatened to
pull her into its undertow, to drown her with too many
unfulfilled wants and needs.

"You say that as if you mean it."

Mason's gaze lingered on her face in what felt like
another heated caress. He pulled her closer, sending her
pulse into overdrive. Her heart rate soared. "There will
be time for us. Later."

Addison couldn't bring herself to glance away. A secret thrill of pleasure filled her heart. There was no
doubt in her mind that he meant every word he said.
"Later can't come soon enough."

Mason leaned forward, cupping one of her breasts.
"I've got a few more hours before duty calls." He
squeezed the plump mound, giving her a quick kiss.

Addison's lips tingled. So did her entire body. The

tips of her nipples immediately tightened into little peaks aching for her lover's caress. "Why did I get dressed so quickly?" And then the sounds of her rumbling stomach crushed the intimate moment.

Mason glanced down at her abdomen and laughed. "Well, I've never gotten that response from a woman before. When was the last time you ate?"

Addison laughed, too. "I honestly can't remember. I've mostly been running on caffeine and adrenaline."

He frowned. "That was two days ago." Stepping back, he tucked his T-shirt back into his slacks. "Webber would have a cow if he found out I let you starve. Guess I'll have to feed you."

Shell-shocked; dazed; definitely confused. Mason felt all that, and more. One minute he'd told Addison that getting involved was out of the question. And the next? He was laying a lip-lock on her as if there were no tomorrow.

He wasn't into games. He didn't lead women on. Hell, he wasn't even looking for a relationship. So, what had happened?

He shook his head. *I still don't know*.

Mason glanced down at the woman striding beside him, walking as if she hadn't a care in the world. Even though the T-shirt and slacks she wore were basically designed for men, he couldn't help but notice she filled out the clothes in all the right ways. He'd like to get them off her again—soon.

He quickly cut the thought short with practiced precision. He wasn't exactly sure what was going on with him, but he knew he shouldn't dwell on it. He couldn't continue to let himself think of her in a sexual manner.

Addison's shoulder brushed his as they made their way through the narrow corridor leading toward the mess room. Somehow they'd managed to make it out of the utility closet without being seen. The late hour and remoteness of the location had helped. He wondered what might be going through her mind, but he didn't dare ask. If she had any opinion about what they'd just done, she was keeping it to herself.

He couldn't help but try to rationalize their actions. They were two consenting adults. Each had enjoyed what the other had to offer. There was no reason to get emotional or attached. It was just sex.

A shiver rippled through him hard enough to make his hands shake. No, it was more than that, but he really couldn't take the time to sort through the mess. He had a mission to accomplish. Putting himself in the middle of a chaotic emotional tangle would only make things worse. He needed to clear his mind.

Mason scrubbed a hand over his jaw. *Focus!* he ordered himself.

At oh one hundred hours, or one in the morning, the dining area was fairly deserted. A few crew members working the night shift had come in for a break, or for a refill from the coffeepot kept on and full 24/7.

A couple of the seamen glanced toward Addison but said nothing. Whether she liked it or not, she still garnered stares of curiosity. That she was a very pretty woman probably didn't help matters any.

He checked his watch. "Looks as though we're on our own. The mess cook won't be on for another few hours."

Fetching herself a cup of coffee, she grinned. "I'm guessing no steak and potatoes."

Mason filled his own cup. "We eat pretty well aboard ship, but those things are above my culinary reach," he admitted, adding cream and sugar to the tarry black brew.

"So show me the galley and I'll try to whip us up something." She took a big gulp of hot coffee. "I'm not the best cook, but I can manage something simple."

Mason pointed the way. "Anything you can come up with is fine by me."

Addison took a few minutes to familiarize herself with the layout, pawing through the supplies. One of the limitations of the *Sea Horse* was food. Sixty days was the max time the ship could spend at sea before supplies would need to be replenished. Although they had a fair supply of fresh fruits and vegetables and eggs and meat, perishables like that wouldn't last long. The ship simply wasn't designed for long-term endurance at sea. Their backup was supplied by the navy's Sixth Fleet, which was currently engaged in keeping the shipping lanes open and sea traffic moving. The electromagnetic interference emanating around Magaera's island was proving to be one big pain in the ass.

Addison dug out a half-dozen eggs, milk, butter, some slices of American cheese, and a loaf of white bread. "I can work with this."

Mason was hungrier for a meal of more than breakfast foods, but he was in no position to complain. He didn't cook. "What the hell does that make?"

Addison cracked six eggs into a bowl, then added a little milk. "It's my version of French toast," she said, dropping whole slices of bread into the egg mixture. "It's quick and simple and tastes good."

He sipped his coffee. Damn, it was strong enough to eat through steel. "French toast with cheese?"

Fishing out a pan and adding a few dollops of butter, she set it on the stove to heat. "Wait until you taste it. It's awesome."

He had his doubts. What she was putting together looked like a cholesterol-laden mess. He could practically feel his arteries clogging. "I'll reserve judgment until I actually taste it."

She arranged the gooey slices in the sizzling butter. "I'll admit most of my eats come from fast-food joints. I never have much time to cook. And my roommates are such pigs. It's hard to find the kitchen in that hellacious confusion they've got going on."

She was right. Her apartment was an unholy mess. "Seems you guys could use a little more room," he ventured.

Digging up a spatula, Addison flipped the bread to allow the egg mixture on the other side to cook. "I'm thinking about moving back to Little Mer soon."

Mason searched through his memory, connecting the reference with the bits he knew about Addison's life. "That's the island your family owns, right? Directly off the coast of Port Rock?"

Cleaning up behind herself as she prepared the food, Addison didn't seem to be giving him much attention. "Yeah. Ken's building us—that's me and Gwen—each a house there."

He watched her cook, quickly and efficiently. "That's awfully generous of him."

She shrugged. "I don't think Gwen will move. She doesn't want to live on the island, and Blake . . . Hell, he's terrified of the water. I'm pretty much thinking they'll say no and stay on the mainland. The hotel business is really good for her, and they're looking at a second location now."

"What about you?"

Arranging slices of cheese on the bread, Addison barely glanced up. "I haven't decided yet. I think I'd like to move back, but not on my own." She layered the slices on top of one another, creating a French toast cheese sandwich. "Not that there's any hurry. Maybe when I get married . . ." She deliberately avoided making direct eye contact.

Mason glanced at her neutral expression. She wasn't playing coy. She was just stating a fact.

He wrapped his hand tighter around the coffee mug. They'd known each other only a few days; yet it already seemed like a lifetime. He couldn't regret their encounter because it had felt so right. Their bodies had fitted together perfectly.

A sudden and unwelcome jab hit his psyche. She wasn't going to be on this ship forever. The idea of losing her bothered him more than he cared to admit.

He shook his head. He didn't like where these thoughts were heading. It would be better to let them go. Neither one of them was in any position to rush into something stupid.

We both have our duty.

Her cheery voice interrupted his thoughts. "Plates, please."

It took Mason more than a minute to locate the requested items. Although the US Navy had once been known for its china and silver cutlery, the twenty-first

century had streamlined the service down to paper
plates and plastic forks.

Addison smiled as she loaded the food onto the
plates. "At least they're the sturdy ones that don't col-
lapse all over you."

Coffee cup in hand, Mason led the way back into the
dining room. "Budget cuts."

She sat. "Ah." She spread a napkin over her lap. "Dig
in."

Mason looked at his food. Coated in egg, the bread
was lightly browned and toasted just enough the give it
a crunch. The cheese she'd layered between the slices
oozed out over the sides. "Looks pretty good." He cut
off a corner, forking the bite into his mouth. He chewed,
then swallowed. "Tastes pretty damn good, too."

Pride flashing in her eyes, Addison grinned and took
her own bite. "It's just my version of an egg and cheese
sandwich."

Hungrier than he'd first thought, Mason dug into his
food. "It's really edible."

Forking up a bite, she offered a smile. "Thanks. I was
about to starve to death."

Mason sneaked a glance at her. He couldn't look at
Addison without feeling that particular funny twist in
his heart. "So, how does it feel?" The question popped
out before he even had a chance to think twice about it.

She lowered her fork. "How does what feel?"

"Being here. Aboard ship."

Addison chewed thoughtfully, swallowing her last
bite. "Honestly? I'm scared. I know you humans are
wondering what the Mer are all about, but believe me
when I say I am, too. I don't know what Magaera's got at

her beck and call. Now that's she's got Tessa, she controls the sea-gate. We may not be ready for what's coming." The edge in her voice was unmistakable.

Mason pushed his empty plate aside. The food had definitely hit the spot. He'd practically shoveled down every bite. The gnawing in his stomach had settled, too, taking the nervous tension with it. "The last time we encountered her, she wasn't in the mood to be diplomatic."

She let out a disgusted breath. "I have a feeling engaging the Mer isn't going to be easy or pleasant. But sometimes what we want and what we get are two different things."

Tension coiled its way up Mason's spine. He wasn't sure where the notion came from, but somehow he had a feeling the same fate that had brought them together wouldn't hesitate to pull them apart. "What are you saying?"

Addison met his gaze. Worry creased her brows. "Call it intuition, but I have a feeling these next few days are definitely going to put a strain on the relations between humans and Mer." A sad little smile of resignation crossed her lips. "You may regret sleeping with the enemy, Captain."

Chapter 13

One week later

Kenneth Randall wasn't a happy man. By the look on his face, he was definitely pissed and struggling to hold his anger in check. "Why didn't you tell me they took Tessa?"

Gwen's knees trembled as she stepped closer to his hospital bed. She'd been dreading the moment when Kenneth realized his wife was nowhere to be found. Through the last couple of days, he'd been willing to accept that Tessa was resting to keep her strength up for the babies she carried. But the deception had fallen apart after Kenneth had demanded to see his wife. If she couldn't come to him, he'd said, then he would go to her.

Tired of putting on a smile and lying through her teeth, Gwen gave it to him straight. "We didn't tell you so that you'd be able to concentrate on getting well." Subconsciously, she reached for the crystal hanging around her neck. She'd put a lot of energy into healing his burns and stabilizing his system. His recovery was nothing short of a miracle.

Shifting uncomfortably in his bed, Kenneth scowled. "If I had known Tessa wasn't here, I'd have worked twice as hard to get well," he flung out ungratefully.

Sitting a few feet away, Blake listened intently. He didn't look happy, either. "Your heart stopped twice from the shock Magaera delivered, and the doctors were afraid the damage was permanent. There was no reason to tell you about Tessa until you were stronger."

Kenneth frowned. "I feel fine." He looked around the private room. "Another hour in this place is going to drive me insane. Where's the doctor, anyway? I'm ready to be discharged."

Gwen and Blake exchanged a look. With her help, Kenneth had recovered from his injuries much faster than expected. The fact that he had the constitution of a bull had probably helped. As it was, there was no further reason for him to remain hospitalized.

Running his hands through his hair, Blake stood up. "Maybe you should think about taking it easy another day or so," he ventured. "Just to make sure."

Kenneth adamantly shook his head. "I'm not staying in this bed one more minute, knowing my wife's life is in danger."

"It's not as though nothing's being done to recover Tessa," Gwen pointed out. "The navy has put together a special team to go after Magaera. Addison is acting as an adviser on all things Mer."

"Let the professionals handle it, Ken," Blake added. "They're doing everything they can to control the Mer now that they've come out of the water."

"You can't even turn on the news without another story about the Mer," Kenneth grumbled, looking sideways at the TV. "People have gone crazy about mermaids."

Gwen shrugged helplessly. Since the Mer had been exposed to the public following Queen Magaera's vicious attack, she felt as though every nerve in her body had been stripped bare and exposed. Every bit of new information that leaked out to the public had her nerves jumping. Her entire world had been rocked off its foundation when the government had decided it was time to pull the veil of secrecy away.

It all made her want to crawl under a rock and hide— forever.

She sighed. "At least they don't know our identities." She sank into a nearby chair. "We've still got a bit of anonymity."

Kenneth snorted. Reaching for the remote, he flipped the television off. "How long do you think that's going to last, Gwen? The people in Port Rock who know about the Mer are starting to fall to the lure of cash these exposé shows are offering. They're singing like canaries." He pointed toward the agents guarding his hospital room. "And no one with eyes can miss the boys in black. Those guys stick out like sore thumbs. They're as useless as tits on a hog."

"Thanks for that thought," Blake muttered under his breath.

Kenneth tossed aside his bedcovers. Determination burned hot and bright behind his gaze. His unshaven jaw deepened his hostile countenance. The lines around his mouth were much deeper than they'd been before the attack. "Well, if they think I'm going to sit here and do nothing while my wife is in danger, they're wrong."

Gwen looked at her brother-in-law in alarm. "What do you think you're doing?"

Grabbing the back of his hospital gown so that his bare ass wouldn't show, Kenneth headed toward the closet. "I'm going to get dressed, get out of here, and get going to the Mediterranean. The *DreamFever* is just sitting, gathering dust. Might as well put it back in the water. It's not fair to let all this fall back on Addison. She isn't the only one in this family who has something to offer."

Gwen gave him a sharp look. Her nerves coiled a notch tighter. What was Kenneth up to? "I thought the ship was for sale." A dozen scenarios rushed through her mind, each worse than the last.

Kenneth shrugged. "It's a tight economy and people aren't buying. Even though Jake screwed me up one side and down the other on it, I'm glad to have it."

"And what do you think you'll do once you get there?" Blake demanded. "The navy is running interference between Magaera's island and the shipping lanes, keeping traffic out of the area. There's no way they'd let you through."

"They may cut me off at the pass, but at least I'll be there. Tessa needs me, and that's all that matters." Kenneth opened the closet, staring into its empty depths. "Didn't you guys bring me any clothes?"

"I packed a bag for you, but it's still out in the car." Although Gwen silently applauded his devotion to her sister, she wasn't quite sure she could sanction his crazy idea of taking off after Tessa. The idea of tangling with the Mer queen again sent a shiver up her spine.

"So get it in here," Kenneth demanded. "I'd like to get dressed in some real clothes instead of having my rear end hanging out for all to see."

Blake stepped in. "Not so fast, Kenneth. I know you're angry, but I won't have you ordering my fiancée around like a maid."

Nostrils flaring in annoyance, Kenneth cursed mildly and slammed the closet door. "You might feel different if Gwen was the one who'd been taken." Suddenly furious, he turned and paced to the opposite side of the room. "It's driving me crazy, doing nothing."

Blake cut him a hard look. "I understand where you're coming from, but you'd be even more of a crazy man to head out now."

Kenneth barely spared his future brother-in-law a glance. "It's none of your business what I do," he grumbled between clenched teeth. His strong hands flexed with anxiety. "I'll take care of everything myself."

"It's a difficult situation for all of us," Blake said. "You need to calm down and think things through."

Kenneth stared at them through narrow eyes. "I have. If it were just Tessa . . . She's good at taking care of herself. But she's carrying my children, Blake. She's alone, she's scared, and who knows what kind of pressure she's under. I swear to God, if she's hurt or loses our babies, there will be hell to pay."

Gwen pressed a hand against her stomach. His words felt like a sharp knife being shoved between her ribs. The pain she felt radiating off him was so sharp that she couldn't take a breath.

For the first time, the layers of Kenneth's fury thinned enough for her to see the raw pain lurking beneath, and she knew his concern and love for her sister were genuine. The realization touched her, and she felt her emotions shift.

She was suddenly overwhelmed with guilt. She'd managed to worm out of the first trip to the Mediterranean, mostly because she'd been afraid of what they might find out. In her heart, she'd hoped nothing would be found and they could continue living their lives in quiet obscurity.

By the goddess, she thought. *How I wish I had never heard of Ishaldi!*

But it hadn't happened that way, and now they had to deal with the consequences.

"If you're going, I'm going, too," she said firmly.

Kenneth relaxed. "Good."

Blake wasn't so happy. He stared at her, his expression incredulous and betrayed. "What are you saying?"

Since they'd gotten together, Blake had stood by Gwen one hundred percent, supporting her fully. He'd never complained that he was the one who'd walked away from his career to be with her. She appreciated it more than he could ever know. But she still needed him to stick by her side. "If Kenneth's going, I'm going. As sisters, we've always hung together, through thick and thin. If I can help in any way, I should."

Never taking his eyes off her, Blake nodded. "If that's the way you feel, I can't stop you."

"There's plenty of room, Blake," Kenneth said. "You coming?"

Gwen couldn't miss the vague sense of uneasiness rippling through Blake. His fear was palpable, transmitting itself straight to her. The chill in her own heart turned into a block of ice.

The one thing that scared the hell out of Blake Whittaker was the one thing she relished as a mermaid. Thanks to early abuses in his childhood, Blake was terrified of deep water. He couldn't even take a bath, always choosing a shower instead.

Blake's muscles bunched with tension. "I—I can't," he said after a moment's silence.

Kenneth didn't beat around the bush. "No swimming required."

Blake shook his head. "There's enough to take care of here. The hotel, repairs on Little Mer, the media . . . Someone should hold down the fort." He had a legitimate argument.

His refusal didn't surprise her. "You don't have to go. Nobody expects you to," Gwen said.

He cut her a sharp look. "Jesus, Gwen. You make me sound like a coward."

His words chilled her anew, but Gwen didn't let herself react. The tension of late had set everyone on edge. Although she'd been afraid of exposure all her life, she had begun to realize that she couldn't continue to live in fear. The Mer were out, and they were known. Too soon she would be identified as one. It was time to hold her head high and let the consequences fall where they might.

"Kenneth's right," she said. "Even if we can't do anything, we need to be there for Tessa."

"Believe me when I say I'm just as concerned for Tessa's safety as you two are," Blake replied stonily.

Kenneth waved a hand. "You're off the hook, Blake. I know you have a problem with the water."

Blake closed his eyes. "I'm going, damn it," he spat

through gritted teeth. "I may be sick and vomit all the way, but I'll go."

Pride and hope melded together into a single wonderful emotion deep inside Gwen's heart. "Thank you." She reached for his hand, savoring the warmth of his big fingers curling around hers.

Blake pulled her to him and kissed her hard on the mouth. It was a kiss born of desperation and the very real fear that he was just as afraid of losing her. "We're family, honey," he said after their lips had parted. "If we can't stick together, we'll fall apart."

Gwen didn't know how she found the strength to pull away, but she did. Meeting his gaze, she saw the sincerity behind his words. Despite his own fear, he meant everything he said.

Tears shimmered in her eyes, blurring her vision. Once again it occurred to her how lucky she and Tessa had been to find men who loved them unconditionally.

She closed her eyes, leaning her head against his shoulder. "Thank you," she murmured under her breath.

"I guess it's settled, then," Kenneth said from behind. "We're going."

Chapter 14

From a distance of ten miles, Queen Magaera's island looked oddly gray and unfocused. Cloaked in a shimmering mist, the strange landmass loomed atop the sparkling sea like a specter of doom. Its size and shape, too, were eerily indistinct, giving no clear indication of its resources and population.

Addison sighed as she pulled away from the telescope. She wasn't sure what she'd expected to see once the anchor dropped on the perimeter of the magnetic zone surrounding the strange landmass on all sides.

She bent toward the lens again, squinting hard. "Is this as close as we can get?"

Captain McKenzie nodded. "Once a ship starts drifting onto what we call the 'dead zone,' everything electrical begins to go haywire. Engines die, radio signals turn to static, nothing electrical works. It's a total shutdown of all systems. Right now the sea traffic between Crete and Egypt is being rerouted to keep any ships from straying into the area. Fortunately, it's just a ten-mile stretch in all directions, which isn't too difficult to contain."

"Thank goodness it isn't the one point five million square miles the Bermuda Triangle encompasses or we would have a real problem," Addison commented.

A brief silence followed. Then McKenzie asked, "Do the Mer have anything to do with these phenomena?"

"As far as I'm aware, no, the Mer haven't cornered the market on inexplicable sea phenomena," she said with a slight smirk.

But Mason's face was totally serious. "So there's no chance other sea-gates could exist, perhaps leading to yet more wormholes?"

She shrugged. "I suppose anything's possible. If there's one, there could be dozens, even hundreds more. Who's to say how many more intelligent species actually inhabit this planet?"

He frowned. "I don't think people are ready for many more surprises. From the bits and pieces I've caught on the news, political pundits are debating whether or not to grant the Mer recognition as a legitimate nation."

Addison blinked to clear her vision. She'd been peering through the telescope for hours on end, trying to make some sense of the island and how to best approach it. So far she was stonewalled by the sheer inaccessibility of the place. She suspected the fog wasn't a natural phenomenon but rather something Magaera purposely conjured to keep her movements veiled from the eyes of the outside world.

"I suppose that depends on how Magaera continues to respond to the presence of humans in these waters." She looked at him levelly. "The Mediterranean is pretty small when you've got thousands of mermaids teeming in its depths. She's going to want to move into wider waters, I'm sure."

His eyes widened. "Pretty much a diplomatic nightmare, no matter how you slice it."

"Thank the goddess we're not the diplomats." She laughed. "Think we could sort out the problems between humans and Mer?"

A small smile curled up one corner of Mason's fine mouth. "I'd like to think we could work through our differences," he said, perfectly aware their conversation wasn't a private one. But the look he gave her was one laced with longing and intimacy.

Addison felt heat warming her cheeks. Even though they hadn't found the time to be alone again, she hadn't been able to get him out of her mind. Thinking about him sent waves of desire rolling through her. Her attraction to Mason, as evidenced by the insistent heat boiling in her core, couldn't be denied.

"Me, too," she murmured half audibly. The huskiness that had suddenly overtaken her tone was unmistakable. Such was the power of attraction—raw, unadorned attraction. All she wanted to do was be with this man who made her heart beat wildly against her ribs.

Mason stepped back, breaking their locked gazes. "So, how are we going to do this?"

Addison mentally flipped through all the details he'd given her about the last aborted attempt to breach the perimeter and reach the island. "I guess the only answer to that is to hit the water and see how far we get before we encounter resistance from Magaera's soldiers."

He frowned. "This doesn't sound promising. The last

time we barely had a half hour in the water before they
closed in. They just came out of nowhere."

"I don't imagine you saw much of them since a Mer
can swim up to twenty-five miles per hour." Her own
personal speed had been clocked at just about twenty-
two, but that was for a mermaid who didn't spend all her
time in the water.

From what Tessa had told her, Ishaldi didn't have
many large bodies of water remaining, and their food
supply had dwindled from slim to almost none. This was
why the Mer had evolved from a species that depended
on the intake of food. The Mer now subsisted on crystal
energy, which had inadvertently helped hasten the death
of their world as the crystals began to burn out and dis-
integrate.

Any Mer emerging from the dying city would probably be impatient to hit the water. Sea crystals and other
rock-based minerals were plentiful enough in the wider
world, and those mermaids would most likely be eager
to take advantage of the bounty the sea had to offer.

"They definitely have the advantage over us," Mason
grumbled. "Being loaded down with clumsy equipment
that's malfunctioning will certainly slow a man down."

Addison cocked her head. "Tell me again what happened."

"Pretty simple, really. Once we'd penetrated the magnetic zone, maybe half a mile in, our rebreathers began
to malfunction. Not getting any air will bring you to the
surface pretty fast."

"Ah, that electronic problem." As a search and rescue
diver, Addison knew that rebreathers, more complex
than sport open-circuit scuba, required special training

and maintenance to be safely used. "I suppose it's the same with single-hose regulators?"

"Pretty much. All it leaves us to work with are snorkels." He allowed a bit of bitterness to creep into his smile. "Not very effective when you want to go deep and sneak up on the enemy."

Addison's jaw tightened. "I'm afraid the Mer have you whipped. There are no limitations to the depths we can achieve, and we certainly don't have a problem breathing underwater. All we have to do is put our tails on and go."

Mason snorted. "If only it were that easy for us. Guess we humans do look kind of inferior when compared to mermaids. You can survive on both land and water."

She nodded, but her mind was tumbling in a thousand different directions. "What can I say? We're just that damn wonderful." The biggest problem they seemed to face was putting the divers in the water, while not crippling the men with useless equipment.

"Looks as though we're stuck with the snorkels," he commented sourly.

Addison shook her head. "Actually, I think I know a way to get around the little problem of depth and equipment failure."

"How?"

She grinned. "Remember when I told you a Mer can share her breath underwater? I don't see why it couldn't be done with a conscious volunteer."

"Are you proposing to kiss all thirty divers aboard this ship?" By the tone of his voice, he didn't care for that idea one little bit.

Her hands settled on her hips. "I don't see why not.

It's just a matter of what you'll be carrying while you're under. The Mer have their Ri'kahs, which probably function nicely since they're crystal powered."

"We have a new prototype of underwater defense gun, or UDG," he said.

"Which is?"

"Instead of firing bullets, the UDG fires a stiletto-type dart that's pretty accurate and lethal underwater. The effective range is about a hundred feet. A single clip can carry seventy rounds. It's still in the development stages, but so far tests have shown it to be our most promising weapon against the Mer in the water, barring mines or torpedoes."

The impact behind his words had an unsettling effect on Addison. For the first time she began to realize just how serious humans were about retaining and defending their dominance as the number one species on Earth.

No wonder the Mer were vicious toward humans. The notion came unbidden. Yet Queen Nyala had chosen humans over the Mer. Would she have made the same choice had she known sealing the wormhole would bring her kind to extinction?

Right now, there were too many questions and complications for her to consider. The only thing Addison was sure of was that there had to be a way to broker peace between the two. Surely this world was big enough for everyone.

The weight of his hand on her shoulder jarred her out of her thoughts.

"Did I say something wrong?" Mason asked. He was looking at her steadily, as if trying to read her thoughts.

Addison took several quick steps back to put a little

distance between them. In a flash he'd reawakened all her cravings. She felt starved for him, and just thinking about the night before caused a knot to form in the pit of her stomach.

"No. Not at all. I was just thinking there had to be a way to resolve our differences peacefully."

"That seems to have been a problem since the beginning of time," he countered ruefully. "Peace on Earth and good will toward all men would be wonderful."

"And Mer."

He shrugged. "If only you and I ruled the world," he murmured beneath his breath.

She didn't have a chance to answer. Another voice broke in. "You'd never get anything done because you're too busy making goo-goo eyes at each other," Commander Hawkins said.

Addison and Mason whirled at the same time. The commander looked at them both, his grin growing progressively wider by the second.

Although they had been nothing but professional around each other since her first night aboard, Addison had the unnerving feeling that everyone on the ship knew about her brief interlude with Mason. It was suddenly as if she had PROPERTY OF CAPTAIN MCKENZIE stamped across her forehead.

Mason's gaze narrowed. "Can it, Hawkins. There's a time for kidding around, and now isn't it."

The captain's second-in-command shrugged. "I wasn't being flippant, Cap," he shot back with an absolutely straight face. "Just stating the facts as I see them."

Mason immediately stepped away from her, locking

his hands behind his back. "Well, then keep your statements to yourself, Commander."

Hawkins immediately put away his smirk. He glanced across the water. "Any idea how to proceed?"

"We're exploring a couple of ideas," Mason answered. "It seems there may be a way for our men to hit the water without having to worry about their equipment malfunctioning."

"That's been our biggest obstacle so far," Hawkins said. "The Mer have us outclassed, hands down."

"Addison reminded me of the mouth-to-mouth breathing trick she informed us of yesterday."

"Really?" Hawkins cut a look toward Addison. "I take it that means you'll need a volunteer to practice on," Hawkins said without batting an eye. "In that case, allow me to be the first in line."

"If anyone's going into the water first, it'll be me," Mason said gruffly. "I won't send my divers back into the water until I know they have a fighting chance against the Mer."

Hawkins immediately protested. "With all due respect, sir, it seems to me that the captain's place is aboard, making the tactical decisions. We do have several capable divers. If someone's going to take a risk, it should be someone who isn't in the direct line of command."

Mason shook his head. "You're capable enough, Hawkins. I need someone who's got my back when I go into the water. We'll do an exploratory dive outside the perimeters of the dead zone. Right now the Mer don't seem inclined to venture beyond that point. It should be safe enough."

Hawkins looked doubtful but made no protest. "If that's what you think we should do, then I'm behind you all the way."

A satisfied glint settled in the depths of Mason's eyes. "Are you ready to suit up?" he asked Addison.

Addison nodded. In a way, she was glad Mason had volunteered himself as the first guinea pig. She wasn't quite sure she could pull off locking lips with another guy who would be fully awake and aware.

"Let's do this."

Only when he was suited up and ready to dive did Mason feel truly alive. As a boy he'd always been drawn to the sea and its magnificence, as well as intrigued by the mysteries lurking deep beneath its surface.

In a lot of ways he considered the sea to be female—capricious, beautiful, and deadly. On the calmest of days, she could be welcoming and warm. At other times she could be a storm-tossed tempest, thrashing with anger as she threw angry waves around. It didn't come as any surprise that mermaids were a female-centric race. The feminine mystique seemed best represented by the sea.

Although she really didn't need to go through the pretense, Addison, too, donned a wet suit. The form-fitting neoprene clung to every curve, exposing her terrific figure.

Every crew member who wasn't tied up with other duties had gathered on the diver's deck to observe. Although most of the action would be taking place underwater, no one wanted to miss a thing.

Mason had already taken a few catcalls from the other divers about the hardship of volunteering to be kissed underwater by a pretty woman. Beneath the easy joshing, though, a sense of unease simmered. These men had already encountered the Mer in action. Being loaded down with bulky, malfunctioning equipment was like having rocks tied to their legs and then being tossed into the water. Even armed with UDGs, they didn't have a chance.

"You ready?" he asked as she approached.

Addison flashed a nervous smile and gave the thumbs-up sign. "As ready as I'll ever be, Captain." Unlike him, she wore no swim fins or other equipment. "See you down below." She dived over the edge. The water barely rippled as she disappeared beneath the surface.

Drawing his mask into place, Mason followed her in. Water closed in from all sides as he began his descent.

Although he preferred the full face mask, which allowed for better vision and communication, he'd had to settle on a half mask and mouthpiece that could be removed.

They'd agreed beforehand to meet at a level of about one hundred fifty feet beneath the water. The day was clear and calm, lending its brilliance to the shimmering sea. Although it took a minute or two for his vision to focus, he soon caught sight of Addison.

All he could do was stare, entranced.

With a movement as graceful as any ballet dancer, she stretched out and rolled through the water. A series of flashy sparks briefly engulfed her body, chewing away the wet suit covering her skin. As quick as a blink her legs disappeared, replaced with a long tapering fishlike tail. As though lit from within, her scales glowed with a strange iridescence. The scale pattern covering her upper torso swirled over and around her breasts, offering the illusion that she wasn't fully exposed.

Catching sight of Mason, Addison twitched her tail, zipping through the water. A second later she floated a few feet away, like a hummingbird hovering in front of a flower. Her lips offered a welcoming smile. She gave him the diver's signal for "okay."

Mason signaled back, and Addison made a few gestures indicating that he should remove his breathing apparatus.

Mason was suddenly filled with anxiety. Once that precious source of oxygen was removed, he'd have absolutely no way to breathe. Images of being grabbed and dragged to the bottom of the sea flashed across his mind's eye. Drowning wasn't a pleasant or easy way to die, especially if the victim was conscious.

A curse echoed through his mind. *I've got to trust her.*

Mason removed his mouthpiece. *Oh God, let this work,* he silently pleaded. Addison swam in closer. Her hands automatically circled his shoulders, drawing him into a tight embrace. For a moment their gazes met. Mason felt the impact like an out-of-control semitruck plowing into a row of parked cars. Goose bumps rose along the back of his neck when she licked her lips. Feeling lust stir within, he tried not to think about the night they'd made love or of the deep kisses they'd shared.

But he did, and his body responded with a vengeance that surprised him. It unnerved him a little to realize what this woman could do to him with the merest touch.

Having lost his concentration, he accidentally swallowed a mouthful of water and began to choke. Air seeped from his lungs in a single quick rush. Without thinking, he started to thrash.

Addison immediately reacted. Cupping his face between the palms of her hands, she pressed her mouth to his. Her tongue sought deeper penetration.

Forcing himself to relax, Mason was vaguely aware of his hands circling her slender hips. The scales beneath his palms felt as smooth and soft as silk. For an instant all he could think about was what it had felt like to run his fingers across her bare skin.

The frisson of heat between them sizzled as their kiss deepened. The air shared between them shifted and thickened. A pleasant buoyant sensation overtook every muscle in his body. His panic faded as much-needed oxygen filtered into his chest.

Addison slowly pulled away. The small, crystal soulstone hanging around her neck glowed softly.

Mason took an experimental breath. Though he'd half expected to suck in another mouthful of water, he was shocked to realize he could breathe.

Damn! It felt wonderful. He flashed the okay signal.

Addison smiled and nodded. She reached for the crystal around her neck. Closing her eyes, she extended her hand until her palm was pressed flat against his chest. A thrumming sensation buzzed over his skin akin to a light electric shock.

She opened her eyes. *"Can you hear me?"*

Though her mouth didn't move, Mason could clearly hear her question echo through his mind. It was strange to have another's voice in his head.

"Yes," he said, and almost choked on a mouthful of air.

Addison laughed. *"Don't answer with your mouth,"* she warned. *"I've opened a light psi-channel between our minds so we can communicate with each other. I can sense your responses."*

Mason nodded to show he understood. *"I've got it, I think."*

She gave him a quick thumbs-up. *"It's strange at first, but you'll get used to replying with your mind instead of your mouth."*

"I'd wondered how Mer might communicate beneath the water."

She gave a saucy flick of her tail. *"Now you know."*

Suddenly feeling weighed down, Mason slipped off his oxygen tank. Several pounds of cumbersome weight immediately dropped away. He struck out, skimming through the water with strong, easy strokes. Startled by his presence, an array of fish scattered every which way.

"My God, this is wonderful." He did a quick flip, and then another. *"It's like walking on air. This must be how astronauts feel in space."*

Addison joined him. *"There are a few advantages to being water-born."* Her laugh chimed through his mind.

"You don't have to convince me. I'm sold." He looked at her with pure admiration. The sight of her in her mermaid form touched him as nothing else in the world could. His pulse spiked. He wanted her so much, it hurt just to look at her.

She didn't seem to be listening.

Addison turned her head. *"Do you feel that?"*

Mason stilled his body, letting himself drift with the current. He hadn't noticed it at first, but the water buzzed with some sort of strange pulse. Just behind his hearing he thought he sensed some sort of low hum. The sound didn't seem to be generated by a mechanical engine, and he couldn't identify its source. Vaguely, he was aware of the high-pitched whine growing stronger. The water around them took on an eerie glow.

An instant later the sea exploded, sending him flying through the water. He somersaulted head over heels, aware of searing heat tearing through his wet suit and burning its way across his back.

Fighting to regain control, Mason propelled himself around to face his attacker. It took a moment for his vision to adjust to the murky depths.

Slicing through the water at top speed, one of Queen Magaera's Mer soldiers prepared to take aim again. He caught a flash of something that looked like a chain of colored lights encircling her right forearm. This, he knew, was the bejeweled weapon the Mer called the Ri'kah. Composed entirely of various crystals set into gold, it looked benign to human eyes. In the hand of a mermaid, the thing acted like a laser and could burn straight through flesh with no problem.

For ten, maybe twenty seconds, he couldn't move. His entire body felt paralyzed. None of his training had prepared him for this.

Chapter 15

Damn it! This was the first time Magaera's soldiers had ventured outside the perimeters of the dead zone surrounding the island. Once again, they'd been caught with their pants down. At least he wasn't totally unarmed. The UDG was loaded and ready for firing.

Mason thrashed around in a panic, trying to reorient himself in an upright position even as his hand automatically reached for the weapon holstered at his waist. His heart went into double time, pumping at an alarming rate. Amazingly, he could still breathe. Addison had told him the spell wouldn't wear off unless he surfaced and took in air. That was the last thing he intended to do.

Another sizzling blast tore past his face mask. Without knowing where he was aiming, Mason lifted the heavy gun and pulled the trigger. A flash of steel bolts tore through the water. His aim was true, striking the Mer in the chest. A mix of bubbles and blood emanated from her open mouth. Her body quickly disappeared into the swirling depths.

A flash of movement caught the corner of one eye.

Mason whirled around. He saw Addison thrashing between three Mer soldiers. The women had her covered no matter which way she turned. She was putting up one hell of a fight, making sure the women couldn't get a solid grip on her. Their scale patterns were entirely different from Addison's iridescent one, making it easy to identify her.

Fury boiled inside him, but he wrestled it aside. He had to stay focused. Losing his concentration would be more than detrimental to the task. It would most likely cost him his life.

And Mason didn't intend to die today.

"Addison, are you okay?" he screamed into her mind. Adrenaline seared through his veins. He'd been drilled in underwater combat, but he'd never imagined using it against a cadre of nasty mermaids. It almost seemed too ridiculous to comprehend.

"I've got my hands full," she responded. Shoving an elbow in the gut of one of her assailants, she launched herself toward yet another.

But this was a fight Addison couldn't win.

Mason caught a flash of silver, long and sharp. One of the Mer soldiers was armed with a blade, which was another very effective underwater weapon. Even though Mer technology might seem primitive, the creatures knew how to defend themselves. No wonder they'd once ruled the seven seas. No man stood a chance against an angry Mer in the water.

Mason raised the UDG a second time, aiming his weapon toward the nearest target. Another laser blast split the water in front of his mask, almost blinding him with its brilliance. These Mer clearly weren't going down without a fight.

Without really thinking, he let instinct guide him. His forefinger mashed down on the trigger. A series of bolts flew out, silent and deadly. Less than a second later an eerie red blossom spread around the Mer's abdomen. She thrashed and jerked violently. But she wasn't giving up.

Mason propelled himself closer. As much as he hated the brutality of war, he'd have to deliver the kill shot. Even if they were women, these bitches were bad to the bone.

The Mer's weapon was still in her hand. Catching sight of her aggressor, she slashed the blade toward him in a vicious arc. Although she had no chance of making contact, her move clearly proved her to be a dangerous foe.

Mason lifted the UDG. This time he took care with his aim. He didn't want to miss or accidentally strike Addison. The single bolt he unleashed found its mark immediately, smacking the soldier right between the eyes. Her scream of rage came out as a flurry of furious bubbles.

Gotcha, he thought as the Mer's now-motionless form was dragged into the depths.

Refocusing his attention, Mason looked around quickly to get his bearings. The water was churning all around him now, making it difficult to see. He squinted through the murk, trying to locate Addison. Horror swept through him when he realized she'd been snared. Magaera's soldiers had somehow surrounded her, then subdued her with some sort of netting that looked like long strands of silver webbing.

"Addison!" Her name roared through his mind with such force that his temples pounded from the intense pressure. Terror rippled through him, overriding the pain of the searing flash burn across his back.

"Surface!" she said silently to him. *"Get out of the water!"*

Mason shook his head. There was no way he'd abandon her. By God, there was no way he'd let her be taken captive. Not Addison. She was too much a part of the team to lose. They needed her—desperately.

He refused to let himself acknowledge the other thoughts lurking beneath his subconscious mind. *He* needed her.

Mason swam furiously toward her attackers. Suddenly hands appeared out of nowhere, gripping his ankles and jerking him backward.

Flailing in surprise, he kicked out hard, desperate to dislodge the Mer who'd caught hold of his legs. His movements to defend himself felt clumsy and sluggish beneath the water. *Let go, bitch!* he snarled even though she couldn't hear or understand him. He caught a flash of her twisted grin. She was holding on tight and wasn't even close to letting go.

He swung his weapon around, aiming for her face. But his finger never mashed the trigger. More hands darted out of nowhere, curling around his wrist and pulling his arm in a violent backward motion. Seconds later he felt a sharp rush of heat as his shoulder and arm separated. Shock almost caused him to lose his breath. His hand involuntarily opened. The UDG slipped from his grip and disappeared.

Cursing and groaning as white-hot pain radiated up

his arm, Mason struggled to wriggle away from his assailants. But his efforts were for naught. Magaera's remaining soldiers quickly overpowered him, wrapping him up like a fly in their silvery netting. He'd been bagged.

Damn it, he didn't want to go down like this.

Mason thrashed around, determined to give the Mer all the hell he could muster. His efforts were for naught.

The mermaids swimming around him simply smiled. They'd won and they knew it. He was little more than deadweight to be towed.

Mason twisted around in the netting until he was able to catch sight of Addison. She was wrapped up tight from her neck to the tip of her tail. A mixture of fear and anger contorted her expression.

"They want us alive," he said, hoping their telepathic link was still intact.

"That might not be a good thing," she responded.

In Mason's opinion, being a prisoner of war was a step up from being dead. As long as they were alive, they had a chance to fight their way out of captivity. If Magaera thought she'd be able to pump him for information, she was wrong. He wouldn't say a word, no matter the torture levered against him.

Suddenly, Mason caught sight of a dozen long bodies, straight as missiles, skimming through the water at top speed. At least six feet long, maybe longer, they undulated gracefully as they propelled themselves toward their targets.

He jolted, swallowing a scream along with a mouthful of salty seawater. *Sharks?!* Spluttering and choking, he fought to regain his breath. *Oh, shit.* There was blood in the water, and the beasts were probably on the prowl.

Immediately breaking into two groups, the creatures sped toward the Mer. One big white body collided with the nearest soldier holding Mason. The impact of the blow forced her to release her hold on the webbing. They rolled together, a mass of flailing fins and tails.

As the second mermaid holding his netting attempted to drag him out of the melee, a second creature barreled toward them. As it came closer, Mason caught a glimpse of its head before it smacked into his captor. These weren't sharks, as he'd first believed, but dolphins. The dark stripes covering their leathery blue-gray skin had thrown him off. He couldn't pin down a species that bore such a distinctive pattern.

The dolphins came from all sides, ferociously attacking the Mer soldiers by using their massive size and girth to separate them from their captives. Their bodies whipped furiously, turning the water around the Mer soldiers into an unfathomable vortex.

Mason tore at his bonds. He was drifting helplessly, swept away from the action by the current.

One of the dolphins broke away from the group. Swimming toward him, it stopped when they were almost nose to nose.

Relief flooded through him even as he squirmed against his bonds. As if understanding his plight, the dolphin swam around him, working its long snout into the silvery strands and tugging them away. A few minutes later, the netting was loose enough for him to work his way to freedom. During the fracas he'd lost both his swim fins, but that didn't matter. He hadn't even noticed. He was free.

By now the water around them had calmed enough

for him to see clearly again. Swimming forward, he caught sight of Addison. She was still snared. A couple more dolphins swam around her, tugging at the webbing with their teeth. The remaining Mer had vanished.

Relief flooded him. Addison was safe, and that was all that mattered.

Addison struggled to remain calm as the dolphins tugged at the net binding her arms and tail. Magaera's Mer had trussed her up tighter than a Sunday chicken, giving her little room to wriggle. *Those bitches came out of nowhere,* she thought angrily. She believed she could handle herself, and she'd been proven wrong. She wasn't as good a fighter as she wanted to believe. The fact was she had very little experience fighting against others of her kind. She'd gotten her ass whipped, and more.

She eyed the dolphins. Four were swimming the perimeter around her while two more worked to free her from the clinging strands of webbing. One didn't often encounter dolphins in the waters of Penobscot Bay. She'd heard stories of dolphins aiding humans in distress, but these creatures had certainly gone above and beyond the call of duty. Like a brigade on the march, they'd charged in from nowhere, ready to fight. They'd easily outnumbered and overtaken the Mer, driving them back.

She'd just managed to free an arm when Mason swam up. A couple of dolphins followed in his wake, guarding his flank.

"You okay?" His words came through their psychic connection.

She nodded. *"I think so."*

"Let me get you out of this." He tugged at the thick

netting, helping her work it down her hips. A moment later the tangled mass fell away.

Addison flicked her tail in relief. She hadn't liked the feeling of the rough material rubbing against her sensitive scales. *"Thank the goddess,"* she said.

Mason smiled and gave her the thumbs-up signal. Everything was going to be okay. *"I think we're in the clear."*

She smiled back. *"Thanks to our new friends here."* The dolphins were much larger than any she'd ever seen, stretching to what had to be at least six feet in length, maybe more. Up close she could see their skin had a strange bluish, white-green tinge that really made it stand out.

"You think they understand us?" Mason held out a tentative hand toward the closest dolphin.

The dolphin swam closer, nudging his palm with its snout the way a dog would its master's hand when it wanted attention.

Mason tentatively petted the creature's massive head. Delighted by his touch, the dolphin rolled in response, briefly going belly up. *"They seemed to understand we needed help."*

Addison eyed the creature. *"As much as I'd love to stay and make friends, we should get back to the surface."*

He reluctantly nodded. *"We should let the others know what happened. There's no telling what they must have seen from above."*

She tipped her head back, looking toward the surface. They were perhaps a hundred feet under now, maybe more. *"Probably a lot of thrashing water."*

Mason gave the dolphin a final pat on the head. *"Thanks for the help, buddy."*

As though it understood him, the dolphin doffed its head.

Addison put a little twitch in her tail. Stretching out her arms, she propelled herself toward the surface.

Mason followed at a slower rate. To prevent the excess formation of bubbles that led to decompression sickness, divers had to limit their ascent rate to about thirty-three feet per minute.

"You're fine to surface," she called out through their psi-link. *"No bends from a Mer's breath."*

They shot toward the surface together, breaking through within seconds of each other. Right before she hit the surface, Addison shifted back into her human form. A series of sparks covered her skin, returning the wet suit she'd initially dived in.

Mason immediately rolled over onto his back, arms and legs splayed out. His chest rose and fell as he took in great gulps of air.

Sensing the disintegration of their psi-link, Addison paddled over to him. "You okay?"

He didn't open his eyes but instead just concentrated on breathing. "I think so."

She glanced around, catching sight of the *Sea Horse* in the distance. They were a quarter of a mile away from the ship, maybe more. They hadn't intended to go so far, but the circumstances had been beyond their control.

She reached for one of the waterproof flares tucked into Mason's utility belt. Even though she could have easily towed Mason to the ship, there was no reason to exhaust herself any further. A passing glance told her the holster for his UDG was empty.

Addison winced as she activated the flare. She was fully

aware he'd used his weapon and had killed a couple of the Mer soldiers. Even though they were her kind, they were still the bad guys. Although she could mourn their loss, she couldn't condemn human actions toward them. Mason had fought to save not only his life, but hers. The idea of a long and bloody war was discouraging, to say the least.

She hoped Mer and humans could find common ground for peace—soon.

Rather than risk taking the *Sea Horse* into the dead zone, which would possibly cripple the ship, Commander Hawkins sent out a manpowered raft to retrieve them. Two burly divers manned the small craft, expertly navigating across the water. The wind was beginning to kick up, creating a flurry of difficult waves. By the look of the sky overhead, the weather wasn't going to remain clear much longer. Leaden gray storm clouds brewed on the horizon, their bellies fat with thunder and lightning. The rumble of thunder warned of trouble ahead.

One of the dolphins unexpectedly surfaced, its sleek body briefly arcing above the water before disappearing beneath the surface. It surfaced a second time, nudging Mason in the side with its snout.

"What the hell?" Startled, Mason immediately rolled over, kicking water with his feet to keep his feet above water.

The dolphin gave him another little push.

Addison grinned, then gestured toward the oncoming raft. "I think he's trying to help you out." She looked around. More dolphins were surfacing, swimming around them in a protective circle.

Mason caught sight of the unusual formation. "You think they're trying to tell us something?"

A second dolphin broke away from the group, swimming up to Addison's side. It gave her a curious poke. When she didn't respond, it followed through with a harder nudge. A moment later it disappeared, skimming around her legs. She gasped when it darted between her thighs. "I think it's looking for my tail!"

Mason chuckled. "You think it's looking for a girlfriend?"

She shot him a narrow look. "Very funny, wise guy."

Laughing, he quirked a brow. "These are some well-muscled fellows. I've never seen them this big."

"Hey, you guys," one of the divers called from the raft. "Where did you pick up the company?"

Addison recognized one of the petty officers, ranked a master diver. Given the freedom to choose his own crew, Mason had chosen only top-notch talent to serve aboard the *Sea Horse*. She vaguely recalled his surname was Donner.

"Right now we're glad to have them," Mason answered as the second crewman reached out to lift him into the raft. He collapsed in an exhausted heap.

The man held out his hand for Addison. "Climb on, ma'am."

Addison shook her head. "Get Captain McKenzie back to the ship. The Mer came after us, and he's been hurt."

Both seamen's faces took on a look of concern. "Then shouldn't you get out of the water, too?" Donner asked.

She paddled out of his reach. "I can make it to the ship easily enough. I'd like to spend a little more time in the water with the dolphins, if you don't mind."

Donner eyed the massive creatures hovering just beneath the water like silent sentinels. "Are you sure they're friendly?"

The sight of the dolphins circling their small group touched her more than she cared to admit. Even though she couldn't explain it, she felt some sort of a kinship with another creature of the sea. Her heart pinged against her ribs when one of the larger dolphins brushed against her a second time.

She reached out to touch its cool, leathery skin. It zipped out of her reach, then surfaced and playfully cocked its head. "I don't know." She made a wry face. "It's not as if I speak dolphin."

You want to talk, she thought with a shiver. She couldn't begin to imagine where that notion had come from. Somehow she had a feeling the dolphins were a lot smarter than anyone was willing to give them credit for. The fact that they'd risked their own lives to save a human and a mermaid spoke volumes. They'd recognized danger and responded quickly. Even though she was a Mer herself, they'd made no attempt to attack her. They'd even tried to help her out of the net.

Mason sat up. "You should come out of the water before they decide to regroup and come back with more. I don't know about you, but I counted a lot more than four Mer."

Addison cursed. "If there're more than four, then she's definitely gotten control of Tessa's soul-stone and reopened the sea-gate."

Mason sighed. "This really isn't looking good for us." Leaning over the edge of the raft, he held out his hand. "And I still think you need to get out of the water. No telling when they will come back and bring reinforcements."

Addison reluctantly accepted his hand, allowing him to haul her aboard. Although she wanted to spend more time with the dolphins, Mason was probably right. It would likely be best to make themselves scarce until they had time to rest and regroup. Based on today's dive, they had no chance of even getting close to Magaera's island.

Some nagging inner suspicion told her the dolphins knew something they didn't.

Chapter 16

Sitting on the exam table, Mason moaned as the doctor cut away at his wet suit. "Ouch, damn it! That hurts." Addison and Commander Hawkins stood nearby. Both of them wore expressions etched with worry. He couldn't be sure, but it seemed Addison's face was also lined with guilt.

"Sorry," Dr. Robinson said from behind. "But it looks as though whatever hit you seared your wet suit to your skin. You took a really bad burn. Going to have to be careful this one doesn't get infected."

The physician lifted away another patch of burned material. "Shit, it feels as if you're skinning me alive," he groused as another patch was discarded onto a stainless steel tray.

"In a way, I am," Dr. Robinson remarked drily. "Care to tell me how you got it?"

"He was hit by a weapon the Mer call a Ri'kah," Addison said. "To people it looks like a pretty piece of jewelry looped around the arm, but in the hands of an experienced soldier, it is absolutely deadly, above and below water."

Robinson shook her head. "I still don't understand how something like that works." She indicated Mason's seared flesh. "The damage extends almost all the way across his back. The burn is at least five inches wide and has taken off the epidermis layer."

"Basically, it works like a laser beam."

"How very interesting," Robinson commented. "From what little I've heard about it, the science behind the Mer is amazing."

Mason wasn't in the frame of mind to sit through a science lesson. His pride had taken a beating, and he'd had enough of licking his wounds. This was the second time the Mer had bested them in the water. So far they hadn't made one viable gain. He hated feeling like a loser. "Just patch me up, Doc," he growled. "I need to be able to get back into the water, ASAP."

"I wouldn't recommend that," Robinson warned. "It's going to take time to heal, and you'll have one hell of a scar."

Addison stepped up. "I think I can help him heal a little faster."

Mason's brows rose. "Oh?"

She nodded. "I think I can generate enough energy to help you out."

"I'd like to see this," Robinson murmured.

"Me, too," Hawkins chimed in.

"I'll need a healing stone." Addison looked around. "Does anyone have a diamond?"

Robinson held up her left hand. I have a couple of stones in my wedding ring," she volunteered, sliding the ring off her finger. She handed it over. "They aren't very big, though."

Addison smiled. She was struck by how open the doctor was to alternative forms of healing. Not everyone she encountered felt this way. "They'll do fine. And I won't hurt it, I promise. I just need the energy inside."

Mason felt the fine hairs on the back of his neck prickle. He wasn't sure he liked the idea of being a guinea pig for unknown experimentation. He held up a hand. "Now hold on," he said. "I'm sure it's not that bad. Just throw a bandage on it and I'm good to go."

A hurt looked crossed Addison's face. "I can help," she said softly. "I won't hurt you."

Dr. Robinson stepped in. "Really, Captain. If you leave it up to me, you'll be spending some time in sick bay, lying on your stomach so this can heal properly. The bandages will need to be changed several times a day to make sure infection doesn't set in."

Mason didn't like what he was hearing. If there was one thing he hated, it was sickness in any form. Even the idea of having a simple cold bent him out of shape. Illness and infirmity did not exist in his world. "I haven't got time to be in sick bay."

"Then I suggest you see what she can do," Robinson said.

Mason glanced to his second-in-command. "What say you, Hawkins?"

Hawkins gave a wide grin. "I say if she cooks you, I'm captain. So go for it."

Mason glanced at Addison. *I don't suppose I have anything to lose,* he thought. *She is supposed to be on our side.* Guilt pinged his heart. It was hard to balance the faith he had in Addison against the mistrust he harbored against the Mer and their powers in general.

"Let's do this," he said after a moment's silence. "I want to get back into action as soon as possible."

Addison took over from Dr. Robinson. "I think I'd work better if you'd stretch out on the table. I want to be able to focus the energy precisely."

Mason obeyed, going belly down on the exam table. Pain lit up every nerve in his body as he repositioned himself. He didn't relish suffering through days of agony and discomfort. He propped his chin on his hands. "This okay?"

"Yes." Addison stepped closer to the table. Clutching the doctor's ring in one hand, she let her other hand hover about an inch above his back. "Hang on. Gwen's been trying to teach me the healing techniques. I just have to make sure I focus the energy right, without too much intensity."

"What are you doing, exactly?" Robinson asked.

"I'm going to try and amplify the magnetic forces of my mind to penetrate the crystalline structure of the diamond," Addison explained. "Once I make a connection, I can refocus the energy and use it to heal the affected area." She shifted a little. "Close your eyes," she said softly, "and just breathe."

Mason did as she instructed, settling himself as comfortably as he could. Drawing a breath, he closed his eyes, attempting to sensitize himself to the feel of Addison's open palm hovering above his back.

Seconds ticked by in silence.

And then he felt the thrust of her psi-kinetic energy connecting with his skin—a cool breeze caressing his skin and a strange rhythm that pulsed gently against his exposed nerve endings. His flesh seemed to crawl in response. He tensed, forcing himself to remain still. The sensations weren't painful, just . . . different. It was as though the two of them were slipping into some kind of unspoken rapport, meshing together into a seamless whole.

"My God," Dr. Robinson said, "that's amazing."

"It's the stone," Addison murmured gently, and continued her healing work.

Closing his eyes, Mason let himself relax. Soft prisms of color pulsed behind his lids. The throb between Addison's palm and his back quickened, and he became aware of his own heartbeat and the feel of blood coursing through his veins.

Already he was beginning to feel adrift, as though floating on soft currents of cool air. The pain began to blur, fading from his memory as a pleasant vibrating sensation replaced it. He sensed rather than felt the regeneration of his skin, aware of nothing except how wonderful the cooling sensation felt across his back.

A random thought flickered through his mind. *This is heaven.*

Time unraveled, reeling away. Half an hour passed in blissful silence.

But the peaceful interlude was short-lived. With a brief, tingling shock, it was over.

Seconds later Mason heard a gasp, followed by a thud. He blinked and immediately sat up, breaking the eerie paralysis that held him. "What's happening?"

"Addison fainted!" Robinson exclaimed.

Without thinking twice, Mason propelled himself off the table without feeling a twinge of pain. He quickly knelt beside Addison's prone body. "What happened?" Worry gripped his heart with icy fingers.

Checking Addison's pulse and vitals, Robinson shook her head. "One moment she was fine; the next she just toppled over."

Mason gently lifted Addison off the floor, stroking her face with one hand. Her head dropped heavily against his shoulder. Eyelids fluttering, she sighed deeply, fighting to regain control of her senses. Dr. Robinson's diamond ring dropped from her lax fingers, rolling onto the floor.

Commander Hawkins scooped it up. "Holy hell!" he exclaimed, letting it drop again. "This thing is hotter than the face of the sun."

Fear gnawed deep in Mason's belly. Had Addison harmed herself trying to help him? "Addison," he whispered in a voice meant only for her ears. "Come on, babe. Wake up." He felt a sharp stab of guilt, as if he'd somehow inflicted the damage to her system.

"Get her into one of the beds," Robinson instructed.

Sliding one arm under her legs, Mason lifted her off the floor. Though she was a tall woman, her weight felt like nothing as he cradled her in his arms. He carried her toward the nearest bed in the cramped sick bay.

Laying her down with the gentlest of movements, he knelt beside her. As he felt a lump form in his throat, he experienced an immense and completely unfamiliar tenderness toward her.

"Addison—" He fought to keep his voice steady and impassive despite the worry clutching at his throat. "Can you hear me?" It drove him half mad to think she might be hurt.

Addison slowly lifted her head, trying to orient herself. "I—I think so," she answered weakly. She lifted a hand, pressing her finger to her temple. "I have a hell of a headache, though. Feels like someone kicked my head in." Her voice gained strength, losing its tremble as she spoke.

Relief washed through him, a reprieve so great, it felt almost like physical pain. "What happened?"

She let her hand drop and then lay back on the pillow. "Pushed too hard, too fast." Pale but controlled, she seemed to be recovering.

"Are you going to be all right?" Dr. Robinson asked. "Is there anything we can do?"

Fumbling with clumsy fingers for the crystal around her neck, Addison flashed a wan smile. Her features were white and drawn. Deep inside the small stone, ribbons of color moved through it, slowly, like a beating heart. "Now I understand what Gwen meant when she said healing sessions left her drained to the core."

Mason caught her hand between his, wishing desperately he could return the energy he'd taken from her. She'd given her all to help ease his pain. *And I can't even help her,* he thought bitterly. *She is beyond me in so many ways.*

He felt a sickening sensation, as if he stood on quicksand. Not for the first time he began to wonder if the two species—human and Mer—could find common ground.

Addison had learned the hard way that using her Mercraft was taxing and demanding on her body. She needed a quiet place to rest.

"I'm sorry," Mason said softly. "I didn't mean to hurt you."

She gave his hand a little squeeze. "I'm actually feeling better now."

Relief softened his strained features. The press of his anxious concern lessened. "I'm glad." He leaned in closer, as if to touch her cheek lightly with his lips.

Addison turned her head. *Yes,* came the forbidden thought. This was what she wanted—needed. She needed physical contact. She needed to cling to him and to draw strength from him.

But it never happened.

At the last moment Mason held himself back, as if suddenly remembering they were not entirely alone. He immediately straightened. "Is there anything you need?"

Feeling strangely embarrassed, Addison shook her head. On one level she felt an intimacy with Mason that went down to the very bone; yet she was perfectly aware that this was a man who barely knew her—and whom she barely knew—except for the brief moment of passion they'd shared.

The profound emotions she felt toward him were confusing and disturbing. She was finding it harder and harder to keep him at arm's length and to work with him on a nonpersonal, nonsexual basis. All she wanted was for him to crush her in his arms and smother her with kisses.

She inwardly groaned. Surely she wasn't . . . *in love.* It was so simple and so obvious that her throat squeezed tight in panic.

What now?

It was something she didn't want to think about. She wasn't ready.

"Caffeine and sugar always put me back on my feet,"

she said with forced enthusiasm. "Let me grab a soda, and I'll be ready to get back to work."

Pushing herself off the bed, she rose, swaying a moment before regaining her bearings.

Hovering at a discreet distance, Dr. Robinson stepped up. "Are you sure that's all you need?" she asked in the voice of a concerned medical professional. The look on her face was more than a bit skeptical.

Her eyes closed briefly. Pressing a hand to her stomach, she resisted the urge to lie back down. This was no time to be as delicate as a hothouse bloom. They had work to do. "I'm fine."

"If you say so," Robinson echoed doubtfully.

She turned to Mason. He was still dressed in the tattered remains of his wet suit, and the tight material clung to his muscular body like a second skin. It was all she could do to keep herself from staring at the way it hugged around his hips.

She quickly thrust naughty thoughts out of her brain. "If you don't mind, I'd like to get back to the water. My gut keeps telling me there's something up with the dolphins. They seem to want to communicate."

Mason turned to Commander Hawkins. "Are the dolphins still following us?"

Activating the nearest com-link, the commander requested an update. "Yes," he answered, "the dolphins are still circling the ship."

Addison nodded. "Good. Looks as though they're willing to stick around."

Mason indicated the rueful state of his wet suit. "Give me a few minutes to get changed, and I'll join you."

His words reminded her that she, too, was still dressed

for diving. Fortunately, her suit hadn't been damaged like his, which pretty much meant she was good to go. Although she much preferred swimming au naturel, the taboos humans had about nudity prohibited her from discarding her clothing until after she dived. She'd never understood why people wanted to hide themselves under layers of clothes when being in the buff felt so much better.

Their world, their rules, she thought. Yet she couldn't help but wonder what things would be like if her kind had prevailed. How different would the world be today if mermaids had never been driven from the water?

"If you don't mind, I think I would like to go into the water alone," she said.

Mason's gaze hardened. There was a faint sense of resistance about him, as though he were putting up some invisible wall to shield himself. Suddenly he was the captain helming this mission. "Why?" he asked curtly.

A strange prickle went down Addison's spine. She couldn't miss the vibrations emanating from him—a wave of resentment and suspicion. It completely startled her. Why the sudden shift in emotions? And how could she even tell what he was thinking? Was the psi-link still intact in some way? She felt totally keyed to his emotions. She wondered if it had something to do with his being conscious when she'd shared her breath with him underwater.

She forced a smile. "I can't keep you from coming along. I simply wanted to see how they would react with just a Mer in the water. They only attacked Magaera's soldiers, which seems to mean they know the difference between us."

"It is interesting that they didn't go after you." He looked away uneasily.

Cold awareness rushed over her. The conflict Mason felt against the Mer was unmistakable. She sensed he was trying to temper his mistrust, and failing.

For an instant, she felt the sting of revulsion. People were sometimes dumb as rocks. Mason was no exception. Not only had she proven herself loyal to humans her entire life—she'd just drained herself to the point of fainting to heal him.

She quickly pulled back her resentment. *It's not personal,* she reminded herself. *He just doesn't trust my kind.* People just needed to be educated about the Mer.

Addison tamped down her own annoyance. She knew he was doing his best to be open-minded. She would have to be patient. "That proves to me that some kind of thought process must be at work."

"Are you sure you can handle going in so soon?" His even, neutral voice betrayed nothing. Nevertheless, his body language betrayed a hint of antagonism.

Refusing to drop her gaze, Addison squared her shoulders. It was true she was tired, but the time to rest would have to wait. She didn't want to let the opportunity slip through her fingers like so many grains of sand. If there was a way for her kind to perhaps communicate with another seafaring species, she wanted to find it.

"I'm ready," she insisted.

Chapter 17

Kenneth Randall wasn't the kind of man to stand around and do nothing. Whenever there was a problem to be taken care of, he went to work to solve it. Usually he managed to find a solution, however impossible it might seem to others.

But having his wife literally snatched out from under his nose put him up against a wall. To make things worse, Mermaid mania was in full swing. Curious eyes looked toward the Mediterranean Sea, watching and waiting with bated breath to see how Magaera would choose to present her people. Would the Mer queen continue her open hostilities toward humans, or would she choose to open diplomatic channels and negotiate peacefully?

Even though the news hadn't caused mass rioting in the streets, it did bring out several factions and religious groups that were firmly against the Mer and their integration into human society. It seemed every political pundit or talking head on television had something to say about the matter. Many were worried about immigration and the social impact a water-bound species might have on the economy.

No one could seem to agree where the Mer truly belonged.

Even though he'd managed to get a crew together and get the *DreamFever* back into the water, the return trip to Ishaldi was proving to be a difficult one. The US Navy was running a blockade along the perimeter of the dead zone, redirecting all seagoing traffic away from the problem area. Only ships carrying authorized personnel were allowed in.

His wasn't one of those ships. But Addison was aboard the *Sea Horse* and working with the USET team. And since his wife was a hostage on Magaera's island, he felt he should be allowed in to offer assistance. Although the powers that be had given him a flat refusal when he'd requested to join the team, he couldn't be stopped. He'd simply go around the blockade and rendezvous with the *Sea Horse*. They'd have to torpedo the ship to get him out of the water.

Hands tightening around the railing of the port bow, he sighed. It was stupid. It was stubborn. But it was the only plan he had to work with.

They can't stop what they can't see. Gwen was going to try to use her Mercraft to shield the boat from all eyes when they passed through the prohibited zone. Although she wasn't sure she could project enough energy to conceal something as large as a ship, she was willing to give it a try.

Walking across the deck as though his feet were made of lead, Blake slowly edged his way toward the railing. "Why the hell do you have to stand so close to the water?" he groused.

Kenneth turned. Despite his fear of deep open bodies of water, Blake was doing his best to keep his nerves under wraps. The man did not enjoy sailing; he had no use for the sea. He was there only to support Gwen. Even though Blake spent most of his time in their cabin bent over the toilet, the man earned an A for effort. It couldn't be easy for him to put aside a lifelong fear.

"There's no way to fall overboard," Kenneth said. "It's perfectly safe."

Blake eyed the roiling clouds in the distance. The wind skipped across the choppy water. "Say that when the storm's tossing our asses overboard."

Kenneth shrugged. "The weather report says the worst of the storm will probably detour around us. We're on the edge, so it shouldn't be bad."

"You can bet I'll be nowhere on deck when the damn thing hits," Blake grumbled.

"You should get Gwen to work on easing that sea sickness."

Blake adamantly shook his head. "No, I'm not going to be a baby and whine. I'll tough it out." He reached for his belt line, pulling his waistband out. "Hell, if nothing else, I'm losing those pounds I'd started to put on. The woman can cook."

"Where is she?"

"She's in our cabin. She can't make a connection with Tessa. She thought maybe you could."

Disappointment twisted his heart. "That doesn't sound good. If her own sister can't communicate with her—" His throat tightened. He couldn't finish the sentence.

Sensing his unspoken distress, Blake raised his hands. "Now, let's not worry until we know for certain. Gwen says harming Tessa would only defeat Magaera's purpose. She's got to keep her alive."

Even though it was a difficult thing to do, Kenneth tamped down his worry. He knew that much to be true. When a Mer died, so did her soul-stone. If Magaera wanted to use Tessa's psychic resonance, she'd need Tessa alive to do so. Otherwise, Tessa's stone would be useless, devoid of psi-energy."

Kenneth nodded. "So, what does Gwen want to try?"

Blake shrugged. "I don't know. Come and see, I guess."

They left the deck, making their way to the cabins below.

Gwen sat on the floor in the middle of the room. An assortment of crystals and other semiprecious stones were spread out around her.

Kenneth stopped in his tracks. At first glance she looked exactly like Tessa, so much so that strangers often mistook the sisters for one or the other. It was only after spending time with them that their individual personalities came to the forefront.

He watched as Blake bent, giving her a quick peck on the cheek. "Figured it out, honey?"

She smiled up at him. "Slowly but surely."

"Anything I can do?" he asked.

"You can leave."

Blake's brows rose. "Excuse me?"

She gave him a cheery smile. "The less psychic interference in the room, the better. I just need Kenneth here."

Blake sighed like a put-upon man. "I always get left out of the fun," he said with a mock pout.

Gwen kissed the tips of her fingers, then waved him the kiss. "I'll make it up to you with a long shoulder rub later this evening."

"Okay," Blake grumbled. "I get the hint. I'm going." He left the room, shutting the door behind him.

Watching the two of them together, Kenneth felt a twinge of jealousy. It wasn't right that Tessa had been taken from him. He brooded, thinking, *She should be here. With me.*

Gwen sensed his dissatisfaction. "I'm sorry," she said quietly. "I know how you're feeling. She was snatched right out from under our noses, and there was nothing we could do to stop it."

Her words unleashed a torrent of guilt that pummeled him from all sides. "I couldn't defend her." His hands curled into tight fists, which he drove into his chest. "I had a gun in my hand and it still wasn't enough to protect my wife." He cast a dark look toward the stones scattered on the floor. The impulse to grind them into dust beneath his heels was hard to resist. Damn the Mer. It was because of them that he was in this situation.

A look of fright crossed Gwen's face. She held her hands over the stones as if to protect them. "Ken, don't do it. I need these."

Kenneth reined in his anger. He'd forgotten how sensitive Gwen was. Not that she needed the talent. His frustration was probably broadcasted loud enough to be picked up through radio frequencies.

He drew a calming breath. "Sorry. Every time I think that Magaera's got her hands on my wife, I get a little crazy. It doesn't help that she's got that fucker Jake nipping at her heels like a faithful hound." He shook his head. "I'm dying to kick his scrawny ass."

Gwen relaxed. "Make yourself comfortable and pay attention. I'm going to need you to concentrate."

Kenneth hunkered down in front of her. He eyed the glittering assortment she'd spread out around her. Although he didn't exactly understand the science behind a Mer's magic, he knew they used various stones for the transmutation of energy. Each stone had a meaning and use. Used separately, they could be dangerous. Grouped together and arranged in a certain configuration—such as in the Ri'kah—the stones could become a weapon of mass destruction.

Because they had never been trained, Tessa and her sisters had been forced to learn the hard way. Sometimes their efforts were hits; other times they were misses. Of the three sisters, Gwen showed the most talent with psi-kinetic work. It wasn't hard for her to make small objects appear and disappear at will. Unfortunately, the side effects were severe, leaving her exhausted and in the grip of massive migraines.

He eyed the stones. "What if we tried to teleport her out? We've managed it a few times successfully."

Gwen nodded. "I've thought about trying it, but there are too many variables against success." She held up a finger. "First, we have to assume that Magaera has taken Tessa's soul-stone, at least to rob her of her abilities. I would also guess that she's tried to manipulate it in order to let her through the sea-gate. So we have no real way to home in on her." She held up another finger. "Second, we don't know how magnetic interference from the sea-gate will alter psi-kinetic travel." She held up a third finger. "Last, we don't know what we'd be pulling back to us even if we managed to catch hold of something on the other side."

He tried another tactic. "What if we went to her?"

Gwen shook her head and raised a fourth finger. Kenneth didn't like the way the odds kept stacking up against them.

"Four, we don't know where, exactly, we'd be landing. One miscalculation and you could end up in the middle of a wall or the floor. I can pretty much guarantee you would not survive physically materializing into an inert object."

He grimaced. "It does sound gruesome."

Gwen stuck out her thumb. "Here's the last one. Even if I got you there in one piece, I can't guarantee I'd have the energy to pull you both back out again."

He scrubbed his hands across his face. "I guess that makes sense," he said reluctantly.

"But there are other things we can try to communicate with Tessa."

"How?"

"I've been working with a few of Tessa's stones, trying to pick up her vibrations."

"Can you do that?"

Fingering one of the stones, Gwen nodded. "Since these are Tessa's stones, they are mostly keyed to her rhythmic energies. I'm hoping to be able to tap into that and use it to open a psi-channel."

"I don't understand a word you're saying, but if it can be done, do it," Kenneth said firmly.

Gwen picked through an assortment. Closing her

eyes, she rubbed each between her palms. After a few minutes, she selected one stone in particular, a rough cluster of crystal quartz. "This one," she said. "I can feel her vibrations inside. She works with this one a lot."

Kenneth looked at the mass of milky white stones. "What's so special about that one?"

Gwen held the stone, about two inches in diameter, between her thumb and forefinger. "This is also a base stone of all magic. The clusters can be used to amplify other stone energies. It's also used to enhance psychic ability, especially when used in meditation."

"What do I do?"

She handed him the stone. "It's pretty simple. Just hold it."

Kenneth accepted her offering. Cradling it in his palm, he lowered his gaze to the whitish cluster. Small ribbons of color flashed deep inside, as though a tiny heart pushed the illumination through its veins.

"It's still energized from the last time Tessa worked with it," Gwen explained quietly. "I'm hoping we can use this to connect with her."

He lifted his eyes. "How?"

Gwen made a certain hand movement, graceful and birdlike. "Focus deeply on the stone," she advised. "Keep your breathing level and even."

Kenneth looked at the stone and tried to relax.

"Watch the lights inside the crystal and try to make your heartbeat match its rhythm."

Attempting to follow her instructions, Kenneth gazed at the tiny sparks of light inside the crystal. *Pretend it's Tessa,* he thought. *Just reach out and touch her.*

Although it took a few minutes, he soon picked up

the rhythmic pulse. It quickened and brightened, seeming to imitate the beat of blood through his temples.

Suddenly, he felt a buzzing sensation emanating from the crystal. Faint, at first, it gradually grew in strength until he was sure he felt another presence trying to break through some invisible barrier.

"I think I can feel something." His voice was strained with anticipation and more than a little excitement.

"Try and concentrate harder," Gwen murmured softly. "See if you can visualize Tessa."

Kenneth nodded. Without any further instruction he closed his eyes. He tried to drown out every other sensation in his body, focusing his concentration on only his hand and the crystal thrumming against his palm.

For an instant nothing existed except the vast shadowy cavern inside his own mind. He was no longer conscious of anything except the expanding darkness—an inky black sea rushing in to drown him.

With a brief, tingling shock, Kenneth was out of his body. A strange light glowed around him. He lifted a hand, shocked to see his skin pulsing with a soft slow. The light, it seemed, was coming from within.

Kenneth?

The sound of his name, not spoken but projected, caused him to raise his head.

Far in the distance he saw a glowing figure. As he came closer, it took on form and solidity. Recognition flooded through his senses. "*Tessa*—"

Suddenly, a shining figure appeared before him. Her face and figure were a little blurred and indistinct, but her psychic resonance was unmistakable.

She looked terrified . . .

*   *   *

Having been stripped of her soul-stone, which felt like a violent rape within itself, Tessa huddled in the farthest, darkest corner of her cell. The Mer were not known for providing more than basic necessities for their prisoners. She had a small cot, a couple of thin blankets woven out of some material she couldn't begin to identify, and sustenance. Past that, Queen Magaera seemed determined to make her incarceration as miserable as possible.

It didn't even touch the icy monarch's heart that Tessa was pregnant. As Magaera saw it, she carried the spawn of an inferior, thereby making her children inferiors, too.

Sighing deeply, she shifted her body, trying to find a more comfortable position on the uncomfortable bedding. Since her soul-stone had been taken from her, she had no way to communicate with her sisters; all her senses felt blunted and dull. She had no idea how many days had passed—more than a few, she was sure.

The isolation was beginning to get on her nerves. Even though she could barely stomach the sight of him, she would have welcomed Jake's company, even if all he wanted to do was gloat. Yes, it was true he was a rat bastard. She wanted nothing more than to rip off his head and use it as a bowling ball. She supposed she'd be willing to let him live, if only for the sake of hearing a familiar voice. The Mer soldiers guarding her cell were all dour-faced bitches, speaking hardly a word whcn they delivered her food.

Tessa made a face. The food definitely sucked. It was fruit and seafood, and the thought of eating it made her gag. Most people would go nuts over a diet of steamed crab, shrimp, and lobster. But since she'd become pregnant, her olfactory senses were unusually sensitive. To her it all reeked of a fishy odor.

But curling up and dying simply wasn't an option. For one, she had her children to think about, those two—possibly three?—precious babies she was determined to see born into this world. She also had no doubt whatsoever that somewhere, somehow, Kenneth was looking for her. The man had a will of iron and the determination to move mountains. If there was a way for him to come after her, he would.

Thinking about Kenneth caused her throat to tighten. Did he even have a clue as to how much she loved him?

As if she could use it to project her thoughts, Tessa focused on the stone wall directly across from her. She drew a deep breath and relaxed. Her heartbeat began to settle, slowing into a calming rhythm.

Concentrate, she told herself. *Send your thoughts outward.*

Closing her eyes, she gradually became conscious of the pulse of blood beating at her temples, of the small interior feelings deep inside her own body. She sensed rather than physically felt the relaxing of her muscles as her conscious self slipped away.

The hours reeled away, sliding from her grip. The darkness around her seemed to thicken.

And then it happened—something no words could describe.

With a brief, tingling shock, she was out of her body. Blurry, indistinct shadows surrounded her on all sides, but she felt no fear. Seconds later she thought she saw a solid figure forming in the strange mistlike illumination.

Her eyes widened in disbelief. "Kenneth?" A rush of welcome relief flooded through her. Her husband was alive!

Catching sight of her, he motioned for her to join him. "You can come to me now," he murmured from afar. Indistinct shadows drifted in the distance surrounding him, an endless, barren space of no discernible form.

A strange, tingling sensation washed over her skin. Sharp, intense physical awareness filled her. He looked so real. "I don't know how."

He held out a hand toward her. "Think of me," his voice whispered through her mind.

Tessa moved, gliding, unconscious of taking any physical steps. "I'm trying." She was afraid that, if she moved too fast, he would immediately vanish, never to be seen again.

Abruptly, and without any transition, she was standing beside him. Warmth and comfort radiated from his strong presence. It didn't look real, but it *felt* real, and that was enough for her.

"Where are we?" she whispered, as if speaking more loudly would destroy the delicious illusion.

Kenneth shook his head as a flicker of faint amusement passed over his face. "I'm not sure. Some kind of astral level Gwen's projecting for us. She can't sense you through your soul-stone, so we've been trying to make contact using other psi-channels. I haven't got much time. She tires fast."

Tessa followed his explanation sketchily; she caught

the gist of what he was saying rather than the whole. It made sense in a cockeyed sort of way. She had an idea of how astral duplicates traveled on the celestial plane. "Queen Magaera took my pendant," she confirmed. "She's mimicking my psychic resonance."

Kenneth's jaw tightened. "We figured as much. So now she has control of the sea-gate?"

Tessa nodded. "Yes. No doubt she's bringing out more of her soldiers as we speak."

Kenneth paused a moment, as if listening to some faraway voice. "Are you on Magaera's island?"

"I—I think so."

He raised his shadow fingers to lay them gently across her cheek. His ephemeral touch was light as a feather. His features radiated a beauty only the eyes of love could see. "We're coming for you," he said. "You won't be alone much longer, I promise."

A rush of unbidden tears fractured her vision. Her eyes were brimming. "Kenneth," she said, suddenly desperate to speak the words that had been on her mind through hours uncounted. "You know I love you."

Pulling her close, he pressed a quick kiss against her forehead, even as his open palm spread against her swelling abdomen. "I know, honey." Tenderness and concern poured through his faraway touch. "Keep yourself strong, for our girls."

Tessa reached for him, desperate to pull his strong body closer. But it was no use. The psychic connection was beginning to fray. Without saying another word, he faded abruptly from her sight. Only a gaping black void occupied the space where he'd stood. Then the darkness flowed through her like a thick boiling cloud. The ground seemed to tremble under her feet.

Tessa felt an enormous thrust of power, a great blow that sent her reeling. A hard jolt followed as her body and spirit reconnected on the physical plane.

Aching and desperate to call him back, she gripped the edge of the cot with her fingers. She'd lain for so long in a half curl that her muscles had begun to cramp. She suddenly felt unbearably tired, as if she'd run for miles without a break. Her flesh prickled with strange sensations, as if thousands of tiny insects crawled beneath her clothing. Even though the stone cell was uncomfortably cool, she was burning up, perspiration drenching her skin.

Was it a dream? she questioned herself. *Or real?*

Thinking the encounter no more than a hallucination, she felt blank with despair.

Pain lanced through her. She'd never had a dream, no matter how nightmarish or surreal, that left behind such devastating physical consequences. Her head and heart were pounding; her teeth were chattering. She was vaguely conscious of an intense lethargy and of hunger—of the depletion of energy that was the unavoidable consequence of psi-kinetic exertion.

A thought niggled, demanding attention. She would have sworn on her life the event had actually taken place. Gwen's powers were growing rapidly, after all.

Tessa pressed a hand to her clammy forehead in an attempt to lasso her racing brain. Too many impressions tumbled inside her brain, and she couldn't make sense of anything—what was real or unreal.

Only one thing was absolutely certain. She had to believe her family had indeed found a way to communicate with her.

They're close. The notion warmed the chill on her soul. Such a hope wasn't much to cling to, but right now it was all she had.

Chapter 18

After the attack in the water, Mason had ordered the *Sea Horse* to withdraw from its present location. A storm was brewing, and a harsh and heavy wind was beginning to kick up high waves. To keep the ship from accidentally drifting into the perimeters of the dead zone, he'd set a course to move beyond it. The storm would drive them in the general direction of Egypt.

Much to everyone's surprise, the dolphins continued to follow the ship. Addison had figured that the bad weather would drive the creatures back underwater, where they would be safe and relatively untouched by the wrath of Mother Nature. Instead of diving, one of the larger dolphins continued to launch its massive bulk into the air, making quick graceful arcs above the surface. It would disappear briefly, then reappear to repeat the process.

Addison clung to the deck railing, watching the dolphin perform. "It's really into it," she called, trying to project her voice above the wind. It wasn't too bad now. Later it would be fierce.

"It's a real show-off," Mason grated back.

She laughed. He still wasn't quite ready to admit the dolphins had pulled them out of one hell of a jam. It was as though he couldn't admit the beasts might actually possess an above-average intelligence. "I think it's cute."

Letting go of the railing, she headed toward the diver's deck. Though the ship lurched more than a little beneath her feet, she easily kept her balance. A Mer always had her sea legs, and the incessant up and down motion of a seagoing vessel didn't bother her in the slightest. Some members of the crew weren't so fortunate, and more than one person had retreated belowdecks to ride out the storm. More than a few were violently seasick.

Humans and water don't always mix well.

Mason didn't seem to be affected. He matched her step for step. "Where are you going?"

"Back into the water." She didn't glance up when she answered. She already knew he'd negate the plan, possibly even try and pull rank. When she'd agreed to accept the position, she'd put herself under the obligation to obey his command. If worse came to worst, she'd simply pretend she didn't understand him.

The other reason she couldn't quite bring herself to look him in the eyes hovered in the back of her mind: his discomfort with her Mer side. Even though he seemed to admire her abilities at times, particularly when they were underwater together, the attack by Magaera's soldiers had brought him back to square one. She could tell by the way he kept his distance that he was struggling with his distrust of the Mer. Did he think she had a dark side that would turn against humans on a dime?

I don't know if he'll ever fully trust me. It was a disquieting thought.

That little fact alone put any chance they had of building a relationship into a dead stall. She couldn't stop being a Mer any more than she could change the color of her skin or stop her heart from continuing to push blood through her veins.

And that was too bad. She really liked Mason. She would even have liked to see what the future might hold for them if they decided to explore the possibilities.

Mason shook his head. "Are you insane? I'm not letting you go down there."

Addison shrugged. "I'm still in my wet suit and ready for diving," she said, flashing him a smile that barely concealed her impertinence. "Besides, it's not as though I'm going to drown. Mermaids and water kind of go hand in hand, you know."

He grabbed her arm. "What if the dolphins aren't the only ones following?" he demanded. "Magaera's soldiers are well capable of keeping up with this ship, too. Those dolphins might not come through a second time."

More than a little pissed, Addison wriggled out of his grip. "I'll thank you to unhand me, Captain," she said, putting a measure of steel in her tone. "In case you've forgotten, I'm the one you came to for help in dealing with the Mer."

His hand immediately fell away. "In case you've forgotten," he countered, "I'm the one leading USET, and I'll make the decisions as to how *all* team members proceed, including those civilians." His blue eyes glinted with cool determination.

Addison knew he was in the right, but she refused to listen. "I'm the Mer here, and you don't tell me what to do." It was a childish and stupid thing to say, but she didn't care. The resentments she'd kept bottled up were beginning to boil to the surface, and she didn't feel like acting as a reasonable adult.

"Either you follow my orders or I'll put you off this ship at the next opportunity," he said, biting off each word in a precise manner that left no doubt of his seriousness. "I won't have your pigheaded ways endangering any member aboard—including you."

If there was anything Addison hated more than being backed into a corner, it was being given an ultimatum. Of course, she should straighten up and fly right, but she just didn't feel like it. "I'll save you the trouble."

With that, she climbed over the rail and dived into the water.

She hit the choppy waves, then proceeded to propel herself several hundred feet beneath the surface. The clinging wet suit annoyed her as she swam. She quickly shifted out of it, putting on her tail.

That feels better.

Even though she knew Mason would be worried, she felt no compunction to surface immediately. *Let him stew a bit,* she decided.

Addison tore through the water with strong, sure strokes. When she had to get away from the stresses of living in the human world, she often returned to the sea. She'd never been like Gwen, wishing desperately to be human. She liked being a mermaid. She relished it, as a matter of fact. Where others were ordinary, she was extraordinary.

A flash of shadow caught the corner of one eye.

Addison stopped, whirling around to confront whoever followed her. A weak laugh bubbled from her lips when she saw one of the dolphins. It swam in her wake, expertly mimicking her moves. Not only was it the biggest; it seemed to be the leader.

Even though she didn't know much about dolphin anatomy, the massive creature practically radiated an overpowering, almost possessive, maleness. From the tip of the snout to the tip of the tail, it had to measure at least seven feet in length. A series of dark stripes wove its way over the dolphin's leathery skin, as if to mimic a tiger shark. Although unusual, it wasn't entirely unexpected. To ensure survival, many creatures often took on the characteristics of predators.

Addison stilled her movements, swishing her tail against the current so it wouldn't carry her away. The dolphin swam closer, closing the distance between them until its long snout was perhaps less than a foot from her nose.

She reached out a hand and touched the dolphin's head. Its butter-smooth skin was cool beneath her palm. *"Well, aren't you a pretty boy,"* she said, sending out her remark on a psi-kinetic level. She doubted the dolphin was capable of receiving her thoughts, but it didn't hurt to try.

Suddenly, a strange tingling sensation shot up her arm. And then it happened. A series of strange blue-gray sparks whooshed across the dolphin's body, like fireworks under the water. Before she could even blink, the dolphin had vanished. A humanoid figure took its place.

Startled beyond reason, Addison held out her arms in a protective gesture. She had no idea what had happened, or how. One minute she was giving the dolphin a friendly pet. The next moment she was looking at a very tall, very naked man.

Long silver-blue hair spread out in a halo around a face composed of sharp lines and angles. His eyes were spaced widely apart, the irises a strange silvery color that seemed to glow with a curious radiance. His features were well defined, with angular cheekbones, an aquiline nose, and a wide but oddly sensual mouth. His long lean body, definitely a swimmer's physique, rippled with pure muscle. Even after shifting, his skin retained the unusual striped pattern. As for any hint of a tail—there wasn't one.

Her gaze tracked over his chest, following the cobbled path down his abdomen. Heat crept into her cheeks. He was definitely all male.

Addison blinked. This thing couldn't possibly be real. Her hand shot out, giving him an experimental poke. The flesh beneath her fingers was solid.

Flustered, she opened her mouth to speak, which only resulted in a big gulp of salty water going straight to her stomach. Spluttering, she gagged down the terrible taste and reminded herself to project her thoughts. *"Who the hell are you?"*

Apparently a connection had been made on the psychic level, for the man-dolphin smiled. *"I am Jovon."*

Addison's eyes widened at the sound of a clear male voice echoing inside her own head. *"You understand me,"* she said.

He nodded. *"Of course. Quite easily, as a matter of fact."*

Confusion hit her from all sides. *"I don't understand. I've never seen a male Mer."*

Jovon laughed, emitting a rich deep sound of amusement. *"We do not call ourselves Mermen,"* he replied. *"I am a Nyx."*

Lips pressed into a tight line, Mason McKenzie stared into the choppy sea. More than an hour had passed since Addison Lonike had disappeared into the choppy water. As yet, he had spied neither hide nor hair of her.

Mason tightened his grip on the railing. Knowing full well the danger that lurked beneath the surface, he'd already imagined the worst—that Magaera's soldiers had returned and taken Addison hostage.

Despite the lure of dry clothes and a hot drink, he forced himself to remain in his place. The remnants of his wet suit clung to his skin, leaving him feeling cold and clammy.

Commander Hawkins approached. "Would you like me to take over the watch?" he asked.

Mason shook his head. After Addison had gone into the water, he'd ordered the ship to come to a full stop and drop anchor. The winds from the pending storm were already beginning to kick up, pushing the ship several miles away from her dive site.

"No, thanks. I'll keep watch."

Hawkins checked his watch. "She's been gone quite a while," he ventured. "It might be she isn't coming back."

Or she can't, his mind filled in automatically. The dolphins had long since disappeared, abandoning their watch and returning to the deep. Perhaps they'd again tried to defend Addison against Magaera's soldiers—and lost.

"How the hell am I going to explain to the Secretary of the Navy that I've lost the mermaid?" he demanded. "That she jumped off the ship, disappearing without a trace into the sea." It was too damn dangerous to go into the water. Otherwise he'd have put on his gear and gone in after her. As it was, there was nothing he could do but wait.

"I wouldn't want to be in your position, sir," Hawkins ventured carefully. "All you can do is tell the truth."

"And watch my command and my career go down the toilet," Mason finished.

Hawkins clapped him on the shoulder, attempting to offer some reassurance. "If it's any help, I'll testify that you warned her not to go back into the water. That she ignored your advice."

Cramped and weary from standing so long in one place, Mason rubbed his eyes. He'd looked at the water so long that his vision was beginning to blur. "Thanks. I doubt that will help much, but it might be the only thing that saves my ass."

"Apparently, the Mer have their own way of doing things," Hawkins said.

That brought Mason's ire up. "I've never met such a stubborn woman," he said. "She's going to do exactly what she wants, and damn the consequences." He hated the feelings of helplessness and the fact that he was worried sick about her well-being. In his role as a leader, he found his instinct was to ensure the safety of the men and women serving under his command. He would never ask any man to do something he hadn't or couldn't do himself.

Hawkins released a chuckle. "Well, whether or not we like it, we're going to have to get used to dealing with them. It doesn't look like the Mer are going away any time soon."

Mason rolled his eyes. "If I could go back to the beginning, I think I'd refuse this assignment."

"You just don't like having anyone talk back to you, Cap."

"I like things orderly," he admitted. "And I like people who know how to take orders and do their jobs right."

"She may look human, but she isn't one of us. She's a mermaid, and our rules and our regulations just don't apply."

"Tell me about it."

"And it may just be me, but I think there's more than a little personal friction between you two."

Mason's brows rose. "Oh?"

Hawkins grinned. "It's hard to miss it when you two are around each other."

Mason forced himself to blank his face. "Think what you want," he said, putting a measure of ice into his voice. "But I assure you I have no interest in Addison Lonike beyond her role as an adviser."

His second-in-command looked at him levelly. "It happens to the best of us seafaring men," he said. "Sooner or later we all fall to the siren's call. Of course, you would have to go one step farther and actually bag yourself a mermaid."

Mason felt uncomfortable under his friend's knowing

gaze. "She's not *my* mermaid," he said, refusing to be baited. Being tied down to one woman—any woman— was unthinkable. He liked his freedom, coming and going as he pleased. It would take more than a little redheaded Mer with an attitude to capture his heart.

To his relief, Hawkins was wise enough to leave it at that. Instead of pursuing the matter, he tipped his head back, staring up at the leaden sky. "Looks like the worst of it might go around us." Even as he said the words, the sun dropped beneath the clouds. Golden shafts of light spread out over the water, almost blinding in their intensity.

Mason immediately lifted a hand to shield his eyes. "Looks like you could—," he started to say, then froze. Right at that moment a figure broke through the shimmering surface of the water. He caught a flash of red as the woman threw back her head to clear her hair out of her eyes.

His heart seized in his chest, missing one beat, and then two, before resuming its regular rhythm. *Thank God she's safe,* was his first coherent thought.

"Looks like our Mer has come back," Hawkins commented.

"It's about time."

Catching sight of the ship, Addison headed toward it. She swam like an Olympic champion, propelling herself through the water with strong, sure strokes. Her scale pattern shimmered in the sunlight—a kaleidoscope of blues, pinks, and greens.

Mason leaned over the edge of the railing. "I see you've decided to come back." He could barely conceal his smile.

She tossed him a saucy grin. "Were you worried about me?"

"Pissed is more like it," he shot back.

Shifting out of her tail and back into her wet suit, she reached for the ladder. "As if that'll last."

Mason felt his heart roll over, pounding against his breastbone with enough force to shatter it. Everything about Addison drove him crazy.

Drawing himself up to his full height, Mason squared his shoulders. "You'll be confined to quarters if you don't start behaving and acting like a member of this team." He motioned toward Commander Hawkins. "I've got to think about the welfare of the people aboard this ship."

"I understand."

Mason cut her off. He wasn't finished. He'd eat her up one side and down the other, just as he would any crew member who acted against his orders. "I can't have you going off half-cocked just because you have some notion you need to swim with the dolphins. What's in these waters isn't exactly welcoming to our presence. If something happened, I'd have no way to help you."

Her smile immediately faded. "You're right," she conceded after a moment's hesitation. "It was a stupid thing to do, and I apologize."

Her admission caught him short.

Mason had expected to be blown off. But she'd taken the shakedown like an adult. Every time he thought he had Addison pinned down, she showed a different side of herself.

"Just don't do it again. Okay?"

She nodded. "I won't."

"I don't suppose you saw anything while you were in the water."

Her smile returned. "Actually, I did." Walking back to the diver's deck, she made an odd whistling sound.

A graceful figure broke through the surface. Head and torso appeared, skimming across the water. Seconds later, strong hands grasped the side ladder.

Commander Hawkins's eyes went round. "What the hell is that?"

Mason's jaw dropped. "I don't know . . ."

Tipping back his head, he stared at the being climbing onto his ship. The creature offered a commanding presence that unnerved him more than the sight of any enemy soldier he'd ever encountered. All he saw was broad shoulders, lean hips, and well-muscled legs that seemed to stretch on for at least a mile.

The man—or was it a *creature*?—stood at least seven feet tall. Silver-blue hair streamed over his shoulders, all the way down his back. His skin, too, was silver—shiny, smooth, and hairless. Obviously a male, he stood naked and proud. Like Addison's, his skin bore a distinctive pattern. Unlike her, he had a slash of gills on the right and left sides of his neck, extending down from under his ears. He also had fins on his forearms and calves. Something that looked like a thin leather cord attached to a small rock hung around his neck.

Mason swallowed hard. "What, uh, *who* the hell is this?" Even from a distance he could smell his scent, a cloying mixture of salt and brine. Intelligence and a subtle cunning glinted in the depths of the creature's silver eyes.

Addison glanced up at the tall figure. "Remember when I told you I thought the dolphins were trying to communicate with us?"

Still disbelieving his eyes, he nodded. "Yes."

"They weren't just dolphins," she explained. "This is Jovon, and he's king of the Nyx."

"So I see." His gaze immediately locked with that of the visitor. A brief moment of wariness and suspicion passed between them, two territorial males checking each other out.

Mason refused to blink. *This is about to get complicated.*

Chapter 19

"**A**re you telling me that he's one of those dolphins?" Mason asked after an excruciating minute had passed.

"I am."

Mason eyed the tall, naked figure. "Is this"—he swallowed hard—"a merman?"

Much to Addison's relief, Jovon answered for her. "Mer is the name our females chose for themselves," he said, speaking perfect English in a low but pleasant baritone. "Our true forename is Nyx, which roughly translates to 'water spirit' in your language."

Addison's brow wrinkled. She'd had no clue males of her species even existed. She'd been raised to believe that humans were the natural mates for Mer.

Apparently we're still missing a lot of pieces about our history. She hoped Jovon could answer the questions pinging around in her mind.

Mason's eyes widened in surprise. "You understand me?"

Jovon flashed a smile. "Of course. As telepaths, we can pick up and interpret many languages quite easily. Just because we are a water-bound people doesn't mean we are as mindless as insects."

Mason cleared his throat. "I'm sorry. I wasn't meaning to imply your kind had a lesser intelligence."

Jovon cocked his head. "Yet your companion is wondering about the naked idiot standing with his privates dangling in the wind."

Mason whirled toward Commander Hawkins. "Put a lid on it, Commander."

Hawkins turned ten shades of red. "Sorry, sir," he mumbled, dropping his gaze. "How was I supposed to know he could read my thoughts?"

Addison forced herself not to laugh. No, from what Jovon had told her underwater, the Nyx couldn't read minds, but they would pick up and interpret impressions based on a person's vibrations and body language. Everything about the Nyx was oversized, including his genitals. Except for his head and eyebrows, his body was devoid of hair, giving everyone who cared to look a clear view of his male assets.

She had to admit his build was magnificent. Muscle rippled beneath taut flesh. When she'd first seen him, the sight of his magnificent body shook her to the bone. There was no ignoring the sinew beneath his skin or the jut of his manhood, impressive even when flaccid. The strange pattern on his skin only added to his masculinity.

Feeling a hot blush singe her cheeks, she forced herself to look elsewhere. Her thoughts were beginning to stray in a most inappropriate way. She'd seen a lot of good-looking men in her life, but nothing had quite prepared her for the sight of a man who hailed from a species comparable to her own.

I wonder . . . She quickly squelched the thought, hoping she'd put the kibosh on her body's physical emanations before Jovon picked up on them.

Clearly struggling to regain his composure, Mason said, "He meant no offense. Among our people, it's customary to cover our, ah, privates."

Jovon eyed the two men. Although Mason still wore his wet suit, Commander Hawkins looked crisp and sharp.

"I understand," he said. A crackle, followed by a brief shimmer, covered his body from shoulders to feet. When the glimmer faded, he was dressed in a simple tunic that looked like linen dyed a muted blue shade. Short breeches were cut off at the knee, and leather sandals laced around his ankles. It wasn't anywhere close to modern, but it looked comfortable enough. "Is this acceptable?"

Mason nodded. "Yes, thank you."

"I do not understand the human need to cover up from head to foot. Bare skin is much more comfortable."

"We do it to spare our more, ah, delicate parts exposure," Mason said by way of an explanation. "Also, it is unacceptable in our society for males and females to go unclothed around each other."

Jovon threw back his head and laughed. "Ah, you humans and your strange taboos."

More than a bit self-conscious, Addison glanced down at her clinging attire. "Well, since we're being proper here." She thought about excusing herself to change, then realized she didn't have to.

Closing her eyes, she focused her own inner energies. Picturing the clothing she'd left in Mason's cabin, she mentally transferred the garments onto her own body. Within the blink of an eye, the wet suit had vanished and she was suitably dressed.

Jovon looked at her in surprise. "So the Mer haven't lost their craft."

She shook her head. "Nope. It's still as strong as ever."

By now, word of the strange visitor had spread among the crew. People were beginning to gather, albeit at a cautious distance. Addison could almost feel the weight behind their stares boring straight through her.

Mason noticed the crowd. He leaned over, whispering to Hawkins, who immediately set off to disperse the onlookers. "I think we should find someplace more private to talk," he said. "Would you care to accompany me belowdecks? We have a dining area that's more suitable for entertaining guests."

Although his regal face revealed nothing, Addison picked up a ripple of uneasiness from the Nyx. Despite his great size and the sheer power of his bulk, he was nervous about leaving the open water behind.

She laid a gentle hand on his arm. "They mean you no harm. But perhaps you would be more comfortable speaking to the captain in private."

Jovon hit her with a direct, unblinking stare. "So he is the leader of his people?"

"I'm not the leader," Mason corrected. "But I do represent my government in our efforts to make contact with the Mer."

"And the Nyx," Addison hastily added.

"We should talk," Mason added. "I'd like to know why you helped us." He paused, then added, "And I will give you my word that you will not be harmed in any way while you're aboard my ship. You can leave anytime you like."

A long minute passed, and then another.

Jovon finally nodded. Even though his face carried a neutral expression, the currents emanating off his tall frame indicated that he didn't trust humans. He was all adrenaline and raw nerves. "That is satisfactory."

A look of relief crossed Mason's face. "Please, come this way."

Jovon looked to Addison. "You will come as well." It was not a question but a statement.

Addison nodded. "Of course." There was no way she'd miss this.

She glanced toward the horizon. The sun had begun to descend in the west, appearing to sink into the water. The surface of the sea rippled with a strange gold-red-orange glow. It was a beautiful and breathtaking sight. The sky, however, remained ominously dark, as if the elements were plotting their next move against the earth below.

There are so many secrets hidden in the depths of the sea, she thought. As a little Mer raised in Maine, she knew almost nothing of her people or their true origins. More missing pieces of the puzzle were beginning to fall into place.

Mason led them belowdecks, through the narrow corridors and into a small recreation room off the galley. As the communal area aboard ship, this was the place where people gathered to decompress after a long stretch on duty. Hawkins had cleared out the area, leaving only a few seamen on duty.

"Please, sit."

Jovon eyed the narrow, benchlike seats bolted to the floor to prevent them from moving during inclement weather. Even if he had tried to sit on one, his bulk would have made the fit uncomfortable. Nothing was designed to accommodate a seven-foot-tall male. "I will stand."

Mason elected to stand as well. Addison compromised by propping her rear on the edge of a nearby table. No one said anything for a while.

She decided to be the one to break the ice. "I don't understand why I've never heard of the Nyx," she said by way of an opening. "I've been in the water a long time, and I've never seen one. Where have you been all this time?"

Jovon's mouth drew down in a severe frown. "Trying to survive." He cast a glance toward the humans. "Which is why I am glad to see the Mer have reappeared in these waters. It gives me hope that we may have a chance against the humans who slaughter our kind."

Mason broke in. "Whoa," he said, making a time-out gesture with his hands. "Just what are you talking about when you say we slaughter your kind?"

Jovon didn't blink. "Humans continue to rape our waters, and many of the Nyx die after becoming entangled in fishing gear, or colliding with vessels. You also do not stop to think that fishing depletes our food sources, or that coastal habitats are destroyed by development. Even more demeaning is that some species are targeted to supply the demand for aquariums."

"We have laws against that," Mason said.

Jovon laughed unpleasantly. "Please, spare me from being treated like a stupid, unknowing creature. Such laws are largely ignored."

Sensing his anger with the humans, Addison laid a gentle hand on his arm. "Then why have you come out of hiding now? You didn't have to help us."

Jovon looked down at her. "Because I wish to seek an alliance between Mer and Nyx."

Pulse pounding like a jackhammer, she stared up at him. "You mean against the humans?" She shook her head. "If you're asking me to turn against them, I can't."

The Nyx stared at her with those strange eyes. "The Mer have always stood for themselves," he corrected quietly.

She shook her head. "I don't understand."

Jovon cocked his head. "Allow me to go back to an earlier time, when the Nyx still inhabited Ishaldi."

Mason folded his arms over his chest. "Go on."

"As you have probably guessed, our society is a matriarchy. The females are the stronger of our kind, and they control every level of our culture and its development. This includes reproduction."

Addison glanced at Mason. Although they had been together only once, she couldn't fail to notice that he'd used a condom. Although the gesture wasn't necessary—as Mer were immune to human disease—she'd appreciated his taking care to protect both of them.

"That's true," she said. "We do decide when to reproduce. Until we settle on our breemas, our breed-mates, nothing happens. We're basically infertile."

Mason rubbed his hand over his chin. "Good to know."

Jovon continued. "The males also have their place, mostly as artisans and craftsmen."

"So the females rule and the males do the heavy lifting?" Addison asked.

A cold smile touched Jovon's mouth. "That is a clumsy way of phrasing it, but correct. Our place in the hierarchy was valued until the Mer females began to discover that if they mated with humans, they could ensure the look and sex of their offspring."

"We have only girls," Addison broke in. "I thought that was simply nature's way to ensure the Mer species didn't die off."

"I wish it were so," Jovon answered with a sad shake of his head. "The truth is, the Mer wanted to become more like humans, to breed out our more aquatic traits." He held up one hand, spreading his fingers to reveal the webbing. Along with his gills and fins, not to mention the silver-blue shade of his skin, there was no way he'd ever be mistaken for human.

"So they chose selective breeding?" Mason asked.

"Yes. And as time passed, the Mer began to resemble humans. Some could even begin to pass as such. In the meantime, breeding with the Nyx was considered undesirable, and any female who did so was shunned. If she was unfortunate enough to bear a Nyx child, it was destroyed—especially if it was a male."

Addison pressed a hand to her heart. The Mer had always been known for their savage nature, but she'd had no idea that her own people had resorted to some sort of ethnic cleansing in an attempt to become more like human beings. "That sickens me."

Jovon let out a long breath. "To survive, the Nyx were

forced to leave Ishaldi. We became nomads of the seas, with no real place to call home."

Addison could barely withhold her shudder. "And the Mer simply replaced the Nyx with human males, whom they could more easily control."

"Eventually humans became their slaves," the Nyx confirmed. "And Ishaldi became one of the more powerful seagoing nations as the Mer began to leave the water and move onto land."

The more Addison learned, the less she liked. So far Jovon had revealed nothing redeeming about her own people. "Were you aware when the sea-gate was sealed?"

"We had hope when the Tesch dynasty came to power. Queen Nyala attempted to make peace with the humans and ease the restrictions against the Nyx. Once a year, during the spawning season, the Nyx were allowed to return to Ishaldi with the hope of making a suitable match with a Mer female. Returning to our homeland seemed possible."

"But that didn't happen."

Jovon's gaze was ravaged when it met hers. "No. Although some welcomed our arrival, many did not."

Addison felt his words, like a whiplash striking her naked skin. "I think I know the rest of the story. Queen Nyala's ministers began to plot her assassination and overthrow the Tesch who had taken power. But she outsmarted them by sealing the sea-gate."

"The plan was to start a new settlement," Jovon confirmed with a nod.

Unnerved by the way he was looking at her, she glanced at her feet. She couldn't even begin to guess what had gone wrong after the sea-gate was sealed. "But it never happened."

The Nyx narrowed his eyes. "By then the humans had begun to prevail. They quickly cut a swath through our numbers." A sound of frustration escaped him. "The few who survived moved to other waters. The females had a better chance of integrating because they had lost many of the traits carried by the sea-born."

Mason frowned savagely. "I hate to break it to you, but the Mer are still as savage as ever."

Addison shot him a look. But his words chilled her because she knew they were true. She didn't want to think too hard about all the unpleasant things the Mer were capable of.

Jovon pretended not to notice the brief tension. "I suspected as much," he said. "But the only ones who could have opened the sea-gate are among Nyala's descendants. And that is why I helped free you. We are aware the current monarch is not of a mind to forge any ties with the humans that would benefit both our people. We, the Nyx, would like to join your cause against her. We would like to see a Tesch queen restored to the throne of Ishaldi."

"There is no Tesch queen," she corrected in a quiet voice.

For several moments no one said a word.

The Nyx looked at her through his silvery eyes, a gaze that seemed to penetrate all the way to her bones. "There could be," he said levelly. "Are you not a direct descendant of Queen Nyala?"

Mason felt the Nyx's words like a dull knife twisting in his gut. Although he knew Addison and her sisters were Mer, he had no idea they would be considered royalty among their people.

Exiled royalty, he quickly reminded himself. From the sound of Jovon's narrative, the Tesch queen who had tried to reverse the savage course her people had taken had come close to losing her life to assassins.

"Why didn't you tell me you were some sort of Mer princess?" Mason asked.

His questions spun her around. "I didn't think it was important," she snapped in her own defense. "Almost two thousand years have passed since that sea portal was closed. I'm pretty sure our claim to the Tesch dynasty has expired."

"But your family had the jewels of Atargatis, right?" Even as he asked the question, Mason could see her muscles bunching with tension.

"A couple of pieces," she reluctantly admitted. "But they were only the orb and choker. The scepter was the most important piece."

"You have the scale pattern of the Tesch," Jovon said quietly. "It is a trait that appears to be the one thing the Mer cannot breed out of their bloodline."

When Addison didn't say anything, a little swirl of uneasiness went through Mason. She looked both confused and uncomfortable. He had a feeling she didn't know just exactly how savage her people really were. Learning the truth must have been a shock. It would be like learning his grandfather was a war criminal. In rejecting the Nyx as mates, the Mer had attempted to control the physical look of their offspring, each successive generation losing many of the traits that had once been common in their kind. Of course, it wouldn't have happened overnight. It would have taken centuries for the females to lose the gills and fins so prominent on the Nyx males, not to mention their odd skin tone.

Things had suddenly gone from merely complicated to tangled beyond reason. "Is that true?" he asked quietly. "Are you really marked as a member of the Tesch dynasty? Could you ascend the throne?"

Addison held up her hands. "Mason—"

He stared hard at her, wondering if the situation could get any more convoluted. It was hard not to let hostility and suspicion cloud his judgment.

Although he would never admit it out loud, the Nyx male offered a commanding presence that thoroughly unnerved him. He had the most fascinating look of any sea creature he'd ever encountered, not to mention an intelligence and subtle cunning that burned bright and hot behind his gaze.

"Just tell me the truth, Addison. Are you really what Jovon says you are?"

She nodded slowly. "I—I think so. At least that's what Tessa told us. But I'm the youngest, so I wouldn't be the next Tesch queen. That would be Tessa."

"Who is presently a hostage," he reminded her.

"Then Gwen would be next in line," she offered.

Mason shook his head. "She isn't here."

"If we have to act now, then I guess I'm all you've got."

He stared at her for a moment, trying to ignore the storm of emotions cutting through him. In the back of his mind he had been trying to figure out all the ways a Mer and a human could be compatible. On a conscious level he'd resisted the idea, and now he knew why it would never work. Whether she realized it or not, she had a destiny to fulfill. There was no way she could step down from the lofty position of princess to be with a plain old navy officer.

It just wouldn't work.

Jovon gave him a penetrating stare, and Mason wasn't so sure the Nyx couldn't read his thoughts down to the last letter after all. "The Nyx would like a chance to return to our homeland," he said. "We can do that only if the ruling monarch will allow it."

"Even if the Tesch could come back to the throne of Ishaldi, what makes you think you'd be accepted?" Addison asked.

"The Mer are emerging into a world that has changed around them since the time the sea-gate was sealed," Jovon explained with quiet patience. "They will need a leader who understands the times." A small smile turned up one corner of his mouth. "And we are hoping they will embrace males who know these waters well."

Addison ran her fingers through her messy curls. Her hair went every which way and resembled a fiery halo. "Tessa told me there are many Mer in Ishaldi who still value their human mates as equals. The revolution has torn Ishaldi apart and has put our world on the brink of extinction."

Jovon blinked. "What do you mean?"

"Those who follow Queen Magaera have shed the physical needs of the body in order to survive solely on crystal energy. But their hunger produced some kind of psychic burning. They take so much to survive that the elements around them began to burn out and crumble." She shook her head in frustration. "The animals are gone, much of the vegetation stripped away. Even the humans trapped there when the sea-gate closed have begun to die off."

"They have the crystal sickness," Jovon said.

Uncertainty flickered in Addison's eyes. "What's that?" she asked uneasily.

Jovon's mouth drew into a tight line. "When Mer begin to depend on crystal energy to feed their bodies, it can become an addiction."

Addison swallowed hard. "And we all know what happens when someone suffers from something like that."

Mason regarded her for a long moment. "It eats him up and destroys him," he finished.

"I know Mer can live for several centuries," she said in a hollow voice, "but Magaera told Tessa this practice could make them immortal."

"It can—if they have a fresh and constant supply of energy," the Nyx confirmed. "With the sea-gate closed, I doubt there was enough in Ishaldi to sustain the hunger of thousands. That is most likely how our world burned out and our resources decreased, as you say."

Mason didn't like where the conversation was heading. "But that isn't a problem now. The sea-gate is open."

Jovon frowned. "And there are a lot of humans to feed their hungers."

Mason's heart thumped. "What is that supposed to mean?"

Addison's face dawned with comprehension. "He's talking about the D'ema, the death magic," she answered quietly. "When we don't have a supply of crystals to take energy from, we can substitute humans. Your bodies also have the same minerals and nutrients . . ." Her voice suddenly cracked with strain.

"Aw, shit. So that means those who have taken on this strange eating disorder will need something to rejuvenate themselves." It was stupid, but Mason couldn't stop his mind from racing toward the worst scenario. The idea of Mer latching on to humans and sucking the juice out of them like some sort of sea spider chilled him to the bone.

Addison seemed to home in on his unspoken apprehension. "It's forbidden to use," she said quickly.

"You think that's going to stop Magaera?" Mason shot back. "Not all Mer may ascribe to the practice, but what about those who do?"

"Those will be the soldiers she brings out of Ishaldi," Jovon warned. "A Mer queen rules with an iron fist. Those who oppose her, she will crush." He shook his head. "It saddens me to learn that a world filled with such promise has destroyed itself. Perhaps there is nothing for the Nyx to return to."

Addison laid a gentle hand on his arm. "We can always try and save it, Jovon. If returning a Tesch to the throne will give our world a chance, then we'll do whatever it takes."

Jovon's head dipped. "We have waited a long time to go home."

Mason stared at them, struck by how strangely alike the two seemed to be. Although he didn't want to admit it, they looked as though they belonged together.

He gave himself a little shake as if trying to wake himself from a bad dream. A thousand emotions tangled inside him, but he forced every one of them back. Now wasn't any time to let his personal feelings for Addison impede the success of the mission.

"That's something we can't guarantee," he said, firmly stepping on her promise. "We're here to establish contact with Magaera, not stage a coup."

The Nyx didn't blink. "If Magaera wanted peace, she would not have sent her soldiers to attack your men the first time they went into the waters near her island. She is asserting her power to prove she rules these waters now."

"I think he's right," Addison said. "Magaera has had a lot of chances to establish peaceful communication. Instead, she's attacked us, not once, but twice. She's not interested in talking, but taking. And until she's stopped, that's all she's going to do."

Mason weighed their words. His own experiences with the Mer queen would have him agree with their assessment. Were he the one calling the shots, he'd be inclined to agree that Magaera needed to be deposed as soon as possible. The trouble was, he had superiors to answer to.

No one could have anticipated the arrival of the Nyx. Their appearance threw a monkey wrench into a matter that was already too complicated. He needed to communicate with Secretary Webber as soon as possible, updating his commander on the latest developments.

He was about to say as much when Hawkins reappeared. "Sorry to interrupt, sir," he said, giving the Nyx a wide berth, "but we've got a problem."

Mason's heart seized. "Have the Mer returned?"

Hawkins shook his head. "It's Tessa Randall's husband."

"What about him?"

"He's here."

That was impossible. The waters around Magaera's island had been declared to be in quarantine. Although a few other countries had protested the US government's authority in the matter, few were prepared to confront the Mer themselves.

"How the hell did he get past us?" he snapped.

Hawkins shrugged. "No telling, sir. But he is here, and he is requesting a meeting with you at your earliest convenience."

A sinking sensation settled into his gut. The last thing he needed was more interference. He briefly considered having Randall's ship picked up and escorted out of the area.

He glanced at Addison. His attraction to her gnawed at him, and he suddenly knew how Tessa's husband felt. *If that were my wife, and she were in danger . . .* , he thought. Yeah. He supposed he'd do anything he could to try and reach her.

"Tell Randall I'll meet with him shortly." He looked at Jovon. "I hope you're prepared to stay awhile. We've got a lot of talking to do."

Chapter 20

Kenneth Randall had invited them to meet aboard the *DreamFever*. Mason had accepted. Even though the *Sea Horse* wasn't officially recognized as a navy ship, it was still a government outfit and subject to the rules and regulations of such.

As a search and recovery vessel, the *DreamFever* was outfitted with much of the same equipment carried by the *Sea Horse*. Unlike the *Sea Horse*, Randall's ship catered to the comfort of its crew and passengers. Although the company he'd bought into, Recoveries, Inc., was presently out of business, Randall had been savvy enough to hold on to the equipment, docking the ship in Crete.

Having read the dossier, Mason knew Randall's attorneys had gone to court to file a record of the discovery of Ishaldi's ruins and had subsequently won the right of ownership over any artifacts that might be raised from the site. Since the actual physical location of Ishaldi lay in waters unclaimed by any country bordered by the

Mediterranean Sea, it had been relatively easy to stake a claim.

That entitlement had subsequently been negated by the US government once the existence of the sea-gate and the Mer had been confirmed as fact. Because Tessa and her sisters were legal residents of the country, the United States had also assumed the burden of what to do with the Mer now that the species had reemerged from what was considered to be a self-imposed exile from the world stage.

"We're doing our best to find a way to breach the island," Mason said, attempting to keep an even and neutral tone in his voice. It hadn't taken him long to figure out that Kenneth Randall wasn't the easiest man to deal with. He charged ahead like a bull in a china shop, unmindful of the damage he might cause.

Randall cut him short. "Whatever you're doing isn't enough as long as my wife remains a hostage."

Mason reminded himself that arguing wasn't going to do any good. "We also don't want to do anything that might antagonize further aggression on Magaera's part. Although we're no longer in the mood to negotiate or recognize her authority, we don't want to risk another attack on civilians."

Having listened silently to the entire conversation, Jovon stepped up. "She is not going to give up without a fight. The Mer do not recognize humans as equals and will not respond with anything other than aggression."

Mason forced himself to hide his smirk as Kenneth Randall stared up at the tall Nyx. Although he was a pretty big guy himself, Randall had been caught short by the appearance of a being that dwarfed him. "If they won't treat their own males as equals, then I'd say we damn sure haven't got a chance."

"So you're saying our only recourse is to depose Magaera?" Mason asked.

Jovon nodded. "I am."

A ripple of uneasiness went through him. "But even if we could manage that, the question is, would her people respond to a new monarch with a new vision for the Mer?" From what he could gather, Queen Nyala had tried that and was almost assassinated for her trouble. She'd ended up leaving her homeland—and her people—to perish.

"The Mer have been cut off from the world for a long time," Kenneth said. "When Tessa and I were in Ishaldi, there were those who expressed a desire to live peacefully with humans. Many are part of an underground rebellion and have fought for a long time to dethrone Magaera and her ilk."

Mason nodded. Okay, a small but dedicated band of rebels could turn the tide within Ishaldi. That made the odds a little bit better.

Jovon cut him a look. "And the Nyx are willing to join with you." He spread his big hands in supplication. "All we have ever wanted is to return to our homeland, to find the mates who will bear our children."

Kenneth eyed the massive being. "So why did you let the females run you off, anyway? It seems to me you guys should have been big enough to take care of yourselves."

Jovon merely laughed. "In your eyes we may be large and capable of taking care of ourselves, but in the olden times Nyx males were trained to be obedient to their women." He cocked his head, a little glint lighting his gaze. "But times have changed, and we are ready to approach our females as equals."

"So your kind have managed to survive by mating with human females?"

Jovon nodded. "Some of us actually have Mer mothers, though it is rare to find a purebred among the seaborn nowadays. If a Nyx is lucky enough to entice a female to take him as a mate, such mothers are usually reluctant to send their sons to face the perils of the sea."

"So a Nyx mating with a human only engenders a son?" Mason asked.

"Yes, one who retains many of our natural traits." Jovon touched the side of his neck, tracing one of his gills. "Fortunately, most of these do not become truly visible until the child hits puberty. It is then that the changes begin."

"What about the soul-stones? You seem to have something similar around your neck," Mason remarked.

Jovon indicated the thin leather cord around his neck. A small gray stone with a hole bored through it hung there. "This," he explained, "is a piece of hematite or iron ore. We males absorb the energy of stone minerals in a different way. Whereas females can absorb and manipulate crystal energies, we males can do so only on a very limited basis, such as to communicate telepathically or clothe ourselves. We can, however, achieve a full shift into our water-bound forms. A trick of the eyes conceals the presence of our soul-stones from humans who might glimpse us. We are also much faster and stronger."

Kenneth let out a low whistle. "Wow, you guys really got the short end of the stick."

A familiar voice broke in from behind. "And you think the women have it easy, fellas?"

Mason felt the fine hairs on the back on his neck rise. Even before she spoke, he could sense her presence. It was uncanny, the feeling that crept through him whenever she was close. His chest tightened, and his stomach knotted.

It's never going to work, he reminded himself for the thousandth time. *Stick to business.*

Everyone turned.

Fresh from working in the galley, Gwen Lonike carried a tray of food. "While you men have been standing around having a power meeting, we were sent to slave over the meal."

Carrying a second tray loaded with a selection of flavored malt coolers and bottled beers, Addison followed at her heels. "We're still the ones who have to have the babies," she added. "It only makes sense that we should have more tricks up our sleeves, to protect our offspring."

Stumbling in with a third tray, Blake grumbled as he deposited his load on the table. "Not all of us were in on the manly powwow," he reminded the women.

Gwen smiled at her fiancé. "Don't grumble too loud, dear. Otherwise I'm going to have to tell them you only ducked out because you wanted another beer."

Blake pasted on a devilish grin. "It helps settle my nerves, sweetheart." He patted his stomach. "You wouldn't want me being all seasick, would you?"

"I've told you a banana and ginger ale will work just as well," Gwen said.

"It doesn't taste the same," Blake said in his own defense.

Gwen rolled her eyes in mock disgust. "When you pass a six-pack a day, dear, we'll talk."

Blake shrugged. "I guess it's true," he said, addressing the men. "These girls have all the power."

Kenneth nodded in agreement. "I owe Gwen my life. I'd still be lying in that hospital if she hadn't used her Mercraft to heal me."

"The Mer can do a lot of good—if they can learn to overcome their savage natures," Jovon added quietly. "Though it is not commonly known, we males exude a pheromone that helps calm our females and makes them more receptive to breeding."

"My wife often struggles with what she calls the 'Mean Mer' inside," Kenneth said.

Gwen reached for one of the malt coolers. Uncorking it, she poured herself a healthy glass. "There are certain times during the month when it just feels like something furious is building up inside you." She took a sip of her drink. "Unless you've experienced it, it's hard to explain. My best guess is that it has something to do with the psi-kinetic side of our minds. If it doesn't have an outlet and begins to build up, things are going to blow."

Claiming one of the beers, Addison flicked the cap off with practiced ease. "For me it's like a tiger, locked in a cage. It's biting and tearing at the bars."

"And that is the time when a female would require the ministrations of her male," Jovon added smoothly.

Addison swigged down a healthy gulp. "Oh, for the sake of the goddess. Why is it that men think that thing between their legs will solve every problem a woman has? Sometimes we like to let loose and kick a little butt." Flipping the cap into the air, she made a neat flicking motion with her fingers. A spark shot out of nowhere, dinging the cap higher.

Mason reached out and caught it. The metal was sizzling hot against his palm. "Shit!" he yelped, letting it drop.

"I should have warned you that those girls can pack quite a punch," Kenneth called out.

Mason knelt, retrieving the cap. Balancing it between thumb and forefinger, he saw a neat little hole burned precisely through its center. "That's amazing."

Addison shrugged modestly. "It's just a little something I've been practicing. I've never really been as good at projecting my psi-energies without a crystal to focus through. Tessa's pretty good, though she doesn't do it much anymore. Gwen's always been best."

"But Addison's best at crystal projection," Gwen said, returning the compliment. "She can use a Ri'kah. I can't even make one pop."

Mason fingered the cap. "So all Mer don't have the same abilities?"

Gwen shook her head. "No, just as people have different abilities, so do Mer. Some of us are very kinetic; others do better on a psychic level."

Mason absently pocketed the cap. Now he had a clearer idea of what they were fighting. A leader was only as strong as the soldiers he sent into battle. Magaera would have only the best at her command—highly trained and battle ready. No wonder they hadn't been able to make any advances in the water. The Mer had every advantage.

Somehow we have to even the odds.

His gaze settled on Jovon. Whether he liked it or not,

it looked like the Nyx were going to have to become a part of their strategy. They were the only ones who stood a chance in the water.

Although she knew Mason wasn't pleased with Kenneth's interference, Addison was more than happy to see some familiar faces. The crew of the *Sea Horse* had treated her with the utmost deference and respect, but she couldn't bring herself to ignore the undercurrents of fear born of curiosity emanating from the people around her.

She didn't agree with the stance her kind had taken against humans, but Addison understood Magaera's desire to see her people survive and thrive in a world they had been cut off from for close to two millennia.

It promised to be a long and bloody war, with neither side willing to make a compromise.

Magaera has to be deposed, she thought. But merely taking the virulent Mer queen down wasn't going to solve their problems. Her people would need a leader, someone strong enough to seize control and set the Mer on a new path toward peace with the humans that also inhabited—and controlled—more than ninety-nine percent of planet Earth.

It wouldn't be an easy path, but neither could it be avoided. Whether she liked it or not, she and her sisters had been born to inherit Queen Nyala's legacy. What their ancestor had begun those many centuries ago had now come full circle.

We've got to step up and take control.

Easier said than done.

Addison sighed and looked at her plate. More than half her food remained untouched. Although Gwen's signature roast beef sandwiches were usually one of her favorite meals, she just didn't have an appetite. Except for herself and Jovon, everyone else had dug into the food. Even Mason seemed to be enjoying himself. Away from the *Sea Horse*, he'd loosened up a little. And while he wasn't partaking of the alcohol Kenneth offered, he'd made himself welcome to the food.

She glanced toward Jovon. The Nyx had refused all offers of anything to eat or drink, explaining that human food had no taste or appeal to him. Since he lived and survived in the depths of the ocean, his diet consisted of seafood—raw fish.

The idea of living on a diet of sushi all the time curdled Addison's stomach, though she imagined that was what the Mer must have lived on before they began to adapt to human ways.

The differences between the Mer and Nyx were fascinating. Although he could come onto land, Jovon felt more comfortable in the water, his natural habitat. She, as a Mer raised on land, could go into the water, but did she really want to live there? No. Although she enjoyed being a Mer and embraced the advantages it gave her in the water, at the end of the day, she wanted to go home to a warm, and dry, apartment.

If Jovon were to be believed, however, there was a time when the Nyx also inhabited Ishaldi, which would have made them land-walkers as well. He'd mentioned the males were the craftsmen. Based on what Tessa had told her of the architecture she'd witnessed, both deep beneath the earth's surface in the ruins of the island and in the realm beyond the sea-gate, the Nyx must have designed and built the original structures.

Because of Ishaldi's proximity to Egypt and Greece, it seemed that the Mer had taken many of their influences from those early peoples. Or perhaps those early peoples had taken their influences from the Mer. Hapi was the Egyptian god of the Nile, just as Poseidon was a revered god of the sea. It was possible those early peoples had some interaction with the Mer, who, as shifters with psi-kinetic abilities, would certainly be able to present themselves as deities.

It was easy to understand Jake Massey's fascination with archaeology and the Mer. Tracking down and verifying the influences of the various human cultures on that of the Mer was enthralling work.

Hiding it was harder, and she wasn't going to do it anymore. *We have our place,* she decided. *Now we just have to reclaim it.*

She glanced toward Jovon. He'd removed himself from the group, taking refuge in a small atrium that offered an unobstructed view of the sea.

Setting aside her food, Addison slipped away from the group. No one would miss her. Right now everyone was deep in conversation, plotting a way for Mason to persuade his superiors to allow Kenneth to provide additional backup for the USET team. The fact that he'd brought Gwen along would probably add to the success. Having another Mer around wouldn't hurt. And although Blake was no longer an agent of the A51-ASD, he did have experience in dealing with the hostiles. Two of Magaera's former soldiers were still being held in confinement in the Virginia facility.

Jovon stood quietly, lost in his own thoughts. With his strange clothing and unique features, he definitely stood out among the humans. There was no way he could pass for one, even if he wanted to.

Addison stared at him, wondering what it would feel like if the Mer had retained their sea-born traits. She had to admit that she didn't find the Nyx unattractive. Taller than any man on the ship, he offered a commanding presence. His features, too, were well-defined. Intelligence burned behind his intense gaze. The hair streaming over his shoulders and down his back was iridescent, shimmering with soft blue-green highlights. His skin, too, had an odd luminescence.

"You find me strange to look at?" He didn't turn his head when he spoke.

Addison jumped in her place. She should have known he'd be able to sense her presence and pick up the vibrations radiating from her body. "Not strange," she said. "Just . . . different."

He turned to face her. "Yet there was a time when our females rejected us in favor of humans."

"I don't understand why. It seems to me the Mer would want to preserve the traits of our people rather than try and erase them." Self-conscious, she lifted her arm and traced her scale pattern. "I can't imagine not having these marks or not being able to shift."

He cocked his head. "Yet you have to admit you were embarrassed when you began to develop the traits, while the rest of the people around you did not."

She shrugged. "It was a little hard when puberty hit. All the other girls were getting their menstrual cycles and breasts." She laughed. "And we were getting scales and tails."

Jovon eyed her with appreciation. "Looks like you didn't exactly miss out," he said.

Addison wasn't sure how to respond to the remark, but a part of her preened at the compliment. Even from three feet away she could smell him, an alluring scent that reminded her of the wind ruffling the water of the ocean, clean and brisk. She was trying to keep her thoughts on the conversation at hand, and failing miserably.

"What about you?" she finally managed to ask. "Were you land-born to a human mother?"

"Actually, yes, I was. My mother was the daughter of a British soldier stationed in Jamaica in 1862. As you can imagine, it was quite a scandal in the family. She was, of course, disowned for her choice of taking a lover out of wedlock."

Her eyes widened. "Wait a minute—that would make you"—she did a quick mental calculation—"about a hundred and fifty years old."

A low chuckle escaped him. "You are correct. As you are aware, our people do have the ability to outlive humans by several centuries."

"So you were raised among humans?"

"Yes, in the proper English way." He held out his hands, showing her his own strangely tinted skin. "Until puberty, I was a very pale, very scrawny English boy. Then my body began to change, and I began to develop the traits of a Nyx male. There came a time when I could no longer fit in with the humans. Many people who saw me believed me to be diseased or some kind of strange oddity. My mother shielded me in the only way she knew how—by sending me back to the water."

"So you had no choice but to return to the sea?"

His knowing gaze met hers. "It was the only place to go. Had I stayed on land, I would have been a curiosity, a—"

Her stomach knotted. "Freak," she finished, saying the word for him.

Of all the words she'd ever heard in the world, Addison hated that one the most. Before she'd come to accept her Mer side, Gwen had often used the word to describe herself. Her greatest fear was to be identified as an aberration in a world that didn't easily accept such things.

She stared at him, unable to imagine having to leave her home because she didn't fit in. Little Mer Island had given them more than shelter. It was a private sanctuary from the outside world, a place where nothing could touch them. Although her mother had always warned her girls to keep their Mercraft under wraps, they'd never been ostracized by the locals for how they looked. But then again, it was easy enough to explain away a scale pattern. People often mistook the markings for an elaborate tattoo—which was perfectly acceptable among human beings.

"The Nyx have no place in this world, really," Jovon continued. "Our females rejected us, driving us from our homeland. And the humans can't accept us because we do not look or act as they do." She sensed that his calm demeanor merely masked an inner self deeply affected by a life that hadn't been easy. His experiences had made him hard, and more than a little bit bitter.

The sadness behind his words gnawed at her. *The Nyx may look different from us,* she mused, *but they are our people.*

"It must be hard, living in two worlds and belonging to neither."

He stared at her through unblinking eyes. "Now that the sea-gate is opened again, we would like a chance to return home," he said softly.

Because she couldn't bear to look at him, Addison lowered her eyes. "I wish I could make it happen for you."

Jovon stepped closer. His hand slid under her chin, tipping her head back.

Addison felt the contact like a blast of dynamite. He was so damn tall. The top of her head barely reached his shoulder. Her breath stalled as she became aware of the gentle rise and fall of his magnificent chest. Muscles rippled with every breath he took. His vivid silver eyes took in a lot more than they revealed.

"I think you can," he murmured in a low voice meant only for her ears.

A current of uneasiness went through her. "How?"

"By returning the Tesch dynasty to power. I truly believe you are the one to do it."

She grimaced. "I'm not so sure about that."

"You've seen the Mer soldiers in action. They are ruthless. Once Magaera begins sending them out into these waters, they will stop at nothing."

His words chilled her, but Addison didn't let herself react. "The humans aren't defenseless outside the dead zone," she said slowly. "They are well prepared to protect themselves."

Jovon cut her a hard look. "Do you not think I know that? Why send them to die when the slaughter can be stopped?" For the first time the layers of his anger thinned enough for her to see the raw pain beneath. His concern, she recognized, was very real. He wanted what was best for everyone.

She stepped back, realizing she needed to put a little distance between herself and the huge Nyx. The emanations coming off his powerful body were intense, slamming into her like rogue waves.

As she gazed into the electric silver of his eyes, something connected between them. The pang of his longing was so powerful that for a moment she couldn't catch her breath. The urge to comfort him pulled at her like a dangerous tide.

She hesitated for an interminable moment. He was waiting for an answer to a question that he had not quite posed but that was lurking there all along. It was one she hesitated to give because she knew it would change the entire course of her life. Once she said the words, there would be no turning back.

Addison felt heat rise in her core. Their gazes met, clashing together. There was no way she could refuse him. He was one of her own.

A strange ache came to life inside her. *He needs me. My people need me.*

"I'll help you any way I can."

One side of his mouth curved upward. He lifted a hand, gently cupping her face. "I knew you would not fail our people."

When he touched her, Addison felt her breath leave her lungs in one quick breath. The air between them shifted, thickened. The roar of the sea outside faded to a pleasant hum.

Addison knew where this moment was leading, but she couldn't seem to stop it. She wasn't sure she wanted to.

Jovon bent. His face was only a few short inches away from hers. He was so close, she could see the thrum of his pulse at his neck, rippling his gills. The long hair cascading around his shoulders shimmered like silk. He looked strong and incredibly handsome.

Addison felt protected by his massive girth. The sensation of his skin against her cheek was incredibly pleasurable. She started to shift away but couldn't make her limbs obey her internal commands. His scent rose to titillate her nostrils, filling her lungs. Her body stirred in response. She felt strange tremors of heat rising inside her. Anticipation burned through her. "I want . . . ," she started to say, but got no farther.

Jovon touched her lips with the tip of his finger to hush her. Something primal and possessive simmered in his gaze. "I am unmated," he murmured in a low voice.

A quiver of need clenched deep inside her. Her hands curled around his. The skin beneath her palms pulsed with warmth. "Are you saying you want to be with me?" She knew she was playing with fire. But his presence overpowered all logic. Electricity snapped between them.

He nodded. "I am."

Addison closed her eyes, trying to ignore the rapid beat of her heart and the slow ache building between her thighs. Even though she'd just met him, she couldn't deny that something powerful was brewing between them.

Only one question remained: *Am I crazy enough to say yes?*

She opened her eyes. His mesmerizing gaze held her suspended. "I'm not sure," she breathed.

Sensual energy poured off him in electric waves. "Then allow me to persuade you."

Addison felt the fine hairs at the nape of her neck prickle. Her brain raced to take control of her body, but it was no use. She was as immobilized as a fly wrapped in a spider web.

Her chest felt tight and for the moment she couldn't take a breath. She knew only that her heart was pounding, and she was floundering, unable to make a decision.

Every nerve in her body zinged with sensation as Jovon lowered his mouth to hers.

Chapter 21

Hands resting palms up on her knees, Queen Magaera sat cross-legged and naked. On each side of her, brass braziers were positioned, fashioned into the shape of octopuses. A variety of stones were piled in their depths, each chosen for the power and strength it provided.

Directly in front of her, three small statues of sea creatures were precisely arranged. Their outstretched tentacles provided the base for a circular pane of cut crystal with a silvered back, which faced Magaera. A fourth statue placed slightly to her left, that of the mythical Cracken, acted as a catchall for various pieces of jewelry. Tessa Lonike's soul-stone hung suspended from a delicate gold chain. It glowed softly, exuding a soft pink illumination.

Magaera's face appeared haggard in the reflective surface of the crystal, her skin stretched taut over her cheekbones, her lips colorless. It was completely at odds with the appearance she projected to others. But the reflection looking back at her was no deception. Underneath her beauty and her youth, lurked an aged crone. It was a cruel trick that she had to pull off every day. She constantly practiced the rites that kept her body intact and ageless through the ravages of the centuries.

Magaera cursed under her breath. By the goddess, why did she not know the use of Atargatis's scepter would come with such a great price?

She groaned, turning her head away and hiding her face in her hands. Every time she used it, the scepter sucked the energy right out of her.

This, the most powerful tool granted to them by the goddess, was to be used only in times of great need or distress. It was not a wand, to be waved at one's convenience. The imperative to use it wisely fell upon the ruling monarch. And if she did not, the scepter would punish her—dearly.

Frowning slightly, Magaera could not stay a shiver that coursed through her with unexpected force. A slight moan of despair broke from her lips—half gasp, half whimper. Her right hand flew up to her shoulder as if a lash had come down across her naked skin.

Was it courageous to go through with her plans, or was she being foolish? She quickly squashed the doubt. It was not that she wanted to proceed with her plans.

I must.

Recent events had revealed that the Mer were not the only sea-born shifters inhabiting these waters. Although she would have believed them to be extinct, her soldiers had encountered one of the only beings who could match them in the water, stroke for stroke.

The Nyx.

Like salmon going upriver to spawn, the exiles seemed to be once again trying to return to their homeland.

A shiver coursed up her spine, sending a slight, telltale trembling through her. It did not come from fear or cold; it came from hatred—hatred directed at the rogue queen who had single-handedly tried to destroy the Mer's domination in these waters. Queen Nyala had almost wrecked their entire civilization.

She alone must rebuild it. But now she had not one enemy to face, but two.

Extending her hand, Magaera reached for Tessa's soul-stone. Since claiming it, she'd been able to fool the sea-gate into believing she was Tessa by mimicking the young Mer's psychic resonance. It had also enabled her to pick up psychic vibrations sent out by Tessa's sisters in an attempt to contact their older sibling. Tessa's stone often flickered with surges of energy her sisters were attempting to feed her way to strengthen and reassure her that they were close.

Closing her eyes, Magaera rubbed Tessa's stone between her palms. Both her sisters were close—very close.

She concentrated, attempting to sort through the mass of psychic visions filtering through Tessa's stone.

Her chin dropped, then lifted in resolution. "Those girls could be the key to my damnation," she murmured. They were strong, and they were determined to reach their sister. They had help. The humans who presently kept her island quarantined from the rest of the world had weapons the Mer could not even begin to imagine . . .

Shaking her head, she frowned and raised her hand,

sending the hateful visions away. Control somewhat regained, her mind began to tick, methodically planning.

Nothing must be allowed to stand in the way of what she wanted.

She made a brief gesture, snapping her fingers. It was a signal. A silent figure glided out of the shadows.

"Jake?"

"Yes, my lady." Ever vigilant and sensitive to her wants and needs, her human consultant was ready to serve. Since revisiting Ishaldi, he walked as if on shells, treading carefully and doing nothing to offend her.

"The Nyx. Are they still in the water?"

He wiped a nervous hand across his forehead. "Yes. They remain outside the perimeters of the dead zone, guarding the ship Addison is aboard. According to the latest report, one of the Nyx has joined them on deck."

Magaera digested his reply. "The Nyx will seek an alliance with the humans, and with Nyala's descendants."

"Would peaceful relations with the humans and the Nyx be so unacceptable?" he asked. "The world has changed in so many ways since Nyala sealed the sea-gate."

She lifted a single brow. "Do you think that fact has escaped me?" she returned coldly. Although she could foresee some form of truce with the land-walkers, she didn't envision the Nyx in the bigger picture. Her people had worked long and hard to breed out the more undesirable traits of the sea-born. The gills and fins and webbed fingers were hideous.

As it stood, the Mer had evolved into the perfect species—intelligent, long-lived, and aesthetically pleasing in face and form. They were as close to godlike as beings of flesh and blood could be.

We must keep our bloodlines pure, she thought with concentrated bitterness.

To do so meant not only continuing to deny the Nyx access to their homeland, but also weeding out those humans who didn't meet the criteria for perfection.

She'd once found Jake Massey attractive. Now, not so much. Still, he had his uses . . .

"It is time for us to make our peace with the humans." Her voice tightened with command.

He smiled uncertainly. "Is that what you wish?"

Magaera nibbled her lip. He was afraid, as he should be. "Yes."

He seemed disappointed. "How shall we go about it?"

Magaera fingered Tessa's soul-stone. "We are going to offer a truce with the humans—but only if they turn over Addison and Gwen."

Jake Massey's gaze darkened. "They would never do that."

Magaera tapped the face of her crystal mirror. "They will, if we present them as enemies of the Mer. As descendants of Queen Nyala, they must pay for her treason against our people. In return for giving us the girls, we will offer to reconstruct the damper around the seagate and remove the obstacle that so cripples their instruments. It is then we can begin to negotiate how the Mer will fit into this world."

His eyes flickered with understanding. "And you will need an ambassador to arrange this."

She smiled to herself. Though she was outwardly calm, anxiety twitched inside her heart. She was nervous. She had to do this in a convincing way. It would be best not to arouse his suspicions. "Of course."

She was still in a vulnerable position. Several members of her council had yet to completely agree to an alliance with the humans. They were wary, watching her every move, analyzing her every word. If they withdrew their support, the Mer would be divided. Divided, her people would turn against themselves.

Lose them, she warned herself, *and they may seek to depose me.*

There was only one more thing she had to do.

She glanced toward the braziers loaded with crystals. Such energies were no longer sufficient to sustain her hungers. She needed a more vital source of nutrition, one that would ensure her continued use of the scepter just a little while longer.

Nothing mattered except her own selfish wants and needs. Insanity had made her temperament a strange and uncertain thing. She would do anything necessary to satisfy her desires. Lying, conniving, and murder were all within her realm of operation.

Allowing Tessa's soul-stone to slip through her fingers, she rose from the floor. Naked, she stood, stretching her arms. Jake smiled, eyeing her figure. "You are still a beautiful woman," he murmured.

"Do you think so?" Magaera's hands skimmed over her slender, perfect figure. Her body was in its prime, as she had rejected the needs of the physical body at an early age. Physically, she was merely twenty-two years of age, even though more than seven centuries had passed since her youth experienced its first bloom.

Jake gave a courtly, almost ritualistic bow. "Absolutely. It has always been my pleasure to serve you." Lust glinted in the depths of his blue eyes.

She gazed at him in silence through a long moment. She had other plans for Jake. As her lover and adviser, he'd served his purpose. He had something else she required—desperately.

And it was time to take it.

Magaera held out her hands in a welcoming gesture. "Come to me," she commanded, offering her most alluring smile.

Jake closed the distance between them. His hands eagerly circled her slender waist, drawing her into a crushing embrace. She could feel the hard ridge of him against her belly, shocking her senses and igniting the brief desire she'd held for him since when they were lovers. He had satisfied her.

But not enough to keep him.

Catching both his hands, she laced their fingers together palm to palm to form a contact point.

Jake grinned. "Oh, you want it a little rough today?"

Magaera tightened her grip, digging her fingernails deeper. "Oh, it will be rough on you," she purred, "but very fulfilling for me."

Jake betrayed his confusion and made to pull away.

Magaera held on. Forcing him back against the wall, she brought her knee up between his legs, crushing his balls against his body. She did it with such practice and dexterity that he didn't have a chance to resist. Her strength more than matched that of any human male.

"Your essence to mine," she murmured in a breathy voice. "Your youth to me, your life to me."

Bucking beneath her hold, Jake shook his head vehemently. "No! I don't deserve this. I've served you . . ."

She smiled. The sharp, sweet dizzying scent of his fear

burned her nostrils. He didn't have a chance against her, and he knew it. "And you have proven where your loyalties are, many times." Her voice had a knife's edge, sharp and cutting. "Unfortunately, I can no longer sustain myself through crystal energy alone. I need a more vital life force to keep up my strength."

Jake shook his head numbly. "I will get you other humans," he rushed. "As many as you like."

"Others like you will come," she replied softly. "There will always be humans to feed us. To breed with us. To serve us . . ."

Redoubling her grip, she closed her eyes and focused her concentration to make a psychic connection. As she groped, her own soul-stone, which was almost black from inner decay, began to flicker.

She psychically delved beneath his skin to attach herself to the spark of vitality within, which was the life force of every human. The connection was easy and instantaneous. She felt a spasm of panic closing his throat. He stiffened, every muscle going tight and rigid with agony. The screams that built in his lungs were never unleashed.

It was time to sacrifice her pawn. If Jake had seriously expected to play any part in the rebuilding of her regime in the human world, he was horribly wrong. She had no respect for a man who would turn on his friends to save his own ass. For a while, Jake had proven useful.

Now he could serve her, one last time.

The tension grew, throbbing between them. Beneath her grip, Jake's skin started to shrivel, aging at an incredible rate as she lapped away the energy from his body.

As a sponge takes in water, Magaera felt his vitality

pour into her veins, an almost visible pulsing of power that lit her skin from within. Seconds later her nerves exploded, sizzling as if on fire.

Beyond the point of reason, she kept her grip tight, refusing to let loose until Jake crumpled to the floor. One last fretful whimper fell past lips stretched taut in horror. His emaciated body twitched one last time, shriveled and lifeless.

Her feeding was complete.

Magaera's mouth twisted with disdain. The air around her felt strangely void and empty. It was the blackest of blasphemies for a Mer to use the D'ema, the death magic. It was little more than psychic vampirism, and forbidden to all. But she no longer had the power to know the difference between right and wrong.

There was only her way.

Filled and flooded with a sense of infinite strength, Magaera raised eyes that teemed with devious plans. But her throat tightened with an emotion long unfamiliar and unwelcome. She squashed it like an insect beneath her heel. She didn't regret her decision. She'd decided a course for the Mer people. Now she must make it happen.

"This will satisfy my need for the present." Casting a final look at Jake's withered corpse, she made a brief dismissive gesture. There was only one drawback to using the death magic to sustain her physical self.

Soon, she would need another.

Chapter 22

I'm not seeing this, Mason told himself as he walked into the atrium to find Addison. The sight of her locked in an embrace with the tall Nyx felt like a punch to the gut. Fury and desire and a thousand other emotions suddenly poured through him with every beat of his heart. *No. How could she be with him?*

The ship shifted a little beneath his feet. For an instant he considered turning around and walking away, pretending that he'd seen nothing. Instead, he held his ground.

He cleared his throat. "Sorry to interrupt," he said, fighting to keep his tone even and neutral, "but we should return to the *Sea Horse.*"

As if caught in the middle of doing something illegal, Addison pulled out of Jovon's embrace. She turned. Her mouth was moist and bruised with kisses.

She blinked as if his presence surprised her. "Sorry," she murmured, swiping at her mouth as if to conceal the evidence. A flush of embarrassment colored her cheeks.

Mason shrugged, fighting to project nonchalance. "No big deal." He eyed the Nyx, consciously sizing up his competition. "Looks like you two found plenty to talk about."

Jovon, not the slightest bit embarrassed, inclined his head. "Indeed, we did." He lifted one massive hand to Addison's shoulder and gave it a reassuring squeeze. "In case you are wondering, I have asked Addison if she would consider an alliance between the Mer and the Nyx by becoming my breed-mate."

Barely aware that his heart was pounding hard against his ribs, Mason wasn't sure he'd heard correctly. "I'm sorry—I didn't catch what you said." Inside, he refused to acknowledge he was upset.

Addison folded her arms across her chest, her movements uncomfortable and self-conscious. "Jovon has asked me to consider becoming his wife."

"Is that so?" Mason countered, surprised by the tightness of his voice. His heart continued to thud against his rib cage, driven by a hot burst of emotion.

"He believes we'd have a better chance of deposing Magaera if our people reunite," she explained, avoiding his eye.

Her words hit like a punch in the stomach. "I see." Mason stared at her through narrow eyes as resentment and jealousy melded into a single ugly emotion. He wanted to lash out at her. Make her feel his hurt.

Addison stepped back as though physically struck. "I haven't decided anything yet," she added in a rush.

Mason barely spared her a glance, focusing his gaze on Jovon. *The rat bastard,* he inwardly raged. *He has no right to her.*

Clearly sensing his spiteful thoughts, Jovon let his hand drop from Addison's shoulder. "I will let you think it over. Perhaps now would be a good time for us to say good night," he suggested. "I will return to my people."

Addison glanced at him. "Will you be nearby?"

Jovon reached for her hand, pressing it briefly to his lips. "Of course, my lady. You can rest assured the Mer will not get near your ships."

As he struggled to tamp his anger down, Mason's brows rose. *My lady?* What kind of bullshit was this? Treating Addison as if she were some kind of princess . . .

He swallowed thickly. But she was royalty. Jovon was treating her with the deference and respect rightfully hers in their hierarchy.

Bidding them both good night, Jovon strode past him with all the reassurance of the male who'd marked his territory.

Mason forced himself to slow down and think. Sorting through his emotions wasn't a pleasant task, but it was a necessary one nevertheless.

They'd shared an attraction and had made love, but that was all. He'd cut her short after the Mer had attacked. After all, what kind of future did a mermaid and a man married to his job have together?

At least that was what he'd believed until he saw Addison in the arms of another man. The idea that she might accept Jovon's proposal sent him over the edge with jealousy.

He briefly closed his eyes, refusing to acknowledge he was upset. He was a big boy. He'd slept with women before, knowing full well that another man would slip in between the sheets once he left port. That came with the territory of being a man with no real place to call home. The sea was his calling, and he'd always given it preference over the women who drifted in and out of his life.

But he didn't want to repeat this pattern with Addison.

Mason clasped his hands behind his back. "Looks as though you two are getting along well," he said coldly. Jovon had stopped to speak to the others in the adjoining room, which irritated him to no end. Despite his odd looks and manner of dress, the Nyx was polite and well-spoken to the nth degree.

Addison seemed to pick up on his mood immediately. "Why do you care, Captain McKenzie?" she said evenly.

"I don't," Mason said, trying to remove the edge from his voice but failing. "I just marvel at your ability to have sex with one man and then move on to another, just like that."

Addison folded her arms across her chest. "You're one to talk. Seemed to me you were just trying things on for size. After Magaera's soldiers attacked, you didn't exactly seem interested." Her tone was laced with a tinge of bitterness.

"It wasn't like that at all," Mason said tightly.

"What was it, then?" she demanded. "I thought we had something there. You know, that little spark that says this is the one for me."

Her words caught him short. Guilt punched through him. That spark? Yeah. It was there. He'd felt it, too.

And then he'd told himself that it wasn't the real thing; that love at first sight was often a hormonal attraction otherwise known as lust; that men such as he didn't commit.

But it suddenly occurred to Mason that having no

place to call home didn't mean he was independent. It meant he was alone—always alone.

And he hated it.

Now that he'd met a woman he could possibly commit to, everything about their getting together was totally messed up.

He stared at her for an interminable minute, secretly loving her to pieces even as he wished he'd never laid eyes on her. "It's there," he said slowly. "But it's nothing we can take advantage of. We both belong to different worlds, and we have different responsibilities to fulfill."

It was the sensible, sane, and logical thing to say. With the mission foremost in his mind, he couldn't let his personal feelings get in the way. Whether he liked it or not, he'd have to let Addison make her own decisions. If she wanted to mate with Jovon in order to unite their people, then that was her prerogative.

He didn't like the idea, but he'd accept it.

Addison's gaze darkened. "I see. It's always duty first with you."

Mason wasn't sure how he found the strength to nod, but he did. "I've got twelve years in the navy," he said. "I can't be like Whittaker and risk everything for what I think my heart wants."

Tears shimmered in her eyes. She blinked hard. "I guess that makes sense." Her voice was little more than a whisper.

I love you, he thought. *But I can't have you.*

Addison offered a tremulous smile. "I feel the same way." She shook her head sadly. "If it's any consolation, I wish things had been different; that we could have met under other circumstances."

Because he didn't want to break down in front of her, Mason turned away and started walking. He had to get back to the *Sea Horse*, to a familiar environment where the rules made sense. He forced his limbs to move, bidding his host good-bye stiffly before boarding the skiff that would take him away from Addison.

He was barely aware that he'd left her behind. He couldn't even begin to wonder how they'd come to this point. He hadn't meant for anything to happen between them. It just had. But with every action came a consequence. For now it was better that they spend some time apart.

Tomorrow they could go on pretending nothing had happened.

Thick clouds lumbered overhead, and the night sky glowed eerily. Gusts rocked the smaller vessel, and a spray of cold salty water drenched him.

"Looks as though we're getting the tail end of the storm," one of the seamen called over the lashing wind.

Tightening his hold, Mason nodded. "Steady on. We've seen worse than this." A sudden hard gust snatched his words away and carried them off.

Retreating back into silence, he marveled at the eerie beauty of the Mediterranean Sea. There were times when it seemed to resent man's arrogance in assuming they could conquer its depths. Tonight was definitely one of those times when he'd have preferred to be on dry land. Singapore. Yeah. That would be all right— trolling one of those shady little out-of-the-way bars where the drinks were cheap and the women were beautiful.

Trying to distract himself from thinking about Addison wasn't working. No matter how hard he tried pushing her out of his mind, the memories of that stubborn little mermaid refused to budge. She was the best thing that had ever come into his life. He admired her courage and tenacity, her loyalty to family, and her determination to do the right thing, even if others didn't always agree with what she had in mind.

She'd opened up a whole new world to his eyes, showing him all the wonders of the sea in an entirely new way.

An inner voice deep inside niggled at him. *You, my man, are a fool,* it said. He'd mapped out a course for his career, but he'd forgotten to allow for the one vital element that made any man's life worth living—having someone special to share it with.

It suddenly occurred to him that he'd viewed his parents' marriage in the wrong way. He'd always assumed his mother was weak because she'd continually deferred to his father's wishes. Looking back as an adult, he realized she'd been strong in so many other ways; she had been a quiet feminine presence in a house full of domineering males. Where his father had been a rough-and-tumble man who demanded his sons toe the line, she'd been there to soothe their anguish, bandage their wounds, and offer gentle words of encouragement that turned defeat into victory.

Hindsight, as it was always said, was twenty-twenty. It was as if he'd been walking around half blind. Seeing Jovon with Addison had opened his eyes. The image of him touching her went all over him like a bad rash. The thought of her being with another man was unacceptable.

At that moment he made up his mind. The next time he saw Addison, he was going to throw all his hesitations to the wind and tell her how he really felt. And then he was going to spend every day after that making up to her for being a jerk. Somehow they'd find a way to work through their differences. *If you want it bad enough,* he reminded himself, *you can make it happen.*

He wondered what Jovon would think of that.

But he never had a chance to consider the answer.

Just as Mason was about to climb aboard the *Sea Horse*, all conscious thoughts vanished in a detonation of multicolored lights . . .

Addison stared in Mason's wake. Watching him walk away was the hardest thing she'd ever done; yet she didn't have the courage to speak up to tell him how she felt.

A single tear streaked down her cheek. She quickly wiped it away, refusing to acknowledge the ache deep inside her soul.

"Correct me if I'm wrong," Gwen said from behind, "but that sure looked like a lover's quarrel."

Feeling lost, confused, and utterly lovesick, Addison quickly shook her head. "You heard wrong. We're not lovers."

Folding her arms across her chest, Gwen frowned. "If there's one person you can't lie to, Addled Brain, it's me. The vibes are all over you." She narrowed her eyes. "You slept with Captain McKenzie, didn't you?"

The sound of her childhood nickname jerked Addison's head up. "Slept with? No. Had hot sex with . . . ? Yeah, that kind of accidentally happened."

Her older sister's jaw dropped. "How do you accidentally happen to have sex with a man?"

Confused, Addison turned and paced to the opposite side of the atrium. Her heart thudded against her rib cage. Regret stormed through her. Even though she wouldn't admit it out loud, she'd liked Mason on sight. Tall, blond, tanned, he was obviously a man of the sea. If ever a perfect match was brewing, she was sure this was it. But her attraction to him went beyond the physical. McKenzie was a man who valued the same things she did: dedication, honesty, and the integrity that came with serving a greater purpose, even if it meant putting aside one's own selfish needs.

She frowned. *Except I can't have him.*

Mason had made it clear he was a career officer, wedded to the US Navy first. He had no inclination to be anchored to a woman, even if she had ten times his skills in the water and a tail to boot.

Addison threw up her arms in frustration. "You know how it is, when you just meet a man. Suddenly the sparks fly and your clothes fly and you're just having wild monkey sex."

Gwen's brows flew halfway up her forehead. "No," she said, shaking her head, "I really don't know how that goes. I've only ever been with one man, and Blake's the only one I'll ever be with."

Addison pulled in a breath. "Prude," she muttered under her breath.

Gwen shook her head. "Waiting to have sex doesn't make me a prude," she said. "It makes me careful and responsible. I'm not like you and Tessa, you know. Flashing your tail in front of every man who gives you a wink and a tingle in a certain place isn't the way to find your mate."

Addison barely spared her older sister a glance. "How you kept your legs welded together for twenty-seven years, I'll never know. Haven't you ever heard the old saying? That you have to kiss a lot of frogs to find your prince? At least Tessa and I have lived a little."

"You've both kissed a lot of frogs, too. As for Prince Charming, it looks like he just turned on his heel and walked out on you."

Addison felt her words like a red-hot poker being shoved straight through her heart. The agony was intense, as if her life's blood flowed from a wound that would never heal. "We had agreed it was just a one-time thing, you know. An itch to be scratched."

Gwen made a face. "Sounds like poison ivy."

Addison offered a weak smile. "It felt right, though. When we were together, it seemed as if we just fit together in all the right ways. I'm not a stupid little virgin—"

"I'd rethink those words," Gwen broke in drily.

Addison rolled her eyes. "I'm aware you think I've been a little generous with my affection, but I know the difference between just sex and something else . . ."

"And it's something else with McKenzie, isn't it?" Gwen asked quietly.

Feeling like a miserable fool, Addison felt the sting of tears all over again. "Yeah." Her head dropped. "I think so."

Gwen crossed to her, throwing an arm around her shoulder and pulling her close. "What about him? Does he feel the same way?"

Closing her eyes against the barrage of emotions trampling through her, Addison leaned her head on her sister's shoulder. Even though she and her sisters often picked at each other and squabbled unmercifully, when push came to shove, they'd always stuck together. That was the way it had always been, even before their parents had died. If you messed with one Lonike girl, you messed with them all.

"He says he doesn't," she admitted, "but the vibes I picked up when he saw me with Jovon said something else."

Gwen pulled back. "You were with Jovon?"

"It was nothing," she hastened to add. "We were talking, and he, uh, he kissed me."

Gwen took her arms and gave her a shake. "What the hell were you doing locking lips with Jovon? You just met him a few hours ago, and he put the moves on you?"

For several long seconds, Addison stood, breathing hard. Her mind was muddled, as if she'd pulled off her head and tossed it into the dryer. All her thoughts tumbled wildly, oddly incoherent.

"I don't know why I was kissing him," she said, crestfallen. "We were talking, and then one thing led to another. The Nyx are our natural mates, and they want to be able to return to Ishaldi. Jovon had just asked me if I would consider being his breed-mate when Mason walked in."

Gwen let her hands drop. "Oh, little girl," she lamented, shaking her head, "you certainly do have a talent for putting your feet in deep piles of shit. First, you sleep with Captain McKenzie, who, I should add, is in no position to be sleeping with you if he's any kind of an officer. Then, when that doesn't work out, you trot off into the arms of the next male who happens to find you attractive."

Addison's palm connected with her forehead. "By the goddess, I've really made a mess of things."

Gwen shot her a disgusted look. "Yes, you have. If McKenzie happened to have any feelings for you, you probably strangled them right then and there. All he probably saw was a tramp who couldn't keep her legs closed and her panties up."

Back to the wall, Addison slid to the floor. She drew up her legs, resting her chin on her knees. "I'm not really sure what happened with Jovon," she admitted. "I mean, yeah, I think I find him mildly attractive, and maybe it wouldn't be a bad idea for the Mer and the Nyx to get back together."

Gwen sat down beside her. "And did you happen to forget what Jovon mentioned?"

Addison shook her head. Right now she wouldn't recall being run over by a truck, even if it had reversed and backed over her twice. Jovon, Mason, the alcohol she'd consumed, her emotions . . . Everything was one big muddled mess. "I don't remember."

"Apparently you weren't listening when Jovon mentioned that the Nyx exude a pheromone to help calm their females. I'm going to assume that pheromone also puts a Mer in the mood for love."

Addison stared back. "You mean that bastard put the moves on me?"

Gwen clicked her tongue. "Appears so. As a Mer, you know we're susceptible to those kinds of things."

Addison lifted a hand, fanning herself. *Somehow I*

have the magic touch, she thought. *Taking a good thing and screwing it up.* On one hand, she wanted Mason. But he'd made it clear less than ten minutes ago that he wasn't interested. On the other hand, Jovon had indicated he would be more than happy to have her as his mate.

Except what she'd felt for the Nyx was somewhat dishonestly produced, seeing as he'd whammied her senses with some Nyx love potion. In contrast, she had no doubt about what she'd felt when she was with Mason.

That was real—very real.

Hands down, there was no contest.

Mason would win every time.

Regret tugged at her. The trouble was, Mason McKenzie had made it perfectly clear that he wasn't in the running. He'd bowed out.

Gwen laid a hand on her arm. "It isn't as bad as it seems, kiddo. As the humans always say, it's better to have loved and lost . . ."

Addison stared at her older sister for an interminable minute. "Oh, spare me the bullshit." She snorted. "I've been dumped before. It isn't the first time a guy's sent me packing."

Gwen forced a laugh. "What can I say? You're just too damn much Mer for one man to handle."

Addison nodded a little overenthusiastically. "That's right. It's not as if I don't have options, you know. I'm young, and a Mer's life is long."

Gwen gave her a reassuring squeeze. "Don't be in such a hurry. The right man will come along. And you'll know when he does."

Addison knew it was a stupid moment, but she

couldn't help but smile back. "Meanwhile, I guess I kiss more frogs."

Gwen laughed. "Right."

She reached up, smoothing her hands across her burning face. Damn, it felt as if she'd been put through the wringer and squeezed dry. She must look a fright, too, with her red-rimmed eyes and snotty nose.

"Do you think Kenneth would mind if I stayed here for the night?" She really didn't want to go back to the *Sea Horse*. Even though she had a private cabin, it was Mason's space. No matter how impersonal he'd tried to make it during her occupation, the entire room had his scent stamped all over it.

"You know Kenneth. He would love it if we were all next-door neighbors and raised our kids together."

Addison let out a long breath. "Yeah, he does seem to be a family kind of guy. I've never seen a man so thrilled his wife was pregnant. By the way he talks, you'd think he was the first man on Earth to have babies."

Gwen leaned back. She was about to say something that was probably profound and thought provoking, but she never got a chance to speak.

Blake sped in. "We've got trouble."

Chapter 23

Both sisters were on their feet in a flash. "What happened?" The words tumbled out of their mouths in unison.

"Jovon and several of the Nyx have been wounded, badly. And it looks as though McKenzie's gone. We need help, now!" Blake grabbed his fiancée and pulled her after him. "It's a bloodbath."

Addison's blood turned to icy chips in her veins. "Gone where?" Pressing her body into motion, she sped after Blake.

"Gone. Just gone!" He tossed the words over one shoulder without looking back. "It looks bad."

They reached the deck in time to see two of Kenneth's crewmen dragging an inert form out of the water. They carefully laid one of the Nyx out. No one had to look twice to see the creature was dead, slashed to pieces.

Gwen's hands flew to cover her eyes. "By the goddess . . ."

Addison gave her a quick shake. "Get it together," she barked. "These are Nyx. They're going to need a Mer healer."

Hands dropping, Gwen nodded. Her fear drained away as purpose reinserted itself. Pale but controlled, she started giving orders for the treatment of the Nyx.

"Good girl. Don't think; just do." Heart stalling, Addison frantically looked around. Relief drizzled through her when she saw that Jovon lay nearby. Kenneth knelt over him, applying pressure to his side. A gush of crimson seeped between his fingers.

Addison headed over. "Let me," she ordered. Wiping away all emotion, she fell back on her training. *Render aid, don't think about the victim. Just concentrate on saving his life.* The terror ripping through her was temporarily forgotten.

Kenneth moved aside, allowing her all access. "Be my guest."

"Get me some light," she ordered. "I can't see a damn thing." The entire deck was chaos, but she refused to let herself be distracted. *Cold and impersonal,* she reminded herself.

Kenneth commandeered a flashlight from a passing crewman. He angled the illumination over Jovon's writhing body. "It is bad," the Nyx gritted, struggling to remain conscious. He lay there, a ragged, soaking wet mess. There was a long slice down one of his forearms—a defense wound—and another in his side. He was in danger of going into shock from blood loss.

"Give me your shirt," she ordered Kenneth. "I need to make a tourniquet."

Kenneth complied, handing over the garment. "What else do you need?"

Addison grabbed his hand. "Pressure here, against his side." Ripping the shirt into shreds, she quickly bound Jovon's forearm. By the look of things, he'd need stitches—a lot of them.

The Nyx fought the hands pressing him down. "The Mer soldiers ambushed us," he grated angrily. "They came out of nowhere. We never saw them coming."

"Don't think about it," Addison ordered automatically. "You've got a sick bay on this ship, right?" she asked Kenneth.

He nodded. "Yeah, we've got a medic. Whittaker insisted he wasn't going near the water without one."

Addison placed a hand on Jovon's shoulder. "We've got to get you into sick bay," she said. "Try and relax."

Eyes glazing over, Jovon tried to push her hands aside. "I promised my men would defend you." A groan broke from his lips. His voice was hardly stronger as he added, "I just need a little time to heal."

"You won't help yourself by being a stubborn ass," Kenneth broke in.

Closing her fingers around one of Jovon's hands, Addison caught and interpreted the Nyx's vibes. He had no trust of human doctors or their methods. That made sense, as a human physician wouldn't know jack about Nyx anatomy. "Let me get you into sick bay. I'm a crystal healer," she said to reassure him.

Jovon resisted her attempt to soothe his fear. "They took the human captain." His eyes, dulled with pain and sorrow, dropped shut. "They capsized his boat and pulled him into the water."

Addison's eyes flew to the *Sea Horse*. Jovon must be referring to the skiff they'd been taking between the two boats. "What about the rest of the men?"

"They are all unharmed. Magaera's soldiers wanted only one man."

His words unleashed a strange ache inside Addison—an ache so strong and gnawing, she almost lost her concentration. She tightened her clasp a little. "Don't think about that now," she managed in a strange rasp. The thought of Mason in the hands of the rebel Mer sickened and frightened her. She'd witnessed Queen Magaera's soldiers in action before and knew them to be utterly ruthless in their methods.

Recollecting himself, Jovon closed weak fingers around hers. "Get me back on my feet, and I swear I will make right this terrible wrong."

Addison was one step ahead of him. If Magaera and her ilk harmed Mason in any way, she would defy Atargatis herself to make sure they paid—and dearly.

"I'll do the best I can."

Motioning to Kenneth, she snagged a passing crewman. "Help us get him to sick bay."

The man nodded, hefting the Nyx's massive weight off the deck. Somehow the three of them managed to get him below. They had to settle on the floor since the other beds were occupied by the wounded. Those remaining from McKenzie's escort on the skiff looked dazed.

Gwen and the medic were already tied up with another of Jovon's warriors. By the look of things, he'd taken a cut in an awkward spot that was hard to bandage. Gwen's face was tight with concentration, and the stone in her hand glowed with healing light.

Addison dropped to her knees beside Jovon. *We're spending way too much time tending the wounded,* came her frazzled thought. For the second time in a single day Magaera's soldiers had struck a devastating blow.

Jovon was slipping in and out of consciousness.

Kenneth glanced at the blood oozing between his fingers. He'd been trying to keep the pressure on Jovon's side firm, but it was a losing battle. "It's bad," he said. "I don't think I'm doing one damn bit of good." His gaze connected with hers. "Can you do anything?"

"Oh goddess," Addison muttered. She didn't really have the skill or strength for a second go-round. Just tending to Mason's burns earlier in the day had drained her dry, and his healing hadn't been easy. "I don't know."

"Try anyway," Kenneth urged. "He'll die in a few minutes if you can't stop the bleeding."

As if she didn't know that.

Addison fumbled with numb fingers for the soulstone around her neck. *"Gwen,"* she psychically called out, trying desperately to make a connection with her sister. *"I need help."*

Gwen didn't even look up from what she was doing. *"Tell me what you've got,"* she replied wordlessly.

"Deep slashes. One can't be staunched with stitches and packing. It has to be closed or Jovon will bleed to death."

Across the room, Gwen's brow tightened with concentration. *"Hang tight,"* came the quick reply. *"I'm sending Goldstone and hematite your way. One's a heal-*

ing stone, and the other harmonizes mind and body, sending negative energy away."

Seconds later, two small stones, one rusty red and the other slate gray, materialized in the palm of her hand. Both were smooth and felt cool against her palm.

Addison fisted her hand around the stones. *"Got 'em,"* she said, then let the psi-connection close.

"It always amazes me the way you girls do that," Kenneth commented.

Addison shook her head to clear her mind. "It ain't easy being Mer, Ken. Believe me. But it can be handy sometimes."

She stared into the stones, concentrating on delving within their essences and sucking out the vital energy crackling inside their stone hearts. The crystal around her neck began to glow softly as she made the connection and began to draw out the energy.

Heat fused with light thrummed through her veins, delivering a much-needed burst of strength, like a shot of adrenaline straight to every nerve ending. She inwardly prepared to turn the energy around and remanifest it outside her physical self.

Slowly, she focused her heightened psychic awareness on Jovon's grievous wound. Placing her hand palm down on his torn skin, she began to delve into the molecular level of his body, then beyond. She could feel the pulsing of his blood and the struggling beat of his heart.

Careful, she warned herself. *Don't go too deep.*

For an instant her mind merged with Jovon's, and she could tell that his life was unbearably close to draining away. His fear eddied up as he fought the darkness threatening to embrace him. She felt a mixture of embarrassment at witnessing his most private thoughts, as well as a deep, heartfelt agony for his pain.

Addison concentrated on the blood vessels severed by a sharp and unforgiving blade. With just the lightest touch of her mind, she applied her telekinetic psi-force and slowly began repairing the damages. All sounds around her became a dull hum in her ears, and her vision slowly began to tunnel in, fading to a single bright pinprick of light as she sucked the energy from the stones and reapplied it to Jovon's wounds. Pure energy poured from her body into his ...

A touch on her shoulder brought her back to consciousness. "It's working," she heard Kenneth saying. "The bleeding's stopped."

With a long sigh, Addison felt herself go dead limp inside. The stones rolled from her weak grip, scattering into nothing but ashes as they struck the floor. She'd drained out every last bit, sucking them dry. Under normal circumstances, it would have taken centuries of erosion to have ground them down to little more than dust.

She nodded, exhausted. It took her a minute to gather her blasted senses and refocus her eyes. Funny, but she couldn't seem to feel her hands, even though she knew they were there and probing Jovon's wound.

Examining her handiwork, Addison could see that stitches would still be needed. She'd managed to repair the worst of the damages, though, and he'd suffer no internal trauma. Another few inches and the blade would have taken his bowels out of his abdomen. Good thing that Nyx anatomy was a little bit different from that of humans.

Jovon muttered groggily, "I felt you inside me."

She forced herself to take a head-clearing breath. "You'll be all right," she muttered, more to herself than for his benefit. "Just hang in there." Letting her mind slip into autopilot, she rapped out a few orders, requesting the implements she'd need for more traditional first aid.

Someone—she wasn't sure who—shoved a needle in her hand.

Addison grimaced. Sewing up flesh wounds was always a messy business, and one she tried to get out of. There was no shirking it this time. She knew she could have asked Gwen to send more stones, but she just didn't have the energy in her to go for another round of healing. She'd have to make do with what she could do by hand.

Through the next few hours, she had not a breath to spare or even a thought of what might have happened to Mason. Once Jovon was taken care of, she turned her attention to the others who had been wounded. All in all, ten of the Nyx were patched up. Their casualties, too, were great. Five had perished, hacked up to pieces to feed the sharks.

It was gruesome, bloody, and one of the greatest acts of aggression Queen Magaera had struck against them.

This means war. It was a grim thought.

For a long time, Mason's sleep was like that of a dead man—without dreams, a total blotting out of mind and will.

When he finally began to struggle back to consciousness, he was dimly aware that his clothes were wet and clung uncomfortably to his body. Although he couldn't be sure, it felt as though there was stone beneath his body, cold and hard and uncomfortable.

Half in a feverish daze, he rolled over on one side and drew his limbs into a tight ball. He would do anything to warm the terrible chill that had settled in his bones. All he had to do was go back to sleep. That would end it all.

Something shook him. "Wake up," an unfamiliar female voice pleaded. "Please, wake up."

Mason shook his head. The voice was like an echo inside his skull. "No," he moaned. "Leave me alone."

A strong hand rolled him onto his back. A palm connected with his cheek. "Get up," the mystery woman demanded in a firmer tone.

Regretfully bracing himself against the chill and discomfort wracking his body, Mason opened his eyes. At first his vision was blurred, and all he saw was an indistinct shape.

A gasp broke from his lips. *Addison?* He wondered vaguely and silently to himself whether it was.

The woman reluctantly smiled and shook her head. "You're okay," she said to reassure him.

Mason didn't feel okay. He blinked hard, and things slowly came back into focus. Wow. The Lonike sisters looked so much alike that it was almost impossible to tell them apart at a glance.

"You must be Tessa, the sister I haven't met yet."

Tessa nodded, visibly surprised that he knew her name.

Mason struggled to push himself up. The best he could manage was a semisitting position. As he'd suspected, he lay on a bare stone floor. A wad of some filmy material had been shoved under his head to ease his uncomfortable rest, and his boots and socks had been removed. The rest of his clothing remained intact, if somewhat soggy.

Memories of the recent past simmered in the back of his mind. He sorted through the images in an attempt to recall what had happened. He remembered being on Kenneth Randall's ship, talking to Addison, and then making a return to his own vessel. He was just about to board the *Sea Horse* when some dark form sailed up out of the water, flipping his boat and sending him headfirst into the sea. Grasping hands had closed around his wrists and ankles, dragging him deep, even as a rush of icy salt water poured down this throat and into his lungs.

He pressed a hand to his forehead. His skin burned beneath his palm. "Where am I?"

Tessa Randall settled back on her knees. "You are a guest of Queen Magaera." She cast a glance around the dim, shadowy chamber. "And this is the cell where she keeps her prisoners."

Mason grimaced. "Looks like a lovely place to be," he commented drily.

Tessa snorted. "Oh, of course. I've enjoyed every day I've spent here. Best vacation I've ever had, hands down."

His hand dropped. By the look of things, Tessa hadn't had an easy time in captivity. Her white cotton shirt was dirty from too many days of wear, and her faded blue jeans were torn in a way that wasn't intended to be a fashion statement. A pair of tennis shoes and a thin jacket completed her shabby outfit. Her long hair was a tangle. She'd attempted to braid her tresses, but all she'd gotten was a mass of knots. But aside from the dark circles ringing her eyes and the pale cast of her skin, she looked healthy enough.

"At least you're still alive." That fact gave Mason some hope for his own well-being. If Magaera's soldiers had wanted him dead, they could have easily drowned him. No, he'd been spared for a reason. The Mer obviously wanted him to keep breathing. What for, he had yet to find out.

"Barely. I was beginning to wonder if the outside world existed anymore. I don't know who you are or what you did to get here, but I hope you're one of the good guys."

Mason grimaced and shifted uncomfortably. Damn, he hated clingy wet underwear. If he'd been alone, he'd have stripped off to the buff. To spare her the sight of his naked body, he'd grin and bear the discomfort. "Captain Mason McKenzie," he said. "My team and I are exploring the magnetic interference caused by the exposure of the sea-gate."

Tessa winced. "My fault," she admitted. "I'm the one who blew the temple apart and exposed it to open water."

His brows rose. "Must have been one hell of an explosion."

"I was trying to destroy it, to keep Magaera from regaining control," she explained. "I don't think I did a very good job."

He nodded. *No shit.* But he wasn't about to give her a hard time. "I've actually been working with your sisters."

Tessa's face brightened. "I keep thinking I feel Gwen and Addison nearby. And my husband, Kenneth . . ." Biting her lip, she glanced down at her hands. "Can you tell me, please, if Ken's all right? I was afraid he was"—she choked, but quickly recovered her composure—"that he was hurt when Magaera attacked us."

"Actually, he's fine." Mason didn't feel there was any

reason to tell the woman her husband had been critically wounded in Magaera's attack. Thanks to Gwen Lonike's healing, he was back on his feet and stronger than ever. He was a stubborn bastard, too.

"Oh, praise the goddess," she murmured under her breath.

"He's here, anchored off the perimeters of the dead zone. Your sister Gwen is with him."

"And Addison? Is she here, too?"

Mason nodded. "Yes." As they talked, he couldn't help but notice the striking resemblance of the three sisters. They looked so much alike, they could almost be triplets. Tessa was a beauty, even in torn clothing and a face smudged with grime. Those emerald green eyes could pull a man in and steal his heart. He knew that to be a fact. He'd lost his own heart, and he was still reeling from the shock of realizing he was in love with Addison.

"All this time I've been thinking the connection I felt to them was the illusion of a desperate mind." She tapped her forehead with her index finger. "I've been driving myself insane, wondering what's been going on. All these quiet hours are driving me stir-crazy, you know?"

Mason nodded again. He couldn't even begin to imagine what it would feel like to be locked away, alone, with no information coming in from the outside world. Such solitary confinement wasn't only brutal; it almost bordered on torture.

"Your instincts haven't led you astray," he said. "Addison has been working with the USET team, and your husband and Gwen arrived just a few days ago."

Tessa's eyes widened. "Kenneth's put the *DreamFever* back into the water?"

"He has." He frowned. "And he even managed to get it past navy patrol ships. These waters have been declared off-limits until we figure out what's going on with the Mer."

She rolled her eyes. "What's going on with the Mer is just a whole lot of trouble. I rue the day we rediscovered Ishaldi. What was at the bottom of the sea should have stayed there, for good."

Mason would have been inclined to wholeheartedly agree, except that he never would have met Addison and been introduced to the wonders of a mermaid and her magical kiss. The hair at the nape of his neck prickled. *You have to take the pain with the pleasure,* he reminded himself.

A crackle of lightning followed by the roll of heavy thunder warned that the storm wasn't finished for the night. He dimly recognized the sound of rain pattering against the stone above their heads. At least the roof seemed secure.

Tessa turned her gaze toward the ceiling. "Looks as though we've got a long night ahead."

Mason winced. That might present a problem. Feeling a full sensation in his bladder, he looked around. A chill lingered around the edges of the walls, and save for the meager illumination by something that vaguely resembled lamps, there was no other light. The cell was small, dark, and cramped, but it was clean. Primitive didn't even begin to describe their conditions. He saw a cot, some filmy-looking blankets, and a few washbowls that looked to be fashioned out of clay. A couple of basins carved into the base of one wall brimmed with water.

It was a brutal way to have to survive, and he hoped his incarceration wouldn't be a lengthy one. *Stay here more than a day and I'll go over the edge,* he thought.

Tessa recognized his distress. "The facilities aren't the best, but they're workable. You have to remember the Mer civilization is still kind of stunted. They're still working with Greek- and Roman-style plumbing."

"Guess I'll have to make do," he muttered. "When in Rome, do as the Romans do."

She glanced toward the entrance. "You get one meal a day here, mostly fruit and fish." She stuck out her tongue and made a gagging motion. "It's definitely not the finest dining experience."

"If it's food, I guess I'll be glad to have it." Since there wasn't anything to do but sit and wait, he stretched out his legs and leaned back against the wall. That helped ease some of the cramps in his legs. He had no idea how long he'd been unconscious, but, judging by the dampness of his clothes, it had not been more than an hour, maybe two.

Tessa settled into a more comfortable position on the hard floor. Her clothes were more than a little loose. "The fish is usually raw. It's nothing I can put in my mouth." She offered a weak smile, but Mason thought he detected the shimmer of nerves beneath the surface of her calm.

"Sushi isn't exactly my favorite food, either," he allowed. "Though I guess if I get hungry enough, I'll eat it."

"I try pretending it's all steak and potatoes." Tessa stuck out her tongue. "But my imagination is wearing thin."

"I hope I'm not here long enough to really sample the cuisine." Mason laced his hands behind his head. Frankly he wouldn't mind a few good hours of shut-eye.

But even though exhaustion weighed him down, he knew he wouldn't get a moment's rest. By the look of things, Tessa was trying hard to hold herself together. The best thing to do would be to keep her calm and get her talking. "If you've got the time, I'd like to hear the beginning of your story. So how did a little mermaid like you end up in Maine?"

Tessa's mouth curved up. "It's a long story."

He shrugged. "I've got all the time in the world."

Commander Hawkins nervously paced the narrow confines of the *Sea Horse*'s communications center. It was clear by the look on his face that he hadn't expected to be thrust into the position of senior officer.

"I can't believe how they just came out of the water," he said. "I've never seen anything like it."

Addison felt more than a little sorry for the man. Not only had he just watched his captain disappear right before his eyes; Hawkins had witnessed the ruthless slaughter of the Nyx by Magaera's soldiers. Between the Ri'kahs and the wicked blades the Mer wielded with expertise, the Nyx had little chance to defend themselves. It was a bloodbath from beginning to end.

As it stood, the entire ship was on red alert. Although the *Sea Horse* wasn't a vessel equipped to carry devices of defense, the crew was armed and trained in hand-to-hand combat. Out of the water, people had a chance to defend themselves. But beneath the surface, no one stood a chance. It appeared that Magaera had gone on the offensive and was stepping up her control of the waters bordering her island.

They wouldn't be unguarded for long. Hawkins had already sent out a distress signal to the navy ships patrolling in the region. Reinforcements were on the way.

As for what had happened to Mason McKenzie, they could only wait and see.

It bothered Addison that she and Mason had parted on such bad terms. There was so much she wanted to say to him, and now she might never get a chance to make things right.

"It'll be all right," she heard herself saying as crewmen swarmed in and out with regular updates. After the Mer had retreated, Jovon and the remaining Nyx had returned to the water to search for Mason. No one knew whether he was dead or alive. Had the Mer drowned him in retaliation, or had they taken him prisoner in an attempt to extract information?

Not knowing had everyone on edge.

Jovon strode in, his skin still damp from the water.

All eyes present turned to the Nyx.

After Addison had stitched him up, Jovon had insisted on returning to the sea. Although a bit pale and shaken, he refused to let anything stop him from leading those Nyx who'd survived. She had to admire his tenacity. As it was, she barely had the energy to swat at a fly. Two intense healings in one day had completely wiped her out. She needed to rest but knew it would be futile to try. She was too keyed up to close her eyes for more than a second at a time.

"Anything?" Hawkins didn't bother to conceal the anxiety in his voice.

Jovon shook his head. "Nothing. We have scoured as much as we can without impeding on Magaera's territory. There is no sign of your captain in the water."

Thank the goddess. If the Nyx hadn't found Mason's remains, then there was a good chance he was still alive.

Hawkins nodded stiffly. "Thank your men for returning to the water so quickly. I know you suffered steep losses of your own."

Jovon lifted a hand, making a strange gesture near his chest. "My men and I have pledged to join humans against Magaera. We will fight to the last breath."

The commander quickly raised his hands. "At this point my orders are not to engage the Mer in any further way until reinforcements arrive."

The Nyx nodded his acquiescence. "Of course."

Addison watched the brief exchange without comment. She already knew that Hawkins had been in communication with Secretary of the Navy, Adam Webber, updating him on events. As Mason hadn't yet revealed the existence of the Nyx, Webber was more than a little surprised at the emergence of a second sea-born species. The Secretary of the Navy would get back to Hawkins when the government had decided on a course of action. Until they knew otherwise, Mason McKenzie was classified as MIA—missing in action.

Her own angst wasn't helping matters. As much as

she wanted to put Mason out of her mind, she couldn't. She ached for his touch something fierce. It unnerved her more than a little that she'd fallen so hard and so fast for a man. He made her want things she was a fool for thinking about, such as a home and children.

The back of her neck heated as she remembered how he'd touched her and kissed her. She felt a stir of longing in her core. Her body had responded to his touch in ways she couldn't even begin to describe.

Addison closed her eyes, blanketing her mind in soothing darkness. Damn it. Mason had made his feelings crystal clear. Mooning over him was a wasted cause. The more she thought about him, the more it felt like another stab to the heart. She would be better off taking a whip and lashing herself across the back.

Physical pain would be so much easier to bear than the agonies of watching what she believed to be love slip away.

He doesn't want you, she reminded herself. *Don't be a stupid little girl. Grow up and get over it.*

A hand settled on her shoulder, warm and firm. The scent of salty water and musk tickled her nostrils. "I never thanked you for healing me," she heard Jovon say.

Addison reluctantly opened her eyes. "No need to thank me." She shrugged his hand from her shoulder. "I'm an EMT. It's my job."

Jovon accepted the slight with good grace. "I could have died from such wounds. It makes me realize again how dependent the Nyx are on their females."

His words made her shiver a little. She glanced up at his face, stark and austere. He bent a little closer. "Do you know what *satki-annahdis* means?"

Addison shook her head, feeling more than a little stupid. Even though Tessa had tried to teach her, she didn't know much about the Mer language and could barely speak it more than to say a few simple greetings. "My mother didn't exactly immerse us in the Mer culture or language before she died," she explained. "She wanted us to live as much like humans as we could."

"To blend in better, I suppose," he finished, suppressing a slight frown.

She nodded. "Pretty much."

"Satki-annahdis means to have a mate who uses her powers to lead and support her male's strength."

Addison didn't respond directly. A creeping sensation in the back of her mind warned her where Jovon was heading. "And you're telling me this, why?"

The Nyx's strong warm laughter filled her ears. "Since you are not a foolish little girl," he said, lowering his voice to almost a whisper, "I refuse to make a game out of what I consider to be a most pressing matter."

Addison stiffened, every muscle going rigid. Clenching her fists behind her back in an almost uncontrollable anger, she forced herself to keep a tight rein on both her mouth and her temper. There was a time to pop off and be a smart-ass, but now wasn't one of those instances. "I am aware of what you want from me," she answered, keeping her voice level. "For the moment, let's just say I'm giving it due consideration."

Jovon eyed her, seeing straight through the deception. "Because you have feelings for the human captain?"

Addison quickly shook her head. "I want to be sure the decision I'm making is the right one." She glanced toward Hawkins, who was attempting to keep calm under the pressures of an unwelcome and unwanted command. "Those in government haven't yet made a decision as to how they're going to proceed against Magaera, if at all. It would be irresponsible of me to enter into any kind of agreement with the Nyx if that's not what our allies view as a wise move."

"Ah, it all comes down to the politics." He offered a small nod. "Already you think like a future queen."

Addison offered a thin-lipped smile. "Assuming makes an ass out of you and me." Okay, so she couldn't resist a little smart-assery. She wanted to let him know she had a mind of her own and knew how to use it. She might stumble and put her foot in shit now and again, but when push came to shove, she knew how to shove back—hard.

Jovon stood still. The line of his stern jaw betrayed not a hint of self-doubt. If he felt stung by her glib retort, his features did not betray it.

Lieutenant Sam Russell, now serving as second-in-command, rushed into the control center. A burly, darkly tanned man, Russell had been chosen by Mason not only because he was a skilled diver but also because his analytical temperament meant he would accept neither double-talk nor bullshit.

"We've got trouble," he announced.

Commander Hawkins's gaze immediately sharpened. "What is it?"

"I'm not sure, but I think Queen Magaera has sent an envoy to speak to us." He took a breath and then added, "She doesn't appear to be armed."

Hearing his words, Addison immediately felt suspicious.

Hawkins ran a hand across his stubbled face and muttered, "What fresh hell is this?" He cut a glance toward Addison and Jovon. "I think I'm going to need some backup here. You two coming?"

"Of course," Jovon murmured.

"You bet your ass," Addison added. She wouldn't miss this meeting for the world.

Chapter 24

The blond, blue-eyed siren emerging from the waters of the Mediterranean could easily have been mistaken for a cover model caught in the middle of a photo shoot.

Although the Mer emerged from the water as naked as the day she was born, a shimmer of energy quickly enveloped her from head to toe. It took only seconds for the glimmer to fade, and then she was clad in a formfitting outfit fashioned out of fish leather. Leather boots were laced up her calves. Her outfit was studded with an elaborate array of gold and other semiprecious stones. A dagger was sheathed in its hilt at her waist.

There was a moment of awkward silence as each looked the other over.

Addison's eyes widened. Good grief! She'd never seen such a perfect specimen of female beauty in her life. The Mer was tall, thin, and angular. Her hair had been shaved away into a strange Mohawk-like style, and a strange marking had been imprinted on one of her flawless cheeks. Although her civilization had existed thousands of years, she looked like some kind of futuristic badass bitch—and definitely ready to kick some ass.

Jovon leaned closer to Hawkins. "One of Magaera's fiercest warriors," he whispered under his breath. "By the marking she wears on her face, she has pledged to fight and die for her queen."

Hawkins looked the Mer up and down. "Shit, she looks as though she could kick our asses to hell and back."

Jovon nodded. "Trust me when I say the Mer are ruthless fighters. Their vow to serve their queen is absolute. Most will kill themselves rather than allow themselves to be taken hostage by the enemy."

"How many do you think Magaera's got?"

The Nyx eyed the newcomer. She held herself very stiff and erect. Her expression was fixed, revealing no emotion.

"Now that she has control of the sea-gate," Jovon murmured back, "thousands."

Hawkins pressed his lips together in a tight line. "We're so screwed."

Overhearing their whispered conversation, Addison raised her brows. "Maybe," she allowed. "Maybe not. Let's see what this bitch has to say."

Hawkins squared his shoulders and stepped forward. "I am Commander Hawkins," he said by way of an introduction. "And you are aboard the USET ship *Sea Horse*."

The Mer soldier pressed the palms of her hands together as if in prayer. She gave a slight, stiff bow. "I am Arta Keria," she said in a mannered, strangely accented tone. "I bring greetings from my queen."

Never one for diplomacy, Hawkins cut straight to the heart of the matter. "Your recent attack on our people is unacceptable. We are viewing it as an act of aggression that will force us to take measures to defend ourselves."

Keria's expression remained set. Despite her manner of extreme discipline, it was clear by the look on her face that she considered herself to be surrounded by menials. "My queen wishes to express her regret for the unfortunate occurrences of recent days," she returned stiffly. "She wishes to assure you that your man is safe and has not been harmed in any way."

"Yet you have attacked us in the water before, and that cannot be overlooked," Hawkins reminded her. "And you have committed acts of aggression against our people, on our own land."

"We did not intend to attack or harm any humans," the Mer soldier hedged. "However, your vessel harbors those we consider to be an enemy to our people." Her tone was low and steady, but it held an overlay of effort, as if she were afraid of losing control.

Hawkins indicated Jovon. "You mean the Nyx."

"The Nyx," Keria allowed. "And also those Mer who have been declared traitors of our people."

Hawkins frowned. "I assume you speak of those Mer who were on the outside when the sea-gate was sealed by Queen Nyala?"

Keria's face took on a shadow of anger. Nevertheless, she managed to hold her displeasure in check. "I am not here to discuss the transgressions of times past," she said slowly. "Rather, my queen is looking toward the future and forging peace with the humans who presently cross our seas."

"And she thinks we will be more inclined to talk if she takes hostages?" By now Hawkins's voice trembled with emotion. He was pissed, and it was beginning to show.

Keria's unblinking gaze settled on Jovon and Addison. "I refuse to speak further until the inferiors are removed from my sight."

Again, there was silence as each side regarded the other. Keria's bold stare of disdain made Addison feel dirty and tainted. "I'm not leaving," she said.

"I will leave only if that is what Commander Hawkins desires," Jovon allowed.

"Nobody's leaving," Hawkins said flatly.

Arta Keria didn't move, but the sneer on her lips silently communicated her displeasure. "If that is what you wish," she allowed, "so be it."

"I do," Hawkins said tonelessly.

Keria quickly regrouped. "To show that she is willing to be reasonable in further exchanges between our people, my queen has authorized me to tell you she will release your man into your custody within a day's time."

Addison couldn't hold her tongue "Why the delay?" she broke in. All this beating around the bush was starting to get on her nerves. Whether politically correct or not, she had to say something.

The Mer soldier didn't even blink. "For her generosity, my queen also requires that those who are known to be descendants of Queen Nyala be returned to Ishaldi to stand trial for their crimes against our people."

Addison nearly choked. "You have to be joking?"

Hawkins's eyes narrowed. "So that's what this is. A hostage exchange."

Keria's face was impassive. "We prefer to think of it as a way to begin building mutual trust between our people. And if your man were a criminal in your society, you would not wish for the Mer to offer him sanctuary."

Hawkins jumped into the argument with both feet. "In our society, the sins of a parent are not passed to their offspring."

The Mer's tense features tightened even more. "Yet you must also recognize and respect the laws of Ishaldi if our people are to continue to build mutual trust. How we deal with those we deem to be criminals is not of human concern."

Hawkins was thinking fast. "The Mer born here have human fathers and are therefore citizens protected by the laws of the country into which they were born."

Keria shook her head. "Males have no rights or recognition in our society," she pointed out. "If the mother is Mer, then the daughter is also considered such, and is therefore bound by the edicts of our society. No matter when or where she may have been born, all Mer, regardless of generation, are considered citizens of Ishaldi. It is the cradle of our origins, and that is indisputable."

Hawkins glanced at Addison and Jovon. "Is that true?" he asked in a hushed voice meant to carry no farther than their own ears.

Jovon bent his head. "It is true that males have few rights in our society. We are considered property with the sole purpose of serving our females."

Hawkins gave him a look of horror. "Jesus, that's archaic."

Addison bristled with offense. What rock was this man living under? Apparently he didn't care to remember that mankind had a long history of abuse toward the fairer sex. "Uh, correct me if I'm wrong, but there was a time when women were treated much the same way in human society. And in many countries, sons are still favored over daughters, to the point where female fetuses are aborted or abandoned at birth."

Hawkins forced a smile. "Touché, but if we allow her argument to stand, you and your sister will be back on your way to Ishaldi to stand trial for the treason committed by Queen Nyala centuries ago. I hardly think that's reasonable."

Jovon's face was grim. "Yes, in our society it is perfectly acceptable for the offspring to undo the offense committed by a parent. The practice is called *amarak*, which means to repair a transgression committed by another."

Hawkins looked away, temporarily silenced. "There's no way Mason would want this to go through, especially if it meant someone else was going to die."

Addison glanced toward the Mer soldier. Keria stood as stiff and still as a statue. "I don't think that's going to be your call, Commander."

Hawkins scowled fiercely. "Unfortunately, you're right." He turned to Arta Keria. "I will need some time to speak with my superiors."

The Mer soldier gave him a look of derision. "If you do not accept our terms, my queen has instructed me to tell you that she will strike out against the ships in these waters." She made a sweeping gesture of finality. "There will be no mercy against any who harbor the criminals who have so grievously wronged our people."

"I'll need to discuss this with my superiors," Hawkins repeated firmly in an attempt to buy some time.

The look of scorn Keria shot at them was withering. "You have until the next sunrise to send word that you will agree to an exchange. If you say nothing, my queen will strike with vengeance. These waters will be safe for no human"—her steely gaze cut to Jovon—"or Nyx."

The morning sky was lit with brilliant hues of pinks and yellows bursting up from the horizon to wipe away the bruised purple face of the fading night. A vague luminescence, too dim for moonlight yet too wispy to belong to an artificial source, hovered above a cobbled path.

Although he was trying to keep his cool, Mason's head turned every which way as he walked between two of his captors. Even though he knew little about Mer society, it didn't take a rocket scientist to figure out the statuesque women were soldiers. They escorted him politely but firmly. He dared not try a dash for freedom. Though their weapons looked somewhat pedestrian when compared to modern armaments, he didn't fancy tangling with any Mer armed with a Ri'kah. A well-aimed blast from one of those bejeweled gewgaws could burn a hole through a man.

Though the hour was an early one, the walkways and paths woven between spacious temples teemed with life. With its high green hills, wide lawns, and blossoming gardens, the island of Ishaldi was a wonder to behold. Mason felt as if he'd stepped through a rip in the fabric of time, traveling back several thousand years to witness firsthand the glories of the ancient world.

It was easy to identify the humans. Unlike the Mer, who were well outfitted in the clothing they considered fashionable, the people were barefoot and clad in little more than loincloths. Women were allowed a binding to cover their breasts. The humans, wearing thick collars and bracelets, were chained like animals. He could immediately tell the difference between those who were slaves, and those who were kept like companion animals. It deeply disturbed him that those humans the Mer considered to be pets were also the ones they considered to be optimal for breeding. Those they favored looked very much like him: tall, fair skinned, and blue eyed.

They're starting to emerge, he thought. Although they had amazing technology, Mer society was still a primitive one. The humans he saw now were obviously descended from those unfortunate enough to be left behind in Ishaldi when the sea-gate closed. They had been thoroughly picked through and culled into two separate castes.

Mason shook his head. How would they ever assimilate the Mer into the modern world? It was going to take a lot of work, especially since their monarchy also seemed to be more akin to a dictatorship than a democracy.

"Where are you taking me?" he asked.

Taking his arm, one of the Mer soldiers guided him up the steps of an elaborate sanctuary.

"Our queen wishes to speak with you," she answered in a short, clipped tone.

Mason's brows rose. Although her voice was accented, she spoke clear English. "You know our language?"

The woman nodded. "We have a working knowledge of most dialects of the seagoing peoples, which we are able to pick up through our psi-abilities."

Mason glanced at her neck. As expected, she also had a crystal pendant identical to those he'd seen Addison and Gwen wearing. He wouldn't mind having such an ability himself.

The soldiers escorted him into an enclosed court where a fountain spouted cool water into a wide oval pool. All around, sheltering trees and neat hedges concealed the entrance from prying eyes. The air was a heady mix of the scents of many flowers and the salty breeze winnowing off the nearby sea.

Paradise regained? he mused.

One of the women beckoned. "This way, please."

Walking up a short set of wide marble steps, Mason found himself in some sort of antechamber.

"Our queen awaits you." The women gave a brief bow and retreated.

Mason looked around. From what he could see, it was truly a place fit for a queen. Across the vaulted room, three wide stone steps led up to the second level. A large bed took up nearly the entire space, built especially to fit into an aperture dominated by two more hearths set into the stone walls behind the bed. Sunken fires burned behind low black iron grates that protected the bedding and skin from popping embers. Colorful tapestries hung from ceiling to floor, and luxurious rugs covered the chilly marble underfoot. Shades of silk hung over windows and doorways, lending the chamber an illusion of dreamy disconnection from the outside world.

In one corner of the room was an array of tables topped with an elegant cloth. A bounty of fruit, fish, and other delicacies was spread out, welcoming all visitors. No doubt the silver carafes were full of rich red wine. A nude blond man, wearing only a collar and bracelets, hovered nearby, waiting to serve.

Mason blinked. *Is that Jake Massey?* he asked himself. He shook his head and then decided it couldn't be. From what he knew about Jake Massey, the man had an ego the size of Texas and a mouth to match.

Though stunning, the entire place felt artificial. It was more like a movie set than a place to be inhabited.

A figure in the bed stirred. Tossing aside something that looked like filmy white sheets, a blond woman wearing nothing but a smile rose from the milky pile like Venus emerging from the sea.

She undulated down the stairs like a tiger on the prowl—lean, lithe, and utterly dangerous. A tumble of blond hair fell almost to her waist, and her porcelain skin glowed vibrantly.

"I hope you will forgive the rather unorthodox means of conveyance that brought you to our shores," she said by way of a greeting. Her voice was husky with sleep. "I thought it was time we met face-to-face, human and Mer."

Mason wasn't in any mood for coy games. "Since you speak our language, you could have simply sent an envoy to extend the invitation," he replied tersely.

"True. Though you must admit, it added much more intrigue to the mix by taking you unaware." That she was totally nude seemed not to faze her in the slightest.

"Your recent assaults against my crew haven't been viewed as intrigue, but as acts of aggression."

She bristled. "We have the right to protect what is ours. This island, these waters, belong to the Mer."

"At one time, that might have been true," Mason allowed, choosing each word with care. "But times have changed." He'd been in her presence only a few minutes; yet something about her manner was deeply unsettling. It occurred to him that dealing with the Mer queen would be much like handling sweaty dynamite. It was dangerous and liable to explode in his face at any given second.

She made a magnanimous gesture. "So let us wipe the slate clean and begin anew." She spread her arms in welcome, revealing every inch of her luscious body for his perusal. "I am Queen Magaera."

Mason wasn't impressed and refused to be drawn into her web. "Captain Mason McKenzie," he snapped. Refusing to look at her body, he focused on her eyes instead. The irises were blue, a shade that reminded him of a frozen pond on an arctic winter day.

She nodded. "I have seen your ships hovering around the edge of my island."

Mason kept his eyes level. It was distracting to try and speak with a naked woman. Whatever her game was, he wasn't going to play. "I have been sent by my government to make contact with you in the interest of forging diplomatic ties between the Mer and our government," he said, measuring each word carefully. It wasn't exactly the truth, but it would suffice for the moment.

Magaera laughed, but with a particular mirth that seemed forced and false. "Although the Mer have been locked away from these waters for a long time, I have an idea of how the world has developed through the ages. You are a member of a great country called the United States."

He allowed a nod. "That is correct."

"My minister of current affairs has advised me that the Mer would do well to align themselves with such a seagoing power."

"Would that be Jake Massey?" Mason glanced around. "If he is here, I would very much like to speak with him."

Magaera looked at him, bemused. With a flick of her wrist, she sauntered toward the lavish spread of food and drink. She snapped her fingers. "Wine," she commanded the waiting servant. "My throat is dry from sleep." Viewed from behind, her buttocks were round and perfectly firm.

The silent presence quickly filled a silver goblet, handing it over to his mistress before scurrying back to his place.

Magaera sipped. "It is much to my regret to inform you that my minister has fallen to tragedy," she said when the goblet left her lips.

Mason raised a brow. "Oh?" This was news, but not entirely unexpected. From what he knew, Kenneth Randall had managed to clip Jake Massey in the shoulder during the attack on the mall. Perhaps the wound had been fatal.

She glanced at him from beneath heavy-lidded eyes. "Despite his passing, we go on," she said, offering no further information, "though you can imagine I am quite at a loss without him."

"Is that so?"

Magaera's gaze swept him from head to toe. "It leaves me in the unhappy position of having to seek another who can guide me down the treacherous path of negotiation." There was an oddly muted tone in her voice, as of false self-deprecation. "This present-day world is un-known to my people. I would be remiss in my duties if I did not seek an alliance that would be mutually benefi-cial to all involved."

Mason resisted the urge to roll his eyes. He'd been around enough stuffed-shirt politicians and ass kissers to recognize a line of bullshit when he heard it. *They'll smile to your face and stab you in the back the moment you turn around.*

"Is that why you brought me here?"

"Mmm. That and because I was curious to know why you have welcomed the Nyx aboard your ships."

"They are your own people, are they not?"

Her lip curled. "The Nyx are the outcasts of Mer soci-ety. They have no place among us; nor do they have any rights or rank."

"I have been informed by their leader that their only wish is to be allowed to return to their homeland and live in peace. Would that be so hard to grant? The Nyx have survived in these waters a long time, and they could perhaps aid you in your endeavors to embrace the mod-ern world."

Magaera's tongue snaked out, tracing the rim of her goblet. The gaze she aimed toward him smoldered with devious intent. "It is true I could use a strong man's guidance."

Mason let the remark pass with silence. *She's toying with me.*

Drinking down the last of her wine and tossing the goblet aside, Magaera flitted across the chamber to stand in front of him. Her gaze challenged his, daring him to send her away. They stood, almost for a full minute, gazes locked. She was testing his will, seeking his weaknesses, shoring up her own.

"You are well suited to be the consort of a queen."

Mason couldn't believe his ears. "Are you propositioning me?"

She pressed on. "In a word, yes." Her hands rose to his chest, smoothing the wrinkles of his shirt beneath her palm. "You are perfect in every way. We need strong, beautiful men to sire our offspring."

Body tensing, he immediately stepped away from her invasive touch. He felt filthy, degraded. She was looking him over the way a rancher would examine a prized stallion to breed with a filly. He didn't like being picked over like a piece of merchandise. "Not interested," he grated. "The keeping of slaves is unacceptable. In our society, all people are equal."

Having failed to entice him, Magaera passed her hands over her body. A brief glimmer of sparks obscured her from his sight. When they vanished, she was fully clothed in a filmy gossamer-like gown. The virgin white material shimmered like frost; for a few brief seconds she seemed to gather light all around her, weaving it into the form she desired. Her translucent skin practically glowed.

She smiled, flashing a hint of malice that, for a moment, revealed the madness driving her methods. First beguile, then seduce. If that didn't work, she'd pull out the heavy artillery.

"Please," she scoffed. "We know that isn't true. We are all divided in one way or another, through rank and position." She quirked a brow. "Is it not true that you yourself answer to a superior and are subservient to his wishes?"

Her question caught him off guard. "Yes, but it's entirely different."

"How?"

Declining to be intimidated, Mason clasped his hands behind his back. He wasn't sure what her game was, but he wasn't interested in playing. She might have been able to bewitch Jake Massey into taking her side, but she sure as hell wasn't adding him to her harem of males willing to serve, and service, her.

"Because it was my own choice to join the military," he said. "And, as time passes, I move up through the ranks, and my position changes from one who takes orders to one who gives them."

She cut him off with an impatient gesture. "My minister explained this thing called democracy and social equality. It seems to me, though, that little has actually changed. There will always be the leaders. And those who are not in a position of power will be crushed if they do not bend to the will of their superiors."

"That may be so," Mason allowed. "However, now is not the time to discuss the particulars of our differing social structures. My present goal is to open a dialogue that will allow for peaceful negotiations between my people and the Mer."

She gazed at him in silence for a moment, then said, "I am prepared to speak with your leaders and work with them in ways that will see the Mer fully assimilated back into these waters. As a show of good faith, I intend to return you to your comrades, unharmed."

Mason allowed a nod. Relief eddied into his veins.

The stories Tessa Randall had told him about how the Mer treated their prisoners weren't pleasant. "I'm listening."

"I have dispatched an envoy to speak to your people and to let them know what we expect in return."

"And that is?"

"That the descendants of Queen Nyala be returned to Ishaldi to stand trial for the crime Nyala committed against the Mer." She pretended to examine the fingernails of one hand. "I have one of the sisters in my keep now. When I have the other two, then we shall begin our talks of peace."

Mason started, rocked to the core by her words. "I don't think that's going to happen," he said, struggling to keep emotion out of his voice.

Magaera smirked. "Oh, but I always get my way." The ruthless light of the fanatic sparked in her eyes.

"We'll see." The idea of being used in exchange for two innocent women didn't sit well with him.

The rogue queen ignored him. "Meanwhile, I need something to amuse me." Her gaze passed over the length of him.

Raising his hands, Mason took a step back. "Don't even think about it—," he said firmly.

Queen Magaera ignored him. Before he could even think to react, she lifted her hand and flicked her wrist in an outward motion.

Mason felt his feet leave the floor. He cried out in surprise as some invisible force seized him and flung him toward the queen's bed.

The next thing he knew, he was on his back and the Mer queen was bending over him. Though she wore the trappings of an angel, she simmered with pure, unrestrained evil. By the cruel set of her jaw, he knew she'd have her way with him—and he'd be helpless to stop the assault.

No one—and certainly not a woman—had ever touched him like this. Mason struggled to lift himself up, but he couldn't move a single inch. The invisible force holding him down was unrelenting.

He stared at her, frozen. By the look on her face, Magaera took certain pleasure in the cruelty she so easily inflicted on her subjects. "Don't." His voice was an unrecognizable rasp to his own ears. He was vulnerable in a way he'd never imagined.

Magaera's fingers moved along the line of his slacks. Her eyes were as cold as an iceberg, and just as remote. "Be not afraid," she crooned. "I will bring you pleasure such as you have never known with any human woman." A button was unfastened, and then his zipper crunched down.

And then there was only the feel of her insistent hands invading his bare skin . . .

Mason swallowed, unable to speak. Acid rose from his gut, a hot bitter taste in his mouth. He closed his eyes. *This,* he thought, *is not happening . . .*

Chapter 25

Commander Hawkins was not a happy man. "Are you positive that's our only choice in the matter?"

Vice Admiral Harold H. Dalton nodded. "Although we are not in the habit of offering support to despotic regimes, our hands are tied. We want Captain McKenzie back, preferably alive." He glanced toward Gwen and Addison. "At that time, we will begin negotiations to have the Lonike sisters returned to us."

Hawkins shook his head. "There's no way Mason would want that. I know him. He'd rather die than send innocent people to their deaths."

"McKenzie is a fine officer," Dalton countered. "It's why we want him back."

Addison could hardly believe her ears. Her throat tightened as she listened to the man who held the fate of her and her sisters in the palm of his hand. The USS *Evanston*, one of the navy's cruisers stationed in the Mediterranean, had steamed into these waters barely an hour before, bringing much-needed backup to the be-leaguered *Sea Horse*.

Vice Admiral Dalton had assumed command, and with him came orders from the highest level of government. The eyes of the world were on them.

Shaking off her exhaustion, she finally found the courage to speak. "I can't believe you're going to turn us over to Magaera," she spat, unable to keep the bitter tone out of her voice. "Do that and you're signing our death warrants, for sure."

Dalton shot her a look of admonition. A grumpy old coot with a beefy build and a ruddy face, he resembled a pit bull that had seen better days in the dog-fighting ring. "According to what our legal experts have told us, as Mer, you are both bound by the laws of Ishaldi."

"That's bullshit," Kenneth Randall broke in. "My wife and her sisters were born in the United States, in the state of Maine. That makes them legal citizens, and bound by the laws of our country."

Hawkins added his support. "I do believe the four-teenth amendment backs that one up."

Dalton peered over the thick black rims of his glasses. "That's true if you're human," he allowed. "But we have to consider the fact that your wife and her sisters are, essentially, an alien life-form. Isn't it true that the sea-gate is also some sort of wormhole, and that Ishaldi isn't even a part of this planet?"

"Technically, that's not true," Kenneth said. "As Jake explained it, the sea-gate is a wormhole. But one that works interdimensionally within our planet. With a shift in dimension, Ishaldi is essentially located in the center of this planet. Our two worlds are part of the same whole."

"Even if this is true, the Mer are still another life-form entirely," Dalton said.

It was Blake Whittaker's turn to step up. "One that's been entirely compatible with humans for centuries." He slipped a protective arm around Gwen's waist and pulled her close. "And you'll send my fiancée back to Ishaldi over my dead body."

Kenneth stepped in front of Addison, folding his hands across his chest. "Same here. And don't forget my wife is on that island and pregnant. I'm not in the mood to lose her or my daughters to that nut job who calls herself a queen. Instead of turning innocent women over to Magaera, you should be trying to figure out how to get that damn scepter out of her hands. That's what put her in power in the first place."

Vice Admiral Dalton threw up his hands. "And we're going to walk over and pluck it out of her hands how?" His eyes shifted to Jovon. "And correct me if I'm wrong, but even if she didn't have her shiny little toy, doesn't she still have a decently sized armed militia at her command?"

Jovon allowed a brief nod. "It is true Magaera commands many soldiers who would fight and die for her," he said slowly, "but there are also many Mer still within Ishaldi who do not support the monarchy. Were Magaera deposed, I believe they would, in fact, be the majority."

"That's true," Kenneth added. "Those are the Mer who have taken human mates and want peace. They were the ones who sacrificed their own lives to help us escape Ishaldi."

The vice admiral appeared to weigh their words. "I have to admit I am not wholeheartedly in support of turning over women who will surely face execution for a crime some ancestor of theirs committed centuries ago."

Addison stepped around Kenneth. "Queen Nyala sealed the sea-gate because she believed in the human race more than she believed in her own people. Had the Mer continued down their savage path, it's entirely possible the Mer would control the world and you would've been born one of the lessers and doomed to a life of slavery."

"Your point being?" Dalton grumbled.

Addison refused to be intimidated despite the fear gnawing in her belly. She couldn't explain why, but she felt the entire future of the Mer hung on the decisions they were making right now. Magaera was not a leader in touch with her sanity. If allowed to remain in power, the rogue queen would destroy everything she touched.

"It's time for a new regime in Ishaldi, for the leadership of one who will work to bring democracy to the Mer and return the Nyx to their homeland," she said.

"That would be much easier to work with," Dalton allowed. "Now, how do we do it and still make it appear that we weren't the aggressors?"

"Perhaps I can offer a solution," Jovon said quietly.

All eyes turned to the Nyx.

"If you've got something, we need to know," Dalton demanded. "Spit it out, man."

Jovon threw the man an austere look. "Although the scepter grants a Mer queen the command of a goddess, it is a power that punishes as well as rewards."

Addison looked straight at him. "Is that true?"

"Yes," Jovon said. "And the secret lies in the arrangement of the jewels in the scepter. Magaera can use it to move heaven and earth, but at her own expense. Energy cannot be pulled from the jewels and filtered through a Mer for her use—instead, the jewels generate power by siphoning energy from the user."

Everyone followed this explanation sketchily. Even though Jovon spoke the language well enough to communicate, his strange accent made some of the words difficult to understand.

It was Kenneth who put two and two together first. "Wait a minute. Are you saying she's the battery that powers the scepter?"

The Nyx smiled. "Exactly. Atargatis was not unwise when she granted the Mer such a power. A queen who does not wield the scepter sensibly and with restraint will only punish herself in the end. Every time Magaera uses the scepter to strike out against her enemies, it drains a little more of her vitality."

Excitement sent a rush of adrenaline through Addison's veins. Suddenly she didn't feel so tired or defeated. "And the more she uses it, the more it takes."

"Exactly," Jovon said. "Should she continue on her present course, the scepter will eventually drain her dry. Even now she is surely finding it difficult to replace those energies. Cellular degeneration will soon set in. At her age, she would wither before your eyes."

Blake snapped his fingers. "Just like the wicked witch in *The Wizard of Oz*," he said. "Throw enough water on her and she'll melt."

Everyone turned an inquiring glance his way.

Kenneth snorted. "Where the hell did you come up with that analogy?"

More than a little embarrassed, Blake shrugged.

"Hey, I've got a kid, remember? Trevor's really into those flying monkey things."

A rumble of laughter filled the room, a much-needed break from the tension of recent hours. Even as they stood there discussing the pros and cons, vital minutes were ticking away. Queen Magaera had set a deadline. A plan of action wasn't the only necessity; they would need time to implement it.

If that's even possible, Addison thought.

"So that's the key!" Hawkins exclaimed. "We've just got to wear her down."

"I would imagine Magaera is still capable of inflicting much damage," the Nyx warned. "What you must be able to do is counter her destructive acts and keep pushing her to exhaust herself."

Vice Admiral Dalton rubbed his craggy chin. "That's probably going to be one hell of a firefight," he commented. "Is there any guarantee we'd win?"

"You can if you have the right weapon," Jovon continued.

Dalton eyed him. "And would you happen to have one?"

"While it is true the goddess granted the Mer many powers," Jovon said with a wry little twist of his mouth, "the Nyx also have many heaven-sent talents. Although the jewels of Atargatis are the goddess's gift to the Mer, it was her husband, Atar, who fashioned them into their final shape. As the sons of Atar, the Nyx have long retained the knowledge of their creation."

"I've never even heard of Atar," Gwen murmured. "I mean, I know some of the lore surrounding our people, but that's all new to me."

Jovon hesitated a moment, reluctant to reveal more. "The Mer are well-known for rewriting parts of their history they find undesirable." His neutral voice betrayed none of his own feelings about the matter that had so grievously wronged his kind.

Addison nodded. "That's true. Tessa told me that much of the history of the Tesch dynasty was erased."

"It's not an uncommon occurrence for a dictator's regime to rewrite history to suit themselves," Dalton mused.

But Addison wasn't interested in discussing philosophy or the rearrangement of historical facts through the ages. "Can the Nyx create something that will neutralize the scepter?"

Jovon drew a deep breath. "Much of the ancient technology has been lost, but there are a few of us who still retain the old knowledge. I believe Andru—he is the oldest of the Nyx—could create a bejeweled arrangement that would counter that of the scepter."

"I don't suppose you happen to have a treasure chest stowed somewhere nearby," Hawkins muttered.

"I don't," the Nyx admitted. "But these waters are rife with ships that have gone down through the ages. Although their riches mean nothing to my people, I believe they would serve you well now. There is one nearby, a ship of Spanish origin, I believe, once known as the *Santa Maria*."

Commander Hawkins's eyes sparked with recognition. "If I recall my history correctly," he said, snapping his fingers, "wasn't the *Santa Maria* one of the ships Queen Isabella sent out when she was trying to sell her jewels to finance Columbus? For safety's sake, they'd divided them, and half were lost to these waters."

"Those gems could be our salvation." Gwen's voice trembled more than a little.

Addison looked to the man who held in his hand not only her fate but also that of the Mer. "What do you think?" she asked Dalton. "Can we do it?"

A long pause ensued, stretching everyone's nerves to the breaking point.

Vice Admiral Dalton's steely gaze finally connected with hers. The man had the weight of the world on his shoulders, and he didn't look happy. "I'm not always convinced that the boys in charge make the right decisions," he said as he slipped off his glasses. "They're politicians, and too far removed from the action to get a clear view of the situation and how it affects the people whose asses are really on the line. In my experience, it's the men serving in the field who have a better grasp of events, and how to respond."

"Go on," Hawkins said.

"This isn't exactly uncharted territory," Dalton continued. "And certainly the powers that be would not want to be accused of supporting a despotic regime that gives little consideration to the will of the people. Magaera has attacked us not once, but many times over. I believe she will continue to do so unless we take definitive action to stop her, once and for all."

Addison grimaced. "That's saying a mouthful." She couldn't be sure, but she had the distinct impression Dalton wasn't exactly in favor of handing her and Gwen over just to retrieve Captain McKenzie.

"I may soon be facing a court martial for what I'm about to do," Dalton said slowly, measuring each word. "But if there's a chance we can end this now by overthrowing Queen Magaera and set the Mer on the path to democracy, then I'm all for it."

Hawkins didn't hesitate to add, "USET was implemented to function outside naval operations already taking place in the Mediterranean. I could say I received your orders and chose not to obey."

Dalton grunted. "Nobody rakes my ash out of the fire, Commander. When the shit hits the fan, I'll be the one who smells the stink." A little twinkle crept into his eyes. "Besides, it washes off when you've got friends in high places."

Hawkins let out a breath that wasn't quite steady. "I can't believe we're going to do this."

Jovon spoke up. "The Nyx will be there," he promised solemnly. "My men are yours to command."

"There goes my retirement." Returning his glasses to their place, Dalton shook his head and sighed. "Might as well go out with a bang rather than a whimper."

Heart pounding a million beats a minute, Addison forced herself to calm. The generosity behind their sacrifice shook her so profoundly that for a moment she couldn't think straight. The defiance of an executive decision would probably land them all in prison by the time all was said and done.

She decided then and there it didn't matter. If Queen Magaera was spoiling for a fight, she was going to get one.

This wasn't going to be easy, even if they were all in total agreement. She already knew without asking that the job of taking on Magaera would fall squarely in her lap. Jovon had called her a future queen, and she knew without a doubt that his words were absolutely true.

I must restore the Tesch dynasty to lead Ishaldi, she thought boldly. *It is the only way to save my people.*

Lifting her head, she angled her chin. "Let's do it," she said. "Let's take this bitch down."

The countdown had begun.

After a long blurred nightmare of having his body manipulated in ways he'd never imagined, Mason opened his eyes. Sometime during the night he'd managed to fall into a fitful sleep, though rest hadn't come easily or without a price. It seemed to him that he'd wandered through shadows lit by strange flickers of lightning, running desperately away from the beast that nipped at his heels, hungry to take bite after bite out of his vulnerable flesh.

As his vision cleared, he realized he was still in the queen's bedchamber, lying amid a heap of downy cushions and milky sheets. The flames of ever-burning lamps leapt and wavered, and the grotesque shapes they cast on the walls danced with obscene vigor. His limbs were stiff from hours of sleeping in one uncomfortable position. He felt more than a little numb, as if certain nerves in his body had been severed.

With some difficulty he turned his head. He made out the shape of Magaera. She lounged in resplendent nudity beside him, sipping from a goblet.

A shiver wound its way up his spine. *Oh God.* He hoped she wasn't getting ready for round two. Although she'd abused him in ways that most would find unimaginable, he'd been unable to respond in any way. She was a beautiful woman, but he harbored nothing but revulsion for her. She'd coaxed and crooned, using her hands, mouth, and tongue in an attempt to get a rise out of his recalcitrant penis.

Nothing had happened.

When he'd proven unable to pleasure her, Magaera had resorted to other methods to amuse herself. She'd whipped him with a leather strap, repeatedly and without mercy. His back was a raw mass of red welts.

That he'd been able to bear it was a small but bitter victory.

Noticing that he'd awakened, Magaera turned her head. Displeasure continued to simmer in her eyes. "You have disappointed me, pet. I expected more out of such a fine specimen."

Mason's tongue felt as heavy as lead, and it seemed as if his mouth had been stuffed full of cotton. God, what he wouldn't give for a long cool drink of water. "Sorry to disappoint you," he rasped drily, "but I don't perform on command."

Magaera nodded slowly. "I can see you are a stubborn one and have a mind of your own." She cocked her head. "I like that in my males. It amuses me to break a man's will." Her smile was twisted, a mockery of amusement. "You will give me many hours of entertainment."

The idea of spending night after night with this maniac was enough to cause Mason's heart to seize in his chest. "You might be able to abuse my body," he grated, "but my mind will remain my own. That's the one thing you'll never touch."

Magaera inclined her head. "We will see about that." She tipped the goblet toward her full lips. Wine dribbled down the sides of her mouth, running down her neck and onto her bare breasts.

Mason shivered. The red lines reminded him of blood, which seemed to be a thing the Mer queen didn't mind spilling. He hadn't been in her company long, but it was already clear to him that she was irreversibly insane. Her shifts in mood were unpredictable and volatile. She expected immediate attention from her courtiers and servants, and when they did not respond to her satisfaction, she abused them both verbally and physically. It was nothing for her to flick a wrist and send someone flying into the nearest wall.

The trouble was, he couldn't decide which was worse: leadership under a monarch who was insane, or the soldiers who would unquestionably follow her into battle.

She's going to be the downfall of the Mer people, he thought. *They have set themselves on a course of destruction.*

Magaera chuckled wryly, breaking through his silence. "Instead of turning you back over to your people, I think I will keep you."

Mason shot her a sharp look. "I thought you intended to trade me for Tessa's sisters." Not that he wanted that to happen. He'd gladly stay on Ishaldi and bear Magaera's torture as long as he knew Addison and her sisters were safe.

The Mer queen shrugged off his words. "I can lay hands on those girls anytime I wish." Her words slid off into a humming croon. "The power to command land and sea is mine alone. I can part the waters or pull lightning from the sky. The price is well worth . . ." She faltered and her lips twisted.

"Worth what?" Mason prodded. "What is the cost?"

Without glancing his way, Magaera raised her left

hand and slowly made a gesture, as if drawing symbols in the air. "That which the goddess grants, she will also take away. Have a care, oh unwise, for your soul will pay the price of blasphemy."

Her words seemed to hang between them, heavy but laden with a meaning he couldn't even begin to fathom.

Mason blinked. He wasn't sure what was going on, but something seemed to have struck a chord deep inside her.

Hope flickered. Perhaps she wasn't as far gone as he'd first imagined. Maybe, just maybe, there was a grain or two of sanity still within her grasp. Although it was a long shot, he had to try.

"My people only want peace with the Mer," he ventured, speaking in a steady, nonthreatening tone. "Release me and Tessa, and we will work with you. We will help the Mer regain their place in these waters."

Magaera turned her head, staring at him through a blank and uncomprehending gaze. "There was a time when the Mer ruled the oceans of this earth," she said. "Humans who wanted to cross our seas safely had to pay for the privilege. They feared us; yet still they came from all corners—to worship us and to offer their finest males to breed with us and their females to serve us."

"Times have changed," he said slowly. "The days of the gods are no more. Man has science and reason. We have grown beyond the old times when the nights were dark and this earth was lit only by fire."

Magaera looked into the distance. Was she thinking about the glory of past times, or the future that might welcome the Mer if only she would lead her people with reason and restraint? "This earth has changed in so many ways I do not yet understand." She looked around, suddenly panicked. "My minister." She clapped her hands. "I must speak with him. Now!"

One of Magaera's servants came out of the shadows. His hair, heavy and black, fell in lank curls around his shoulders. Even by the light of nearby lamps, his skin was pale with the unhealthy pallor of one who had never stood beneath the sun. His face was haggard. At first glance he appeared to be very young; yet a closer look revealed features lined with the woes of a hard and unrelenting life.

Mason started. *They barely seem human.* He still hadn't gotten used to how the people born in Ishaldi looked. The huslas, or lessers, were those unfortunate enough to be born with dark hair, eyes, and skin. According to Tessa Randall, as the animals of that doomed world had begun to die off, humans had slowly assumed their place, pulling carriages as if they were horses and plowing fields like oxen. Blond-haired, blue-eyed women were prized for their looks and were valued like pedigreed pets, companions to the Mer owners. The males were even more desired. Given a life of luxury, they were to be used only for propagation.

That he'd be considered a prime specimen for breeding wasn't an encouragement as far as Mason was concerned. Having his body pawed disgusted him, causing the pit of his stomach to curdle.

Magaera's servant lifted dull eyes. "You have no minister, my lady," he answered in a voice barely above a whisper. "His body lies now beneath a cairn of stone."

The queen snorted. "Enough with your lies," she hissed. "I saw him just the other day."

Her servant took a step backward. The wringing of his hands intensified. "Do you not remember, my lady? You fed yourself well upon his essence."

Mason froze. *Oh, shit.* So that was what had happened to Massey. Tessa had explained how the D'ema, or death magic, worked. Such a death was agonizing, akin to being tossed alive into a vat of boiling acid. The poor bastard—no matter what he'd done, nobody, not even a dog, deserved to die in such agony.

Much to his surprise, Magaera chuckled. "Ah, now I remember." She smacked her lips in an exaggerated manner and gestured to her servant to refill her goblet. "He tasted quite good."

Christ almighty, Mason thought. *She's as mad as a hatter.*

He nearly jumped when Magaera reached out, running the flat of her palm across his exposed abdomen. What remained of his clothing was in shreds. "I am sure you won't mind taking his place. He had his uses but displeased me so."

Mason decided he'd rather be swallowed by a sea monster than endure another go-round with Magaera. Her decision to keep him wasn't exactly encouraging. It looked as though he was going to be in for a long and miserable stay on Magaera's island.

The notion didn't have long to linger in his mind.

At the sound of heavy footsteps outside her chamber, Magaera came to instant attention. Two of her soldiers entered the room.

Spears in hand and knives sheathed at their hips, both offered a deep bow.

"How dare you disturb my rest!" she snapped.

"My lady," said one, "there is important news to be told."

Magaera stiffened. "Speak now," she barked.

"The humans have sent word," the other answered formally. "They have declined the trade and say they will not turn over the criminals."

A tiny muscle in Magaera's jaw jumped. "How dare they defy my wishes," she said in a voice trembling with emotion. "Do they not know I will strike them down with the wrath of the goddess herself?"

The first soldier took up the message. "The humans say they will meet us on the field of battle, whether by land or by sea."

"They have many ships," the second woman added with terse directness. "And the Nyx have joined them. Although the humans cannot easily make landfall, the Nyx have no impediment in these waters around the island."

Flinging her goblet across the room, Magaera pushed herself off the bed. "How dare they defy my wishes," she repeated. "Do they not know I will bring the heavens down upon their heads?"

One of the Mer soldiers stepped forward. "Curse not their heads, my lady." Dropping to one knee, she brought her fist up against her chest in a gesture of solidarity. "We shall serve your will. The waters around this island shall run red with the blood of any who dare breach our shores."

Magaera ignored her, walking with great deliberation toward the balcony overlooking the shoreline. She held herself very stiff and erect. Her servant cowered, fearing an angry hand. "Deliver a message unto the humans," she said without turning.

The soldier still on her feet stepped forward. Although Mason couldn't be sure, she seemed less eager than her partner to pledge devotion to Magaera's cause. "What shall I say?"

Magaera whirled. "Tell them, come the morrow, they shall see the power and strength of the Mer. I shall walk across these waters as if it is the land itself and drive their ships aground."

After a moment's hesitation, the second soldier offered the salute her queen expected from a loyal servant. "I shall do as you wish, my queen." Giving a final bow, she turned. Just for a second a tormented look flitted across her face. And then it vanished.

Even from a distance Mason recognized her misgivings. He'd seen the same look on the faces of countless other men and women whom he'd served with in wartime. She would fight for her queen, perhaps to her death. But she wouldn't be happy to make the sacrifice.

Why must those in power send us to die without considering the consequences of their actions? There was, he realized then, no clear answer.

The two soldiers left, disappearing back into the night, leaving no doubt in Mason's mind that, come dawn, all hell would break loose. The vision of the bloodshed to come sickened him to the core of his being.

Weary to the bone and aching from head to toe, he closed his eyes.

Chapter 26

Nobody was exactly sure what to expect when dawn arrived, but one thing was for certain. Everyone felt ill at ease and no one had slept a wink. By the time the first rays of light began to peek over the edge of the faraway horizon, the tension in the air was palpable, hanging over the coming day like a giant fist of doom. Veiled in mists, the island loomed in the distance.

Addison, standing on the port bow of the *Sea Horse*, felt uncertainty gnawing in her gut. She glanced at her wrists, now encircled in an intricate arrangement of gold and jewels that extended halfway up her forearms. Andru, one of the few craftsmen remaining among the Nyx, had worked through the night to create the pieces. He was one of the few old enough to recall the lore behind the casting of the jewels of Atargatis. A variety of stones were needed, and the jewels had to be arranged in a certain way to maximize their output of energy. He'd also created a breastplate, which fit around her shoulders and covered most of her abdomen. Andru had worked without ceasing, amazing onlookers with his ability to create a weapon to counter the scepter.

The downside was that it was going to drain away a lot of her own energy. If she expended too much too fast, she'd burn herself into a cinder, both physically and mentally.

It would all come down to who was the stronger. Addison not only had to outwit Magaera; she had to outlast her. If she couldn't counter whatever the Mer queen chose to throw at them, a lot of people might lose their lives. Magaera had warned she would come at dawn and that those who witnessed her coming would tremble and fall to their knees.

Gwen stood beside her, gazing into the distance. Although Andru had had no time to construct a weapon for her, Gwen would be providing as much backup as she could from her own arsenal of crystals. She'd spent the last few hours in meditation, drawing in as much energy as she could without overloading her psychic circuits.

"What do you think is going to happen?" Despite her outer calm, Gwen looked pale and frightened. Getting into a firefight with Magaera was the last thing anyone wanted to do, but Tessa's and Mason's lives depended on their success. They had to win. They just had to.

Addison shook her head. "There's no telling what she's going to throw at us." She glanced around the *Sea Horse*. Vice Admiral Dalton's ship loomed nearby, practically dwarfing the smaller liner with its massive girth.

The sound of footsteps interrupted the lull. "Anything?" Jovon's smooth voice sounded from behind.

Addison turned. Jovon wasn't alone. Commander

Hawkins followed at his heels, as did Kenneth and Blake. The looks on their faces were grim. Nevertheless, they were armed and ready to stand and fight.

She shook her head. "So far, nothing."

Jovon nodded. "My men are in the water and ready to fight."

All nervous energy and angst, Kenneth couldn't seem to control his hands. "This waiting is driving me mad."

Gwen laid a hand on her brother-in-law's arm. "I'm certain she's all right. I would sense if something had happened to her, I'm sure."

Addison vaguely followed the conversation. Goddess in heaven, how was she going to handle this if she couldn't even keep her own thoughts straight? Fear of failure terrified her. Lack of knowledge of what would happen next only made her all the more anxious.

What if I can't . . .

She pushed the notion away. Failure, she decided then and there, wasn't an option.

The sun rose a little higher, lighting the water with a pink-gold shimmer.

Gwen suddenly pointed. "What's that?"

Everyone looked.

Addison squinted. All she saw was the murky fog swirling around. It was like trying to look through pea soup. "I don't see anything."

"There," Gwen insisted. "The water around the edges of the island is turning white."

Commander Hawkins lifted a pair of binoculars to his eyes. "Holy shit," he cursed under his breath. "She's right."

All at once, the mist surrounding the island began to

gather itself, rolling out across the water in a churning mass. As it made contact with the sea, a hard crust of ice began to form, instantly freezing into a solid mass. Its circumference widened, stretching outward and onward with breathtaking speed. Broadening and extending, it soon encased the ships. They were frozen in place, unable to move.

"What the hell!" Hawkins exclaimed.

Jovon immediately ran to the diver's platform. Dropping to his knees, he frantically drove a fist against the chilly white surface. "She's trapped my men beneath the ice!"

No one had a chance to respond to his warning.

Magaera suddenly appeared on the shore. Draped from head to foot in resplendent white robes, she glowed with all the energy of righteous anger. And she wasn't alone. Flanking her to the right and the left, row after row of Mer soldiers appeared. Weapons at the ready, they were prepared to do some serious ass kicking.

Addison felt her blood run cold. She had no way of knowing what Magaera was capable of. She wasn't even sure she had enough firepower to counter what might head their way. It was like fighting blindfolded, with one arm tied behind her back. The odds were against them.

A spike of fear clutched her heart. "Fuck," she gasped. "I think we're in trouble." It was true. People were going to die today, no doubt about that. It was unavoidable. Turning away, however, was impossible. Her fight wasn't only for her sisters, but for the Mer as well. Her people deserved a chance to thrive, to find their own way in the world without the heavy hand of tyranny and oppression hanging over their heads. Today wasn't just history in the making. Destiny, too, had brought them all to this moment.

Gwen shot her a look. "Don't let her get to you," she shot back. "This display is going to cost her a lot of energy. If we can wear her down, we've got her beat."

"Steady now," Blake added. "We've been through this before."

"Piece of cake," Kenneth added.

Wishing she felt as confident, Addison nodded. "You're right. She puts on a good show, but it won't last."

"*She* may not last," Hawkins warned, "but she's got a lot of soldiers. I hope Dalton's got his guns pointed their way."

Addison shivered despite herself. In one mighty stroke they'd lost the Nyx and their ships were totally incapacitated, trapped in thick ice. *What else can go wrong?* she wondered in panic.

They would soon find out.

Queen Magaera stepped down onto the ice. The scepter in her hand punctuated every step. The Mer soldiers followed in her wake. Mason, too, was present.

Addison gasped when she saw him. Although she tried not to let the sight of him affect her, she couldn't stop the trembling that started deep inside her. Shackled and under heavy guard, his presence set off alarms in her head. Was he being presented as bait, or for another darker purpose?

Tension throbbed between the two opposing factions for a minute or so. It didn't take a mind reader to know that Queen Magaera intended to take every last one of them down to their knees.

Addison swallowed hard and tried not to let her ner-

vousness show. "Get your hands off my man," she grated
under her breath.

Gwen shot her a look. "Let's go get our people."

Addison nodded. "Game on, bitch."

Hurrying onto the diver's deck, the sisters stepped
onto the ice. Kenneth and Blake followed close on their
heels. Jovon and Hawkins joined them. And they weren't
alone. Several members of the *Sea Horse* crew also filed
into place behind them. The men were all armed. By
their expressions, they were also ready to face whatever
might come next.

Hawkins quickly shook his head. "You men stay
aboard ship. That's an order."

One of the bigger men was quick to speak up. "There's
no way we're staying behind while women do the fighting. McKenzie's our captain, too, and we've got a right to
go after him."

"That's not a valid argument, Chester," Hawkins said.
"No man leaves this ship without my say-so. You're
needed aboard, to defend the ship."

The burly diver folded his arms across his chest. "That
isn't how we view it, Commander. You've got to have
backup, and the more the better." The men accompany-
ing him all nodded their agreement.

Clearly annoyed, Hawkins cast a glance toward Addison. "What say you?"

Addison sized up the crewmen, most of whom she
knew only in passing. By the look of determination on
their faces, there was nothing she could say that would
deter their stance. They weren't fighting for the Mer, she
realized, but for the captain who'd been boldly snatched
from beneath their noses. No matter the reason behind

their presence, the additional manpower would be welcome. Even with the presence of Admiral Dalton and the USS *Evanston*, they were still clearly outnumbered.

She nodded. "We're glad to have you on our side." She did a quick mental count. Twenty-five people, including her and Gwen, were on the ice. Dalton's ship might have been trapped, but his crew also stood at the ready.

It wasn't nearly enough, but it was all they had.

Addison drew in a breath. "Let's do this."

Everyone nodded. Hawkins and Jovon assumed the stance of bodyguards, walking a few steps ahead.

The group advanced across the ice with grim determination. Magaera, too, began to lead her soldiers away from the island. As they walked, a strange mist began to eddy around them. The sun above their heads became a pale golden halo, which struggled to cast its light through the murk.

"She's cutting us off from our backup," Hawkins warned.

"I have a feeling she'll strike fast and hard," Kenneth muttered from behind.

"You have to counter every move she makes," Jovon advised. "Whatever she throws at you, your mind has to be faster. Don't think; just do."

Addison nodded. "I will." Deep inside, though, she wasn't sure she could.

Magaera halted. Less than a hundred feet separated them. A smile played at the corners of her mouth. "Who among you leads the humans?" Though her words were a bit garbled by her otherworld accent, she managed to make herself understood.

Hawkins stepped up. "I do."

The Mer queen gestured toward Mason. Her soldiers pushed him forward, and he fell to his knees. "If you wish to have your man returned, you must give me the traitors. Otherwise, he will witness every last one of you die at my hand."

Mason painfully raised his head. "Don't do it, Hawkins," he shouted. "That's an order."

Addison's heart seized. His shirt had been torn away, revealing the raw red welts that covered his shoulders and upper abdomen. It looked as though Magaera had tried to flay him alive.

A volatile mixture of emotions bubbled inside her. She loved him so much, and now she was so close to losing him. Unable to contain her anger, she stepped around Jovon. Gwen followed, picking up her flank. "I've had enough of your shit."

Magaera's eyes widened at the sight of the jeweled cuffs circling her wrists and the glittering breastplate. "I see the Nyx have betrayed our secrets." A smirk crossed her lips. "But your weapon won't stand against the scepter of Atargatis."

"We'll see," Addison spat back.

Placing the scepter in front of her, Magaera muttered a few unintelligible words. A lightning bolt appeared out of nowhere, striking the ice at her feet. It cracked and sizzled under the assault of pure unrelenting heat.

Addison jumped back. Quickly gathering her wits about her, she lifted her arms, crossing her wrists in front of her. Forcing herself to make a mental connection with the stones, Addison projected outward. A flash of light appeared out of nowhere, striking a couple of Magaera's soldiers. They dropped in their place, a mass of withered corpses.

In a sudden eruption of violence, more Mer soldiers rushed forward to take their place, barely glancing back at the bodies of the fallen. A volley of spears was launched into the air, aimed with unerring precision toward the human males.

The men scattered, dodging the dangerously sharp tips. Struck in the thigh, Hawkins cried out, dropping to his knees. "I'm hit," he yelled. The words had barely left his mouth before four more crewmen were felled by the burning hot laserlike blasts from Mer soldiers with Ri'kahs. Although the men were armed, they hadn't even had a chance to fire their own weapons before being struck.

"Fuck!" With only a fleeting glance toward the downed men, Blake dodged through the melee toward Hawkins. His clothes were already singed, and blood streaked across his face. Another flare from a Ri'kah blazed across his legs, sending him crashing to the ground. As he lay there, momentarily too dazed to defend himself, one of the *Sea Horse*'s crewmen rushed in front of him.

It wasn't a wise move. The seaman's face was blasted to bits; flesh and bone flew in all directions as he stumbled in agony before collapsing and dying a few feet away.

Moving with lightning speed, Kenneth dragged Blake toward Hawkins, who lay panting on the ground, and shielded both with his own body. It wasn't much of a cover, but it was all he could offer. He fired with deadly accuracy, taking down half a dozen Mer soldiers in quick succession.

Moving even faster than the humans, Jovon boldly snatched one of the missiles out of the air. Without hesitation he returned the stolen weapon. Then, with nothing more than his own bare hands, the Nyx rushed forward and tackled two of the advancing soldiers. Grasping them around the neck, he cracked their heads together with enough force to shatter their skulls. The Mer fell like dolls discarded by a careless child.

Trailing behind Jovon, Chester, too, claimed one of the spears. With a cry of sheer ferocity, he gutted one of the advancing soldiers. A volley of bolts from Gwen sent several of the Mer into retreat.

But the Mer weren't giving up easily.

Hawkins somehow managed to climb to his feet, a spear gripped in his hands. One of the Mer soldiers rushed him. His first attempt to stab her barely creased her fish-leather suit, though the second upward stroke carved a deep welt across her cheek. Wounded, she refused to retreat, grinning as she unsheathed the blade at her hip.

Hawkins was pressed back, dangerously close to the edge of the ice. The first swipe of the Mer soldier's blade caught him across the back of his hand. The second thrust would have surely caught him squarely in the throat if Jovon hadn't struck with an even fiercer determination.

Catching the Mer soldier's head between his massive hands, he savagely bent her backward and snapped her neck. Her face registered incredulous shock as her legs folded under her. She was dead before she fell.

But the casualties were beginning to pile up on both

sides. And, by the look of things, the humans couldn't hold their own against Magaera's forces much longer. They were vastly outnumbered.

Addison barely had time to digest the carnage going on around her. The men were fighting without regard for their own safety, determined not to go down without a fight. She hadn't expected the Mer to strike with so much so fast. The way it was going, this fight was going to be short, and bloody.

And they were going to lose.

But now was no time to waste thought or action. Gritting her teeth, she quickly shook her head to clear her mind. *Focus!*

Addison threw her hands out, pulling more energy from the jewels circling her wrists. The pressure of pulling so much energy so fast was beginning to build behind her eyes, thudding at her temples. She ignored the discomfort, projecting the energy outward. The Mer soldiers she aimed the blast at shrieked with agony as a flare akin to pure fire engulfed them.

But the battle was far from over. Unleashing a scream of fury, Magaera hurled several hot bolts toward the men who were brave enough to stand with them and refused to back down.

Gwen immediately threw up her hands. A radiant beam of light surrounded the men, shielding them for the fatal strike. "I've got them covered," she yelled, "but I can't hold it long."

Without even stopping to think twice, Addison reached out in midair, catching the lightning Magaera threw at the men and tossing them back at her with blinding speed. She saw the electric bolts explode and crash around the queen, knocking over row after row of soldiers like dominoes.

Realizing she'd been bested, Magaera changed her tactics. Her expression hardened. The lightning she'd created faded away, and she smashed the base of the scepter against the arctic pathway beneath her feet. The ice began to melt as rapidly as it had appeared.

"We're going under!" Gwen cried as the solid ice began to crack and separate.

Addison felt a spasm of fear as the icy surface melted away beneath her feet. It was clear that Magaera intended to sink them halfway and trap them alive by refreezing it. "Not going to happen!"

Standing her ground, she stretched out her hands toward the ice. She envisioned a frozen arctic plain—solid, thick, and impenetrable—stretching between them. It wasn't the best plan, but it was the only thing she could think to do to keep them on stable footing. Even as she did so, agony lanced through her mind, squeezing her skull in an unrelenting grip. As Andru had warned, the jeweled weapons he'd provided her with were beginning to exact a physical toll.

"You are stronger than I believed," Magaera snarled across the expanse separating them. "But it's not enough."

Addison struggled to clear her mind and focus. "It doesn't have to be like this. Surrender now, and the humans will talk with you peacefully and without further aggression."

"I bow to no man's will." Magaera's voice, though shaken, was firm with conviction.

Addison stared at her nemesis, reaching out and try-

ing to make a telepathic connection. Magaera flinched
as if physically struck. For a moment, the two of them
were locked on a psychic level, and she felt the woman's
fear and hesitation.

Magaera was weakening.

I can take you, she shot back through their psychic
link.

Magaera immediately severed all contact. "No!" she
screeched. "I am the rightful queen of Ishaldi—" She
wasn't just furious. She was insane and would destroy
them all.

Raising the scepter in front of her, she played her final hand. A subzero blast of wind came out of nowhere,
bringing with it a thick boiling cloud populated with
dark and twisted shapes.

Addison screamed in pain as invisible claws began to
rip at her flesh. The boiling mass around her struck from
all sides, and she caught a glimpse of flashing, silvery
blades.

Thinking fast, Addison clothed them all in thick gleam-
ing armor. She felt the impact of the blades against the
solid steel barrier she created, battering incessantly until
she could barely hear herself think.

Without quite knowing what she was doing, she
cupped her hands together. A harsh electric shock went
through her as she gathered the last bits of her flagging
energy. Centering her thoughts, she imagined herself
holding a bright glowing ball of light, one that emanated
a radiance so luminous it was painful to gaze upon. As
she looked down at her hands, her skin seemed to turn
translucent, stretched so thin and pale that she could see
the fine bones of her fingers.

Lunging forward, Addison threw out her hands. The light blasted outward, striking its intended target.

Queen Magaera screamed and writhed, twisting against the force that picked her up and held her suspended. Her grip on the scepter was unrelenting, but there was little she could do to defend herself as billions of tiny sparks danced over her skin. Her control abruptly snapped. All at once she began to age, rapidly and unceasingly, until little remained of her but a withered old crone.

Magaera dropped to the ground. She gasped one final time, then went utterly still. The scepter rolled free of her grip.

All was still and deathly quiet. The darkness suddenly cleared. Bright rays of pure sunshine burned through the mist, revealing a bright clear sky overhead. What had felt like hours had taken only minutes.

Struggling to identify everybody, Addison quickly performed a mental head count. Hawkins was alive, but he was breathing with difficulty from his wounds. Blake was muttering a string of curse words under his breath as he examined the various cuts and bruises mottling his skin, as did Jovon and Kenneth. Although a bit pale, Gwen seemed no worse for wear. But the news wasn't all good. At least a dozen crewmen from the *Sea Horse* hadn't survived. The ice beneath their bodies was slick with blood. The sight of their sprawled bodies was both shocking and sobering.

Everyone was exhausted and badly shaken, but there was no time to do more than exchange grimaces of pain to assure one another no one had been mortally wounded. Somehow, it looked as though they'd actually beaten Magaera.

As her heart rate dropped to its normal rhythm, Addison let down her defenses. Taking a moment to regain her bearings, she drew in a couple of breaths. The armor she'd created faded away. The jeweled cuffs circling her wrists were completely burned through. They dropped away from her wrists, falling with a tinkle against the ice beneath her feet and shattering into pieces. Only the breastplate remained, but it, too, was almost completely ruined. The walkway she'd reinforced out of Magaera's initial floe was slowly beginning to melt away.

I can't fail them now. Her thought was focused. She had to hold things together just a little bit longer.

Barely aware of what she was doing, Addison staggered to where Magaera lay. She bent, wrapping numb fingers around the scepter's girth. Amazingly, it had suffered no damage and was intact.

Without a word, she raised it above her head. It was all she could do to stand up straight. Tiny black specks were beginning to float in front of her eyes.

She blinked hard, searching for and focusing on Mason McKenzie as he broke away from the guards who'd held him captive. His wrists were still shackled, but that didn't stop him from breaching the distance separating them.

"My God," he gasped. "Are you all right?"

Heart seizing in her chest, Addison felt a brief resurgence of energy burn away a bit of her fatigue. "Yeah." That single word was absolutely all she could manage. He was safe and nothing else mattered.

Through a long moment, silence filled the air around them. Neither of them dared to move.

Mason glanced at the men who'd fallen, and then toward the Mer soldiers. The look on his face was one of loss and dismay. His fists were tightly clenched from having watched good men fight and die. "Do it." His voice was tight, but controlled. "It's time to end this."

Addison nodded. Stepping past him, she lowered the scepter, allowing its base to touch the ground. Her head was spinning, and her feet felt heavy and unresponsive.

Drawing a breath, she cleared her throat. "It's over," she announced, struggling to find the words. Her grasp of the Mer language was tenuous at best, and she could only hope they would comprehend what she was trying to convey. "There will be no more war between the Mer and the humans."

More seconds ticked by, painfully slow. What would the Mer soldiers do without a leader?

A solitary figure broke away from the rest. As she marched slowly forward, Addison thought she recognized Arta Keria, the envoy who'd delivered Magaera's demands. Blade sheathed at her hip, she carried a spear in her hand. Her face was blank of all expression.

Addison stiffened. The image of that spear going straight through her gut flashed across her mind.

Arta Keria came to a sudden halt. "Speak you the truth?" Her question was simple, and rational. A slight tremble at one corner of her mouth revealed her inner anxiety.

Fighting against the darkness swirling at the edges of her mind, Addison nodded. "There will be peace between our people."

The Mer soldier inclined her head. "So swear you?"

Addison grasped the scepter tighter. It was all she

could do to remain in an upright position. Exhaustion clawed at her senses. "I do." Though her voice shook, she made sure her words were audible.

And then something incredible happened.

Keria knelt down. Lowering her spear to the ground, she drew a wicked dagger from its sheath. Extending her free hand in front of her body, she laid the flat of the blade against her forearm. "My blade is yours, my lady. I willingly serve at your command."

Mason shook his head in disbelief. "Holy shit," he muttered.

Addison wasn't sure what was going on, but at that point it didn't matter.

The Mer soldiers who'd survived also knelt. Laying their weapons aside, they offered homage to their new queen. A rumble of female voices rose in unison: "Long live our queen!"

Although she heard the cheer of her people, Addison could make little sense of them. At this point she was beyond comprehending what she'd accomplished.

Her limbs trembled a moment before collapsing beneath her weight. She groaned fitfully, her body shuddering from fatigue. Drained to the max, she didn't have an ounce of energy left. Her eyelids felt unbearably leaden.

Darkness crept in from all sides, and she knew no more.

Mason felt sick with apprehension as he sat in the sick bay of the USS *Evanston* beside Addison. She looked as if she'd been badly beaten; her skin was sheet white and dark circles ringed her eyes. Even her lips, normally so rosy, seemed pale. The trauma she'd gone through was etched into the lines of her face.

Feeling a sharp stab of guilt, he tightened his grip on her hand. He was so focused on Addison that he barely noticed anyone else. Commander Hawkins, Vice Admiral Dalton, even Jovon, had all faded into the background as he lashed himself repeatedly with guilt. His own fatigue and injuries were nothing compared to hers.

I wasn't there when she needed me, came his dark thought. Not that she'd needed him. Even now he couldn't forget the aura of power and majesty that had surrounded her when she'd stepped out to challenge Magaera.

Needing answers, he glanced up. On the opposite side of the bed, Gwen sat quietly over the crystals cupped in her hands. A calming bluish green glow emanated from the stones. Blake hovered nearby, keeping a protective eye on his fiancée.

Mason hated to disturb her meditation. He cleared his throat, trying not to be too damn intrusive. "She will be all right?"

"She sent out a lot of energy, fast and furious. It'll take a bit to recharge." Gwen swept a hand across her younger sibling's forehead, smoothing away the damp strands of hair. "But she's young and should recover pretty quickly."

Mason looked at Addison again. Although he didn't know where she'd gotten such a thing, the bejeweled breastplate she'd worn had left its mark on her flesh; her shoulders and chest were scorched. More blisters ringed her wrists, both lightly bandaged. "You're sure?"

Setting her crystals aside, Gwen nodded. "Of course. All she needs is rest."

He shook his head. "We should have done more to help her."

"Your men did help us," Gwen countered softly. "Several of them gave their lives to stand beside us. Their deaths honor our battle and prove we weren't wrong to stand against a tyrant."

Mason felt his throat tighten. All he could do was mourn the dead and take pride in the fact that the men serving under his command had enough courage to put their lives on the line to defend what they believed in. "Thank you," he said quietly. "That will mean a lot to their families."

Gwen smiled gently. "They were there when we needed them. We never could have stood against Magaera alone. Their sacrifice gives the Mer people a freedom they've long been denied."

Trying to block his reaction to her reply would be futile. "Then it's true—Addison is queen?" Cold awareness rushed over him even as the words slipped past his lips.

A flash of pride crossed Gwen's face. "Absolutely. And when I think back on all we've been through, I know this is the way it was always been meant to be."

"How so?"

"It took us a long time to discover who we really were and where we came from. We had no real identity. It was wrong, I think, to try and hide the truth. In a way, I guess we owe Jake for his obsession with rediscovering Ishaldi."

"In the end it all came around and bit him on the ass.

When Magaera had no more use for his services, she disposed of him."

Gwen lowered her head. "I'm sorry he had to die such a cruel death." Her gaze caught his. "Does Tessa know?"

Mason glanced over his shoulder. Tessa lay nearby, practically smothered by her husband. Even as the others were scurrying to abandon the rapidly disappearing floe of ice, Kenneth had headed toward the island with one thing in mind: recovering his pregnant wife. Whittaker, Hawkins, and Jovon had accompanied him. The Mer soldiers had offered no resistance. He had even managed to reclaim his wife's stolen soul-stone, miraculously undamaged. Fortunately, Magaera hadn't been wearing it when she died, having left it in her private chambers in the keep of her lady-in-waiting.

He shook his head. "I don't think so."

Gwen's lips thinned. She gestured for Blake to join them, pulling him down to whisper a few things in his ear.

After a quick, hushed conversation, Blake straightened. "I'll tell Kenneth," he said. "It would probably be better coming from him. From what I gather, she had a pretty tough time in captivity." He went to pull Tessa's husband aside.

Gwen watched her fiancé walk away. The depths of her eyes sparkled with pride. "I can't think of what I would do without that man. Every day I thank the goddess I found someone who's so good to me."

Mason felt a twinge of envy. The expression on Gwen's face was one of pure love and appreciation for her mate. He wondered what it would feel like to see that same light in Addison's eyes.

A few minutes of silence passed between them, each lost in his own thoughts.

"I imagine being taken by Magaera wasn't easy for you, either," Gwen finally ventured.

Mason didn't want to think about it. He still felt as if he'd been through hell and hadn't fully comprehended the trip. "I'll survive."

Gwen looked at him and cocked her head. "I hope so, Captain. As for you and Addison . . . I know what happened between you two. Although it's probably not my place to say so, I want you to know that my little sister really cares about you. So don't be an asshole. If you don't love her, let her go." Rising from her seat, she brushed the wrinkles out of her blouse. "Excuse me while I check on my other sister."

Watching her go, Mason shifted uncomfortably in his chair. Gwen's warning, however subtle, hit its mark. Once she woke up, Addison had a lot to face—a restless nation and a curious world, not to mention learning how to be a queen.

And what would that make him? Some kind of prince consort, a man standing in her shadow, destined forever-more to walk two steps behind?

If he was going to walk away, now would be the time. *Just get up and go,* he thought. *And don't look back.*

But he couldn't, and he didn't. The hold Addison had on him was too damn strong.

There had to be a way to make their lives mesh. As one accustomed to the protocol of military service, surely he could make the adjustment to the rites and rituals of diplomacy. Those who could not bend under pressure were destined to break. He could be flexible ...

"How is she?"

Lost as he was in his thoughts, the sound of a new voice startled him. Recognizing a superior officer, Mason tensed and rose to his feet.

Vice Admiral Dalton returned the gesture. "At ease, Captain."

Mason allowed himself to relax. "Thank you, sir."

"How are you holding up?"

Mason rubbed his hands across his face. "I'm not sure. I've never lost anyone under my command."

Dalton's face took on a grim cast. "You never get used to it." He tilted his head. "It'll stay with you until the day you die. But their deaths weren't wasted, and you can take pride in that."

Mason clasped his hands together. Though his heart had ceased to pound in his chest, his brow was still clammy. And the taste of rage and bitterness was strong in his mouth—rage at his own helplessness and rage over the loss of the valiant men who'd fought and died. "It doesn't seem to be enough."

Dalton's expression softened. "That's the reality of our situation, Captain." His gaze turned toward Addison. "How is she?"

Mason forced himself to swallow the acid rising from his stomach. It would be easy to turn his anger toward the Mer people. But he couldn't do that. Not when he loved Addison so damn much. "According to Addison's sister, she's going to be fine. She just needs rest."

Dalton eyed the unconscious woman. "She did a brave thing." He shook his head. "I've never seen anything like it. Incredible doesn't even begin to describe the scope of what these things are capable of."

Mason stared directly in his superior's eyes. "With all due respect, sir, the Mer aren't *things*." He looked down at Addison, an ember of warmth growing stronger in his heart. "I made the mistake of thinking the Mer don't belong in our world. But they're just like us. They think, they feel, and they love the same way we do."

Dalton's brows knitted. "I misspoke," he allowed. "And my apologies. It is my hope that we will be able to help the Mer expand their horizons in the near future." His gaze moved back and forth between Addison and Mason. "Correct me if I am wrong, Captain, but I take it you two have become very close."

It was a fact Mason couldn't deny—not that he wanted to. "That's right," he allowed. "In the time I have known Addison, I've come to admire her skills, both in and out of the water."

Dalton nodded. "You'd better make sure she's what you want, Captain. Despite what happened here today, it won't be easy facing a future with her."

Mason bristled. "What's that supposed to mean?"

Dalton's expression turned grave. "I'm saying there are still a lot of people who aren't as welcoming to their kind. Once the new element wears off, it's going to be tough bringing them into the twenty-first century."

Mason held his gaze for several long seconds before answering. "I'll be there, right beside her." The decision had been made. He'd charted his course. And he intended to follow it, as he promised, every step of the way.

The older man released a grunt of approval. "You're a good officer and a better man, McKenzie." He shook his head in admiration. "Somehow I think you'll make it work."

"I intend to, sir."

Dalton laid a hand on his shoulder. "I know you will." Without another word, his superior turned and walked away.

Mason watched him go. Although he wasn't really sure what had gone on after he was nabbed, he had a feeling that Dalton had played a large role in the coup d'état against Queen Magaera. Whether the vice admiral had acted in conjunction with Washington was something he had yet to find out. When push came to shove, Dalton was known to be somewhat of a wild card.

Mason scrubbed a hand over his jaw. Everything in his life had suddenly been turned upside down, and he was still struggling to catch up.

His gaze traveled back to Addison, lying so pale and still. He'd always believed true love was a myth. He'd always believed himself to be smarter than that, unwilling to confuse the needs of the physical with those of the heart.

But he'd been wrong, damn it—entirely wrong. Since making love to Addison, she was all he could think about, night and day. He couldn't imagine being with any other woman ever again.

Taking his seat, Mason bent closer and pressed her hand between his, silently willing his strength into her weakened body. Even though he felt absolutely wasted, as empty and dry as a husk in the desert, he would give every last ounce to help Addison. She was all he wanted now—deeply, and without reserve. *Open your eyes, honey. Please . . .*

As if in response to his silent prayer, Addison's eyelids fluttered. Fighting for control, she tried to raise her head. "Mason?" she mumbled half audibly.

He reached out, stroking Addison's cheek. Her skin felt so icy. "Welcome back."

She gasped painfully, swiping her tongue over papery lips. "F-fancy meeting you h-here." Her voice was strained, barely above a whisper.

Mason drew a deep breath of relief. He felt wholly exposed to her. "You're going to be all right."

Addison tried to raise herself but fell back with weariness. "Magaera . . ."

Mason hushed her. "She's gone. It's over."

His words did little to calm her. She shivered. "And Tessa . . . Is she all right?"

Mason leaned forward, narrowing the distance between them. The only thing he wanted to do was put his arms around her and hold her close. Just thinking about all he wanted to say made his heart beat faster. "Your sister is fine. You can see her in a little while." He allowed a smile. "I think Kenneth's hogging her attention right now."

"Thank the goddess," she murmured. "I never want to go through anything like that again."

Tightening his grip on her hand, he nodded. "What you did was amazing. I've never seen anything like that before in my life."

Staring at him pitifully, she shivered again. "I don't w-want to be queen," she mumbled weakly.

Mason stared at her in silence for a moment. He could see the uncertainty in her eyes and the fear hovering just beneath her calm façade. In one momentous event, everything about her life had changed. She was no longer just Addison Lonike, an EMT who happened to be a mermaid. She was Queen Addison of the Tesch dynasty, and her life was no longer her own. The Mer people would need a steady head to guide them as they rejoined the modern world.

"Well, damn it, you are, so you'd better get used to being called Your Highness." As he spoke, need jolted through him. *Damn it.* He couldn't remember the last time he'd kissed her. He'd make up for that, as soon as he could.

Addison stared at him in confusion. "I don't want to be"—her breath caught—"without you."

Mason briefly shut his eyes. Before Magaera's soldiers had grabbed him, he'd made a resolution to tell her exactly how he felt. Now was that time. "You won't have to. Whatever arrangement you might have with Jovon, it's done. Call it off."

She gave him a strange look. "It was never on to begin with," she admitted.

Somehow he'd misjudged the situation. Badly. "And you never gave it a moment's thought?" he asked, just to make sure.

"Not one single minute." Despite her exhaustion, a twinkle lit up the depths of her eyes. "So tell me—do you think you'll have any problems being a queen's consort?"

Mason couldn't answer right away. He felt a lump in his throat; it was an immense and completely unfamiliar sensation. It had to be love, as there was no other word to describe the emotions welling up inside his soul.

He managed a laugh. "Can you live on a navy captain's salary?"

Without warning Addison blinked. "That's a lot to ask." Her voice sounded surprisingly strong as a smile tilted her lips. "But I'll try. Real hard."

Mason smiled back. "And so will I," he murmured. *With all my heart.*

She pushed herself upright. "So I guess this is the moment where I should say those three magic words." Though her expression was serious, her gaze danced with mischief.

Mason lifted his brows. "Oh? And what would that be?"

Addison angled her lips toward his ear. "I love you." Her words were spoken in a hot, breathy whisper.

Unable to resist, he leaned forward and brushed his lips against hers. "I love you more," he breathed before sealing his words with a kiss. She nipped back, playfully catching his lower lip between her teeth.

Oh, yeah. Addison was going to be just fine. He'd make sure of it. With his entire being, he knew a single kiss would never be enough to satisfy his need for her.

Their lives lay ahead of them now, a path that wouldn't be an easy one. Nevertheless, it would be one they would travel together, walking always hand in hand.

As for the Mer, a new day had dawned and the future of Ishaldi and its citizens lay ahead. And not only were there the Mer to be dealt with, but there were also the Nyx who wished to return home. Although it would take much time and patience for diplomatic ties to be established, one thing was certain: The mermaids had returned to the waters they'd once called home.

ABOUT THE AUTHOR

Devyn Quinn lives in the scenic Southwest, though she has called several other states home. She is a huge fan of dark gothic music and shoot-'em-up action movies. But reading is her first love, and Devyn spends too much time with history books, as well as feeding her addiction for celebrity biographies. She especially enjoys reading books on Hollywood before the 1960s and is crazy about Marilyn Monroe, her legend and her myth. Visit www .devynquinn.com for more information.

Read on for a sneak peek at the first novel in
the Vampire Armageddon series,

Darkness Descending

Available from Signet Eclipse.

Jesse Burke crouched beside the grave of Candace Ackerman. Her gaze raked the freshly turned soil, her grip tightening around her flashlight. Its weight felt solid, reassuring in her hand. A good thing, too. Her heart pounded so fiercely, she could barely think straight.

Her breath caught as a wild thought popped into her head. *What the hell am I doing?*

Most people didn't sit in cemeteries after dark waiting by a grave the way someone would wait for a bus. Most people, even bereaved family members of the recently deceased, had the good sense to go home after the sun set. And most people didn't believe the dead would awaken, return to walk again. After all, the deceased were no longer alive.

Jesse believed. Because she believed, she'd traveled to the Metairie Cemetery to do one thing and one thing only—to slay her first vampire.

No matter if she died in the process. As far as she was concerned, she'd passed away months ago and just didn't have the sense to stretch out in a coffin herself. No matter if she had to endure a lot of pain to make it happen. She wasn't leaving until one of them stayed put.

Permanently.

She'd already examined the temporary metal plate marking the grave several times with the beam of her heavy Maglite, reading and memorizing the brief stats of the occupant.

CANDACE DENISE ACKERMAN.
BORN 1984. DIED 2006

The girl had been only twenty-two years old. Found wandering in a delirium, she had appeared to be uninjured save for a few bruises and ragged punctures dotting her throat and arms. Feverish and vomiting, she'd died shortly thereafter. The source of her strange wounds and sudden onset of illness was unknown. Whispers about the plague were beginning to spread among the population.

Remembering the newspaper's retelling of events, Jesse felt chills scrape up her spine. Beneath her feet lay Candace's body, occupant of the nice satin-lined coffin her grief-dazed parents had recently purchased.

"All the signs are there," she said aloud, as if saying the words made them true. "This means only one thing." The cult that had taken her and her twin was on the move again, recruiting new members to its ranks. Barely a month had passed since the identical death of a twenty-one-year-old man.

Memories she couldn't easily suppress rose to the forefront of Jesse's mind. Bitter acid welled in the back of her throat as strange, distorted faces swam out of her mind's dark corners. Soulless eyes stared; they were empty, terrible things. Taut ruby red lips were drawn back over sharp white fangs.

Unwilling to let the beasts out of the cage locked tight in the back of her mind, Jesse closed her eyes hard. A thin film of sweat coated her skin. Icy fingers grasped her spine, holding on tight. Like the girl in the grave, she knew how it felt to be taken, her blood sucked away drop by precious drop to feed an unholy hunger.

Unlike the girl in the grave, she'd survived.

At this point in her life nothing scared her—nothing at all. She'd spent almost a year preparing for this moment, waiting for the chance to be something more than a victim. She had to get it right this time.

Opening her eyes, Jesse blinked several times, wiping beads of perspiration off her clammy skin. Refocusing on the freshly filled grave, she strained in an attempt to see through the dirt. Although not quite full, the moon provided sufficient light, bathing the beautifully manicured cemetery in an unearthly silver-blue glow. The night air smelled clean. The wandering breeze stirred stray leaves and tugged at her hair, tousling the strands around her face and shoulders.

She heard the vampire before she saw it. The muffled sound of a strange wail cut through her like a knife. Hands braced against the cool ground, she lowered her head and stilled her breath, listening. She easily detected the distressed scrabble of fingernails tearing through wood. The beast had awakened and was beginning to dig itself out.

Heart hammering in her chest, Jesse pulled herself to

her feet. As her gaze darted from side to side, she saw all, yet at first she comprehended nothing. At last she saw the ground heave upward as though the corpse below were attempting to take great gulping breaths of air.

"I can do this," she murmured.

Dressed in jeans, a T-shirt, and army boots, she'd filled every pocket of her secondhand Levi's jacket with her meager arsenal. Her research had narrowed down the weapons best used for slaying vampires: garlic, a cross, and, of course, a wooden stake, its end sharpened to a deadly point.

Suddenly, the stone-walled cemetery wasn't so peaceful or calm. The temperature dropped significantly as the breeze kicked up, winnowing among headstones.

A voice, a grating whisper, echoed on the breeze, caressing her ears. The fine hairs at the nape of her neck rose. "Get the hell out . . ."

Was it her imagination . . . or something more sinister?

Fingers wiggling like pale worms unexpectedly jabbed up through the soil. The tips were shredded; the nails ripped away. Groping hands came next, followed by a head shrouded in wisps of blond hair, and then shoulders. The earth had rejected the demon-tainted corpse, giving birth to a foul and terrible thing.

A torso and legs followed as the newly risen cadaver broke free of its grave.

Shaking off the dirt the way a dog would shake off water, the girl-cadaver climbed to its feet. No more than a slender wisp standing perhaps five feet tall, it was dressed in a frilly pink confection, the kind of dress perfect for a senior prom queen.

The demon once known as Candace Ackerman looked pale, frozen, as if its features were chiseled from ivory. Fathomless eyes burned with inhuman recognition. A twisted grin split parched lips, revealing fangs. The girl-cadaver had fangs—big fucking fangs. They looked pretty damn sharp, too.

A smile curled one corner of Jesse's mouth. This was what she'd been waiting for. Her hand dipped into her coat pocket. Her fingers closed around the solid length of her weapon. "Gotcha."

Her daddy always told her that if she planned to attack someone, to do it first and do it fast. It seemed like good advice.

Unfortunately for Jesse, the vampire didn't plan to be put back in the ground anytime soon.

The girl-cadaver stared with a gaze lit by an evil spawned in the deepest pits of hell. The low feral growl of a predator emanated from its throat. Uncoordinated limbs were pressed into motion.

The beast charged, striking Jesse with a full-body tackle.

Jesse flailed helplessly. She hit the ground hard, knocking the breath from her lungs. The back of her head smacked the headstone marking a neighboring grave. Bright shards of color zipped past her eyes. A gush of air, mingled with a groan, rushed past her lips. The feeling she was ten feet tall and bulletproof vanished like a wisp of smoke.

Oh, shit! Candace Ackerman was strong—and heavy. Despite its diminutive size, the demon bitch weighed a ton, maybe two.

Fighting to keep the vampire from straddling her,

Jesse lashed out, determined to stake the beast. The projectile struck her assailant squarely in the center of the chest. Silky material ripped. Fragile flesh tore.

The stake, however sharp and expertly aimed, did not penetrate the vampire's rib cage. Skidding across bone, it barely made a dent.

Giving her a half-quizzical look, the undead girl plucked the useless weapon right out of Jesse's grip. No blood flowed from the gaping tear she'd inflicted all the way down to the vampire's breastbone.

"Imbecile," the creature snarled, tossing the stake aside. "Fool." The vampire's borrowed human vocal cords gave its speech a guttural tone, its words spoken as if the language were wholly unfamiliar.

Astonishment flooded Jesse. Panting and lightheaded from her effort, she felt tremors course through her.

Strike one.

The vampire reached for the cross around Jesse's neck. A jerk snapped the chain. Mutilated fingers closed around the silver ornament, crumpling it into an unrecognizable mass of metal. Pale lips lifted into a crazed grin. "You lose."

Strike two.

Jesse tensed. She'd pretty much bet that the garlic might have been good only for spaghetti sauce. Past that, it probably wouldn't have been much help in warding off the evil undead. Her investigation obviously had a few serious flaws. She'd believed herself strong, ready for the battle she'd chosen to pursue.

Wrong. So wrong.

She stared into the creature's fathomless eyes, letting

it see that she wasn't afraid. "If you're going to kill me," she panted, "make it fast. I haven't got all fucking night."

The vampire's gaze glittered with menace. The smile it offered wasn't pleasant. "I do."

Jesse swore under her breath. It occurred to her she was going to die—really die.

Maybe it was better this way. The life she'd been attempting to hold on to seemed futile now, wasted on the revenge she'd envisioned herself delivering with a terrible and swift justice. She had to remember where she stood in the grand scheme of this world. To society, Jesse Burke was nothing, a transient drifter.

Nobody would miss her. Nobody would mourn.

Jesse's heart shifted into overdrive. Adrenaline seared her veins. There was a low throbbing throughout her body, but it was all far away, as if she stood outside her own body watching the scene unfold. Helplessness only added to her panic as her senses reeled. "We really don't have to do this," she said, backpedaling.

Catching a handful of Jesse's hair, the vampire grinned. "Oh, but we do. Painfully." Mouth ratcheting open, its lethal fangs hovered.

A faint whimper escaped Jesse's lips. Holy cow. She'd really screwed up—the latest mistake of many she'd made during her poor excuse of a life. A wild thought zinged through her mind. *No way I'm going to live through this*.

Certain she was about to be toast, Jesse caught a quick rush of motion out of the corner of her eye. A shadowy blur moving at top speed charged in, knocking the creature off her. Candace Ackerman went akimbo, arms and legs flying.

Immediately taking advantage of freedom, Jesse rolled onto her stomach and pushed herself to her feet. She knew she should run. She wanted to run, but her legs felt like lead stumps. Fighting to control her uncooperative limbs, she forced herself to take a step, then two.

Climbing back to its feet, the confused vampire rounded on her. Heart lodged in her throat, Jesse froze. The time to bend over and kiss her ass good-bye would be about now.

Like a hummingbird coming to rest midflight, the blur reappeared, positioning itself behind the advancing threat. All at once, a man's figure materialized in its place, silhouetted in the shadows. Tall and lean as whipcord, he was dressed in some sort of lengthy trench coat. Untangling a long, slender object from the folds of his coat, he lifted his weapon and placed it against his shoulder. The moonlight glinted off the cool gray metal of a sawed-off shotgun.

Time spun away. Everything around Jesse ground down into disorienting slow-motion movements.

The stranger pulled the trigger without hesitation.

Boom!

Ambushed from behind, the vampire, formerly known as Candace Ackerman, stared down at the newly formed holes in its chest, courtesy of the blast of a double-aught buckshot.

A toothy grin replaced its scowl of bewilderment. Swinging around to face its new assailant, the she-beast growled. "Not good enough."

The stranger reloaded, calmly jacking another shell into the chamber. "This is," he said, and fired.

Another shot rang out, kick-starting Jesse's breathing

with a burst of adrenaline. The vampire's head exploded, its fanged menace vanishing in an instant. Jesse's mouth dropped open.

The mutilated corpse wavered, balance and footing all of a sudden unsure. Seconds later it dropped to the ground in a crumpled heap.

For ten, maybe twenty seconds, Jesse couldn't move. Nothing had adequately prepared her to see a body so gruesomely mutilated.

This time Candace Ackerman was unquestionably dead.

Without warning, the corpse began to splutter and spark. Flesh dissolving like overheated wax, the remnants of skin and bone crackled and grew blacker, oozing a thick puslike substance. A stench like rotting eggs emanated from the fizzing mass.

Jesse gagged when the sickening odor of burned flesh permeated her nostrils. Unable to tear her gaze away, she watched the cadaver devour itself. At the same time, thin strings of gray-white mist gathered above the remains. It slowly took shape, curling into the figure of a bat-headed, clawed mutant.

The demon laughed.

Then, with a flick of its reptilian tail, it vanished. A strange luminescent afterimage lingered as if scorched into the fabric of the atmosphere. All that was left of the body was something that looked gummy and sticky, like tar poured on top of the newly turned soil. Immolation had happened so instantaneously, it was almost hard to believe the thing had existed.

Knees going weak, Jesse collapsed. It was all she could do not to scream or break into hysterical sobs. She hadn't imagined anything like this would happen when she'd climbed over the fence surrounding the cemetery. A stake to the heart and the vamp would turn into a neat pile of ashes—game over.

Only this was no game.

Gun in hand, her rescuer sauntered over like a soldier armored in the pride of an enemy's defeat. He stopped within a foot of Jesse, overwhelming her with his presence. His lanky body filled her vision. The power he radiated enveloped her, kept her sitting.

"First time you see a demon face-to-face is a shock."

Struggling to calm her erratic heartbeat, she barely managed a nod. "No shit."